WHEN PROPERTY FLEES

A NOVEL

GREGORY LeFEVER

*To the brave souls who risked all, both those who fled
and those who helped.
And to Christine, who made this book possible.*

"I do not think there is a mother among us all, who clasps her child to her breast, who could ever be made to feel it right that her child should be a slave; not a mother among us all who would not rather lay that child in its grave."

Harriet Beecher Stowe
Author of *Uncle Tom's Cabin*
February 6, 1854

CHAPTER ONE

FUGITIVE

ONE DAY IN MARCH OF 1854 ON A REMOTE ROAD SOME miles north of where the river flows between Ohio and Kentucky, two horsemen lean against the stinging grit in the wind. Just behind them, a third man yanks on reins to steer a wagon along ruts of hardened mud.

Meanwhile, on a bluff a distance back from the road, Adam Porter perches high on a ladder propped against a wall of his house. He pounds an iron nail into the clapboard siding till a gust threatens his balance and he clings to a rung for steadiness. He waits for the wind to subside and looks past the barn and across a field of corn stubble to a few surviving patches of dirty snow. He squints to see the distant road with its tiny figures of men on horseback and the horse-drawn wagon following.

He turns back to his hammer and nails. Soon his wife, Hannah, rushes to the base of the ladder. She pulls her blue wool shawl tighter and calls up to him. The wind blows away her words so she shouts again.

"Some men are here, Adam, some men."

He climbs down the ladder and hands her his hammer. "Stay here. I'll find out." He rounds the corner of the house and sees the two men standing beside their horses and the third man seated on the bench of the long-bed wagon. One of the men waves his hat in the wind and calls, "Hello there." The wind tugs at the man's coat and blows strands of black hair across his face.

Adam eyes the Colt hanging from the man's hip. "You need something?"

"Troubling you for water," the man calls out as he jams his hat back onto his head. "We been blown to hell and back and got more ground to cover before nightfall. Like to get these filled." He holds up two metal canteens.

"Here, let me," Adam says. "You can water the horses at the trough over there."

The man walks toward Adam and hands over the canteens. "Name's Summerfield. I'm federal marshal for this area. Haven't been out this way much. Still getting acquainted." The lawman points toward the other dismounted man, large in a wool coat and wearing a battered hat low over his eyes. "That's Klemmer." Summerfield then gestures toward the gnarly man seated on the wagon. "Abe Williams." The driver touches his brim and nods.

Adam walks to the water pump with Summerfield following. "Seems winter just might be behind us at last," the marshal says. "Some say this one's going down as Ohio's coldest far back as memory serves. I never before witnessed so many folks digging through so much snow just to get wood to keep warm. Odds are, we'll soon be finding what's left of some of those folks who got froze in their beds."

Adam hands him the full canteens.

"You been here long?" The lawman rambles between gusts. "Myself, I come up from Nashville last October and can't attest to being warm since."

"Three years next month," Adam answers. "Farm belonged to my wife's uncle. We were living up by Akron—my wife and two boys—when the old man died. We came down here for a new start and found the place a fearsome mess. Still working on making it our home."

Summerfield glances toward the farmhouse. "That her? Your wife?"

Hannah approaches slowly, shawl flapping in the wind.

"That's my wife."

"Ma'am," the marshal nods. "Marshal Summerfield at your—"

A nearby tree branch cracks in the wind loud as a gunshot and the mare hitched to the wagon shies. The wagon rolls directly in front of Hannah. She clasps her hands over her mouth. "Oh, my goodness."

"Stand back from there, ma'am," the lawman orders. "Runaway colored we're taking back to Kentucky."

Hannah peers into the wagon's bed to see the beaten boy, no older than fourteen. His canvas pants are ripped and muslin shirt is smeared with blood. His wrists are wrapped with twine soaked red where it sliced through the boy's tender skin. A rusted length of chain crudely encircles his thin waist and is padlocked to the wagon's seat.

"Found him holed up in Elmer Mitchell's barn," Summerfield says.

"To his misfortune," the man named Klemmer mutters.

The boy flinches at the sound of Klemmer's voice.

"Have you done this to him?" Hannah asks Klemmer as she slips the shawl from her shoulders and spreads it over the boy's chest. "Help me cover him. He's freezing."

Klemmer picks up a corner of the shawl and tosses it back toward her, exposing the boy. For a moment no one moves. Then Adam gathers up the shawl and hands it back to Hannah. He edges away from the wagon and gently pulls her with him.

Summerfield breaks the silence. "He'll be warm soon, ma'am, I assure you. We'll leave now." The marshal hoists himself onto his horse. "I thank you for the water." He nods to Hannah. "And I do apologize for this, ma'am."

Klemmer mounts his horse and slaps the rump of the harnessed mare so the wagon lurches forward. The boy cries out. Klemmer shifts his weight on the saddle and turns his horse to follow the wagon.

CHAPTER TWO

ACCUSED

TWO DAYS SOUTH, ON THE OTHER SIDE OF THE OHIO River, twilight settles over a small Kentucky settlement of one large house, a few barns, and four small cabins. In one of the cabins, a woman named Nettie opens the shutters and peers through the square hole cut into the plank siding.

"Don't be letting in more cold," the man known as William complains. "How many times you got to look out there? That boy be home soon."

Nettie squints at the darkening landscape and then closes the shutters. She shuffles across the dirt floor to the table. "Sky's getting dark and he's supposed to be in by now. You know that."

"Must be Bobby Hill got him doing something. Don't be worrying." William lights a third candle for more light. He walks to the window himself and opens the shutters, but all he sees are the squat silhouettes of the other slave cabins and bare tree limbs. Up the hill, the Leyden house is framed by the sunset's final flare. He closes the shutters and turns to watch his boy Alfred snitch a piece of cornbread from a dented tin. The youngest boy, Dan, splashes water in a basin while the baby Lucy coos in her crib.

"I know he's in some trouble." Nettie says. "You eat. I can't."

"I say there's no trouble and that's what I'm going to do—eat." William looks at the boys. "Alfred? Dan?" He picks up the pan and puts pieces of fried pork onto the boys' plates and one onto his own. He takes the tin of cornbread from Alfred. "Give us some of that afore you eat it all."

Nettie glances toward the door. "Somebody's coming." She pulls open the door and her boy Richard stomps into the cabin. At twelve, he's tall for his age and lighter skinned than the other three children. He keeps his eyes to the floor. "You hurt?" his mother asks.

A ruddy man named Bobby Hill steps into the cabin behind the boy and shuts the door as Nettie looks over her son. The overseer's black frock coat is flecked with mud. His face is pale and fleshy, making him look younger than his thirty years. Reddish curls poke from beneath his felt hat.

"Everything all right, sir?" William asks nervously.

"We have ourselves a situation." Bobby Hill looks around the cabin. "The boy's been up to no good."

Nettie puts her arm around Richard's shoulders but the boy pulls away.

William gives the boy a stern look. "What he do?"

"He and his friends seem to delight in inflicting damage around here." Bobby Hill looks directly at Richard. "I caught them pushing down a fence."

William reaches out quickly and grabs Richard's chin. "Why you do such a thing, boy? Why you wreck a fence?"

Bobby Hill keeps his eyes on the boy. "I suppose they were hoping the hogs would stray over and trample the tobacco in the north field. That right?"

Richard twists his chin free of William's grasp.

"I didn't do it. I was there. But I didn't do it."

"Come now," the overseer chides the boy. "Lying makes everything worse."

Nettie picks up the baby Lucy, who squirms in her arms. "What's going to happen, Mister Hill?"

"As I said, we have a situation. First it was little things like mud thrown against the buildings. Tools been coming up missing and equipment getting busted. Couple of times I've found cured leaf thrown in the dirt and ruined." He turns to William. "You know what I'm saying, William. You've had to fix a number of these things."

"Yessir. You let me fix this, too. I promise the boy won't be no more trouble."

"I'm afraid it's beyond that now. I'm taking the whole situation to Mister Leyden. It's not just your boy. It's the bunch of them doing things that's costing the farm money. That's when Mister Leyden gets involved, when there's money at stake."

"What you think the master going to do?" Nettie whispers with worry.

"That'd be solely up to him," Bobby Hill says. Without another word, the overseer opens the cabin door and is gone into the night.

William digs his fingers into Richard's shoulder. "What's got in your head, boy? You going to get beat. If Bobby Hill don't beat you, I will."

Nettie pulls on William's hand to loosen his grip. "What's the boy got to say?"

Without raising his eyes, Richard tells how he and two other boys, Frankie and Louie, were stacking wood at the Leyden house. They'd finished the chore and wanted to tell Bobby Hill so. Then the brothers Ben and Reuben showed up and all five headed toward the north pasture to look for the overseer. They'd romped through the field in the fading daylight. Richard said Reuben had run into a fence post. "That post busted and fell over so we tried to put it back in the ground. That's when Mister Hill showed up."

"And what'd he do?" William asks.

"Made us put those posts back."

"What you mean 'posts'? You said Reuben knocked just the one over."

"Could be two or three. Can't say."

William groans. "Oh, you done it now, boy. You telling tales and you going to be punished for sure."

Nettie leans close. "You tell me the truth, Richard. You and those other boys been causing all that harm Mister Hill says? Stealing tools and stuff?"

"We ain't."

"What about the other boys?"

"Maybe Reuben. Can't say."

"Can't say?" William grabs Richard's shoulder again. "Let me tell you something. Any of those boys—Reuben, Ben, any of them—could be making trouble and you could get beat or whipped for just being around. You could get sold away."

"Leydens don't whip us and they don't sell us." Richard takes a step back from William.

"You a fool, boy!" William says, voice rising. "They ain't beat or sold us because there ain't been no trouble all these years. I ought to know. I been here for more than twenty. And what about Bobby Hill? We never had no overseer before. Now we got the missus' own brother looking over us and telling us what to do and how to do it. Who knows what he's liable to do? No, this don't look good."

William looks down at his plate of food. "Now I ain't hungry. Not at all."

CHAPTER THREE

WARNING

IN THE SPRING IN THIS PART OF SOUTHERN OHIO, SUN-
sets blaze pink and orange through the trees like a fireplace as wide
as the horizon. After a long day clearing brush and rocks from a
muddy field, Adam rests his pitchfork on the barn wall and kicks a
stump to rid his boots of muck. He pauses to watch the sunset and
the braid of smoke rising from the kitchen chimney into the evening
sky.

Hannah calls to him from the back door, "Coming in?"

In the glow of the kitchen, Adam watches their boys, John and
Robert, scrub themselves with warm water from a metal basin.
Hannah helps them into their flannel nightshirts and prods them up
the stairs to their bedroom.

Adam turns up the wick on the oil lamp on the table just as the
sounds of men and horses come from the road along with another
sound like none he had heard before—a low wail rising to a chilling
howl. From the upstairs bedroom Robert, the younger boy, cries out
to his mother.

Adam rushes through the dark house to a front window where he sees three men on horseback in the road. Two are swinging torches in slow arcs of flickering light. He sees two or more men walking in the torchlight.

Again the horrible howl erupts, this time ending in two distinct barks.

Adam grabs his musket from a nearby cupboard and returns to the window. He half cocks the gun and slips a firing cap in place as Hannah comes up behind him. "You and the boys stay here," he tells her as he opens the door and steps into the night with the musket held high.

At the sound of the door opening, one of the horsemen wheels around and raises his torch higher. Two large dogs on leashes sniff the ground, pulling their handlers along with them.

"What do you want?" Adam calls out.

One of the dogs snarls at him, lunging and straining against its leash. The man holding it struggles to control the animal. "Down!"

The horseman farthest away turns his sorrel stallion toward the commotion, the tip of his cigar glowing red.

"That you? Klemmer?" Adam says.

"You know I am Klemmer. You got fugitives here? Hiding maybe in your barn? Tell me!"

"The only fugitive who's been around here is that boy you brought here chained to the wagon."

One of the men on foot strays closer to the house as his hound drags him along.

"That's far enough." Adam turns the musket toward the man. "I said there's no one here."

Klemmer asks the dog's handler, "Does he find the smell?"

"Can't say for sure," the man says.

"Then come back."

Klemmer dismounts, holding his sorrel's reins. He grinds his cigar into the dirt with his boot. "These dogs—they are my own breeding." His breath is frosty in the torchlight. "They have the noses of the hunting hounds."

Adam detects an accent in Klemmer's speech.

"I say even in the wind these dogs can find the one smell. Sometimes even after many days." The torches throw shadows across Klemmer's face. "I get a piece of the colored man's clothes from his owner, even a little piece"—he reaches into a pocket of his wool coat and carefully pulls out a shred of dirty cotton—"like this." He holds the scrap in his palm. "I give it to a dog to smell and the dogs will find the man. Maybe now or maybe later. Did I tell you these dogs can bite a man to death?"

"You and your dogs have no business here." Adam keeps his musket pointed toward the man and hound close to the house.

"And you are not foolish enough to help the colored when they run from their owners—am I right?" Klemmer folds the scrap of cloth and returns it to his pocket. "You would not deny a man the return of his own property. No, you would not spit on the law—am I right?" Klemmer hoists himself back onto his horse. "And I think you would not put your family in danger by bringing the fugitive into your home—am I right? No, you would not be so foolish."

The group wanders farther down the road by torchlight as one of the hounds lets loose another long howl.

CHAPTER FOUR

LAW

MIDMORNING CLOUDS HANG LOW AND THE THREAT OF rain mounts with each minute. Sitting on the wagon seat with Hannah, Adam slaps the reins and the black gelding Othello breaks into a trot. Their sons are in the wagon bed—two giggling bumps bobbing beneath a sheet of oilcloth.

"Boys, if it starts to rain, stay under that cover," Hannah tells them.

A cluster of tumbledown houses and outbuildings line the road as the wagon rolls into the small town of Buford. A few hundred yards farther, Adam halts the wagon in front of Pope's Store just as a wind-driven wall of rain pelts the family. He jumps from the wagon and helps Hannah, who holds the brim of her bonnet as she runs toward the door. Then he lifts the oilcloth and yells, "Out, out!" and the boys leap from the wagon and follow their mother into the store.

Adam secures the oilcloth. Through the downpour he sees Joseph Summerfield walking toward the Buford Inn across the road, shoulders hunched against the storm. Adam dashes across the road and follows the lawman into the inn.

"Quite the storm," Summerfield says as he brushes water from his coat and hat onto the wood floor.

Adam draws close to the marshal. "Let me come straight to the point. I believe your men are acting well beyond their duty."

"My men?"

"They came to my farm with dogs a couple nights ago on the pretense of chasing a runaway."

The lawman eyes Adam. "I don't recall—"

"Adam Porter. You and two others came to my farm with—"

"Ah, the boy in the wagon. The one we found at Elmer Mitchell's place. Now I remember."

Adam follows him into the dining room, past two windows dulled by soot. They sit at a table in front of a large fireplace holding some sputtering wet logs.

"Why do you say my men? I have no men unless I swear them in."

"Even Klemmer?"

Summerfield wipes his face with his bandanna. "Julius Klemmer is not one of my men, as you put it. What's he done?"

Adam describes Klemmer's sudden appearance at the farm. "He said he was after a runaway slave but he seemed more intent on frightening us with dogs and guns and torches. Threatening my family."

Summerfield stands and walks to a cupboard, where he grabs an amber bottle and two glasses. He places the glasses on the table in front of Adam and pours bourbon into them.

"Rids the chill." The marshal takes a gulp. "Where'd you say you hail from?"

"Up by Akron." Adam sips from his glass and feels the whiskey burn its way down his throat.

"I'm certain you got runaway slaves going through Akron, too," Summerfield says. "But nothing like down here. Here we sit, a few miles from the Ohio River. There's thousands of the coloreds just on the other side and they're dead set on crossing over to find freedom on this side, in this here Canaan or wherever."

Adam wipes his mouth. "We'd hear of a few around Akron who made it that far."

"Take that boy we brought by your place. He'd never make it up to Akron." Summerfield toys with his glass against the tabletop. "He got across the river and couldn't find anybody foolish enough to help him. So he just kept wandering north. Three or four days he must have stumbled around with nothing to eat. Then he got desperate and saw Elmer Mitchell's farm. He found a cow in a barn and tried to suck milk from her teat and that's what caused the ruckus. Elmer and his sons caught him in that barn. They tied him up and one of Mitchell's boys rode off to get me."

"So how'd Klemmer get involved?"

"How do you think? Money, of course. Mitchell's son sought out Klemmer first so Klemmer would give them a cut of the reward."

"Who beat the boy?"

"I can only guess. They had him chained in the wagon when I got there."

A spindly man with gray stubble approaches the table. "Darkie had no prayer with Klemmer there," he drawls.

"Morning, Ogden," the marshal nods. "Helped myself to the bottle."

"Heard the boy fetched a good price. Klemmer didn't even cross the river afore a trader made him a good deal."

"You know him—Klemmer?" Adam asks.

"Ought to. Stays here frequent enough. But can't say I know you."

Adam tells Ogden his name and holds out his hand for a greasy handshake. "You say a trader purchased the boy this side of the Ohio?" Adam turns to Summerfield. "Is that even legal?"

"Let's not split hairs," the marshal says. "The boy broke the law just by being over here. Hell, I don't care who takes him back."

Ogden pulls an oily cloth from his belt and wipes the table between Adam and Summerfield. "He's lucky Klemmer got him. Any slave boy creeping around this place going to be one dead darkie, reward or no." He forms a pretend pistol with his right hand. "Pow!"

"Nope, makes no difference to me after a certain point," the marshal goes on. "The slave law Fillmore signed four years ago says I got to catch these runaways and get them back to their owners. Period."

"The Fugitive Slave Law?"

Summerfield leans forward to pour himself another glass. "If you know about our Fugitive Slave Law of 1850, then you know I got no choice in the matter. Let's say a man—let's say Klemmer—spots a runaway. If he tells me about the runaway, as federal marshal I've got to go after that slave or risk having to pay a fine of a thousand dollars myself." He takes another sip of bourbon. "If the fugitive gets away, I might have to pay his owner the full amount of his worth. Could be well over a thousand dollars. You better believe I don't have that kind of money."

"That's the law?"

"I'm telling you that's the law. And if I capture a runaway and take him before the court and the judge says the colored is a fugitive then the judge gets ten dollars himself. But if he thinks the colored ain't a runaway and should be let go, he gets only five. So how many of the coloreds we bring into court aren't fugitives by the time they leave? Nary a one. They're all fugitives in the eyes of the law and got to go back across the river. No more Canaan for them. So you may not like it, but that's the way the law works."

Ogden drifts away to the fireplace, where he kicks a smoldering log.

"And tell me again where Klemmer fits into this?" Adam wonders.

"As I say, there's the reward and whatever other money he gets from owners or traders in exchange for the unlucky bastards he captures. He might demand near full value from the fugitive's owner. The owner might not want to pay that much. That means the slave hunter might take the fugitive to a trader. Sometimes a trader's able to pay more for the slave than the slave's owner is willing to pay. There's money to be made, and we've got slave hunters all around this here part of the country to prove it. As for Klemmer, he's got just himself and his horse and some hounds, so he stands to make a decent living, I suppose."

"I don't know how decent it is."

Summerfield leans back in his chair and pushes away his empty glass. "All I know is I've never seen a man more intent on tracking down slaves, ever. I don't know much about Klemmer except his accent sounds like some German folks I know, but I can't be sure. He doesn't say much about himself."

"He told me the other night to be sure not to hide slaves at my place—not while he's around."

"Best keep that in mind. He has no liking for abolitionist types. If he's got you pegged as one, I'd advise you to steer clear of him."

Adam rises from the table.

Summerfield looks up at him. "Can I ask where you stand on all this? This slavery thing?"

"Sure, you can ask." Adam leans down with his hands on the table. "I want nothing to do with any of it. I've got no answers as to what to do with the three million slaves in this country. But I do know it's not something you can just legislate away and no amount of agitation is going to solve a thing. That's where I part company with my younger brother and his precious Anti-Slavery Society. He's the abolitionist, not me."

The marshal rises alongside Adam and puts on his hat. "You sound like a wise man."

"But let me be clear," Adam adds, his voice tightening. "I don't want any runaway slaves coming to my place and I don't want Klemmer or any other slave catcher scaring my family, day or night. And, if you'll beg my pardon, I don't want any marshals bringing their prey to my farm ever again."

Summerfield nods. "Can't blame you for that."

CHAPTER FIVE

PLAIN

"ANNIE, WHY ARE YOU WEARING THOSE DREADFUL clothes? You know you're not really a plain person."

Anne Billings struggles to remain calm in the face of her mother's scolding. "I'm not trying to be anything other than what I am." She buttons her gray dress and laces her black shoes. She reaches for her black wool cloak and stiff black bonnet.

"What'll they think?" Peggy Billings persists. "You look like someone in mourning."

"What'll who think?"

"You know very well who. Those people at the church."

"It's not a church, Mother. When Quakers worship they call it a meeting. The Society of Friends doesn't have churches."

"But you're a pretty girl, yet you make yourself look so—"

"Plain? You already said that, Mother. Nobody in this family complained when I had to wear my brother's clothes in the fields. I didn't hear any protests then."

Anne studies herself in the oval mirror on her dressing table. She adjusts the ties on her cloak and brushes her blond curls away from her face. The reflection of her mother's tired face, standing behind Anne, peers back at her.

"It's fine, Mother. These clothes are appropriate for—"

Her mother leans over Anne's bed. "And what are these?" She picks up two newspapers and dangles them from her fingertips. "Oh, I see, something here calling itself *The Liberator*. Well, you can't let your father see these."

"I don't plan to."

Her mother lays the newspapers back on Anne's bed. "He won't want you troubling yourself with matters that don't concern you."

"What if these things do concern me?"

"It's not your place to be thinking about such things, Annie. You know that."

An hour later, Anne stands in front of John Pope's house and tugs nervously at her bonnet. The white frame house with its broad porch sits just a hundred paces from Pope's Store along Buford's main road. A small stable stands between the store and house. Anne watches as a dozen Quaker men and women with children in tow walk from their buggies to the house—all clothed in shades of gray and olive and black.

A man in his early twenties squeezes past a family on the porch and walks toward Anne, the breeze ruffling his sandy hair. She smiles at Jacob Pope, whose father, John, is proprietor of the store. "It's good to see thee, Anne. I saw thee step from thy buggy." Jacob clasps his hands together and a tint rises in his cheeks. "I do hope thee enjoys this."

"You needn't be nervous, Jacob. I'm nervous enough for the both of us. We aren't church people in my family and I don't know what to do."

"Thee needn't do anything but sit and be with the Lord."

They step into the entry hall. Jacob nods to a man and wife holding a sleeping infant and steps past an aged man who touches the wide brim of his black hat. They all file into the dining room with its whitewashed walls. No decoration detracts from its starkness. A walnut dining table has been pushed to one side to make room for several mismatched wooden chairs and benches now arranged in rows throughout the room.

Jacob leads Anne to a chair near a window and sits next to her. She feels people watching her. A moment later John Pope stands to face the seated group, clearing his throat. He adjusts his wire glasses and opens the meeting by asking for God's guidance. Everyone sits in silence with heads bowed. Anne closes her eyes. She feels the sunlight from the window warming her hands on her lap. She hears only an occasional cough and the sound of a few children in a nearby room. Soon a woman rises to her feet and tells the group that the Lord has been good to them and they should reflect on this goodness when they encounter troublesome people. The woman does not elaborate and quickly seats herself again.

Once more the room is silent.

A few minutes later a tall man Anne recognizes as Abner Blair—gray hair streaming from his black hat, his long beard white with age—stands to loudly proclaim, "And I will bring the blind by a way that they knew not. I will lead them in paths that they have not known. I will make darkness light before them and crooked things straight." He pauses and turns his closed eyes toward the ceiling. He finally adds, "Isaiah, forty-two, sixteen," as he seats himself.

Several more minutes of silence follow and then the meeting is over. Some men move the table back into place and arrange chairs as the women talk among themselves.

"I fear my father and I are not the best of housekeepers," Jacob says.

"No, it's fine," Anne tells him as the couple steps into the home's parlor. The room is so barren their voices resonate. "May I ask when your mother—"

"My mother passed when I was three," Jacob says. "The cholera. My parents had been without children for many years till I came along. So now there is only my father and I. It has not been easy for him. Sometimes people mistake him for my grandfather but we—"

John Pope enters the room breathing heavily. "I tell thee, Jacob has been a blessing to me. Though sometimes I believe he is here with the express purpose of strengthening my patience." He chuckles and adjusts his glasses. "I'm pleased to see thee this fine day, Anne. What did thee think of our meeting?"

"It was beautiful, peaceful," she says. "I thought there would be more said about Quaker opposition to slavery. I mean you've exerted God's will so bravely for so many years and surely have given the slaves hope that one day soon their bondage will end." She paused. "I apologize. I have no right."

The storekeeper holds his glasses at arm's length and searches for smudges. "But even among the plain people confusion reigns about slavery," he says. "Thee speak of God's will. Even today there are Quakers who take action in the name of God's will, and there are Quakers who question whether those actions are only interfering with His will. I recall one man during our worship in this very house who spoke of the Lord's tenet that we not resist evil. This man said the abolitionists were attacking another man's institution, and if the Lord considered that institution to be evil, then the Lord would abolish it—that it's not our place to resist it. And there are many Friends worried that the abolitionists are so inflaming our southern neighbors that one day our land will run red with the blood of war."

"But that's not what thee believes," Jacob says to his father.

"No, it is not. But the few of us who worship here have agreed we'll each follow our own conscience. For me, I try to influence—not fight nor preach nor coerce, mind thee—but simply influence others to do the Lord's will. Each of us in our own way is given this opportunity to help."

"That's what I believe as well," Anne says with visible relief.

"I am a storekeeper," John goes on, "and much of our merchandise comes from Kentucky and some from Virginia. I've been a merchant all of my life but had not realized until a couple of years ago how much of my inventory bears the stain of slavery's sweat. So Jacob and I have quietly replaced some of our merchandise with goods untouched by slaves. It's not an easy thing to do and it's not practical. Thee can understand, Anne—knowing the sentiment of some of our neighbors—that I cannot disclose this activity to them without the threat of reprisal. Not here, not in this town."

"Oh, I know the sentiment well," she tells him. "Very well indeed."

CHAPTER SIX

DECISION

"NETTIE, IS SOMETHING TROUBLING YOU?" GRACE Leyden looks up from the mound of clothing on her bed.

"Just got things on my mind, ma'am."

"Is there something you want to tell me?"

The two women are on different sides of the canopied bed, culling the mistress's apparel and setting aside garments that no longer fit or have fallen from fashion. Grace moves to her vanity table and sits on the padded stool. She snaps her fingers to get Nettie's attention and then points at an overstuffed chair.

"Sit down right there, Nettie, and tell me what's bothering you. I know something is."

Nettie moves to the chair. From this seat she glimpses her own reflection in the vanity mirror against the backdrop of the room's plush furnishings. She looks down at her feet.

"Ma'am, it's my oldest boy, Richard. Mister Hill says Richard and some other boys did something bad to a fence. My boy says he didn't do nothing wrong. But Mister Hill says he's going to tell Mister Leyden about it."

"Nettie, you know my husband is a fair man."

"I know he is, ma'am. I never seen him do wrong by any of us."

"So why are you worried?"

"I don't want Mister Leyden thinking my boy is bad."

"Nonsense." Grace brushes lint from the sleeve of her dress. "You and William are among our most trusted servants. William's been here since he was a child and you and your boy have been here, what, ten years now? You know I've liked you from the very beginning. I made you my maidservant and put my trust in you to take care of my May. You know these things. So you shouldn't worry about what my husband is thinking."

"I know, ma'am. It's just you been so good to me and I don't want nothing bad to happen. I get scared."

"Let me put your mind at ease," the mistress says. "I'll talk to my husband about this and I'll talk to my brother. I'll make sure your boy is treated fairly." Grace steps over to her armoire and swings open its doors. She runs her hand across the dresses hanging there. "If it turns out Richard did behave badly—and I'm not saying he did or he didn't—I'll make sure the punishment is mild. I'm sure he's a good boy."

Raindrops spill from William's hat brim onto his hands as he pounds a steel pin through the flanges of a barn door hinge. He steps back and slowly swings the door open and closed to test the hinge.

Bobby Hill suddenly appears at his side in a rubber slicker. "Come to the house."

The overseer's words strike fear in William.

"It's nothing bad. Bring your measuring tape."

The two men walk up the muddy path toward the house, past the deep front porch with its graceful lines. "I'll bet you're familiar with every inch of this place," Bobby Hill says. "How long you been taking care of it?"

"Ever since Mister Leyden made me his carpenter. Been a good many years now."

The overseer leads William past the outbuilding that serves as the summer kitchen. They enter the house through a rear door and wipe their boots with rags. They step quietly through the dining room and then down a wide hall to another room where Philip Leyden stands beside his desk.

"How are you, William?"

"Good as can be, Mister Leyden, sir."

Leyden pulls himself to his full height and straightens his green satin waistcoat. "Come over here, William. Take a look at this wall." Three framed landscape paintings hang on it. "I want bookshelves built right here. Enough for a small library. Yes?"

William looks across the room to a set of shelves already holding several books.

"And I want those old shelves removed. I want you to build a cabinet where those shelves are, a place where I can put papers and files." He turns back to the first wall. "Yes, the books will go here." Then he turns toward the center of the room. "I'll want the desk to face the door, my back against that window and I think perhaps some shades on the window itself. But we can talk about that as you go along."

"Yessir."

Leyden puts his hand on William's shoulder. He is an angular man, tall enough to look down on the slave. "William, I want your work in this room to be of your highest quality. I'll be having important men in here and I want them to be impressed. I want them to see by this room that I'm a man worthy of their utmost respect. A man to be trusted. Do you understand what I'm saying, William?"

"I can only build what I know, sir."

Leyden chuckles. "That's very true and I have every confidence in your abilities. I'll see you get good lumber—the best—and whatever hardware you require."

"Yessir."

Leyden turns to face his brother-in-law. "Bobby, perhaps you can take William to see the old judge's chambers in the courthouse in Washington. I know most of the building is a school now, but I believe those old chambers still convey the sense of authority I'm seeking. Do it soon."

"We can do that," Bobby Hill answers.

Hours later, back in their cabin, Nettie and William and the children squeeze around the table. On it sits a pan of sweet potatoes Nettie has just boiled from the small stash they buried last fall in the root cellar. William folds his hands. "Hush, you children," he begins, "Lord, we thank you for this food—"

"And for protecting Richard," Nettie interjects, glancing across the table at her son.

"And for watching out for the boy, Lord, that's true. We thank you. Amen." William opens his eyes and says to Richard, "I sure hope you learning something about not messing up no more."

With that, William spears a potato and divides it between the two younger boys' plates. As he slices it, he tells Nettie about his visit to the house and Philip Leyden's plans for the office. "That man says he trusts me to do a good job to make him proud," he says, beaming.

"Glad you had it so good," Nettie laughs. "The missus had me sorting clothes and made me hem a dress for their girl. Whew, I say that girl's got some temper. Something don't go Miss May's way and she shouts so loud the angels got to cover their ears."

Two raps on the door bring a sudden end to the talk. Bobby Hill enters the cabin, rain dripping from his hat and slicker.

"Just sit, keep eating. I'm bringing news."

"About Mister Leyden's new room?" William wipes his hand across his mouth.

"Not that. No, I've talked with him about the trouble around here."

The overseer's words fall like a shadow over the family.

"You know our boy didn't do nothing wrong," Nettie says and reaches over to take Richard's hand. "You know that."

"What'd you expect him to say?" The overseer glares at Richard. "Same as Reuben and Ben say. Same as Louie says. Same as Frankie. I told Mister Leyden what I saw."

The baby Lucy bangs a spoon on the table.

"I know your boy and the others are making trouble around here, like I told you. But this time I caught them red-handed. And you're the ones who should be keeping these culprits in line."

The overseer paces around the cramped cabin, moving closer to the fireplace for warmth.

"We try, Mister Hill," Nettie cries. "You know he's a good—"

"You people make trouble and you know who gets in a bind? I do. I'm the one who hears about it from my sister and her husband. So I'm figuring how to make these things stop." He stares straight at Richard. "And I asked Mister Leyden to let me handle the punishment. To let me figure it out."

"Mister Leyden's always been fair all these years," William says.

"I'll be fair. It's just I've got a different way of handling things. For one, there's going to be some whipping."

"No!" Nettie clutches Richard's hand even tighter. "You know Mister Leyden never—"

"Your wish is granted, Nettie," Bobby Hill grins as he rubs his hands together near the flames. "I've decided it's the parents who can't keep their boys in line, so it's the parents who need to be punished. I'll be putting the lash to Willis and Rufe and William here."

"My Pa didn't do nothing," Richard cries out as he pulls his hand free of his mother.

"You see how this boy reacts?" Bobby Hill says. "I think these rascals watching their fathers getting some bloody stripes will hurt worse than if I laid leather to their own nasty black skins."

William looks up at the overseer. "I never been whipped, sir. Never did nothing to deserve it in all these years."

"Tell your boy. Not me."

Everyone falls silent. The only sound in the family's cabin is the banging of the baby Lucy's spoon as Bobby Hill ventures back into the rain.

CHAPTER SEVEN

DISBELIEF

THE RIM OF THE EASTERN SKY IS BEGINNING TO BRIGHTEN as Nettie leaves her cabin with Lucy in her arms. She rushes across the wet grass past one cabin and then another. At the last cabin she stops and pushes open the door.

"April? That you?" she calls to the husky woman rocking a baby in the candlelight. "April, where's Glory?"

"Gone on up to the house. She been up all night worried about getting beat."

Nettie steps over a rumpled mattress on the floor. "Bobby Hill didn't say they was going to beat Glory. He said just William and Rufe and Willis. You think they going to beat Glory too?"

"I got no idea about any of this whipping talk," April says as she wraps a small quilt tighter around the baby she's holding. "I never heard the likes of it. I'm just trying to help Glory with the little ones. She don't seem able."

Nettie lays Lucy in a large crib against the wall. "You know her Frankie was one of the boys Bobby Hill saw with my Richard. But I can't believe they going to whip Glory just because Frankie's got no pa. Bobby Hill didn't say—"

April blurts, "No sir! I don't believe Mister Leyden going to let it happen. It ain't his way."

For a minute or so, Nettie makes cooing noises over the crib as her daughter drifts back to sleep. "April, I got to go up to the kitchen now. Keep a good eye on my Lucy."

"William. How's he?"

"William's like you. He don't believe Mister Leyden going to let the beating happen."

Nettie shuts the cabin door and then squints to make out a figure on the path from the big house. She recognizes her friend, barefoot and dressed in a cotton shift, wiping her eyes.

"Glory, what's happened?"

"I was up to the house. Only Bobby Hill was there and he won't get Mister Leyden so I can speak to him."

"It's too early, Glory, you know that." Nettie looks closely at Glory. "They not going to get the master up just for you. What'd you want with him anyway?"

"You know my Frankie was one of the boys in trouble and now they say they going to whip people and I—"

"Settle down," Nettie urges. "I know all this. What did Bobby Hill say to you?"

"He said I'd get punished for sure for what Frankie done. Just not whipped."

"Then what?"

"What you think! I know what that man wants." Glory steps around Nettie and starts running down the path again.

Once inside the small summer kitchen building, Nettie opens a cupboard holding aprons and caps, folded neatly on the shelves and all in Grace Leyden's favorite shade of pale blue. On the bottom shelf she spots a basket with a card with the word she recognizes as "Nettie" written on it. The basket holds a simple chintz dress she and her mistress had set aside the day before during their sorting. She holds it up against her body and then carefully folds it and puts it back in the basket.

The kitchen door opens and Glory's son Frankie steps in, carrying a pail of fresh milk with both hands. He looks up at Nettie.

"I seen your mother, Frankie."

"What they going to do to her?"

"I don't know."

"They hurt her and I'll kill them."

Nettie quickly puts her hand over the boy's mouth. "You shush, Frankie! You never say nothing like that again."

Frankie shoves her hand away, lips quivering. "She shouldn't get beat for what I did."

Nettie pats the boy's head. "Go get the eggs now, Frankie, and hurry back. It's late."

For the next hour Nettie cooks and carries food back and forth between the summer kitchen and the house dining room. After a while, the aroma of coffee, fried bacon, and hominy fills the big house.

Philip Leyden strides into the dining room, white linen shirt loose at the collar and gray vest still unbuttoned. His tan trousers are tucked into his riding boots. He walks past the table and chairs, over to where Nettie is setting a platter on the sideboard.

"Nettie, I want to speak to you." His voice is low. "I have something to say before Grace and May come down. I know you're likely upset about what's going to happen. This business of the whippings. But I want no mention of it in this house. No mention at all."

Nettie says nothing and stares at the platter.

"Do you understand me, Nettie? Not a word. In fact, it might be best for you to stay out in the kitchen until we call you."

Nettie retreats to the kitchen building, where Frankie is stoking the fire to heat a big pan of water. The boy turns toward Nettie and she sees tear streaks on his cheeks. She puts her arms around his shoulders. "Your momma's going to be all right."

"I hate them."

"I know."

CHAPTER EIGHT

PLANS

ANNE BILLINGS SETS THE BOWL OF STEAMED GREENS onto the dining table, ready for the midday meal. In the adjacent mudroom, a ruckus erupts and her father storms into the room, trailed by her three brothers.

Joshua Billings has fire in his eyes. "I tell you I should get some damn coloreds for this place!"

"Wrong side of the river," says the eldest son, Hugh.

"I know what side of the goddamn river we're on," his father snaps. "A fellow on the other side can get all the slaves he wants to do his damn work. Cross the river and over here we're fighting rocks and stumps by ourselves just to get a measly crop in the ground." He faces Hugh and squints. "You tell me what difference a few miles is supposed to make when it comes to trying to work a farm."

Anne uses her apron to wipe sweat from her face and says, "The difference between good and evil."

Her younger brother Ben speaks up. "Darn if this ain't the evil side, because over here we got to do all the darn work."

"No good or evil about it," their father huffs. "Just some damn laws."

Chairs scrape against the plank floor as the four men seat themselves at the table. Anne jams a serving spoon into a pot of beans. "Are you saying you'd buy a man just like you'd buy an ox and work him the same?"

Joshua reaches for the bread and looks at his daughter. "You better understand that I could buy a couple slaves and feed them and put a roof over their heads for a year and I'd still come out way ahead."

"But you know it's about more than just—"

"Just what? You keep in mind you're talking to a man who's been out in those damn fields since daybreak busting my back to give this family a home and put some food on this table." He thumps the tabletop for emphasis. "We could use a few coloreds to help."

"But you know it's about more than the work," she says. "It's about what happens to these people—"

"They ain't people," Ben says. "They're property."

She turns toward her brother. "You're a fool."

"Enough!" Joshua's voice rings through the room. He points his finger at her face. "I'm about ready to buy me a new daughter who don't talk so much."

The meal over, Joshua Billings gets ready to return to the field with his sons. Anne tells him the family is low on flour and sugar, so their father tells Hugh to hitch a wagon and take Anne into Buford.

Anne and her older brother say little as they travel the two hot and bumpy miles into the village. Once there, Hugh pulls the wagon to a halt in front of Pope's Store and then walks across the street, where Ira Ogden is motioning for Hugh to join him in the inn.

Anne enters the store and sees John Pope on a ladder arranging boxes on the shelves. He calls down to her, "Hello, Anne. Thee picking up thy family's mail?"

"And bags of flour and sugar. Is Jacob here?"

"I'll get him for thee as well," the shopkeeper says as he descends the ladder. Shortly, Jacob emerges from the storeroom. He carries a large, thick envelope and a couple of smaller ones.

"I'd like to talk for a moment, Jacob. Can we go outside?"

Jacob, envelopes in hand, walks with Anne toward the stable between the store and the Pope house. New leaves are unfurling on the tangled tree limbs above them, while small swarms of young flies buzz at their feet.

"Jacob, it's my family. My father, my brothers. They're just brutes." She tilts her face toward the sky as tears well. "Why was I born to such people?"

"Thee never told me much about thy family, really nothing," he says awkwardly.

Anne leans against the hitching rail and wipes her eyes with her arm. "There's not much to tell. We lived north of Milford, this side of Cincinnati, until my father decided a couple of years ago he could make more money growing tobacco if he had more land. It was the only home I'd ever known. He found the farm here in Buford and bought it."

"I recall meeting thee almost a year ago."

"I'd wanted to be a teacher. That was my dream. At least before we moved."

"Thee would make a fine teacher, Anne. Thy mind is so quick."

"That's from growing up with three brothers who can be bullies," she says and manages a brief smile. "These days, there's so much to be done at the farm I can't even dream about teaching. When we moved here the land was fallow and we had to get a crop in as soon as possible. My father made me work the fields alongside my brothers. My brother Ben and I are about the same size, so I wore his clothes, and after a couple of hours I'd be covered in so much dirt and mud nobody'd ever know I wasn't one of the boys. I'd lie in bed at night and dream of wearing a clean blouse and skirt in front of my students. But then I'd wake up to another day of dirty clothes and blistered skin, fingernails caked with soil, and my hair so stiff with dust that it stood straight up."

"I don't know what to say, Anne. It sounds very hard."

"And then there's my mother. On good days she cooks and washes clothes and tends to things. But on bad days she cries and rages through the house in a blind fury. When she's that way, all the housework falls to me. And it's been happening more and more."

"This is awful, Anne. How can thee work both in the house and in the fields?"

"Each day my father decides. Go here or go there. One's just as bad as the other."

Jacob places his hand over hers on the hitching rail. "Thee does not belong in the fields. Not with three brothers at hand."

"In some ways I'm treated better there. Out in the fields I'm like another son. When I work in the house, it's just me. They just toss their muddy clothes on the floor for me to wash. Every hour I spend mending and cleaning up after them they take for granted. I cook their meals and my reward is another heap of greasy dishes. Never are there any words of gratitude." Her voice trails off.

Anne and Jacob turn back toward the store. She looks at the thick envelope in Jacob's hand and recognizes her aunt's handwriting. Following her line of sight, he hands her the package. She opens it and pulls out a folded letter and two newspapers.

"Ah, I see thee reads *The Liberator*," Jacob says when he sees the newspapers. "Thee must be acquainted with William Garrison and his long opposition to slavery."

"I'm becoming familiar, yes. I have an aunt in Cincinnati who attends abolitionist meetings there. She sends these to me." She unfolds one of copies and scans the front page, dense with long columns of tiny type. "Oh, Jacob, it all makes me furious. This is why I'm so upset. To hear my father and my brothers and their ignorant—"

"Thee had an argument?" he interrupts.

"I wouldn't dignify it with that term. Just their usual cruel comments and my usual failure to sway their thinking. Sometimes I wonder how slavery can exist in this day, and then all I have to do is listen to my father."

Jacob spots the large bag of flour and the smaller bag of sugar where his father has placed them. He carries both bags to the buggy. "We're in a troubled part of the land to be sure, living so close to Kentucky. If I lived in Boston like William Garrison, I might never even see a real slave. But here I can leave on Pony in the morning and see slaves working under the whip in the fields before nightfall. The evil practice is so close to us and it's on people's minds much of the time. We all hear of slaves crossing the river to escape and then we have slave catchers roaming our roads and coming into our store to buy rope and chain to bind their captives when they take them back."

"I was so impressed when your father explained how the two of you are stocking your store with free labor goods. It's very noble." She puts her hand on his arm as he sets the bags behind the buggy seat. He smiles.

"You said Pony?" Anne asks.

"She's my horse, a Morgan I raised from birth. I call her Pony. Silly name, I suppose." He turns to face the stable and shouts, "I'm talking about you, Pony. Can thee hear me?"

Anne laughs and then looks at Jacob. "Perhaps we could do something about it."

He looks at her, puzzled.

"Helping the slaves, maybe helping them reach freedom," Anne tells him.

"That would be both difficult and dangerous."

"What else can I do? I've heard about the Underground Railroad. Isn't its purpose to help the ones trying to escape? Aren't Quakers involved in it?"

"Some are. But none close by that I know of. Certainly none from the meeting we hold here."

"Perhaps you could talk with the others to find out if they know how we could help."

"It's possible," he says. "I've heard of fugitives sometimes coming this way. But most people around here would never admit to providing food or shelter."

"I understand why," Anne says. "I heard about that slave boy who was caught at the Mitchell farm a few weeks ago. My father said the boy was captured and then was sold to a trader even before he was taken back across the river. Maybe that boy and others like him who come this way would have a better chance if somebody would help them."

"Anne, thee knows thy family would object most strenuously."

"They wouldn't know."

CHAPTER NINE

WHIPPING

AT ELEVEN IN THE MORNING BOBBY HILL RINGS THE
farm bell to summon the slaves to the open area between the cabins
and the big barn. Eighteen men, women, and children soon gather
near the oak bell pole. Last to arrive are the hands from the far fields.
In a knot at the center of the group stand William and Willis and
Rufe with their women by their sides.

"They really going to do this thing?" the big man named Willis
asks William.

"I believe so."

William looks up at the sky. Heavy rain clouds hang low over
the farm. He crosses his arms over his chest to stop his hands
from trembling.

Bobby Hill climbs onto a bench. "Clear some room around
this pole."

The people move back and open an area at the base of the
bell pole.

"More!"

Again they step back.

"I want these boys to come forward and stand over here." The overseer motions to a spot at the side of the pole. "Reuben. Ben. Richard. Frankie. Louie. All of you—here!" The boys follow the order. They stand awkwardly and hug themselves against the chilly, damp air. Bobby Hill points to an area on the other side of the pole. "Over here I want Willis and William and Rufe." He examines the faces looking back at him. "Glory, you stand there with them for the time being." A murmur runs through the slaves as Glory follows the three men to the pole. She clutches her tattered skirt with one hand and puts the other to her forehead.

All grows quiet as Philip Leyden appears on horseback. A long leather strap lies across his horse's shoulders.

"I want you all to listen to me," he says firmly. "This is an unfortunate day for us. For thirty years I've tried to avoid using strong discipline on my workers. Just look around you." He sweeps his hand across the barnyard. "Do you see stocks here where I could lock you up for days on end?"

Some slaves watch Leyden but most just stare at their feet.

"Well, do you?" he says louder.

A few answer, "No, sir."

"Look at your bodies. Look at the bodies of your family and friends. Do you see scars left by the branding iron? Scars from the lash?"

More answer this time. "No, sir. No."

Leyden's voice rises. "Have I ever turned your kin over to the slave trader?"

They answer in unison. "No, sir."

The wind rises, carrying the scent of rain. Leyden pushes his wide-brimmed hat more firmly onto his head. "Now it seems that some among you don't appreciate the kindness I've shown. They don't seem to comprehend you've been treated better than others of your kind on the farms of our neighbors." His horse grows impatient and paws the ground. "Some among you have stolen my shovels and my hoes. Damaged my wagons. Defaced my buildings and torn down my fences so the hogs could trample my tobacco, my livelihood."

Leyden turns in his saddle to face the five boys and everyone's eyes follow. Frankie and Louie look at the ground. Richard and Ben cover their faces with their hands. Only Reuben stares back defiantly.

"But these aren't just acts against me. These are sins abhorred by the Almighty." Leyden reaches into his trouser pocket and pulls from it a folded piece of paper. He opens it and clears his throat, pulling himself higher in the saddle. "You all know from the Good Book that evil must be punished. So hear the words of Jeremiah when he says, 'But I will punish you according to the fruits of your doings, saith the Lord.' And now hear the book of Ezekiel, 'And they shall bear the punishment of their iniquity.'"

A few slaves utter, "Amen."

The wind blows grit against the group. Leyden bends his brim downward to shield his face. "And so you wonder why we should punish the fathers of these sinners. I will tell you. It's the fathers of these boys who have failed." The paper flutters in the wind and Leyden clasps it with both hands. "Listen to the book of Exodus when it says, 'Teach them ordinances and laws, and thou shalt show them the way they must walk and the work they must do.'" He crumples the paper and shoves it back into his pocket. He prods the bay forward, and the people move aside. He stops directly in front of the three fathers and Glory. "You didn't teach your children to follow the laws as the Bible commands. They have sinned and you are to blame."

Sprinkles of rain sweep across the barnyard. Leyden lifts the leather strap from his horse's shoulders and holds it high. "We've not used this strap at this farm, not once. And after today I intend to put it away for good." He hands it to the overseer. "Mister Hill, administer the punishment."

Bobby Hill steps off the bench to grab the strap, five feet long and two inches wide with one end fastened to a thick oak handle.

Leyden points to the strap Bobby Hill now holds. "This lash is tanned leather. It's not rawhide, which will slice the skin. These men today will feel the lash—it will give them pain, most assuredly—but I've no desire to scar their skins. Let's get on with it."

The overseer straightens his hat and walks to the bell pole, the strap tucked under his arm.

Leyden motions to one of the slaves, a small man with a limp inflicted by years of handling the Leyden hogs. The man steps to Bobby Hill's side and looks around, unsure of what to do.

"Rufe, you're first," Leyden commands. "Take off your shirt."

Rufe slips his suspenders from his shoulders, pulls his muslin shirttails from his trousers, and slips the shirt over his head. He rolls it up and clutches it to his belly. Bobby Hill grabs the shirt and tosses it to the ground. He tells Rufe to face the bell pole and reach around it. The overseer then pulls a leather thong from his own pocket and—still holding the strap under his arm—binds Rufe's wrists together, tying the slave to the pole.

Leyden looks down at the young slaves. "You boys," he says to the five, "I want you to stand right there. You watch and you learn."

Rufe's woman, Sallah, pushes past Leyden, past the boys. She scoops up Rufe's shirt from the dirt and reaches his side, putting an arm around him.

"I'm here, Rufe."

"Sallah, you get back," Leyden orders. "Stand there with your boy if you want. But no closer."

Bobby Hill takes his position several feet behind Rufe. He jiggles the strap in his right hand and cocks an eye toward Leyden.

"Thirty lashes," Leyden says.

A chorus of moans erupts from the slaves.

The overseer takes a single deep breath and then swings his arm back and brings the strap forward with his full strength. The leather smacks loudly against the slave's left shoulder. Rufe does not flinch. Bobby Hill—along with everyone else who's watching—stands for a moment to see what harm the leather has done to the man's back. There is no mark.

"Keep going," Leyden says.

Bobby Hill swings the strap back and slams it down again on Rufe's back. The slave still does not move. The overseer hits him again, this time swinging the strap with a sideways movement. It hits the right side of the man's rib cage, and Rufe jerks his head backward.

"Pa!" Louie shouts.

Leyden looks down at the boy but says nothing.

William whispers to Willis standing next to him, "Bobby Hill never whipped no man before. I can tell. See him playing with that whip like he's finding out how to use it?"

The rain comes down harder as the overseer continues whipping Rufe. He settles on a stroke, bringing the strap straight back over his own right shoulder and then swinging it overhead, reaching as high as he can at the top of the strap's arc. This stroke hits the shoulder blades squarely and leaves the skin deeply bruised. Bobby Hill is so absorbed in mastering his technique that he strikes Rufe thirty-two times before Leyden stops him.

"That's enough! Untie him."

Sallah steps to the front of the group of slaves.

"Sallah, you stop," Leyden orders. "You boy," he points to Louie. "You go to your father."

Tears stream down Louie's cheeks as he runs to his father. Bobby Hill unties Rufe and the man's son hugs him around the waist. Rufe walks unsteadily back to the group, his eyes shut and his lips clamped, his son hanging onto him.

"William," Leyden calls out.

Nettie puts her hand on William's arm. "I'm with you. Be strong."

William steps to the bell pole. He glances up at Leyden on horseback and then pulls his damp cotton shirt over his head. The rain is cold against his bare skin. He embraces the bell pole, its wood slick against his chest and arms. Bobby Hill ties William's wrists tightly with the thong. A twinge of panic strikes William as he realizes he cannot move or breathe freely. He leans his head against the pole as Leyden says, "Thirty lashes."

For a moment, William wonders what being whipped feels like. Then he hears the whish of the strap cutting the air and the loud slap and feels stinging pain radiate from his shoulders to his heart. The pain is like a red-hot poker across his shoulders. Immediately he hears the frightful whish again. Again the loud slap, and his right shoulder slumps under the burning impact. Before he can even think about pain, the strap strikes him again. He has not anticipated the power of the blows. He feels his spine curling and his knees folding. He tries to straighten his legs, but the next blow slams him into the pole. The flesh on his back is on fire. He's hit again and he flings his head backward, scraping his cheek against the pole. He hears himself utter, "Sweet Jesus."

William hugs the pole with all his strength and tenses every muscle in his body. The next blow hurts so much that tears come to his eyes. He tries going limp to ease his muscles, willing the pain to flow through and away from him. But the whip only digs deeper into his skin and the pain reaches down to his bowels. He becomes aware of the rainfall. He knows it's heavier than it was when he stripped off his shirt. He focuses on the rain softly covering his back, cool and soothing. He still hears the sickening slap of the strap, but rain washes away the pain. Once more, the strap hits him hard and drives his chest against the pole. But the rain protects him. He lowers his head and rests in the rain.

"William!"

He hears the voice and feels a slap across his cheek. Bobby Hill is jerking his chin this way and that. He hears Nettie sobbing by his side.

"He's all right," the overseer tells Nettie. "Get him back with the others."

Nettie stands helplessly as William is whipped. Her thoughts tumble. She believes the whipping of William and the other two men is brutal and wrong. But by no means would she rather see her son whipped. She knows William is strong and can bear the punishment same as Rufe or Willis. Yet these thoughts give her no relief as she watches in horror as the overseer swings the strap high and slams it down with all his might across her man's back. Each of the thirty blows is solid and awful. She is helpless, watching William flinch and twist as the leather strikes him again and again. She sees his skin split and bright blood run down his wet back. She sees Richard standing with the other four boys with his hands over his eyes.

Rain falls harder now. It soaks through her clothing. She looks up at Philip Leyden astride his horse, sees him staring with his head bowed and the rain running off his hat brim onto the bay's shoulders. She wonders how this man can do this thing. William was a child when he first came to this farm, and the master has watched him grow into a loyal hand who works hard. The master would never beat a horse this way. She hears moans from the group around her and then sees William has slumped to his knees and is being held upright only by his arms tied around the pole.

"That's thirty. Revive him, Mister Hill," Leyden shouts to the overseer. "See that he can stand."

It takes a few moments for William to come around. Nettie holds him tightly and cries as Bobby Hill unties the leather thong. William struggles to his feet and the overseer slaps his face to bring life back to his reddened eyes.

Then Nettie leads William away.

"Willis!"

Of the three men being punished, Willis is the strongest. He has spent years removing boulders from the land and felling trees to turn into lumber and plowing fields behind ornery oxen. He pulls off his rain-drenched shirt to reveal a hardened torso. He flexes his arms and glares at Bobby Hill. There is anger in the slave's eyes.

Tying Willis's arms around the pole proves difficult because the man's shoulders and arms are so thick that his wrists do not meet on the other side of the pole. Bobby Hill makes him hug the pole tightly and even then is forced to tie one end of the thong to one of the man's wrists and the other end to the other wrist.

"Thirty," Leyden again commands.

Bobby Hill is tiring. Unable to swing the strap as high and hard, he adopts a sideways arc that pounds the ribs and lower back more than the shoulders. The rain has soaked the leather strap, now slimy like rawhide. Bobby Hill and the others see that the wet strap is doing what Leyden said he wanted to avoid—it is slicing Willis's skin with nearly every blow. After just seven lashes, the blood flows freely from the slave's wounds. Bobby Hill changes his stance to hit the slave's back in a different place, but there too it slices the skin. Rain mixes with Willis's blood, and his entire back glistens red.

Willis does not cringe under the lash. He holds himself upright, his muscles visibly tensed. Only once does he yell and violently throw his head backward. Bobby Hill strikes the thirtieth blow. Willis's pants are stained pink to the knees with bloody rain. Only then does Willis allow his head to fall forward.

"Thirty more," Leyden says.

Everyone gasps, and even Bobby Hill turns to look at the man on the horse.

"Willis has two sons involved in this trouble. So he will pay doubly."

"No!" Reuben yells. "Beat me instead." He dashes toward Leyden but the master holds up his palm.

"You stop right there, boy. For every step you take I'll order five more lashes to your father's back." Leyden narrows his eyes as he glares at the boy. "I want you in particular to learn from this, Reuben."

Bobby Hill begins whipping Willis again. Each blow makes the man's back bloodier. Willis tries to hold himself erect but his strength ebbs and he slumps against the pole. Nearby a gaunt woman named Ellen clasps her hands as if in prayer and shifts her gaze back and forth from her man tied to the pole to her sons as they watch their father suffer. Suddenly the woman's legs give out and she collapses into the mud. The slaves near her try to lift her, but Ellen again slides to the ground and stays there.

Near the pole, Bobby Hill suddenly bends over and vomits. He pulls a handkerchief from his back pocket and wipes his mouth.

"Proceed, Mister Hill," Leyden tells him. "You're almost done."

As if with a single voice the group of slaves begins moaning—an ancient, mournful sound growing louder as the slaps of the wet lash cut the man's back again and again. Bobby Hill finally drops the whip to the ground and moves toward the pole to untie Willis's hands.

Leyden looks to Reuben and Ben. "You boys, help your father."

Without warning Glory shouts, "Beat me! Beat me too!" Everyone stands stunned as she runs toward the bell pole. "Beat me," she screams again and pulls hysterically at her cotton blouse. "Whip me, sir! I don't want no other punishment!"

"What are you saying, Glory?" Leyden asks.

"Him," and she points at Bobby Hill.

"Cover yourself, woman," Leyden tells her. "Nothing more will happen. There's been ample penance paid this day." Then he shifts himself higher in the saddle, his pale chest visible through his rain-soaked shirt. "Leave now, go back to your duties. We've all had enough."

Leyden turns his horse toward his house and nudges the bay's ribs. Bobby Hill follows several yards behind on foot. The slaves linger in the pounding rain for a few minutes more before some return to their cabins and others to their chores.

CHAPTER TEN

THREAT

ADAM KNEELS IN THE ROAD IN FRONT OF POPE'S STORE so his horse Othello blocks the midday sunlight. He lifts one of the gelding's forelegs and examines the fetlock and then the hoof to determine why Othello began limping on the way into Buford.

A bulky shadow falls over Adam and he hears a distinctive voice. "You have trouble with your horse?"

Adam rises to his feet and shields his eyes from the sun. He realizes that Julius Klemmer is nearly a head taller than himself. "It's nothing."

"Then your horse is not hurt?" Klemmer reaches out and pats Othello's flank. He wears the same wool coat Adam has seen before, far too heavy for this day's warmth. "That is fortunate. So what do you want to say to me?"

Adam answers Klemmer's question just as bluntly. "Just this. I don't know why you came to my home the other night with your hounds and your torches unless it was to frighten my family. I told Marshal Summerfield about it."

"So he says. You do not believe I was on the trail of the colored?"

Adam removes his hat and wipes its moist band with his hand. "Frankly, I don't."

"And you are wrong." Sweat trickles down the sides of Klemmer's face. "You believe you are so important I would take my dogs out at night only to scare you? You forget about the law. The slave is property and the law says when the property runs away, it is the owner who has the law with him. And when I catch the slave, the law is with me. It is the same with a horse." He puts his hand heavily on Othello's muzzle. "This horse could run away from you and I could catch him and bring him back because he is your property. I catch the fugitive and take him back, just the same."

Adam watches a bony dog lying near the road, tongue hanging limp as he pants. "Of course, there's money in it for you. You didn't mention the rewards."

Klemmer shifts his gaze past Adam to the bony dog. He flicks his hand and makes a hissing sound. The dog groans to its feet and ambles across the road toward some shade.

"You are right. I will take the money the law gives me."

"You profit from another man's misfortune, just like you said about that boy in the wagon. Taking that money is how you live." Adam reaches for Othello's reins.

Klemmer quickly grabs the reins from the hitching rail and holds them beyond Adam's reach. "I should be like you, maybe? I should work like a slave in my own fields. Or maybe run a little store like the coward here?"

"Coward?"

"He will not fight for anything. It is his faith, am I right?"

"John Pope is a Quaker. They're pacifists. They don't believe in fighting. But that doesn't mean they're cowards."

"Ah, I said the wrong word." Klemmer chuckles. "I am still learning."

"Now give me the reins."

The bony dog lying in the shade barks as Ira Ogden saunters across the road from the inn. He unties the stained apron from around his waist and flings it over his shoulder.

Adam again reaches for the reins but Klemmer dangles them beyond his reach.

"I'll tell you the same as I told the marshal," Adam says with no attempt to hide his anger. "I just want my family to live on our farm in peace. I don't want runaways coming there and I don't want people like you coming there to hunt them down."

"You speak like one of the abolition people around here. They tell me there are no slaves hiding here and for me to go away. But they are hiding them. Sometimes they put the fugitives in their barn and sometimes even in their house. They give them food and at night they take them to another house and then to another. They are thieves."

"I assure you I'm not one of them."

"So you say."

Ogden sidles up to Klemmer. He eyes the reins in Klemmer's hand. "Y'all could be one of them," he says as he shifts his gaze to Adam. "Sounds like y'all could be hiding darkies, sure as shooting. Y'all could be a goddamn abolitionist, who's to say?"

Suddenly Klemmer drops the reins and grabs Adam's arm and presses him back against the hitching rail. Adam squirms and the wood grinds into his back.

"You will listen to me," Klemmer says with his face close. "You hide the runaway fugitives and bad things will happen. The law says you can go to jail but I say it will be worse."

Adam smells the cigar smoke on Klemmer's breath and the reek of his sweat. He turns his face away. "I'm not one of them."

Klemmer slowly releases him and steps back.

"Lucky for y'all," Ogden chuckles. "Klemmer here's dead set on catching these fugitives hisself, one and all. Getting them back to the rightful owners and making hisself a living along the way. Ain't that right, Klemmer?"

This time Klemmer gathers up the reins and forcefully hands them to Adam. "You hear of fugitives nearby, you get word to me through Ogden." He juts his jaw toward the inn across the road. "You do that. It will help the law and the owners. Yah, even your own family. Not like the ones who hide the runaways and then the bad things happen to them. You hear what I am telling you?"

Adam steps into the stirrup and pulls himself onto the saddle. As he turns Othello, one of the men slaps the horse's rump.

CHAPTER ELEVEN

PRICES

"GET UP HERE," BOBBY HILL ORDERS. "NOW!"

William groans as he hoists himself onto the wagon, his back still tender from the whipping two weeks ago. He slides onto the wooden seat next to Bobby Hill as the overseer slaps the reins of the two-horse team.

"I've got goods to pick up in Washington," Bobby Hill says as the wagon rolls forward. "When we get to town, we'll stop at the old courthouse first so you can look over the judge's room like Mister Leyden said."

The two men avoid looking at each other. William finally decides to break the silence. "I hear Mister Leyden be getting more hogs." He keeps his eyes trained on the fields and meadows.

"Not with pork prices dropping," Bobby Hill responds.

"But don't we got more hogs than last year?"

"Not for long. We'll be selling them but we'll make less."

"Maybe more sows would make it better."

"Listen to what I'm telling you," Bobby Hill says as he turns to look at William. "I'm saying we've got more hogs this year but we'll make less money. The price of pork is going down. You understand?"

Both men revert to silence. The wagon rolls on in the cool morning and William again concentrates on the countryside and its spring lushness.

A mile farther, the overseer speaks again. "We've got trouble with the tobacco too. Our harvest is bigger and the leaf's the best we've ever grown. But these days more farmers are growing it. There's even good crop coming from across the river in Ohio. So down goes the price just like with the damn pork. And here we are. Doing more and getting less for it. Let me tell you, Mister Leyden can't afford to be losing money."

William starts to speak but stops himself.

"You got something to say?"

"Maybe we just got to work more. Maybe we got to get more tobacco and more pigs."

Bobby Hill casts a sideways glance at William. "That's one way of looking at it. It's the philosophy of more and more and always more. I'm a student of agrarian economics and I'll tell you this. You can't do more of anything these days without spending more money. Raising more pork would take more feed and that means we'd have to clear more land to grow more corn for them to eat. We'd need more pens. Maybe even more coloreds to handle the new hogs. It all means money."

William turns to Bobby Hill and speaks quickly. "Some of our boys be getting big enough to help. My Alfred could help Richard and Rufe with the hogs. And if we could make us one more shed—"

"You've got to think in a different way, William. It's not about putting your boy or somebody else's boy in there with the hogs. It's the whole economics of the thing. You understand what I'm trying to tell you?"

"No, sir," William mutters.

Bobby Hill hunches forward over the reins. "Same with tobacco. What does it take to make more money? It takes more leaf. How do you get more leaf? With more land and more work. We'd need to clear more land and maybe even buy more acreage. We'd need to build more curing sheds and we'd need more hands in the fields. It's all money. The fact is we've got to begin doing things in a different way entirely. My sister and her husband need to get money in ways they haven't tried before."

William watches the sway of the horses' rumps a few feet in front of him. He knows Bobby Hill is staring at him.

"You've been on this farm a long time, haven't you?"

"Yessir, I have."

"My sister and her husband take good care of their coloreds."

"Mister Leyden says we got to work hard and keep clean and be Christian and don't touch liquor. So that's what we do and he watches over us because Mister Leyden is a good master. Sure is."

Bobby Hill flicks the reins again. "That's all fine and dandy, William, but if Mister Leyden starts losing money it won't be good for any of you. His money puts a roof over your head and food on your table and clothes on your back. He provides what's good about your life so you don't need to worry about where these things are going to come from."

"Yessir."

"So, William, you ever think about being free?"

William glances at the overseer and quickly looks back at the road.

"Well, I say you coloreds can complain about your lot and take it out on fences and tools. You could even run away. But I'll tell you, the coloreds who run up North don't have it near as good as you. I've seen it with my own eyes. White people up there hate you coloreds. They won't give them work, so the coloreds starve to death in those bitter cold winters with a few rags on their backs. Starving and freezing right there in the streets. Frozen bodies of coloreds everywhere. I'm talking women and children too. You don't have to believe me, William, but that's the way it is."

Arriving in the town of Washington, William spots the old Mason County courthouse standing two stories tall with a third-story bell tower. Once the center of the town's civic life, much of the courthouse is a school since the county seat moved to Maysville six years earlier. Inside the building, Bobby Hill tells an elderly caretaker that he and William want to look at the room that housed the judge's chambers. They follow the caretaker as he hobbles down a creaking hallway to a small room adjoining the courtroom.

William studies the room while Bobby Hill chats with the old man. He runs his hand along the walnut and cherry woodwork. He looks closely at the expert joinery and smooth finishes on the shelves and cabinets. He traces with his fingers the delicate turnings and carvings. At the chamber doorway he turns around to take in the way the shutters filter the bright sunlight.

"You got what you need, William?"

They leave the old courthouse and walk down a grassy slope toward the wagon. A poster nailed to a tree catches William's eye with its bold black type and crude drawing of a black family.

"I didn't know you could read," Bobby Hill chides him.

"Can't, sir."

"That big word there. That says 'slave.' Now look here." He points to the other words below it. "This word is 'auction' and it says there's going to be a slave auction here on Wednesday."

"Here?"

"Yep, it says six bucks will be sold. Ages twelve to twenty and in excellent health. That's always good. And here it says a wench of twenty-three and one fourteen and another of forty-two. That one's getting old but it says here she's still a good cook. Might fetch a few dollars."

William looks across the lawn toward a wooden platform standing in the shade of poplars and maples. "That it? That where the auction to be?"

"Yep. You got any idea how much you'd bring at auction, William?"

He looks at the overseer and cannot conceal the fear in his eyes.

"Come on, how much? You're a fairly strong fellow. And you got skills. How much you think?"

"Never learned about auctions and such."

"I'd bid nine hundred dollars for you. Maybe even a thousand because you can build things. If it were up to me, I'd buy you and then hire you out and make back a good portion of my investment."

"That's a lot of money, sir."

"Sure it's a lot. But what do you think Nettie would bring?"

"Nettie?"

"Sure, if we sold your woman. What do you think we'd get for her?"

William feels blood rushing to his face. "I don't like this talk, sir."

"No, I suppose not. But I'd say we'd get at least twelve hundred for her. More than for you, even with your skills. That's because she's got plenty of baby making left in her and she can produce a crop of little ones that'll bring good prices in a few years. And she's a good cook, to boot."

"Stop!" William's feels his fists clenching.

"Did you just tell me to stop talking?"

William waits a moment for his blood to settle. "It's that talk about selling my Nettie—even if it ain't true—that talk's so bad I can't even think straight."

"No, I suppose not."

CHAPTER TWELVE

PROFITS

WILLIAM STRETCHES HIS RAGGED MEASURING TAPE across a section of plaster wall in Philip Leyden's office just as Sallah slips into the room holding something draped with a napkin.

"Eat this and be fast about it." She unwraps a warm turkey drumstick. "We really laying out a spread for this Mister Hiram Nash from over by Louisville. Nettie and me been sweating in that kitchen all morning cooking these turkeys and hams and potato salad and bread pudding and—"

"Who's he?" William asks between licking his fingers.

"Somebody worth a big show. That's all I know."

Sallah leaves with the drumstick bone and William goes back to marking off inches on the wall. A few minutes later Philip Leyden walks into the room.

"Hard at it, I see."

"Yessir."

William hears another man chatting in the hall with Grace Leyden.

"Hiram, come join me in here," Leyden calls.

Hiram Nash is squat with long gray hair combed straight back from his forehead. His blue frock coat is slung over his arm and his crimson waistcoat—into which he is tightly packed—remains buttoned on this warm day. He taps the floor with his ornamental cane as he enters the room.

"So, Philip, how are things working out with your brother-in-law as overseer? He seems a studious fellow and a far cry from most who do that work." Nash tugs at his black cravat to loosen it. "And he does have some provocative ideas, I'll say that for him."

"Bobby's a veritable font of ideas," Leyden answers. "He reads agricultural journals dawn to dusk and, yes, I've taken stock of some of his suggestions." Leyden gestures toward a chair near a sawhorse. "Please excuse the clutter, Hiram. Have a seat."

William moves to a far corner of the room and kneels on the floor with his measuring tape. Nash eyes him and then looks back at Leyden.

"It's all right," Leyden assures him. "We can talk." He sifts through the papers on his desk and begins telling his friend about a trip to New Jersey he made this past November. "Grace and I were visiting her cousin and I had the opportunity to talk with his banker friends. I tell you, Hiram, never before had I realized the emphasis those Yankees place on profit, pure and simple. I believe it drives every decision they make."

"Surely there's more to life than purely pecuniary concerns," Nash says and adds a tap of his cane.

"But I must confess it's affected my own ideas about this farm." Leyden thumbs through more papers.

Nash settles back into the chair. "You've always been conscientious in running this place. For heaven's sake, Philip, you've diversified and increased your income without expanding either your Negroes or your acreage. That's saying something in this day and age."

"But now I'm looking toward something else and—"

William is poised to saw a board and looks over at Leyden.

"Go ahead, William. Our guest is familiar with making himself heard above the hollering of his constituents." Leyden and Nash chuckle in unison.

William cuts through the board with four quick strokes and then Leyden continues. "The Yankees I met were sensitive to—how should I put it? —to the forces that drive commerce. They talked incessantly about the growth of the railroads and the new western territories."

Nash leans forward in his chair. "We all have our eyes on the Kansas and Nebraska territories. If we can just get Senator Douglas's bill signed into law, we'll have effectively removed the boundary that's halted the growth of slavery for thirty years. But to do that, we need to squelch the influence of the abolitionists."

"So our southern Congressional delegation is truly intent on pushing slavery into the western territories? I'm not sure the Yankees will want that," Leyden says. "I'm pretty certain they'll try to stop us, Hiram."

Nash taps his cane against the floor with some force. "That's because, fundamentally, they don't understand us." The man's voice becomes deeper and fuller, that of an experienced orator. "Those Yankee bankers don't comprehend that our labor is our capital. One and the same. Our capital is not tied up like theirs in machinery and locomotives and buildings. No, our capital is our Negro workers." He rises slowly from his chair and begins slicing the air with his cane. "And those foul abolitionists would just as soon destroy our way of life and take down the entire nation's economy with it. A damned ignorant lot they are."

Leyden finally pulls a sheet of paper from the pile he's been sorting on his desk. "Ah, here it is," he says and motions for Nash to return to his seat.

Nash sits again but keeps talking and thumping his cane for emphasis. "Don't forget, Philip, that our Yankee neighbors are seeing their own cities teeming with thousands upon thousands of foreigners—Germans and Irish and who knows what else—bringing every manner of language and faith and political persuasion all across the North. It stands to reason these Yankees are dwelling on railroads and telegraphs and the new lands to the west. They also need to expand westward to perpetuate their own way of life, just as we do. So they attack our beautiful southland—the largest producer of cotton in the world. They completely ignore the fact that cotton is the financial blood of this whole United States and we need the Negro to grow it. No, sir, the damned abolitionists would slash our southern arteries for their cause and bleed this entire nation to death."

"I didn't intend to get you riled, Hiram," Leyden says with a smile. "Earlier, you and I talked about the prices of pork and tobacco. As I said, I simply cannot continue along my current path—"

"And you are not alone, my friend." Nash thumps his cane more quietly as he calms down.

"Bobby and I may have come upon something. But I want to hear your thoughts on it before I even discuss it with Grace."

Leyden examines the sheet of paper he holds. "These figures from *De Bow's Review* are the projected growth in American cotton for the next ten years. They predict a substantial growth—along with substantial profitability for the planters—throughout the Mississippi delta and in the Red and Arkansas River valleys."

"That's most interesting, Philip. But you don't grow cotton and you don't live in one of those godforsaken places."

Leyden keeps his eyes on the paper. "The estimate is that for each ten bales of cotton, the planters will get a profit that could reach two hundred dollars or more per field hand. Hiram, I repeat, two hundred dollars per slave. Pure profit."

"That's an attractive return, I admit."

"Now listen to this, Hiram. These growers need to constantly replenish their slave populations and, according to these figures, they're willing even today to pay over twelve hundred dollars per head."

"Far more than we pay here in Kentucky, for sure."

"So you see, here's a steadily increasing demand for slaves at steadily increasing prices."

Nash cocks his head and strokes his chin with his free hand. "So you're planning to transform your farm into . . . what, exactly?"

"A hub of labor supply. I'll hire agents. Good men. Not that contemptuous lot we usually associate with the slave trader. We'll buy coloreds throughout the upper South at our lower prices and ship them to depots closer to the planters, to places like Little Rock and Shreveport and—"

"Franklin and Armfield. Ever hear of them?" Nash interrupts. "Large traders with a business not unlike your plan. They started in the late twenties. Armfield was in Virginia. His agents bought up Negro slaves and shipped them to Franklin in New Orleans, who sold them to planters down there for a hefty profit. They became known for the quality of their Negroes and both were regarded as gentlemen. Very wealthy gentlemen, I might add."

"That's it exactly," Leyden slaps the top of his desk. "My stock will be strong and healthy and obedient. They'll be Christian and not savage. I'll do some breeding here. I'm perfectly willing to invest eight to ten years growing and training young coloreds before I sell them to recoup my investment and more."

"And you're what, twenty-five, thirty miles here from the Ohio River? You could have your own steamer for moving your stock downriver," Nash says, now showing enthusiasm for Leyden's idea. "You'd be in complete control of both stock and delivery."

"And timing, too," Leyden goes on. "We'd ship between October and March. We've learned it would give the slaves time to adjust to the hotter climate so they'd be ready for the growing season. It's that sort of thinking that I hope will set me apart—"

Nash bursts into loud laughter.

"Where's the humor, Hiram?"

"Simply the irony of it all," he says. "It's the irony of you being prompted to think like this by your Yankee friends and their lust for profit. You listened to them and your conclusion is—if I'm following you correctly—to improve your own profitability and become wealthy by providing a steady supply of Negroes to meet a growing demand while taking advantage of the price differential." Nash slapped his knee. "You, my friend, are employing the tactic of a Yankee banker to become an abolitionist's worst nightmare."

Leyden replaces the paper on his desk with a broad smile. "Perhaps so. Let's continue our stroll."

Nash suddenly notices William sitting silently in the corner.

"It's all right," Leyden tells Nash. He puts his arm around his friend's shoulders and leads him from the room. "That fellow has a talent for carpentry but he's stupid as a brick."

CHAPTER THIRTEEN

CONNECTIONS

"I WONDER IF THIS IS EVEN THE RIGHT WAY?" ANNE SAYS as the carriage bounces in and out of the road's hardened ruts and pitches her hard against Jacob. "If it's this difficult for us to find Wendell Childress, what's it like for slaves on the run?"

A short while later Jacob pulls the horse and carriage to a halt. A clapboard house sits fifty paces back from the road, mostly hidden behind a thicket of ivy.

"This must be it," he says.

A delicate black boy of about fifteen with a demeanor mature beyond his years answers Jacob's knock on the door. He leads the couple through the kitchen and past a small cot with a dozen books piled high along one side. He takes them to a small parlor, where they find Childress, a slender man with sharp features and a high ivory forehead framed by lank black hair falling to his shoulders. His cravat and wrinkled blue waistcoat are oddly formal for the rural setting. He holds himself upright with an oak cane in each hand.

After brief introductions, Jacob tells Childress of his and Anne's desire to help fugitive slaves.

"Sit, sit." Childress points a cane at two slat-back chairs beside a window. "Permit me to explain some things." With practiced deliberation he slowly and mechanically lowers himself into a wingback chair and nests his canes between his knees. "Four years ago," he begins, "I inherited a substantial sum upon the death of my beloved parents—certainly enough so that a parsimonious man like myself would be freed from the drudgery of daily existence. I wanted to see the capitals of Europe—perhaps even to live in one of them—and to frequent the finest libraries and museums and to bask in the sparkling conversation of the intelligentsia."

The man's cadenced diction intrigues Anne. Then she watches intently as he goes silent with his eyes clamped shut. "Excuse me," he says as he slowly opens his eyes and resumes talking. "I decided to leave my home in Cincinnati and to head to New York, whence I would embark on a sea journey to London. Has either of you been there?"

Anne and Jacob shake their heads.

"No, I suppose not." Childress closes his eyes again and sits absolutely still. A moment later he opens his eyes and resumes his story. "On the morning of my departure I boarded a coach and not more than a hundred feet from my doorstep a stampeding herd of squealing swine charged at us. The horses reared and the coach tipped onto its side and I cracked my cranium against the cobblestones. I have not been the same since."

Childress explains that his head injury left him stricken with chronic vertigo. Moving his head even slightly in a certain direction—and the direction varies moment to moment—sends his mind reeling for several dizzying seconds and leaves him with no sense of balance. He can go nowhere without his canes.

"You poor man," Anne says.

Childress raises his hand. "I only wish to emphasize that the cruelest of misfortunes can open doors of opportunity." He talks freely—poking the air with his skinny fingers for emphasis—until some slight nod of his head triggers the vertigo and momentarily suspends him in his private, whirling world. He tells Anne and Jacob how he sold his big house in Cincinnati and bought this tiny one fifty miles to the east, settling into the life of a recluse.

"I've heard thee is active in helping the Friends assist fugitive slaves who've crossed the river," Jacob says. "I think thee has contact with some members of our Friends meeting in Buford, but I don't know which meeting thee attends."

Childress leans forward in his chair, holding one cane out in front. "My dear mother was a Quaker who raised me to oppose injustice in all of its forms. But I am not a Quaker."

"I was certain thee would be a Friend," Jacob says, "since it was from Friends that I learned of thee and they encouraged my secrecy about thee."

"It's true, I share many beliefs with the Society of Friends." Childress pauses once more. "But no, I am not a Quaker. I am not plain and I am not a pacifist."

"But thee surely is involved."

"I freely admit that I contribute to abolitionist journals and send missives to newspapers throughout the North. Putting pen to paper is something I can still do and I pride myself on being a master-ful propagandist."

Anne frowns.

"Oh, Miss Billings, do not scorn this teetering propagandist," Childress says. "I take great delight in penning articles about the well-oiled machine we call the Underground Railroad. Oh, the sto-ries we"—he shuts his eyes for several seconds and starts again—"the stories we tell. We describe in detail a network of brave citizens who move hapless fugitives northward to Canada in a matter of days. We tell how we clothe these unfortunate people and feed them along the way and then deposit them in a land of freedom and opportunity. I write profusely about conductors and agents and depots and main lines and sidings and switches. It drives the slaveholders mad."

"But shouldn't it be kept secret?" Anne asks.

"Not in the least. These descriptions convince slaveholders that their beloved institution is headed toward extinction and that the South had best begin learning how to exist without that brutal practice. Such publicity convinces us here in the North that there's a steadily growing anti-slavery movement consisting of brave neighbors. And perhaps best of all, these descriptions encourage the slaves themselves to flee their captivity. It gives them hope there will be people here who will help them." Childress studies the knob of one of his canes. "Of course these descriptions are all greatly exaggerated."

Jacob gives Childress a look of puzzlement.

"Question? Go on," Childress tells him.

"It's just that when I tried to find anyone involved with helping fugitive slaves, there seemed to be no group at all," Jacob says. "No one seemed to know anything. It took me weeks to even find thee—even among the Friends."

"And that, young man, is the true face of things. As you go north—Cleveland, Rochester, Detroit, Albany, Bennington—the Underground Railroad is more formally established because the land there is safer. Whether a so-called conductor is threatened with arrest for hiding fugitives is more a social matter of how well his wife gets along with the judge's wife. Good heavens, some of our people farther north even use newspapers to advertise their homes as shelters for fugitive slaves." Childress closes his eyes and this time shakes his head violently. "Excuse me once again. Down here the situation is dangerously different. We're close to the Ohio River and we're overrun with marshals, sheriffs, and slave hunters of unimaginable cruelty. They prowl our roads like vermin. Federal marshals come after us armed with that damnable fugitive law while our judges wield brutal gavels against the Negro and those who would help his kind. The truth is, aiding an escaped slave in these parts is sure to raise the ire of your neighbors and merchants and preachers alike. You can land behind bars or far worse."

"That's exactly the way it is with our neighbors," Anne says.

"Then keep that in mind, young lady. You should know that our situation"—Childress is again momentarily stricken—"our situation is steadily worsening. Even someone inclined to give only a crust of bread or an old jacket to a poor runaway can be threatened and beaten and often jailed. We see people's homes being torched by slave hunters who are nothing more than scum from across the river or from next door. Farther north the emphasis may be on the word 'railroad.' But down here, it must be on the word 'underground.'"

Childress pauses while Anne and Jacob reflect.

"And think of the runaways themselves," he goes on. "No fugitives are likely to find this particular house where we now sit. Not unless they're brought here by someone associated with the underground. The slaves who decide to flee of their own accord have a desperate plight. Truly desperate. Most of them have never heard of the Underground Railroad and would have no way of reaching us anyway, if it weren't for those of us willing to assist. As for me, I do what I can, when I can. Sheltering those unfortunate people is one activity where the seclusion of this humble dwelling is a distinct advantage."

Jacob tells him, "I believe Anne and I are still dedicated to helping the slaves."

"That's exceedingly brave, my good fellow, considering what I just told you."

Childress shifts his body from side to side, plants both canes in front of his chair, and rises slowly until he is standing. "Permit me one more digression to help you better understand my specific situation. The boy who greeted you at the door—his name is Marcus— will become familiar if you decide to work with us."

Childress explains he first learned of the boy two years earlier in a letter published in the abolitionist newspaper *North Star*. The letter told of a gifted black boy on a farm near Memphis. "It stated that this boy's brilliant promise—and I quote from memory—'will never be fulfilled because of a destiny limited to mindless labor under the pain of the lash.' Upon reading about him, I wrote to friends in Cincinnati and asked them to find the lad and buy him. Simple as that. I had been in despair for obvious reasons and the idea of saving that boy brightened my days. My friends succ ssfully located Marcus and negotiated with his owner, who happened to be the proprietor of a large Tennessee livestock farm. The man was not eager to sell the boy, but neither was he eager for more abolitionist publicity concerning his property. He agreed to sell Marcus for the steep price of sixteen hundred dollars. My friends and I assumed the boy would be overjoyed. But we'd overlooked the fact that he didn't want to leave his mother and brothers, so I offered to buy the boy's entire family. The owner refused. The boy's mother finally convinced Marcus to come north to live here, with his incapacitated benefactor."

Childress walks—using a peculiar cane-foot, cane-foot shuffle that sets his black hair swinging—to where Anne and Jacob are seated. "Marcus is a veritable savant," he tells them. "A towering genius in a boy's body. In the two years he's been here he's conquered much classical literature and philosophy and has exhibited an exceptional aptitude for mathematics—or so I'm told, for I have no such gift myself. He cleans and cooks and nurses this obstreperous cripple you see before you. I pay him well and he is free to spend his money as he wishes. It was Marcus"—another pause until Childress's world steadies itself—"yes, Marcus who sought our involvement with the fugitives. That's his cot you passed in the kitchen. Among that stack of books you'll find everything by or about the former slave Frederick Douglass. Marcus idolizes Douglass both as a former slave and as editor of the abolitionist journal so instrumental in obtaining the lad's own freedom. Like his hero, the boy is committed to freeing his people."

"I wonder if he misses his mother?" Anne asks.

"He does."

Jacob glances out the window at a nearby hedgerow and its shadow lengthening across the yard. "I must ask thee, if we become involved with helping the fugitives, how would it work? What would thee expect of us?"

"Excellent question," Childress says as he shuffles to a small sofa and props himself upright against one of its arms.

"Now, as for the fugitives, sometimes I know in advance when they'll be arriving. Most often I don't. There's only a knock on the door in the middle of the night and they're here. Marcus and I feed and shelter them for as long as necessary—usually a day or two—though I've had some here for a week. The longer they're here, the greater my concern for safety, theirs and ours. There comes a time when the fugitives must continue their journey. And as you can see, I cannot perform that duty myself."

"So Marcus does it?" Anne asks.

"Certainly not." Childress declares. "I absolutely forbid it. Can you appreciate the risk he'd be taking? If at any juncture a young Negro is discovered helping fugitives, he'd be back in chains or worse. I can't even imagine the horrors the lad would face. No, Miss Billings, Marcus serves as a messenger only, my black Mercury. He notifies others when they are to move the fugitives from here to the next location. That's risk enough for the lad."

"But you've made him legally free and he's living in a free state," Anne says.

"The fact of the matter is that free coloreds are abducted all the time, and these unfortunates tend to be taken straight to the deeper South where there's less opportunity for them to be found and where they can be quickly and anonymously worked to death. The brutality inherent in this evil institution becomes magnified the farther south one goes."

Jacob stands and holds out his hand to Anne, who rises from her chair. "Perhaps we can talk as we get ready to leave," he says. "It's much later than we'd expected to stay, but thee has told us what we wanted to know. I believe I speak for both of us in telling you we remain interested."

"Yes. Even more than before," Anne says, her tone excited.

Childress shuffles with them through the kitchen, past the cot where Marcus sleeps, and outside to Jacob's buggy.

"Listen to me," he tells the couple. "Remain silent about what you're doing. Tell no one. Absolutely no one. Slavery's sympathizers are everywhere and the very walls have ears." He raises one of his canes and points it at them. "If the law or the slave catchers find out you're involved, they'll intimidate you. They'll frighten you. They'll even harm you and your loved ones. So consider yourself warned. Now I want to thank you for a most pleasant afternoon."

Childress waves the cane and teeters toward his house.

CHAPTER FOURTEEN

DISCLOSURE

NETTIE DUSTS CAREFULLY AROUND THE ORNATE CRYS-
tal bottles on her mistress's vanity table. She lifts one to sniff its fra-
grance and sees the morning sunlight reflected through the cut glass
and amber liquid. Then she hears Grace Leyden's voice behind the
closed door to the adjoining bedroom.

"That's not decent, Philip. It's not even Christian!"

Nettie moves stealthily across the dressing room and puts her
ear to the door. She hears Philip Leyden addressing his wife in
hushed tones.

"It only makes financial sense," Nettie hears the master saying.
"Think of our future, Grace. This farm doesn't make money the way
it did just a couple of years ago. Everything's costing us more and the
prices we're getting at market are worse than ever. Can you understand what I'm telling you?"

Nettie hears no reply.

A moment later, he continues. "What do you suggest I do, Grace?
Raise more tobacco? We'd need more land. Should we buy more
land? Or would you prefer more hogs? You always complain about

their stink. What should I do? Turn the whole farm into a pigpen? Please, you must face facts."

Then Nettie hears her mistress, louder than before. "How could I hold my head up among my friends? How could I even face them?"

"Listen to me," he answers with growing impatience. "This is business. There's an entire section of the country where planters pay top dollar for slaves. We could do well, Grace. We could—"

"You could do well. You! I refuse to have any part of it." Her voice is rising. "What you're proposing is contrary to every belief we've ever held when it comes to our coloreds and you know it."

"I'm not talking about being some whiskey-sodden trader who speculates in slaves who are ill or criminal. I'm not trading women for the sole purpose of—"

"You said you would breed slaves," Grace interrupts him. "You said that!"

"I said breeding was one aspect of it. Why wouldn't we encourage propagation? Slave children are good capital, and when they're old enough to be sold—"

"I can't talk about this anymore."

There is only silence. Nettie quickly moves away from the door. Just as she reaches the vanity table, the door between the two rooms bursts open and Grace rushes into the dressing room.

"Nettie! I didn't know you were here!"

"Just dusting, ma'am," Nettie says, frightened.

Grace puts her hands on her hips. "Did you hear what my husband and I were discussing?"

Nettie keeps dusting.

"You must have." She throws herself into the overstuffed chair in the corner of the room. "I cannot remember when I've been this angry."

Nettie nervously rearranges the perfume bottles and continues dusting.

"Pay attention to me, Nettie. Now let me ask you something. What would you think if this farm became a place to grow colored babies?"

"We already got our babies, don't we, ma'am?" She keeps her eyes on the group of crystal bottles.

"What if we wanted to grow babies like we grow piglets or foals?"

Nettie looks up and then folds her dust cloth. "Ma'am, we can't have more babies than we already got and still do our work."

"That's right, Nettie. But what if we brought in more colored girls just to have the babies? To have them one after another? What about that?"

"Who's father to these new babies?"

"Who cares?" A flush spreads across Grace's face. "I suppose any colored stud can service the girls. For that matter, who says he's got to be colored? Lighter babies get more on the block anyway."

"Sell these babies, ma'am?" Nettie's expression betrays her confusion.

"Now you're beginning to see. Yes, get young women like yourself—probably even younger—in here to have one baby after another like broodmares. Raise these babies till they're children and then sell them to whoever pays the most."

"Oh, ma'am. I know about these things. Children getting pushed onto the block and men poking at them and looking at their teeth and their parts. Oh, ma'am, that ain't what Mister Leyden wants."

Grace sighs deeply. "I really don't know anymore. This has always been a Christian place where you coloreds could raise your children as a family. Where your children remain your children and not taken away."

"And we sure thankful, ma'am."

"You know, there are people who believe you coloreds don't feel the love of a mother for her child. They say it's not in your blood and that taking a child away doesn't pain you the way it does us white people. Well, I'm not so sure. I'm pretty convinced that what I've witnessed is actual love of a mother for her babies. That's why in all these years we've not broken up your families. Philip hasn't sold one of our servants ever. Not one."

Nettie grasps her dust cloth tightly as if wringing it. "Ma'am, you think this is going to happen?"

"I'd like to say no. I'd like to say it's just an ugly idea that'll never see the light of day." Grace sighs again and stares across the room at nothing. "I don't know. Perhaps I've said too much."

CHAPTER FIFTEEN

CHANGE

WILLIAM FINISHES PAINTING THE FINAL COAT OF SHEL-
lac on the new bookshelves and starts clearing the room of cans and
brushes and rags.

Philip Leyden stands nearby, watching him. "William, you've
done a remarkable job. You've greatly exceeded my expectations."
He leans over to examine a shelf. "When will this be dry? I want to
get my books up here soon."

"Be dry tomorrow, sir."

"Good."

William moves toward the door with his arms full.

"Stay a moment, William. I want to talk. Set that stuff down."

He sets the cans and brushes on the floor and rubs his hands with
a shellac-stained rag. "Yessir?"

"There are two things I want to say. The first deals with a new
project and the other is about you."

William stares at the floor.

"No cause for alarm, William. It appears I'd best talk about the
second point first if I'm to put you at ease. To start with, I want you to

know that there'll be considerable change here at the farm. Probably as much change as you've seen in all your years here."

"Twenty-five."

"Twenty-five?"

"Been here twenty-five years, sir."

"So you have." Leyden gingerly touches the shelf with his fingertip. "The point is, I don't want you worrying. If there's less work needed in the fields and less with the swine, you're still in a good position because of your carpentry skills."

"You mean there won't be so much for us to do?"

"That's my point, William. Even if there's less work here, I can hire you out. You specifically. I can send you wherever your skills are wanted. And here's something else. You and I perhaps could have an arrangement so you could keep part of the earnings I get for the work you do at other farms. You ever thought about that?"

"Never even thought about working away from here, sir."

"It could be a good thing for both you and me."

"I would get some of the money?"

"Some of it. But let's not get into that right now, William. I just don't want you to worry. You and Nettie will be just fine."

"The boys and Lucy, sir?"

"Your children? Of course. Just make sure there's no more trouble around here. No more broken fences and the like. Then everybody will be fine."

"Yessir." He leans down to pick up the cans and brush.

"Now to the other point." Leyden tells William that he is to begin work immediately on a new building to be located near the slave cabins and that Bobby Hill will give him the details and arrange for the materials to be delivered.

"Some of the folks, sir, they going to be real happy."

Leyden walks toward the door but stops and looks at William. "Who?"

"The ones so crowded."

"William, I'll ask you to not jump to conclusions. I didn't say anyone here would be moving into new quarters, did I?"

William shakes his head.

"Just build the building and keep your assumptions to yourself. That's all I ask."

CHAPTER SIXTEEN

PROPERTY

A FEW DAYS LATER, TOWARD EVENING, NETTIE AND William and their small children gather around the cabin's table, where Nettie is setting out plates of hot food. The cabin door opens, and Richard steps inside, glancing at Nettie and William as he catches his breath.

"Where you been?" William demands.

"Me and Reuben—"

"Boy?" William snaps.

"We didn't get in no trouble. I'm telling the truth. But we seen some things."

"Here, eat this." Nettie hands him a plate. "And whew! Put those shoes outside. They smell like the pigpen."

"What things you seen?" William asks.

Richard puts his shoes outside the cabin door and shuts it. "Mister Leyden and another man, they come up to the house in a wagon. They got three coloreds in the back of it and Mister Hill he come to the wagon and took them out."

"When?"

"Just a bit ago. Just before dark. They got chains on."

"Chains?" Nettie says. "What they look like?"

"Two boys same as me. And a girl, near as I could tell."

"Anyone else?" William asks.

"Me and Reuben figured we best get on home."

With that, Richard devours the food on his plate and scrapes it clean. The evening routines continue—washing the dishes, getting ready for bed. Nettie tucks Lucy into her cradle. Alfred and Dan crawl onto a large mattress next to the cabin wall and pull a couple of quilts over themselves. Richard washes off the day's dust and removes his trousers and wedges himself next to Alfred, who pushes Dan closer to the wall.

The cabin door opens suddenly and frightens Nettie, who jerks the crib and sets Lucy to crying. Alfred and Dan sit up as Richard bounds out of bed and pulls on his trousers. William jumps up from his chair and holds a lantern high to see.

"Get more light in here," Bobby Hill shouts as he thunders into the cabin. "Get in here," he orders someone outside in the dark.

Two boys and a girl enter, bumping into each other in the cramped space. The two boys are about sixteen, the girl perhaps the same, maybe younger. In the dim light, one boy is ebony black. His face is tear streaked and the remnant of his shirt hangs loosely on his skinny frame. The other boy is lighter skinned and several inches taller. He wears no shirt and hugs himself against the night chill. He glares at everyone in the cabin. The girl quickly walks past the two boys and Bobby Hill to where Nettie is holding Lucy. Barefoot, her hair closely cropped, she wears a threadbare purple cotton dress that reveals the outline of breasts. The girl pats Lucy's head and grins at Nettie.

"She's Martha," Bobby Hill says and then turns to the two boys. He points at the crying one. "This is John and this other one says his name's Constantine—and it must be because nobody makes up a name like that. They'll stay here with you."

"But where, Mister Hill?" Nettie says. "We got no more mattresses and no more blankets."

"You'll have to come up with something. This is where they'll stay."

Martha holds out her arms to Lucy. Nettie studies the girl's face and slowly hands Lucy over to her.

"How long they going to be here?" William wonders.

"Plan on it being a while. I'll increase your food portions."

When the overseer leaves, there's an awkward moment while everyone in the cabin just looks at each other.

Nettie breaks the silence. "You boys stand by the fire. Get yourselves warm."

"Where you from?" William asks.

No one answers for a moment, and then the boy John speaks up. "We been bought. Your master bought us today. Now we his property."

"I seen you get off the wagon," Richard tells them. "You was in cuffs."

"They was scared we might run," John says.

"What about you?" William asks Constantine.

"What you mean?"

"Where you from? Before you got bought."

"By Orangeburg. Big tobacco farm. We all from there."

For the next few minutes, the three tell how their owner hauled them early today without warning to the auction in Washington where Philip Leyden purchased them. They say each has been sold at least twice before. Their lives have been just hard work, they say, and they are no strangers to the lash.

Nettie sets out some food and the three hungrily scoop the remaining beans from the kettle. She gathers what cloths can be used as blankets and spreads them in front of the fireplace.

"You get some sleep," she tells the young slaves. "Tomorrow's going to be a better day for you."

CHAPTER SEVENTEEN

RUNAWAYS

ADAM WAKES IN THE DEAD OF NIGHT TO POUNDING rain and muffled hoofbeats and a woman's frantic yell. He bolts from his bed as lightning pierces the cotton curtains and thunder crashes overhead.

"Did you hear that?" Hannah sits upright and clutches the covers. "It sounded like a woman."

Adam jumps into his trousers and boots and dashes into the parlor as lightning again flashes. He heads for the cupboard where he keeps his musket. Thunder explodes as someone pounds on the door. He looks first at the door and then yanks open the cupboard and grabs the gun.

"Who's there?" he shouts.

"Please," a woman pleads. "Please let us in."

He holds the musket in one hand and with the other unbolts the door. A drenched woman stands before him in the driving rain.

"Please, it's me—Anne Billings."

He tries to get a better look at the woman on the doorstep with her face hidden behind soaked hair. Hannah comes up behind him. "Anne? Is that you?"

"Oh, Hannah!" The woman steps closer.

Hannah pushes the musket's barrel downward. "I know her from my sewing circle. Anne, come inside!"

Anne hesitates as she looks over her shoulder to the side of the house. Then she motions someone forward from the darkness. Two people step through the doorway, one short and covered with wet blankets and the other a man with a floppy hat concealing his face. Anne follows and shuts the door.

Adam holds his musket ready as he watches the dripping strangers standing uneasily in the room. Hannah finds a lamp on a nearby table and lights it. The boys, John and Robert, have crept down the stairs from their bedroom and are crouching behind a nearby chair. Meanwhile Anne slowly unwraps the smaller, blanketed stranger to reveal a frail black woman in tattered clothing, her gnarled and trembling hands tightly clasped in prayer. The man—also black though much younger, still trembling and chilled—removes his dripping hat, no longer concealing his fear.

"Please," Anne begs as she wavers on her feet. "I must sit."

Adam props the musket against a wall and reaches for a chair. He glances at the gun and then at the black man.

"No trouble," the man says and raises his open hands in reassurance.

Hannah brushes her friend's wet hair from her face. "Are you hurt? Are you ill?"

Anne puts her hands to her face and her shoulders heave. "I was so, so scared," she stammers.

"Who are these people?" Hannah whispers to Anne.

"Slaves. Runaways. Her name is Nancy Blue and his name is David. He's her grandson."

"Fugitives." Adams makes no attempt to conceal his anger. "Were you followed here? Tell me."

"Let her get hold of herself," Hannah says.

"I want to know if anybody followed you."

"I don't know," Anne sniffs. "I thought so. But now I don't know."

Adam steps up to the man named David. "Did you have a buggy?"

"Wagon, sir. I put it in back."

For the next several minutes, in a shaky voice, Anne relates the events of the night. She says she and Jacob were to pick up the two fugitives at one man's place and transport them to another destination.

"Then where's Jacob?" Hannah asks.

"I think he broke his arm. We were ready to leave the first place when Jacob slipped and fell from the wagon. He landed on his arm and was in such awful pain. We knew he couldn't drive the wagon."

"So you drove? Alone?" Adam asks.

"They didn't want me to. But I argued. Jacob said he would ride along but I knew he was in too much pain. He was on the verge of passing out."

"Why didn't this other man take them?" Hannah says. "The one whose place you were at."

"He's housebound. It's hard for him to even walk."

"Was it so important to take them tonight?" Hannah asks.

"Everything had been arranged. And I was as forceful as I've ever been in my life. I insisted that we stay with the plan because we'd only be on the road a few miles. I didn't think anyone would see us."

"And someone did?"

"I don't know who it was."

Adam opens a curtain just wide enough to peer into the night. "I need to know if anyone's out there."

David speaks up. "Sir, nobody seemed behind us when we got to your road."

The two slaves had been concealed in the wagon, Anne explains, and she had directions to the destination, but then the storm broke and she must have missed a turn. Within a few miles they were lost. "There was a place not far from here where we came upon two men on horseback just standing there in the dark in the rain," she says. "We drove past and one of them yelled something but we didn't stop. Then we heard a gunshot."

David continues the account, "We thought we heard horses behind us so I took the reins and drove the wagon fast as I could."

"It was terrible," Anne says. "Sometimes the wagon slid off the road. The horse was scared and running wild. There was thunder and lightning everywhere. Finally we pulled off the road to see if those men would go by. But they never did. We waited and waited."

"Could the gunshot have been thunder?" Adam asks.

"Maybe. Can't say, sir." David shakes his head. "Everything was booming around us. It was a true fright. My granny just kept praying."

Anne says somehow they got the wagon back on the road and tried to find their way either to their destination or back where they started. They were so lost they were unable even to backtrack. Then she recognized the road where the Porters lived.

"I didn't know what else to do."

At that, the old woman named Nancy Blue tilts her head toward the ceiling with her eyes closed. In a weak and raspy voice she says, "It's God's will that we be here and safe."

An hour later Adam shakes Othello's reins to hasten the buggy along the rain-swept road to Buford. Sitting beside him, Anne says, "Nothing turned out as it should have." She stares into the dark road ahead and tugs Hannah's wool cloak tighter. "I'm so ashamed. If I hadn't recognized the road where you live, I don't know what would have happened."

Adam responds with a biting tone. "For one, Hannah wouldn't be left alone with two fugitive slaves and the chance that a bunch of slave catchers could show up. And I wouldn't be hauling you home in the middle of the night."

"I know you didn't want—"

"I don't understand what compels people like you—and my brother, for that matter—to put yourselves and others at such risk. It's one thing to object to slavery. But it's something else entirely to cross the line into foolhardiness. I've seen the bruising my brother's taken at the hands of people who don't agree with his abolitionist talk. And Lord knows how many people you've put in danger tonight."

"But we believe we must do something to—"

"And I don't want Hannah getting mixed up in this." He slaps the reins again. "Keep her out of it, Anne. I implore you. Her heart goes out to anything that's suffering, whether it's an injured dove, a sick child, or a mistreated slave. She's vulnerable and easily hurt. She needs to be shielded from these things. Not thrown into the midst of them."

Hannah runs from the house through the storm to the barn. Her feet slide in the mud and rain pelts her bonnet. She shields a basket she has filled with scraps of ham and some bread.

"Hello?" she calls into the barn's dark interior.

"Back here, ma'am."

Deep in the barn David lights a lantern. Hannah walks cautiously toward its flickering light. She picks her way past the stalls and the stacks of saddles and bridles and around the sharp edges of plows and harrows. The heavy stench of manure hangs in the damp air.

"I brought food."

David digs eagerly into the basket and hands his grandmother a piece of ham.

"Bless you," says the old woman.

"It's good here, ma'am," David says as he rips apart another hunk of ham. "We been in some bad places these past days."

"It must have been terrible being chased through this storm by those horsemen. And even if no one truly was chasing you, it makes no difference. Phantoms can be as frightening as real men."

Nancy Blue nibbles a piece of bread and coughs.

"Let me get some water." Hannah makes her way back through the barn. She passes Othello's empty stall. In the next stall stands the lathered and muddied mare that had pulled the wagon carrying Anne and the fugitives. Hannah feels the horse's frightened eyes following her.

Rain pounds the back of her coat as she fills a bucket from the well. She strains against the bucket's weight as she makes her way back toward the lantern's glow. She stops when she sees David kneeling on the straw-covered floor next to his grandmother. He has one arm around her bony shoulders and the old woman is praying.

"Dear Lord, we seen so much trouble these past days. But now we here with these good people."

"Praise be, praise be," David intones.

"Lord, thank you for the care they give us. For this good food and this roof over our heads this wet night. Thank you for giving me life long enough for me and my David to be free. We love you, dear Lord."

Tears well up in Hannah's eyes. She steps into the lantern's light and sets the water bucket on the floor near them. "Please sleep, and God bless you both," is all she can say.

CHAPTER EIGHTEEN

CARING

DAWN DIMLY LIGHTS THE BEDROOM AS HANNAH WAKES, realizes she fell asleep in her clothes, and sees Adam standing in the doorway. He's disheveled, some of his clothing is wet, and he holds his boots in his hands. Then she remembers the events of a few hours earlier and why Adam is just now returning home.

"Is Anne home? Did it go well?"

"No, it did not," he says as he unbuttons his damp shirt. "Her parents are angry and I don't blame them. She concocted some tale about a lame horse as to why she was out all night and I know they saw right through it and were thinking the worst."

"The worst?"

"Sure, a married man smuggling their daughter home in the middle of the night. What would anybody think?"

He climbs into bed beside her. She can feel the night's chill on his body and she curls around him. "Our guests seem to be good people," she whispers.

His body stiffens. "I don't need guests who can land me in jail."

Soon she hears his breathing settle into the rhythm of sleep. The sky grows lighter and she slips out of bed.

A short while later, deep in the barn, she finds David sitting on the floor against a stall. His grandmother is asleep with her head on his lap.

"Is everything well?" Hannah asks softly.

David nods.

"When you and your grandmother are ready, come into the house. I'll cook breakfast."

She returns to the house to get John and Robert dressed for school. An hour later the boys are sitting at the kitchen table and poking at each other when the two slaves come through the door.

Robert yells, "Ma?"

"Everything's fine," Hannah tells her sons and introduces them to Nancy Blue and David. She tells the boys David is the woman's grandson, to put her sons more at ease.

"You need help?" David asks. He spots the empty water bucket by the sink. "This?"

"That would be good."

David leaves the kitchen, bucket in hand. The old woman settles into a chair across the table from the boys. They look down and barely move. Hannah knows Nancy Blue is older than anyone her sons have ever seen.

"Tell me," Nancy Blue says, "you boys seen a colored person before?"

Hannah starts to answer. "We moved from—"

"Yes, ma'am," John interrupts. "There was a colored boy in a wagon here one day because he'd run away. Some men caught him and were taking him back."

Nancy Blue looks at Hannah. "You had a slave boy here?"

David lugs the pail of water through the doorway.

"There were some men here a few weeks ago—bounty hunters, slave hunters, I don't know—and they'd captured a boy who'd run away," Hannah says. "They wanted some water. They'd beaten the boy and chained him to the wagon. We felt very bad about it."

"Not as bad as that boy did," David says.

The bedroom door opens and Adam steps into the kitchen, eyes red and hair mussed.

"Morning, sir," David says.

"Morning."

"You need more sleep, Adam," Hannah says. "You were up all night."

"What I need is to take care of this situation." He looks at David. "Do you know where you were supposed to go last night?"

"Only know the name's Blanchard. Don't know where they live. Don't even know where we at right now."

"Well, I can't leave you here," Adam says, going out the door and heading toward the barn.

In the next several hectic minutes, Adam saddles Othello and rides away toward Buford. A wagon carrying rowdy children stops in the road to collect John and Robert and haul them to school. Hannah waves them on their way and returns to the house, where David and Nancy Blue are still at the kitchen table.

"How long you think we going to be here, ma'am?" David asks.

"As long as need be. Did you and your grandma get some sleep?"

The old woman nods and says, "Ma'am, we got the best sleep as any night since we left home." She looks at David. "Sounds funny, don't it? Thinking about a place with so much hurt in it and still calling it home."

"I want to learn about both of you." Hannah puts her hand on Nancy Blue's shoulder. "But we need to take care of you first. I'll heat water for bathing."

Nancy Blue claps her hands. "Ma'am, I can't think of nothing better for this old body than a hot bath."

Hannah and David struggle to fill four large pots with water and lift them onto the stove to heat. She studies the old woman's tattered linen dress, once the color of ivory and now stained brown with grime and mended so many times it's close to disintegrating.

"Did you and David live at the same place in Kentucky?"

"No, ma'am," Nancy Blue answers. "Our people been all split up years back. His momma—she was one of my babies—she's been gone a good many years. Sold off. Can't even say where she is now. This boy David grew to be a hand on a farm some miles from me. We didn't even know each other was in this world."

Nancy Blue tells Hannah how slaves are rotated from one neighboring farm to another, following the harvests. A year ago David came to work the harvest at the farm where Nancy Blue was a cook.

"I was putting stew on the plates when one of them boys calls out to me, 'Nancy Blue,' he says, 'Gimme some more stew!' Well, David's momma had told him his granny was called Nancy Blue. So he comes up and tells me his granny's name is my name and we figured then and there that we was kin." She claps her hands and grins. "Lord, that was a good day. So then my David would come see me most Sundays—walking all those miles there and the same back again. Guess that boy likes seeing his old granny."

"It was God's hand bringing you two together," Hannah says.

"Amen to that," Nancy Blue says with a shake of her head.

David smiles at Nancy Blue. "The first day I spent with my granny she tells me, 'I pray to spend just one day of this long life as a free woman.' You remember that, Granny?"

"Could be," she laughs. "Wasn't something I said just the one time."

"I made up my mind then and there that I'd give my granny the one thing she wanted."

Nancy Blue rests her hand on David's knee. "He told me he wanted us to run. And I thought Oh Lord how hard that'd be. Then Jesus spoke to me. He told me I'd be with him soon enough so why not be free now? I knew I had to go with David and the Lord would help us."

David tells Hannah how, two Sundays ago when he visited Nancy Blue at the farm, he stashed a bag with food and matches alongside the road. This time, when it was time for him to leave, they both passed through the front gate and kept on walking.

"Oh, I had such fear," she recalls. "I just kept saying, 'Protect us, dear Lord, please protect us.'" She says David picked her up like a child in his arms and started running. He ran to where he'd hidden the bag and then he ran as fast as he could down the road and veered into the forest, stumbling through thickets and briers.

"Mercy, look at that water," Nancy Blue says as the pots on the stove begin to boil over. "I was hoping to take a bath," she laughs. "Not be made into soup."

"Please take these." Hannah lays a yellow gingham dress and muslin apron on the table.

"Oh, Lord, I couldn't. I'd ruin them right away." Nancy Blue sits naked in the large copper bathtub in the center of the kitchen. "Been so long since I was clean." Her shoulders and arms are little more than worn brown skin stretched over bone. She eases lower into the warm water and her eyelids gently close.

Hannah hears the familiar crack of wood being split and finds David in the woodlot behind the house. He brings the ax down solidly on another chunk of hickory. Hannah asks him again about the journey with his grandmother.

"We always tried by best guess to head north. We moved mostly in the day when we didn't see people around but sometimes at night too." He tells her how traveling on the roads was easiest but dangerous. Fields were better for hiding but the mud made it hard to walk. Forests were safest but hardest to cross because of trees and dense undergrowth. It was three days before they reached the Ohio River, where he stole a skiff to row across.

"Over on this side, we still stayed away from everybody. We couldn't tell who'd help us and who'd take us back." David wipes sweat from his forehead and grabs another chunk of hickory to split. He tells Hannah about two more days when they wandered along creeks and through pastures and across fields, always avoiding the farm-houses they saw in the distance. They slept in woods with insects humming in their ears and crawling into their clothes. The next day they woke to a chill at dawn and ate the last of their food. They walked openly in the roads, hungry and parched and beyond caring if they were seen. "My granny was so weak," David remembers. "I carried her miles and miles that day till I thought my back would break. I feared she was dying." Then a horseman came up behind them so silently he startled them.

"I didn't know what to do," he goes on. "That man could tie us up or shoot us and I couldn't fight back. Too weak. Then the man says he would get someone to help us." A few hours later, another man appeared with a horse-drawn wagon.

"Do you know who the man was?" Hannah asks.

"A friend or maybe an angel. When you running away you don't ask names and folks don't tell you."

"I wonder if it was Wendell Childress? I've heard of him."

"No, ma'am, this man with the wagon took us to Mister Childress." David says he and Nancy Blue stayed two days at the Childress house and slept most of the time. "Then Mister Childress, he sent word for somebody else to take us to the next place. That's when Miss Anne and her fellow came to get us."

He gathers the pieces of wood he just split. "You know the rest."

CHAPTER NINETEEN

ANGER

THE POUNDING OF OTHELLO'S HOOVES ON THE DIRT road jolts Adam's body as he rides the horse hard into Buford. Morning sun now glints in the puddles remaining from the night's thunderstorms. He dismounts in front of Pope's Store, where he finds John Pope finishing a transaction with another farmer.

"I need to speak to Jacob."

"He's in the storeroom, Adam. Thee is welcome to go back there."

Adam finds Jacob bent over a keg of nails in the back room with his right arm in a sling of white cloth. "I know what happened last night," he says with no greeting. "Anne brought those slaves to my house in the middle of the night."

Jacob is startled. "Why would she—"

"She got lost and couldn't find her way in that storm. They were all frightened half to death."

Jacob rubs his injured shoulder. "This is awful. Do her parents know what we were doing?"

"Transporting slaves? I don't know what all she's told them. When I took her home it was nearly dawn and she said something about her horse going lame and her staying with us during the storm. I'm sure they didn't believe her."

"This is my fault."

"I agree."

Jacob pushes a lock of hair from his eyes with his good hand. "Anne and I planned to move the slaves to their next stop. Then this." He holds out his arm and its sling. "It wasn't supposed to be a long trip and then I got hurt when I fell from the wagon. Anne was determined to take them herself. I made a terrible mistake by staying behind."

"Listen to me, Jacob," Adam barks. "I want those slaves away from my home as soon as possible. Right now they're with my wife. Slave catchers have been coming around and I don't want anybody thinking we're harboring runaways. We didn't ask for this."

"I know."

Adam takes a step closer to Jacob. "Anne's been through enough. This is your job. You either take those slaves back to where you picked them up or you take them to where they're supposed to go. Either way, I want them gone from my place by midday."

Jacob adjusts his sling. "I'll tell my father I'm leaving. He's worried about my shoulder. But I'll tell him."

"Do that."

Adam follows Jacob through the storeroom door and past the counter and then leaves the store while Jacob talks with his father. Soon, Jacob joins him outside the store, wearing his black hat and no apron.

"Will thee help me saddle my horse?"

They walk to the stable between the store and the Popes' house. Adam watches as Jacob tries to put the bridle on Pony but winces in pain each time the mare moves her head. "Let me," Adam says and reaches over to adjust the bridle's cheek straps. Then Jacob struggles to lift the saddle onto the mare's back but instead drops it heavily to the ground.

"This isn't going to work," Adam fumes. "You've got no strength in that arm and I doubt you could handle this horse, much less the wagon." He lifts the saddle himself and sets it back on its rack.

"What thee says is true, I fear. That was the trouble last night and I'm not much better today."

"Damn it, Jacob, I'll take the slaves myself," Adam says with exasperation. "Just tell me where."

Jacob tells him what he knows about the location of the Blanchard house as the two walk back to where Othello is hitched to the rail.

"Understand one thing," Adam tells Jacob as he pulls himself onto his horse. "I'm not doing this to help you or Anne or those slaves. I'm doing this to protect my family. Keep that in mind."

CHAPTER TWENTY

SHAME

NETTIE BREAKS AN EGG INTO THE SKILLET OF SIZZLING bacon grease and looks up to see Frankie holding a bucket of fresh milk. Behind him stands the slave girl, Martha.

"Says she's supposed to be here with you," Frankie tells Nettie.

The girl scrutinizes the summer kitchen and tugs at a ragged sleeve of her purple dress. "The boss says to come here to help you. Says I don't go to the fields no more."

"You know kitchen work?" Nettie asks her.

"Just tell me how," the girl says as she grabs a platter.

"No," Nettie says and pulls back the platter. "I don't want eggs on the floor. You just sit here till I get all this served." She studies Martha's dirty dress and bare feet. "You sure Mister Hill told you to come up here to the house?"

"Uh-huh," the girl says as she peruses the pots and pans.

"Frankie," Nettie says, "you take Martha back to Mister Hill. If you can't find him then you take her to your momma." She waves her hand at the girl. "Go now. Git!"

With the morning meal served and consumed, Grace Leyden tells Nettie that Reverend Joseph Barry is arriving soon from Lexington and orders her to prepare the family's finest tea service. A short while later, the pastor appears at the house, chalky road dust clinging to his black clothing. He and Grace go directly to the parlor with Nettie following.

"Grace, how are you? I'm curious as to why you summoned me," the pastor asks after pleasantries and the first cups of tea. He holds out his empty cup for Nettie to fill.

"I've been better, Joseph, much better. I feel so blessed that you could visit at this time."

"I'm at your service, as always, Grace." He sips his tea and sighs deeply.

"Should I leave, ma'am?" Nettie asks.

"You should. But don't go far. We'll be needing you."

Nettie collects some rags and polish from the scullery and returns to a chair in the dining room—well within earshot of the parlor—to shine silverware. No one has closed the parlor door and she easily hears her mistress telling the pastor about matters at the farm.

"My fear is that Philip will be considered no better than a common slave trader and we won't even be able to circulate in decent society."

"But there is a need, Grace. I'm certain you realize that."

"To think of the Christian environs we've established here, Joseph, much of it built up over the past fourteen years through your influence and guidance. Our coloreds live as families. They're taught the Bible. We've nurtured them and their little ones. We've resisted selling them even when—"

A period of silence and then Nettie hears her mistress softly weeping.

"You see, Joseph," Grace says finally, "all of our belongings—this furniture, my dresses, our carriages—all of it comes from the proceeds of this farm. It's one thing for me to wrap myself in a cloak bought with money from the sale of tobacco or swine. But it's quite another thing to wear a wardrobe procured from the sale of colored children."

Nettie stops rubbing the creamer she's polishing.

"You must pray on this issue and discuss it with Philip," the minister tells Grace. "Let your thoughts and your concerns be known to the good Lord and to your husband. Don't demand that Philip change his mind. Ask him instead to join with you in praying for guidance. Confront this situation in a prayerful spirit and I suspect these fears of yours will never materialize."

"It's too late."

Nettie again hears her mistress's voice crack.

"I'm sorry, Joseph. This is very difficult for me. Just yesterday he purchased three young slaves at the Washington auction. He wants to sell two of them—two boys—very soon."

Nettie feels a knot in her throat and a burning in her eyes.

"He says he needs to establish channels—relationships and such—for selling more slaves. Oh, and he bought a young female as well and says he might sell her or might keep her as a breeder. Do you hear me, Joseph? A breeder."

"I see. So it has begun."

"Yes, it has and he's delighted." Grace's voice rises. "Both Philip and my brother. Oh, yes. They talk about the price they paid for this one and how much they'll get for that one and how to reinvest the profit. I cannot stand any of it."

"Grace, your focus may be too narrow," the minister says as he tries to calm her. "Practically anything a person buys these days comes from the labor of some slave somewhere. Providing Negroes to our southern growers is a necessity. Without the Negroes we wouldn't have the cotton that's sustaining our nation's entire economy."

"You sound like Philip."

Nettie turns to see the Leydens' daughter, May, come into the dining room. The girl puts her hands on her hips and glares at Nettie. "So there you are," she snaps. "I need you to help me in my room."

"Your mother's friend Reverend Barry is here, Miss May. I been told to—"

"I am aware of who's here," the girl says with a voice sounding much older than her twelve years. "I'll be joining them later. But I'm telling you I need you now."

Nettie puts down her polishing rag and follows the girl in the starched dress.

CHAPTER TWENTY-ONE

DISCUSSION

A LARGE WAGON TRUNDLES UP THE LANE TO THE LEYDEN farm, its four-mule team straining against the weight of the lumber piled high on its bed. William stands in an open area near the slave cabins. He shields his eyes from the sun and motions the driver to pull up beside him. Ned, a sinewy, bow-legged, and graying slave owned by the man who operates the nearby sawmill, steers the wagon to a halt.

"You in charge here today, William? You drive these bucks real hard, you hear?" Ned grins as he climbs down from the wagon. "Beat the bejeezus out of them. They's a bad lot, each and every one."

"You looking at the meanest slave driver around," William jokes as he puffs out his chest.

"So what's all this fine lumber for? You building you a nice big house?" Ned leans close to William. "Don't build it big as the Leyden place or you going to be in a heap of trouble," he jokes. "They going to think you being uppity."

William tells Ned the lumber is for a larger slave cabin so the Leydens can buy slaves and sell them to planters farther south.

"Maybe he should be growing more little slaves from scratch," Ned says and keeps his grin. "You tell Mister Leyden if he needs a good stud, Ned's his man."

"You too old," William chides.

"Don't you put money on it." Ned jabs at William's ribs and both men laugh.

Then William's smile fades. "My Nettie's real upset about this. She's worried about our boys getting taken away and sold."

"Leyden don't sell his hands. Everybody knows that."

"He might be selling two new boys he just got and then buy more and sell them too. Pretty soon he just be thinking about buying and selling and buying and selling like it's a habit. Some of our boys been in trouble and Mister Leyden might be getting fed up. He might be thinking of selling them too."

"So what you going to do if that happens? Run?"

William is startled. "I don't know nothing about running."

"So what happens if Leyden gets a mind to sell your boy? Then what?"

William studies Ned's face. "Don't know, Ned. I been at this farm since I was little. They treat us pretty good and now I might have some money."

"What you saying, William?"

"Mister Leyden says he could be hiring me out and says I could keep some—"

"Not that. The boy. What about the boy if they come after him?"

"Don't know. Seems nothing could be good after that. But I'd be scared to run." His voice drops to a whisper. "I don't know what's out there. But you do. You been known to run."

"Not like that, I ain't. Sometimes I get tired of old Blake and his ways so I go fishing for a few days. Blake always takes me back and says 'Damn you, Ned, you get back to work.' Like he forgot I ever been gone. When I get away I always stick close to the fishing streams and don't venture far. But you could be talking about taking women and children some great distance and being gone forever."

"I'm not saying I'd ever do it."

"I'll tell you the land gets a whole lot bigger out there when you running and hiding. A place it takes an hour to reach normal, now that place going to be a whole day away because you can't use the road. Best time to run is corn season when you can live off corn in the fields and hide there too. But there's nothing out there now. Not this time of year. No food, nothing. But that ain't the worst."

"What's that?"

"You talking about going into country where people shoot our kind as soon as look at us and you got to cross a lot of that kind of country before you get to a safe place. And to do that, you talking about doing the most dangerous thing of all."

"What's that?"

"Trusting white people."

CHAPTER TWENTY-TWO

BANISHED

ANNE BECOMES AWARE OF HER MOTHER SHAKING HER
shoulder. "Wake up." Sunlight streams through her bedroom window and she hears again, "Annie, you better get up, now."

Then she suddenly recalls the confused mess of the night
before—the fugitives, the terrifying midnight ride to the Porter farm,
and then encountering her parents when Adam Porter brought her
home before dawn. After a loud confrontation with her father, she
had come straight to her bedroom and stripped off her wet clothing
and climbed into bed.

"Your father wants to talk to you."

She pulls on trousers and tucks her chemise into them and puts
on one of Ben's baggy shirts. She pats down the stubborn spikes of
her hair and walks into the dining room, where her father and brothers are eating.

Her brother Hugh looks up. "You look like hell."

"You sit," Joshua Billings commands.

"Should the boys leave?" her mother asks.

"Don't see why."

Anne drops into a chair. Her mother places a plate in front of her. "I'm not hungry."

Her father leans back in his chair as her brothers continue to swab their plates with hunks of bread. "We're going to find out right now what you've been up to. And I don't want smart-alecky answers or lies, you hear?" He stares straight at Anne. "Let's see if I got this right. You told us you were going to the church for that sewing group. You took the mare and left here early afternoon. Am I right so far?"

Anne remains silent.

"By the end of the day, you're still not home. We're all getting worried so I send Ben to the church to see if you women are still sewing. Well, Ben finds nobody there. Nobody at all."

"I wanted to—"

"Wait." Her father holds up his hand to silence her. "It gets toward dark and we still don't know where you are. So I tell all three boys to saddle up and try to find you. They all go different ways and I wait here because we got no more horses, counting the one you took."

Anne can tell her father is relishing the interrogation. "I want to—"

"Not yet, not yet," he says as he strokes his black beard. "So what happens next? Well, here comes Hugh bringing home the mare you took. Seems he found her at John Pope's house. Trouble is, old Pope says you and his boy been gone for hours. Says you two needed his wagon because you—yes you, Miss Anne Billings—you had to pick up some furniture for your parents."

"Oh, Annie." Her mother shakes her head.

"Well, it gets to be night," her father goes on. "We wait. And we wait. I'm expecting you to come sneaking back yourself or maybe with that Pope boy. And I'm getting real mad."

Anne knows the very recollection is stirring his anger anew. Her mother stares at the table. Her brothers are entranced by their father's performance.

"Well, you know what happens from there." Her father's voice grows louder. "You show up near dawn with that other man. A married one at that. I ask where you been and you say you had to stay at his house because your horse was lame."

"But I told you last night—"

Joshua suddenly slams his open hand onto the tabletop. "Lame, my ass! That horse was here in our barn. You lied to me."

Silence surrounds the table. Her brothers turn to watch Anne. She straightens herself in her chair and slowly folds her hands in front of herself.

"Yes, I lied to you and to mother. The reason was because I didn't think you would like what I would tell you."

"I think I know already," her father says with eyes narrowing. "I just don't know which one of these men you been fooling with—the Quaker one or the married one. But you're going to tell me."

"If you think I was romancing anyone, you're wrong. I was helping runaway slaves."

Her mother speaks up. "Oh, Annie, you better tell us what you're involved in."

"Jacob and I—"

"I thought so," her father growls. "I knew no good would come of you and that Quaker."

"It was my idea. Not his. I want to help those people escape their awful lives."

"Those coloreds belong to somebody else," Hugh chimes in. "Why not just steal their horses, too?"

"Who put you up to this?" her father demands. "And for god's sake it better not be your aunt."

"Nobody put me up to it. It's something I believe in."

"You sound like a damn abolitionist."

"Perhaps I am."

Her father rises so suddenly his chair topples to the floor. He leans over her. "My daughter's no damn abolitionist. You hear?"

"Why would that be bad?" she challenges him.

Her brother Cyrus—silent until now—says, "Don't be a fool."

"Who'd you steal?" asks Ben.

"A young man about Cyrus's age and his grandmother. And I didn't steal them."

"His grandmother?" her mother repeats.

"We were supposed to pick them up at one house and take them to another. It wasn't supposed to take very long."

Her father slaps the table even louder this time. "You're breaking the damn fugitive law. It says plain as day that people get their property back." He slaps it one more time. "Don't you know that?"

Her father's voice and the noise of the blows to the table obscures the sound of knocks at the front door.

"Someone's at the door," her mother finally says.

"Ben, go see." Joshua keeps his eyes on Anne. "If someone's got slaves, it's none of your concern. If those slaves run away, it's none of your concern. Your concern is right here. In this house."

Ben returns. "It's your boyfriend. The Quaker one."

Anne starts to rise.

"You stay here," her father orders. "And you understand one thing. It makes no difference to me that you're my daughter. If any son of mine would think about being a damn abolitionist I'd cuff him up one side of his fool head and down the other. Nobody in this family will bring shame on the rest of us."

At that moment Jacob enters the room with his hat in his hands, the white sling standing out sharply against his black coat.

"Well, here's one I don't need to ask about being an abolitionist," her father says to Jacob. "I just want to know why you brought my daughter into this."

"We believe slavery is wrong, sir, and we wanted to . . . " His voice fades and he backs away from this large and thundering man.

"Well, it's not her concern," her father shouts. "Now you tell me what happened last night."

Jacob fingers his hat brim. "As Anne may have told thee, we were to pick up two slaves from one house and take them to another destination. As we were leaving the first place, I fell off the wagon and landed on my shoulder."

Cyrus rolls his eyes.

"He was hurt," Anne says. "He couldn't do anything because of the pain."

"My shoulder snapped out of place. We were able to put it back after some struggle. But that was after Anne left."

"Who's 'we'?" her father asks.

"I won't give thee names. But there was the man whose house we were at and his hired boy."

Her mother looks puzzled. "But you said Annie had left?"

"She left with the wagon and the two slaves."

"Hold on," her father says. "Maybe I'm not following something here. You say you stayed at this man's house with the man and his hired man?"

"He's not really a hired—"

"—And my daughter's driving a wagon around the countryside carrying two runaway Africans? By herself? And the three of you are sitting back at this man's house?"

"I demanded it," Anne says. "They didn't want me to leave but I said I had to take care of those slaves. I had to get them to the next—"

Her father moves toward Jacob until he stands only inches away, the muscles of his jaw throbbing. "You little piece of chicken shit. What kind of man are you?" He grabs Jacob's shoulder and squeezes until Jacob cries out.

"Stop it," Anne shouts.

He keeps squeezing. "You sent my daughter into the night with a buck African you don't even know? What if that African had no god-fearing respect for white women? What if she ran into a slave catcher or a whole patrol and they see my daughter helping the fugitive? You ever think of that?"

"Please, stop!" Anne tries to pull her father's hand from Jacob's shoulder. "It wasn't like that."

Her father ignores her and shoves Jacob down the hall toward the front door. "Get out! You stay away from my daughter."

Anne lunges past her father to stand beside Jacob on the porch. "I'm so sorry," she tells him as her family crowds the doorway. Her father pushes past everyone.

Anne yells, "Get away from us!"

"Joshua, please," her mother begs from the doorway.

"Sir, don't do this," Jacob pleads.

Her father strikes Anne across the cheek with the back of his hand. Jacob catches her before she tumbles backward down the porch stairs. Tears well in her eyes as she and Jacob dash to his buggy.

CHAPTER TWENTY-THREE

DELIVERY

ADAM WATCHES HIS SONS AND THE SLAVE DAVID CHASE the pig named Hamlet through the tall grass behind the house. Hannah and Nancy Blue sit on a bench in the tranquil sunlight and laugh as the hog eludes its pursuers.

Adam approaches the two women. "I found out where the Blanchard farm is and I need to take these two there now."

Hannah holds her hand to her brow as she squints up at Adam in the sunlight. "Does it have to be today? They've had a hard journey and they still need rest."

"With the likes of Klemmer poking around, yes, today."

David joins them. "You mean to take us in daylight, sir?"

"There aren't many folks in the direction we'll be going. If somebody sees us we'll say you're free coloreds."

"We got no papers, sir."

"And we've got no choice."

Adam leaves the sunny yard and walks into the darkness of the barn. He examines the family buggy and his own wagon and then John Pope's muddy wagon in which Anne had carried the fugitives.

He checks the stalls. The storekeeper's gray mare seems to have recovered from her ordeal of the previous night. He strokes her muzzle and she tosses her head and whinnies. He decides to hitch her to his own buggy for the journey.

An hour later the two slaves are waiting in the yard as Hannah hands Nancy Blue a black straw bonnet. She and Nancy Blue hug each other.

"God be with you," Hannah whispers.

"He's with you, too," says the old woman. "I know he is."

David steps forward with his floppy hat in his hands. "Ma'am, you been good to us. We'll remember you in our prayers."

"You take care of your grandma and that'll be remembrance enough."

Adam steers the buggy through the rolling countryside with Nancy Blue sitting on the seat beside him and David crouching behind them. The old woman loudly sings one hymn after another in her raspy voice and claps her hands to the squeaky cadence of the buggy wheels. She laughs and points to the green meadows where unsteady colts test their spindly legs.

A while later, clouds are piling up on the western horizon and the setting sun splashes them with brilliant orange and pink. The road grows narrower, flanked by dense rows of poplar and sycamore whose branches weave overhead to block the remnants of daylight. The mare picks her way haltingly among the road's rocks and ruts despite Adam's urgings to go faster.

They round a curve to see two men in the darkened road ahead. Adam tells David to crouch lower. Nancy Blue keeps her face lowered in the bonnet. The men carry muskets and stand still as the buggy approaches. One reaches for the mare's bridle and the animal stops.

"Whoa there. You lost?" the man asks.

"No," Adam answers. "Let us to be on our way."

"You seeking somebody down this road?" says the other man as he strains to see into the buggy. "Ain't nobody there but a pig farmer."

"I appreciate your concern." Adam flicks the reins lightly and the mare snorts and steps forward. The men stare after the buggy as it pulls away.

"Slave catchers?" David whispers from the rear seat.

"Hunters. Either for food or slaves, can't say."

"Or both."

A hundred yards farther they reach a narrow lane leading away from the road. The overpowering stench of manure fills the air.

"Hogs," David says.

They travel the length of the lane until twilight reveals the silhouettes of a house and two barns. Smoke rises against the evening sky from the house's chimney, but no light escapes its windows. Adam draws the buggy closer as several dark and bulky shapes move close to the ground. He climbs down from the buggy and hogs begin bumping his legs and rubbing against the buggy wheels.

"I'll go," David says.

"You stay. People around here don't take kindly to a colored man at their door at night."

Adam steps over the smaller pigs and around the larger ones lumbering between broken fence posts and pieces of rusted metal. He reaches the doorstep to find curtains drawn tightly over every window and hears the sound of muffled conversation inside the house. He taps on the door and the voices fall silent. He knocks again.

"Who's there?" a deep voice asks as the door opens an inch.

"My name's Adam Porter. I'm trying to find a man named Blanchard."

"What you want with Blanchard?"

Adam pauses a moment. "I have some goods for him. Goods from a man named Childress."

The door opens wider and Adam confronts a stocky black man who thrusts a burning lamp toward his face.

"I'm Blanchard."

Henry Blanchard and his wife, Sarah, embrace the two fugitives as they enter the house. For several minutes the four talk rapidly as if they had known each other for years, their speech thick with a loping dialect Adam can barely understand. Sarah Blanchard sits Nancy Blue in a large wooden chair and lays a threadbare quilt over her lap. Adam moves over to the large hearth where smoke from the fireplace blocks the stink of hogs.

Henry Blanchard is heavily muscled and wears a sweat-stained homespun shirt and baggy denim pants. Soon he joins Adam at the hearth. "I thank you for bringing these people here," Henry says. "Who are you?"

Adam tells Henry where his farm is located and that a friend had arrived unexpectedly the previous night—lost in the thunderstorm—with the two fugitives.

"That boy David says you took care of him and the old one."

"My wife did. I was not as kind," he admits. "I brought them here so there wouldn't be trouble."

"You could've turned them over to the law. Probably got yourself a reward."

"I suppose. But after what they—"

"But you didn't. So you do deserve our thanks."

"Let's just say I'm protecting my own family by bringing them here. And who are you?"

Henry drops two more logs onto the fire. He tells Adam that he and Sarah had been freed ten years earlier in Virginia. They'd traveled to a small settlement of free blacks in southern Ohio and acquired this farm through circumstances he did not explain. Adam could see the man was not comfortable talking about himself and divulged little.

Moments later Adam says goodbye to Henry and Sarah and shakes hands with David. Then Nancy Blue rises from her chair. She throws her skinny arms around Adam and surprises him with the strength of her hug.

"The Lord knows what you done." She steps back and takes one of his hands in both of hers. "You going to do more good. I know that for sure."

"Perhaps," was all he could think to say.

CHAPTER TWENTY-FOUR

HUNTED

A QUARTER MILE FROM THE BLANCHARD FARM, ADAM sees the shadowy shapes of the two men with muskets still walking in the road. He drives the buggy closer to pass them and they both turn to look.

"Howdy again," one man says as he peers into the buggy. A dead rabbit hangs from his belt.

"Seems you lost somebody," the other man says as he grabs a rein and causes the mare to stop abruptly. She whinnies and flings her head up and down.

"Leave somebody at the pig farmer's place, did you?" asks the first man as he leans into the buggy. "Now you just hold on while we—"

Adam yanks the reins free from the man's grasp and slaps them solidly. The mare jumps and the buggy lurches as one of the muskets discharges with a flash and roar into the night sky. The mare panics and bolts, heedless of the rutted road. Adam pulls back on the reins as hard as he can when the right side of the buggy suddenly sinks into a rut and Adam hears the sound of spokes splintering.

The buggy tilts sharply and scrapes to a halt with the mare thrashing against her harness. The two men approach at a run as Adam leaps from the driver's seat. He struggles to unbuckle the mare's harness straps and finally manages to free her. He tries to mount her but she flees into the dark woods with straps trailing behind.

"Grab him," one man yells to the other.

Adam runs after the horse into the woods. Briers snag his pants and branches slap his face. He throws himself onto the ground, figuring it's safer to remain still rather than crash through the woods trying to elude these men. It's too dark to see clearly but he hears them stalking him.

"Man don't run 'less he's got reason," one says.

"He's got reason all right," the other answers.

The brush snaps as the men poke through the woods. They search nearer and Adam huddles closer to the ground. They are within yards of where he's hiding when the distant sound of a gunshot reverberates from the direction of the road.

"Who's that?" one of the men asks, and they both walk back toward the road to investigate.

When the men are far enough away, Adam rises and walks deeper into the woods in the direction the mare had run. He holds his arms in front of his head to guard against briers and branches but still trips over a fallen limb and scrapes his face as he sprawls on the ground. He squints and in a nearby clearing sees the mare standing in the dim moonlight.

Adam moves cautiously toward the horse with his arm outstretched. She lets him unbuckle the hanging straps. He's sore and winded by the time he leads the mare to the road. He can barely make out the shape of his wrecked buggy in the distance. He struggles to pull himself onto the mare's back and prods her gently with his heels to begin the long and dark ride home.

CHAPTER TWENTY-FIVE

WAITING

HANNAH HAD WATCHED THE BUGGY CARRYING ADAM and Nancy Blue and David disappear down the road as she held Robert's hand and John threw stones at a tree. Now she and her sons walk back around the house to the yard behind it, where an hour earlier the two runaways had been so joyful.

"We need to gather the eggs," she says and looks down at Robert. "Go get the basket from the kitchen."

Hannah hears snorting a few yards away. The pig Hamlet is ramming his snout against something on the ground. She recognizes the dirty fabric of Nancy Blue's old dress. She shoos away the pig and picks up the tattered garment and rubs the rough linen against her cheek. Tears well in her eyes.

"Ma?" says Robert, holding the egg basket.

"I just want them to be safe."

Afternoon turns to evening. She and her sons eat a small meal and she scrubs the day's dirt from their bodies. Evening turns to night and she tucks her sons into their bed.

"When's Pa coming home?" Robert asks.

"Very soon. No need to worry."

Her older son is not so easily comforted. "Why did Pa have to take them away?"

"He's trying to find help for them." She strokes John's thick hair and he moves his head away from her hand.

"What about those other men?"

"What other men?"

"The men who had the boy in the wagon and then came back here with those dogs. Are they coming here again?"

"No they're not. Let's say our prayers so you can go to sleep."

The prayers bring little comfort. The boys beg their mother to stay with them. And Hannah is having concerns of her own.

"Would you boys rather sleep in my bed?"

Both jump from their bed and dash down the stairs. She sets a lamp on her dresser and settles her sons into her bed. When they are quiet she goes to the parlor and lights another lamp.

She walks to the cupboard where Adam keeps the musket. She feels the weight of the gun as she examines it and recalls a day shortly after they had moved to Buford, the day Adam taught her how to load and fire the musket. He told her to aim at a distant oak and pull the trigger and the recoil had knocked her backward and left a bruise that took a week to heal. It still was the only time she'd fired the gun.

Hannah returns to the parlor and her rocking chair. She hears the wind pick up and she looks toward the window. She sees the reflection of a lone woman in a chair with a musket across her lap. This is not Hannah Porter of Akron—not the woman who had lived among three thousand other people and had strolled daily among dozens of stores and churches and past busy flour mills and woolen factories—not the woman Adam had courted. She sees in the reflection a woman who has moved with her husband and sons away from all she has known—a woman who has left her friends and family in a town two hundred miles away—a woman now facing a difficult land without the support of parents or friends or parish and who lives without easy access to the necessities of life she has always known.

She sees a woman ready to fire this heavy gun at whoever seeks to harm her or her sons or the new life she knows is growing inside her.

Somehow the fatigue of the day prevails. She stops rocking and her head slumps forward as she drifts into dreamless sleep. She awakes with a start just once when the wind blows grit against the windowpane. Her lamp has long run out of oil and the room is dark. Again, she sleeps.

"Hannah?"

She strains to hear the voice as if in a dream.

"Hannah?"

It's Adam's voice, far away but still distinct.

She rises slowly from her chair to see the first light of dawn filling the room. She rushes to the kitchen and unbolts the door to find Adam muddied and exhausted. She clutches the musket in one hand and throws her other arm around her husband's shuddering shoulders.

CHAPTER TWENTY-SIX

PERMISSION

ANNE WATCHES HANNAH LIFT TWO MOUNDS OF WHITE dough from the breadboard into the waiting tin pans. "So now, after everything that's happened and my father finally realizing that I consider myself an abolitionist," Anne goes on, "after all of that, it comes as no surprise that I've been ordered to leave. I can't go home."

Hannah looks at her friend. "Are they so rigid they can't abide more than one opinion under their roof?"

"They know I lied about that night."

"And they don't like me," says Jacob as he enters the kitchen with an armload of split wood.

"They don't understand you," Anne says. "They don't understand Quakers and they don't understand my respect for them."

Jacob drops the firewood into the wood box and rubs his shoulder where he's removed the sling. "I appreciate what thee says. But this is my fault. I'd do anything to turn back the clock so I could have taken the wagon that night. None of this would be happening."

"I wish you'd stop chastising yourself," Anne tells him.

"Nothing's to be gained by wishing things had gone otherwise." Hannah uses a towel to protect her hand as she swings open the oven door. Hot air spills into the room.

"You know you're welcome to stay here, Anne."

Anne says her one concern about leaving home is that her mother still relies on her help. "Mother does so much work for my father and brothers she might as well be a slave herself," she says.

"Would thee move back if thy mother got sick again?"

Jacob's question startles Anne. She had not contemplated what would happen if she got word that her mother was stricken again. "I can't think about that right now."

"What if thee were married? Would thee leave thy husband to go back to live with them?"

"No, I wouldn't." She glances at Jacob and her face suddenly flushes. She flutters her hand beside her cheek. "That oven is hot, Hannah."

Hannah studies Anne's florid face. "There comes a time, Anne, when children must lead their own lives and parents must lead theirs. That doesn't mean you don't honor your parents or love them."

"I wonder what will happen if I run into them one day. I wonder if we'll speak or just shun each other."

No one ventures an answer. Then Hannah says, "We need to arrange a bed for you." The women decide Anne should sleep on the sofa in the parlor and begin gathering blankets and a quilt.

Hannah is back in the kitchen when Adam comes in from the field. He tosses his hat onto the wood box and dips a ladle into the water bucket. "The crops are in trouble." He sips and then wipes his mouth with his forearm. "The rain the other night has made every-thing worse. The soil's crusted over and the corn's only this—"

He spots Anne standing in the doorway.

"My father says the same thing about the fields," she volunteers. "He says the soil is so hard that no water can …." She stops talking and looks at Hannah.

"Adam," Hannah says, "Anne's going to be staying with us for a while. If you approve." The two women relate to him what happened at the Billings house, how Anne's father raged and struck her.

"Let me tell you this." He points the ladle at Anne. "You can stay but you can't have anything to do with slaves while you're here. I'll not have it."

"I understand," she agrees. "Besides, after the other night I don't think they'll want my help ever again."

CHAPTER TWENTY-SEVEN

PREACHER

REVEREND SHEM MARSHALL RIDES HIS MULE UP THE
lane toward the Leyden house as he does every Sunday. A tall black
man, he wears a black frock coat and black trousers and a bright,
red-and-white checked shirt. His black felt hat is pulled low to keep
the morning sun from his eyes. He tethers his mule near the Leydens'
large barn and brushes the dust from his coat and trousers. He walks
to the bell pole and grasps and yanks the rope. The bell clangs as the
preacher studies the pole where three of his parishioners had been
bound and whipped a few weeks earlier.

Nettie approaches the preacher with two young slaves trailing
behind. She tells him they are John and Martha—two of the three
Philip Leyden purchased at an auction a few days earlier. She says the
other boy, Constantine, refuses to come worship.

"Have these two go sit with William and let's find that boy,"
Reverend Shem says.

Constantine has not strayed far. He leans against a pigpen and
watches the hogs sniff the hard ground.

"So Mister Leyden intends to go ahead with his plan to trade in black flesh?" the preacher asks Nettie as they approach the pen.

"These the first ones, Reverend Shem. The missus says he's to be selling the two boys right soon but I don't know for sure." She stops and puts her hand on the preacher's sleeve. "I'm afraid for my boys. Mostly my Richard."

"Are you going to stay at this place?"

She stares back at him but says nothing.

"Talk to me after worship," he tells her.

Constantine watches them warily. He wears a new blue linen shirt that gleams in contrast to his torn trousers and heavy boots.

"Come join us in the barn," Reverend Shem says.

"No need to." The boy digs a fingernail into one of the pen's boards.

"You do have a need."

The boy glares at Reverend Shem. "I ain't no sinner."

"Never said you were." The preacher moves close to the boy. "You know Jesus said, 'Blessed are they that mourn, for they shall be comforted.'"

"I ain't mourning."

"I say you are."

Constantine looks down at the hogs. Without another word the preacher takes Nettie's arm and turns to lead her back toward the barn. They reach the open barn door and Nettie looks back to see Constantine following several steps behind.

"I'll wait for the boy," she says.

The preacher continues into the barn and walks straight to the makeshift pulpit William built for him a few years earlier.

"Lord," he shouts, "send thy spirit down upon us!"

Several of the people on benches calls back, "Amen!" as Nettie and Constantine enter the barn.

"You, our new friend." Reverend Shem points at Constantine. "Swing that big door shut and stand there by it." The boy falters and then pulls on the door as the barn goes suddenly dark except for slivers of dusty daylight coming through slits between the clapboard.

"My people, feel this darkness surrounding us," the preacher intones. "We are blind. We cannot see our way." He waits till their eyes adjust to the murk. "We have three new friends with us today. Three who have suffered. One is there." He again points at the boy barely visible by the barn door. "His name is Constantine."

The preacher steps from behind the pulpit.

"People, let me tell you the story of Constantine. Oh, not this poor boy in his slave clothes. No, my people, this is the story of the great ruler Constantine in Rome a long time ago. Back when the Christians were hated. Back when they were scorned and they were whipped. Back when they were thrown to the lions like Daniel."

"Amen," someone responds.

" Now this Constantine was a leader of a great army facing a great battle. This Constantine was sitting on his horse and watching his enemy's army growing and growing. 'Where's my god Jupiter?' Constantine asks as he looks up to the heavens. 'Where's my god Mars? Are these gods still on my side or are they with my enemy?'"

Reverend Shem suddenly spins around and waves one hand high.

"Then from out of nowhere this Constantine feels the holy spirit take hold of him like nothing he ever felt before. He looked into that big sky and—glory be! —he saw the Savior's cross right in front of that burning sun and he heard the holy spirit say to him, 'By this sign you will conquer!'"

"Halleluiah," someone else shouts.

Reverend Shem's voice grows softer. "That night Constantine had a dream and our Lord Jesus came to him and told him to have all his soldiers paint the holy cross on their shields. So that's what Constantine told his soldiers to do. They painted those crosses and then they marched into that battle with those shields held high." The preacher's voice rises again. "And they fought and they fought and they won that battle. They beat that enemy. Beat that Jupiter. Beat that Mars. That enemy ran away and the good Lord made Constantine ruler of the whole wide world!"

Shouts of "Amen!" and "Halleluiah!" fill the barn.

"Now, you, boy," Reverend Shem shouts at Constantine over the commotion. "You push that door open with all your might and you let that light pour in!" The boy obeys and daylight streams into the barn and makes everyone blink.

"And when that Constantine was ruler of the world, he said no more punishment for the Christians," the preacher shouts. "No more lions. No more whippings. He made his people free!"

Willis stands by one of the benches and suddenly sings out in his strong voice.

"Oh, Moses, Moses, don't get lost."

"In that Red Sea," the others sing in response and some jump to their feet.

"Smite your rod and come across," Willis sings out.

"In that Red Sea."

Reverend Shem says his final prayer an hour later and the slaves sing and hum as they leave the barn. Nettie approaches the preacher as he slips his Bible into his saddlebag.

"Reverend Shem?" She gulps her breath. "I'm here."

"I must tell you something, Nettie, and I want you to trust me."

"You know I do, Reverend Shem."

"Now listen to me. If your family or any of the others here want to run from this place—if you want to head north across the river to the free land—you must let me know."

She searches his eyes.

"Nettie, you can trust me."

"Me and William talked about it." She clasps her hands together as if in prayer. "Oh, Reverend Shem, I'm so afraid of what's going to happen if—"

"I know a man who can help. He can get you across the river and over to people who will take you north."

William strolls over to join them with a great grin on his face. He grabs the preacher's hand and pumps it. "Reverend, you got some kind of spirit in you. You sing and clap and spin around like a man filled with the spirit for sure. You surely is our shepherd."

"I was telling Nettie about a man I know who can take you north."

"What you been saying?" William asks Nettie.

Reverend Shem puts his hand on William's shoulder. "I asked her if there'd been any talk of running away because of what's going on at this farm. She said you'd talked about it. That's all."

"That's the truth," William admits. "But I don't know—things might be all right here. Might be getting better."

The preacher slips his boot into a stirrup and mounts his mule.

"Let's pray that it's so, William."

CHAPTER TWENTY-EIGHT

SHELTER

IN THE LIGHT OF DAY THE BLANCHARD FARM IS FAR more derelict than Adam had realized. The old frame house is badly weathered. Its siding is splintered and the porch rotting away. Barns and sheds lean precariously. Hogs are everywhere and their stink hits Adam, Anne, and Jacob as soon as they turn onto the lane leading to the tumbledown property.

"Hello?" Adam calls from the rickety porch. "Henry, you there?"

Sarah Blanchard opens the door. "He's out back."

Anne steps into the house with Sarah while Adam and Jacob pick their way through the dung and broken bottles and rusted metal to find Henry filling buckets at the well. Henry pulls a bandanna from his baggy pants and wipes the sweat from his face. A line of empty buckets stretches from the well to a plot of land near the house, where mounds of earth swell with manure and are crowned with lush vines and thick patches of vegetable greenery.

"That's amazing," Adam says as they approach. "Yours is the only garden with any abundance I've seen this year. No rain hasn't hurt it at all."

"I got to be my own rain," Henry says as he points to the buckets. "Always have. Growing food is something I'm good at. That and growing hogs." He looks at Jacob. "You the one was supposed to bring those two here the other night?"

Jacob nods. "I'm afraid that's true. I came today to see where thee lives so I would know."

"It all worked out in the end," Henry says and turns back to Adam. "Glad to see you made it safe. Sorry your buggy didn't."

"I was hoping to find it today. You know where it is?"

"There." Henry points to a shed.

"I brought a wheel to repair it," Adam says.

"No need."

Henry leads them past two large barns—one with its roof caving in and the other lopsided but still solid—toward the shed with axles and wagon tongues strewn around. He swings open the shed door and Adam's buggy is there with wheels and axles intact.

"Good, good," Adam says as he walks around the carriage and examines the repairs. "Good. You did this?"

"With that fellow David you brought here."

"This is as fine as any wheelwright could do," he says as he kneels beside the vehicle. "You even got the side repaired." He runs his hand along the restored panel as he asks about David and Nancy Blue.

"Moved them two nights ago," Henry tells him. "I figured somebody might be back with the sheriff so we got your carriage fixed and I took them on their way. What was it happened to you that night?"

Adam tells him about the two men in the road and how the buggy crashed and the horse fled. He tells Henry about running from the men in the dark woods and finally finding the mare and then the long ride home.

"We heard a shot just after you left," Henry says. "So I took my gun down to the road and fired to scare them off. I found your rig but nothing else. Those men been hanging around this place like buzzards."

Anne is seated at a table in the darkened keeping room. Sarah Blanchard ladles water from a bucket into a metal cup and hands it to her. Anne sips and sputters, "Vinegar?"

"I always put it in the water. Helps keep the thirst down."

Anne looks around the room. All the windows except one are covered by heavy drapes. "Do you shelter many slaves here?" she wonders aloud.

"Been doing it long as we been here. Ten years or so. Can't even say how many come this way—couple hundred all told, I suppose. We go weeks and nobody. Then they start coming. One then another, then could be a whole family."

"From Wendell Childress?"

"Some from Childress. He gets runaways through that underground road."

"Yes, I know." Anne dabs at the sweat beading on her face.

"Others come from free colored folks. And that's where we all got to watch out."

"Of being returned to slavery?"

"That or getting killed. Sometimes getting killed is better." Sarah slides close and lays her arm next to Anne's on the table. "Say your skin was colored like mine. Say you got these white folks telling you all your life your skin ain't as good as theirs. Saying something's wrong with you—that you no better than a mule. Saying you only their property to do with as they want. It ain't at all Christian."

Anne fans herself with her bonnet in the stifling room. "Sarah, these people you're talking about aren't Christians."

"They say so. They go to church and pray to God for their souls."

"I believe the real Christians are trying to help the slaves."

"Maybe so. But a colored person can't tell the difference between the real ones and the others." Sarah says. "That's why a lot of runaways go from one colored home to the next. They willing to go a longer ways and be hungrier between places just to stay away from white people because they can't know what to expect. But don't you get bothered over this. I know you want to help and Lord knows these poor slaves need all the help they can get. Coloreds can help other coloreds when they running. But it's sure bigger than all that. The slave master going to be with us till the white people want him gone. It's only the white people who can stop this slavery for good."

"I want to help. I want to help more than anything."

Sarah drums her fingers on the worn tabletop. "Tell you what I think."

"Yes, do."

"I think you got no business driving around these roads at night with colored folk hiding in some wagon. There's bad men in these parts who would do fearsome harm to you if they caught you."

"I hadn't intended to do it by myself."

"Get us clothes."

"Clothes?"

"You should see some of the rags these folk wearing when they show up here. Some been living in the woods and hiding in barns for weeks. Slave clothes get pretty tore up to start with and there ain't much left after what these people been through." She looks at her own gnarled hands. "My fingers don't sew so well no more. I can't fix their clothes and I got nothing to give them. You get us clothes."

Henry takes Adam and Jacob past two large corncribs to yet another broken-down shed. Inside he tugs on a rope and opens a section of wall to reveal a tiny hidden room with just enough space for a mattress on the floor and a chair next to a small table with a lantern on it.

"You see nothing of this from outside," Henry says. "It's plenty tight and no draft gets in. This is where they hide." He points to a trap door, two feet square on the rear wall. "That's the way out, if need be."

They step back into the sunlight. Henry faces the other two and puts his hands on his hips. "I'm putting my life in your hands by telling you about things here," Henry says to Adam. "I seen you only that one time before." Then he looks at Jacob. "And you I never seen till today."

"We would never harm thee or anyone here," Jacob says. "Thee must get quite a few slaves staying here."

"Some come on the underground and I steal some."

"Steal them?" Adam asks.

"I cross the river into some town and find a few slave folk wandering around and I talk to them to see if they want to run. If they willing I give them a meeting place and we come back over the river at night. They stay here for a while and then go on their way."

"That's unbelievably brave considering thy color," Jacob says. "How many has thee brought to freedom?"

"Maybe twenty. Maybe more."

"Why?" Adam asks. "When you've got men watching your place and just itching to catch you with a runaway, why would you cross the river to steal slaves? Those men would kill you quicker than they'd swat a fly."

"Sure, but they got to catch me first."

CHAPTER TWENTY-NINE

NEXT

WILLIAM YANKS ON THE PADLOCK IN EXASPERATION. The morning sun is high above the horizon and Bobby Hill is late coming to the barn to unlock the tool chest. William steps into the sunlight in hopes of spotting the overseer when suddenly he hears shouts and sees a tangle of bodies writhing in the dust near the cabins. He runs down the dirt path and finds Bobby Hill wrestling on the ground with Constantine while a man William has never seen before pins down one of the boy's arms.

"Hold still," Bobby Hill yells at Constantine. The stranger tries to clamp an iron shackle around the boy's wrist.

Richard stands by the door of the family's cabin crying, "Let him go! Let go!"

Constantine's frantic grappling suddenly ceases. Then his knee shoots upward and Bobby Hill groans and rolls over onto his side. Constantine struggles to his feet but the stranger grabs the boy's leg and topples him. This time Bobby Hill crawls on top of Constantine and slams his head against the ground. Then Richard runs and leaps onto Bobby Hill's back and pounds him with his fists. The overseer twists and flings Richard to the ground. He kicks Richard solidly in the chest and sends him tumbling across the dirt path.

William runs to Richard's side and grabs him to hold him back.

Constantine does not move. Blood runs from his nostrils and down the sides of his face. His blue linen shirt is in shreds. The stranger clamps manacles around both of the boy's wrists and stands panting. Bobby Hill holds his gut and growls at Constantine, "Where's the other one? Tell me!"

William holds Richard tightly. "What happened here?"

Richard spits his words in anger. He says the men were waiting outside the cabin when he and Constantine and John had walked out a few minutes earlier. The overseer told Constantine and John to hold out their wrists and then both men had jumped Constantine as John fled back into the cabin.

"They been sold," Richard says. "That man's here to take them away. That's what's happened."

Bobby Hill storms toward the cabin and yanks open the door. William hears the crashing of the table being overturned and he peers through the doorway to see the overseer trapping John near the fireplace. The boy eyes the iron poker resting on the hearth.

"Don't try it, boy," Bobby Hill warns.

Then John falls to his knees and lets out a sob.

Bobby Hill grabs the boy's wrist and pulls him out the door. The stranger quickly clamps shackles around John's wrists and then links John's manacles to Constantine's with a heavier chain. Without a word the stranger dusts off his clothing and starts up the path yanking the heavy chain. Constantine limps along and John follows in tears.

Bobby Hill picks up his hat from the ground and fastidiously brushes off the dust. He walks slowly over to Richard, still in William's grasp, and puts his hand on the boy's shoulder.

"If I got anything to say about it, boy, you're next to go."

CHAPTER THIRTY

TROUBLEMAKER

NETTIE PREPARES THE LEYDENS' MORNING MEAL OUT OF habit, her hands mechanically turning the thick strips of bacon in the hot skillet. She ignores the sweat streaming down her face.

Philip Leyden startles her when he suddenly enters the summer kitchen. "My wife wants you to serve her in her room. Prepare a plate and tea and take it up to her."

"Missus feeling poorly, sir?"

"Just do what I tell you."

Nettie carries a large tray through the house and upstairs to Grace Leyden's sitting room. She knocks on the door and Grace opens it in her silk robe and matching slippers with her hair neatly brushed. She motions for Nettie to set the tray on the dressing table.

"Nettie, I want to talk to you outside the presence of my husband. I've had discussions with him yesterday and this morning and I suppose he and I have reached an understanding. At least now I understand some of his recent decisions."

Nettie looks at Grace's expensive robe and the crystal bottles on the dressing table and at the large oval mirror in its gold frame—anywhere but at her mistress's face.

"I can no longer protect your son."

Nettie's hands begin trembling.

"I cannot tell you for sure what will happen to him. But I want you to know it will do you no good—and it will do William no good—to come to me or Philip and beg that the boy simply be forgiven."

"Yes, ma'am," is all she can utter.

"I've learned much more about this farm. And the truth is that these last two years have been more difficult than I'd realized. We need to be more careful with money than ever before. You know about the things that have been stolen and broken. There hasn't been as much attention paid to the crops or the chores or—"

"Ma'am, I—"

"I mean it. Do not interrupt me, Nettie. We've tried to give our hands a better life than any other coloreds around here. We've kept your families together at great expense to ourselves. And now when things are—"

"But my boy—"

"Don't even start. Your boy is a troublemaker. He's one of the worst ones we have. I suppose it's hard for a mother to believe such a thing of her son."

"These things, ma'am. They ain't true."

"Just listen to yourself." Grace slaps her cushion for emphasis. "You stand there and argue with me after all I've done for you. You leave Philip and me no choice. We need to weed out hands who cause trouble and replace them with coloreds who understand loyalty and a good day's work. And we will do just that."

Nettie watches Grace pour tea into her cup.

"Whatever happens, Nettie, I want you to remember that we're all in God's hands and that the Lord sometimes works in ways we cannot understand."

Again Nettie can only mumble, "Yes, ma'am."

"Now please leave."

CHAPTER THIRTY-ONE

RUNNING

SALLAH BURSTS INTO THE SUMMER KITCHEN. "HE'S back," she tells Nettie. "The man that took those boys. He's here again."

Nettie stops scrubbing the morning dishes. "Constantine and John?"

"I seen him," Sallah says. "He come up the lane in his wagon. He come to the front door and Mister Leyden let him in."

Nettie unties her apron and removes her cap. "I got to find William." She runs down the path toward the cabins and past the stranger's wagon with its team tethered to the hitching post. She reaches the skeletal frame of the new building and sees William nailing a door casing. She waves frantically.

"That man's back! Who took Constantine and John!"

William wipes his face on his sleeve and looks toward the Leyden house. He puts down his hammer and walks over to Nettie. "That his wagon?"

"Sallah says so. Says he's in with Mister Leyden."

William gazes up at the clear morning sky and down again at the Leyden house.

"Maybe we should go right now," he tells Nettie.

"You mean run?"

"We wait and it could be too late."

She grabs his arm. "Then you get the boys and I'll get Lucy and we meet back home."

William crosses the barnyard in long strides to the hog pens, where he finds Richard prodding piglets toward a sty. He tells the boy to come with him and then spots Rufe shoveling ears of dried corn into a wheelbarrow.

"I got to take my boy."

"Well, there he is. Something wrong?"

"The man who took those boys away the other day—he's come back."

Rufe stops shoveling. "What you going to do, William?"

"Rufe, you can't tell nobody."

"I ain't saying a word."

"We going to run."

"Can't you wait till night?"

"That man's got his wagon here now. Could be planning on taking our boy. I got no choice."

Rufe leans on his shovel. "Then get that boy out of here, William. Don't you wait for nobody."

Nettie runs to Glory's cabin and finds her in the yard plunging diapers and towels into a cauldron of water on a bed of coals. Then she goes inside the cabin where Martha is tending two babies and Lucy sits on a mattress playing with scraps of cloth.

"I got to take my child."

Martha eyes Nettie but keeps quiet.

Nettie lifts Lucy and carries the child into the sunlight. She joins Glory beside the steaming cauldron. "Glory, that man's back and we got to run," she says as she fights back tears. "I can't let them take my Richard. Oh my, I never been so scared in my life."

"Dear Lord." Glory dries her hands on her apron. "What's going to happen to you all?"

"Keep Martha here. Don't let her follow."

"Maybe she could help."

"She's more bother than help."

Glory opens her arms wide and gives Nettie a strong hug. "The good Lord protect you, Nettie. You and all the others. You going to Reverend Shem?"

"We going to try."

William and Richard trot down the lane to the first tobacco field to find Alfred. They see him in a wagon sitting on a pile of gunny-sacks bulging with seed. William runs over to John Little, a slave Bobby Hill brought to the farm to be the driver for this field.

"I got to take my boy Alfred for awhile."

"Mister Hill know this?" the driver asks.

"I'll be sure to tell him," William blurts. "The boy's mother needs us real bad right now."

"When you bringing him back?"

"Hour. No more than that."

"Well, you go. I'll tell Mister Hill when I see him."

William and Richard and Alfred hurry back up the lane toward the cabins. "You stay close by," William orders Richard between breaths. "I can't go so fast. But don't you be alone at all, you hear?"

With no shoes, Alfred is having trouble keeping up. William scoops up the boy and keeps running.

"Where's Dan?" Richard asks William.

"With Glory. Your ma's getting him."

They leave the lane and creep through the tall grass to avoid crossing the open area near the cabins. William sees only Willis and two others still hammering on the frame of the new building. He and the boys duck from tree to tree till they reach their own cabin. William shoves open the door and they all tumble inside.

"Thank the Lord," Nettie says from a dim back corner. "Lucy's here and I'm getting some things."

William's eyes adjust to the shadows. Two gunnysacks are on the table. Nettie puts some ham and cornbread into a small bag and slips it into one sack along with a blanket. In the other sack are more clothing and another blanket and Nettie's wooden keepsake box from under the bed.

Suddenly she stops.

"Dan."

"You get him from Glory?" William asks.

"He wasn't there."

"I thought you said—"

Both Nettie and William are frantic.

"Watch the baby. I got to find my Dan," Nettie yells as she runs out the door. She creeps between the cabins while keeping watch for Bobby Hill or the stranger. She finds Glory still beside the cauldron. This time Martha is with her.

"Where's Dan?" Nettie asks.

"He was here for awhile earlier," Glory tells her. "Then they come for him some time back and took him to the field to help. I thought you knew."

"My Lord, Glory, it's too dangerous for Richard or William to go back to that field." Then an idea crosses her mind, though it gives her little comfort. "Martha, can you get my boy?"

The girl shoots Nettie a calculating look. After a moment she says, "Tell me where the field is."

Nettie tells Martha how to get to the field. "You say we got to have Dan back here. You say I need him at the master's house and say Bobby Hill says so. You say whatever you got to say to get my boy back to our cabin."

"I'll find him." Martha saunters across the yard.

"You run!" Nettie shouts after her.

She and Glory watch the girl disappear down the lane. "Hope you done the right thing," Glory says. "It should be me going after your boy."

"And if Mister Leyden ever found out you helped us, that stranger be coming after your Frankie, and Bobby Hill be coming after you. You know it."

Nettie returns to her own cabin to find William holding Lucy while Richard and John wait by the door. She tells William she sent Martha after Dan.

"That girl? I pray she can do this one thing right. But when she's back, here's what we got to do." William tells Nettie he wants her and the children to make their way from the cabin to the grove of trees lining the lane leading to the house. While they're hiding there, he'll steal the stranger's wagon.

"My Lord, William, somebody going to see you for sure."

"Could be. But it won't look all that rare to see me driving a wagon. Anybody be thinking I'm just moving lumber around."

Nettie shakes her head.

"It's the only chance we got," he says. "Maybe the Lord put that wagon there for us."

Nettie looks through the cabin doorway and sees Martha skipping toward the cabin and holding Dan's hand. "She got him," Nettie cries. "She got the boy."

Once inside the cabin Martha tells Nettie and William how she reached the field and saw an older boy walking toward her with Dan by his side. "I just told that boy I got to take this child and I reached down and grabbed your boy's hand and here he is." She sees the gunnysacks on the table. "What you doing?"

Nettie takes her arm. "We think that man's coming after Richard just like when he took Constantine and John. We going to leave here before he can take our boy."

"Take me with you."

"We can't. It's too many."

"I can help you." She clutches at Nettie's hand. "Take me. Please."

William puts on his wide-brimmed felt hat and steps between Nettie and the girl. "Martha, you just too slow."

Tears well up in the girl's eyes as she stares at William. "You going to be free. You going to get across that river and—" She begins to choke. "They going to put me up for sale and poke at me. Some man going to buy me for hisself and make me do things. I just know it."

William turns to Nettie and Nettie watches Martha rubbing her eyes and sniffling.

"You can come," Nettie tells her. "But you got to help every step of the way."

William pulls his hat brim down and looks only at the gravel path at his feet. He reaches the stranger's wagon and sees scattered in its bed several lengths of rusty chain and two sets of manacles. He quickly unties the reins from the hitching post and the team follows obediently as he turns them to face the lane. He never looks up as he climbs onto the driver's seat with sweat running down his spine. With one gentle slap of the reins the two horses step forward. He expects to hear voices ordering him to stop but instead he hears only the birds and the creak of the wheels and the rattle of the chains on the boards behind him.

William drives a few yards and Richard darts into the lane in front of the wagon. William stops the wagon while Nettie and Lucy and the two younger boys run from the woods with Martha behind them.

"Move fast," William orders.

They toss the gunnysacks into the wagon and they all climb into the wagon's bed.

"Go!" Nettie tells William.

Everyone sprawls flat to hide. William slaps the reins harder this time and the horses quicken their gait down the lane. When they reach the road William turns the horses hard to the right and heads north.

CHAPTER THIRTY-TWO

PEOPLE

ANNE AND HANNAH STEP FROM THE BUGGY ONTO SOLID ground. They brush yellow dust from their dresses and wipe sweat from their faces and swat at the horseflies as they walk up the gravel path to the door of the Buford Methodist church.

"This heat is relentless," Hannah says. "It wouldn't make any difference if I was with child or not. This is miserable."

They enter the church. The afternoon sun spills through small-paned windows and turns flecks of dust into floating sparkles. They step through a door behind the pulpit and enter a small room at the back of the church where five women sit around a table. The women flutter fans in front of their faces and sip from glasses of water, paying little attention to the scraps of fabric and pincushions scattered on the tabletop.

"How's your mother these days," the widow Elizabeth Rumsford asks Anne as she and Hannah seat themselves at the table.

"I hope she's well. I haven't seen her for some time."

"Oh? Where's she been?" Eleanor Crowley asks.

"I'm no longer living at home. I'm staying with Hannah and her family for the time being."

"I hope everything is all right," Eleanor says.

Anne opens her sewing kit. "I didn't leave under the best of circumstances."

"But it's been wonderful having her around to help," Hannah interjects.

"I imagine so," says Mary Franklin with a chuckle. "You're welcome to stay at my place anytime."

"What happened at home?" Elizabeth asks with her fan still flapping. "I don't mean to pry."

"Of course not," Anne answers. "I argued with my father. It was about slavery."

The movement of the women's fans is the only sound in the room.

"A bad argument, no doubt," Mary Franklin finally says. "I'd say you favor abolition and your father doesn't and things got out of hand."

"That's quite perceptive," Anne replies.

"Not really," Mary goes on. "I've seen you around with Jacob Pope. His sympathies are quite evident and I figured you must feel the same way. So the trouble was either your opinion of slavery being different than your father's. Or maybe your father thinks you're seeing too much of the Pope boy."

"You shouldn't say 'boy,'" Eleanor Crowley chides. "He's grown into quite a handsome man."

Elizabeth Rumsford's fan moves so quickly it's nearly a blur. "Again, I don't mean to pry, but perhaps wedding bells are in the offing?"

"Jacob and I are good friends and we enjoy each other's company."

"Then maybe he'd better make his move before some other handsome fellow comes along and takes the prize," the fifth woman, Abby Dillon, says with a chuckle.

With the mood in the room now lighter, Anne tells the women some Quakers had suggested to her that spare clothing would greatly benefit slaves who were on the run. She asks the women if they would be willing to donate some.

"I'd have to keep it from my husband," Mary Franklin tells her. "He won't tolerate people who can't abide slavery. He says they're destroying the country."

"And he might be right," Eleanor Crowley says. "I've read some abolitionist literature."

"This is not about abolitionists," Anne retorts. "It's only about helping people who are in need."

"I'm not even sure we should be talking about this," Fanny Burton mutters. "What exactly are we—"

Hannah interrupts. "We're talking about collecting clothes we no longer need and getting them to the fugitives. Some of them live in the woods for weeks on end and their clothes are filthy and in shreds. A number of them are just children."

"I suppose it's consistent with what we're taught in church," Fanny says.

"Maybe your church," Mary counters. "Not all Christians see fit to interfere in their neighbors' lives."

The widow Rumsford finally closes her fan and tells the others, "I looked into the eyes of a Negro once."

"What do you mean, Elizabeth?" Mary Franklin asks.

The elderly woman sips from her water glass and clears her throat.

"I was staying with my sister down in Franklin County in Kentucky. It was just before she died of the fever in thirty-seven. They kept slaves, maybe a dozen. One of their coloreds—a man named Asa—was hauling bricks one day to build a new privy. He took them from a wagon and stacked them by the house. I remember the day was even hotter than this one. Easily a hundred degrees and Asa was not a young man. He just kept moving those bricks. Stack after stack after stack. There was nobody standing over him— nobody lashing him or such—and I was sitting alone on the veranda drinking my water and trying to catch some breeze. I could see him out of the corner of my eye. He'd go to the wagon and put the bricks into his wheelbarrow and push them over toward the house and then unload them into neat stacks." She pours more water into her glass and drinks it all. "At some point I noticed Asa wasn't there anymore. His wagon was there. I could see his wheelbarrow and his stacks of bricks. But he was nowhere to be seen. I began to think something was wrong. So I picked up my glass of water and walked to the edge of the veranda and saw him lying face down on the ground."

"Dead?" Mary asks.

"I didn't know. I walked down the stairs. I didn't run, mind you. I walked over to him and saw he was breathing a little. There wasn't anybody else around." She wipes perspiration from her forehead and tucks back strands of gray hair that have fallen forward. "I nudged him with my foot. He groaned but he didn't move. So I nudged him harder yet. The same thing happened so I did it again. Only harder each time, again and again."

"Kicking him?" asks Fanny.

"That's what I came to realize. I saw myself standing over the body of this man and holding my glass of water and kicking at him as if he were a lazy hog. My Lord, I thought, what am I doing? I knelt down beside him and set the glass on the ground. I took his shoulders and pulled on his heavy body with all my strength until I finally turned him over. I had never touched a Negro before, mind you. But I was certain he was dying right there in front of me."

"What'd you—" Eleanor blurts and Fanny shushes her.

"I put his head in my lap and I poured some of my water on his face and rubbed it around. Then I opened his mouth and poured some down his throat. He choked and I thought 'Now I've surely killed him!' But it woke him up. It took a little while for him to come to."

"So you saved his life," Hannah says.

"I was only God's tool," the widow goes on. "Then I gave him the rest of my water. He lay there trying to get his strength back. Then he looked up at me in that terrible heat. I looked down into his eyes and I realized that this was a person. A human being."

She studies her water glass. "Keep in mind how I was raised—Negroes were not people. They were somewhere between people and animals. It was our responsibility as humans to give them food and shelter in exchange for the work they did for us. We were taught to do the same for them as we did for our other property, for our horses and oxen. And if we could teach them some Christian ways and make their lives a little better, Jesus would be pleased with us. I thought about how that man had been trained to work just as you'd train a draft horse. And that's when I realized that if we believe Negroes are not people, then there's no harm in working them like animals. There's no harm in ruining their families and selling their children away from them. There's no harm in keeping them ignorant and dressed in rags in their horrible little hovels. Certainly our Christian conscience could not bear to treat another human in this manner —as Scripture teaches us — and that's why the colored man and woman cannot be considered fully human. Not if slavery is to function. That day with Asa taught me the true evil of slavery. My sister wasn't evil and her husband wasn't evil. We'd all been raised with the same beliefs. No, it is slavery itself that's evil. And it's evil because of what it does to people—what it had done to Asa and what it had done to me."

The widow slowly unfolds her fan and again tries to cool herself.

"Elizabeth," Fanny asks her, "do you think we should collect the clothing?"

"Yes, I do," she replies. "Yes, we should help those people."

CHAPTER THIRTY-THREE

HELP

"BY NOW THEY KNOW FOR SURE WE GONE." WILLIAM looks back from the driver's bench at Nettie lying in the wagon bed with Lucy in her arms. "Could be an hour till they come after us. So that's what we got. Maybe an hour."

The sun is high in the sky and a steamy haze covers the countryside.

"You sure you know how to get to Reverend Shem's place?" Nettie wonders.

William remains silent as he steers the team along the dusty road. He drives with his shoulders hunched forward and his hat pulled low, his cotton shirt clinging to his sweaty back. The wagon rumbles along for a few more miles until they reach a road heading east toward Mays Lick. There is no signpost but William turns onto the road anyway. Another mile and he spots a battered barn with a large cross painted crudely in white on its bleached siding.

"Thank you, Jesus," William says. Everyone jumps out and he hides the wagon and team behind the barn. He spots an old coop attached to the rear of the barn with a ladderback chair sitting next to a door. He pounds twice on the door.

Reverend Shem answers with his shirt unbuttoned and sleeves rolled up. "Hello, William." He steps into the sunlight and looks toward the road.

William rapidly tells the preacher about Constantine and John and the brawl and the threat against Richard and how the stranger had returned this morning.

"Does anyone know you were headed here?"

"We didn't know ourselves till we lit out."

Reverend Shem leads them around the building and into the larger part of the barn where he holds worship. A dozen makeshift benches rest on the dirt floor and hand-hewn beams fashioned into a cross hang high on the wall. The preacher walks toward a spindly ladder reaching up to a loft crowded with several bales of hay.

"Don't the law come here looking for folks?" William asks.

The preacher shakes his head. "People don't think I'd be fool enough to risk my neck by hiding runaways."

At dusk Reverend Shem climbs into the hot and dusty loft and sits on a bale in front of William and Nettie. "Leyden's men are bound to show up here."

"You told us they don't look here," William says.

"I said the law hasn't come here. But this is the first time any of Leyden's hands have run."

Nettie looks up from Lucy to the preacher. "We don't mean to cause danger for you, Reverend Shem. But when you said you know people who—"

"You did the right thing." He puts his hand on hers. "But people who run got to have a plan to make it to freedom. The ones running like scared rabbits are the ones who get caught. Sometimes they just turn around and go back because they don't know what else to do."

"We can't go back," Nettie says.

"And we don't want to get caught," adds William.

The preacher promises to ride to Maysville early the next day to find James Pike, a man he describes as an abolitionist friend who's helped other runaways get across the Ohio River. "He may want to take you all in one trip or he might say two trips. I don't know. But you've got to trust him."

"We got to stay together," William says. "You tell him we stay together."

Reverend Shem tells them the next two days will be the most dangerous. Leyden's hunters will be scouring the countryside close to the farm and then fanning out north toward Maysville.

"And if they can't find you, Mister Leyden's likely to offer a reward, and that means every slave catcher in northern Kentucky going to be looking for you."

Late the next day Reverend Shem climbs the ladder once more into the suffocating heat of the loft. He's covered with thick dust after riding most of the day to Maysville and back. He hands Nettie a canteen of water. She uncorks it and tips it to Lucy's lips, then passes it to her boys and Martha. All of them had slept most of the muggy afternoon amid the rich smell of hot hay.

"I found James Pike and he's come back with me," the preacher tells them. "He's getting the wagon and horses ready. So gather up your things."

Reverend Shem leads them down the ladder and around the barn to his quarters inside the coop, a hovel with barely enough space for William and Nettie and their four children and Martha. "Keep in mind James Pike knows what he's doing," he says. "There aren't many white people who put their lives at risk for our kind. So you do what he says."

The door to the coop opens and a tall man with blond hair and goatee stoops to step inside. He holds his hat in one hand and a canteen in the other. "I'm James Pike and we need to leave this place." He quickly looks them over. "We've got quite a ways to go before morning."

CHAPTER THIRTY-FOUR

MISFORTUNE

JAMES PIKE LIMPS TOWARD THE WAGON AND HOISTS himself onto the driver's bench. He motions for William to sit beside him and for Nettie and the boys and Martha to huddle in the wagon bed. "The more we can make this trip look like an everyday thing, the less anybody who sees us will wonder," he says.

They leave Reverend Shem's barn and roll through the farmland north of Mays Lick. They have twenty miles to cover before they reach Pike's home, and the evening sun already casts long and rippling shadows of the horses and wagon and its passengers onto the side of the road.

"Your leg been hurt, sir?" William asks after a while.

"War wound," Pike answers. He tells William he fought in the war with Mexico seven years ago, and at Chapultepec a young Mexican with a bayonet slashed his left thigh to the bone. They ride a few more minutes in silence.

"Sir, why you helping folks like us when you could come to so much harm?" William asks.

Pike flicks the reins so the mares will quicken their pace. "I never agreed with slavery," he says. "Never could understand how one man could treat another so poorly. We never had slaves on our family farm and I'd never contemplate doing anything to perpetuate slavery. Then President Polk called us to war in forty-six with a lot of talk of manifest destiny. You know there's an ocean a couple thousand miles over that way"—Pike gestures toward the sunset—"and the president said we could make all that land between here and the ocean part of these United States. So we fought Polk's war by spilling a lot of Mexican blood and some of our own to get that land. Then I came to realize what Polk was up to." He tugs on the reins as the mares come to a tight turn in the road. "Nearly everywhere else in the world— England and France and even Mexico itself—had outlawed slavery. Then here comes the United States adding hundreds of thousands of square miles so we could put slaves on that land. Polk wanted to spread slavery farther than any man in history, and I'd helped him do it. So now I do this to help make up for the wrong I did in fighting that war."

Back in the wagon bed, Richard toys with the shackles the stranger had brought with him to the Leyden farm. He slips a manacle onto his wrist. "How many slaves like us you helped?" he asks Pike.

"You stop that," Nettie orders when she sees her son with the manacle. "Take off that devil's iron this minute!"

Richard lobs the manacle and a length of chain into the brush alongside the road.

"Slaves? I'd say a good many over the years," Pike answers. "Sometimes I carry them a distance like tonight and sometimes I just keep them a night or two at my home. I'm part of something people like to call the Underground Railroad because we hide people like you so the law and the slave hunters can't find you."

"I got to know how big it is," William says urgently. "This railroad."

Pike chuckles. "Well, I can't say for sure. There's me and I know about three others who can take you. All people I trust. And they know two or three others and it goes on like that all the way—"

"No, sir. The part under the ground. How big is it? I can't be in places too tight where I can't breathe and—"

"No, William, no," Pike says. "It's not actually under the ground. It's been called that because we hide runaways so they seem to disappear. Just like if they'd gone under the ground. We're on the Underground Railroad right now. In this wagon. On this road. This is it."

They reach the crest of a hill and spot another wagon coming toward them. "Everybody just act like there's nothing unusual here," Pike says. The two wagons draw near. Pike exchanges a nod with the burly white driver of the other wagon as they pass by one another.

William waits until the other wagon is a distance down the road and then asks, "Those other runaways you helped—they all get free?"

"I can't say for sure. I never had anybody captured when they were in my care. But I don't know what happens after I send them on their way."

No one speaks as the final daylight fades. The clopping of hooves and rhythmic squeak of the wagon's axles compete with the chirping of crickets. The road winds into hilly land made even darker by thick foliage that blots out all light except the twinkling of fireflies. The two mares stray back and forth amid ruts as Pike steers them away from steep ravines on both sides of the road.

The mare on the right suddenly stops, causing the wagon's tongue to twist and making the other mare stagger. Then both horses snort and shake their heads violently. A sharp and acrid smell fills the air.

William waves his hand in front of his face. "Skunk!"

The stink intensifies and the mares stomp and snort and lunge against their harness and each other. Pike struggles to control them. William watches the horses moving toward the edge of the road.

"Get them back," William shouts. "It's a cliff!"

Both men jump down from the wagon and grab the bridles of the thrashing horses. William can see Nettie and the boys hanging onto the side of the wagon as it rolls closer to the ravine's edge.

"Get out," he yells. "Jump! Now!"

William tries once more to grab the bridle of the nearest horse, but the animal twists her head away. He then runs to the side of the wagon as Richard and Martha leap to the ground. Alfred climbs over the rear gate and falls onto the road with a cry. Nettie drops Lucy into William's arms, and he tosses the child to Richard and turns back to grab Dan as the wagon teeters at the edge of the ravine. Suddenly the wagon tongue snaps loudly and both horses rear high with their hooves flailing.

"Nettie!" William screams.

She swings one leg over the wagon's side and falls toward his arms. He catches her and staggers backward just as the entire wagon tumbles into the chasm. With a sickening scraping sound it drags first one horse and then the other with it. The animals scream amid the cracking and splitting wood as the wagon smashes into trees and bushes till it finally lies shattered on the ground far below.

The stink of the skunk is still strong in the night air.

William peers toward the wreckage and sees one horse squirming. He looks around for Pike and sees him curled up on the side of the road. He rushes over and shakes him. Pike does not respond. William rolls him onto his back and sees a bloody wound on his forehead. With his fingertips he tenderly probes a deep dent as large as a horseshoe in the man's skull. He puts his head close to Pike's face to hear any breathing and then notices the peculiar angle of the man's head and realizes Pike's neck is broken.

He looks up at Nettie. "He's dead."

"What we going to do?" She puts her hands to her face.

"Dead," he repeats.

Their gunnysacks of food and belongings have gone down with the wagon. Minutes later William and Richard descend the steep bank into the dark gully and find the wagon in pieces in the undergrowth. One horse is silent and not moving. The other is on its side with its chest heaving. Richard crawls under the broken wagon and pulls out the sacks. William opens one of them.

"Got to get my knife," he tells Richard. "Go look at those horses, but stay clear. They hurt bad for sure." He finds his long-bladed knife in its leather sheath and stumbles over to where Richard is kneeling.

"This one's killed, Pa," the boy reports. "The other don't seem so hurt. Maybe just scared."

William examines both mares as well as he can in the darkness. The one Richard said was dead is breathing faintly. The large shaft of the wagon tongue has pierced her shoulder. One leg is twisted and her right foreleg is smashed. With a swift movement William raises his knife and stabs the horse's neck and tugs the blade through the thick flesh. He jumps back as blood squirts from the wide wound.

"Wasn't she dead, Pa?" Richard cries. "Now you killed her."

"Had to."

The other mare begins thrashing on the ground as the scent of blood reaches her. William wipes the knife blade on the leaves and then straddles the struggling horse. He slices through the mare's harness and puts his full weight on her as he unbuckles the heavy bellyband. The mare grows quiet and soon is able to stand.

"We can't get her back to the road," he tells Richard. "It's too steep a climb for her."

William picks up their gunnysacks and he and Richard slowly crawl up the dirt wall. They reach the road and look back down into the gulch to see the horse—fireflies twinkling around her—standing silently beside her dead companion.

William and Nettie and their children and Martha gather around James Pike's body and William folds the man's arms across his chest. "God bless you for trying, Mister Pike," he says. "The Lord look after your soul."

Then they head down the road and deeper into the night.

CHAPTER THIRTY-FIVE

OMENS

ANNE DIPS A RAG INTO THE WOODEN BUCKET AND CON-
tinues scrubbing the parlor floor on her hands and knees. The day is
hot and sticky, and strands of blond hair cling to her face no matter
how she tries to pin them back. She hears the kitchen door open and
she rises to her knees and rubs the cramps in her back.

"Hello?" she calls out and then wishes she hadn't. She realizes it
is too early for Hannah and her family's return. She scurries on all
fours to hide behind the sofa.

Footsteps approach slowly from the kitchen as she crouches lower.

"Hello?" a man's voice calls. "Hannah, that you?"

She peeks around the corner of the sofa to see him in the doorway. He resembles Adam and she guesses he must be Adam's brother.

She stands up awkwardly. "No, I'm Anne."

"Why, hello, Anne," he says as he grins at her embarrassment.
"I'm Adam's kid brother, Simon. I see you're getting the place cleaned
up for me."

"No." She again brushes back her hair from her face. "I mean I
didn't know."

"I'm joking. They had no idea I was arriving."

"They've gone to into Buford to pick up some things," she says and looks down at the bucket of dingy water.

"Please go on with your chore," Simon says. "I've got to get my things and tend to my horse." He grins again. "Nice meeting you."

Anne quickly finishes washing the floor and then struggles to make herself presentable. The humidity and sweat has made her hair wild. Her arms and knees are dirty and her dress is soaked. She steps outside the house to empty the bucket and sees Simon coming from the barn.

"Come sit with me," he calls to her. He points toward the bench. "It's shady there."

"I really should be—"

"Nonsense. Come along. Tell me about yourself."

She sits beside him on the bench—painfully aware of how she must look—and tells him how Hannah and Adam have taken her in since her father ordered her from her home.

"Hannah mentioned it in a letter. She said it was because of your beliefs against slavery. Or at least that was part of it."

"A big part, for certain. I told my family that I'm an abolitionist—"

"And?"

"I hardly dare use the term around you. I mean you've been so involved and have done so much and here I sit and call myself an abolitionist and I don't even—"

"Anne, Anne," he says. "If you hold abolitionist beliefs then you have every right to call yourself one. What's more, I've heard you've done far more than just talk about it."

"You mean the way I bungled my first attempt to help those poor runaways?"

"Hannah said you got into some trouble but at least you were doing something. She also told me about the plea you've made to your sewing circle for clothing to help the fugitives. And then there's one other brave thing."

She looks at him, puzzled.

"Being an abolitionist and staying under the same roof with my brother."

By evening, the family is gathered for a meal of ham and boiled eggs and warm bread. The mood is good, even as Anne and Hannah pepper Simon with questions about the political scene.

"Let me put it this way," Simon says as he reaches for more ham. "Even as we help ourselves to this fine meal, the wind outside carries omens of a struggle beyond anything we've seen in our country's history. Here we are in 1854, the middle of June, sitting in this house on this farm, while just a day's ride to the south there are other houses sitting on other farmland where colored men, women, and children are lawfully the property of their masters, to be subjected to whatever those masters choose. And now the forces protecting slavery and the forces opposing it are realizing that blood likely will flow before this matter is resolved. Many of us now believe the conflict we're facing will be magnitudes larger and bloodier than just transporting hundreds or even a few thousand slaves to new homes in free states."

"Simon," Adam says sharply. "I say this talk is not appropriate when we're trying to have a meal."

"I got carried away. I apologize."

Anne turns to Simon, perplexed. "I agree with what you say about the crime of slavery, but do you think our efforts to help the runaway fugitives is of no value?"

Adam interjects, "I believe we're still eating," but he is ignored.

Simon shakes his head. "I'm sorry for how I sounded, Anne. I don't mean to trivialize what you're doing with this Underground Railroad and such. What you're doing is important."

"But?" she asks.

"But we only need to look at where we're at right now," Simon goes on. "Just two weeks ago, on May 30, Pierce put his presidential seal on the travesty we're calling the Kansas-Nebraska Act. After months of debate, the Slave Power finally prevailed in Congress by passing this new law overturning the boundaries we've had since 1820 to confine the growth of slavery. Franklin Pierce has now opened the western territories to slavery."

"I hadn't heard that slavery would be a foregone conclusion in those places," Hannah offers.

"But the scales are shifting, Hannah," Simon says as he places his palms on the table. "People across the North are finally seeing the Slave Power for what it really is. They're seeing the intention is not to simply preserve slavery where it exists today, but to extend it into the West wherever there's new settlement. Slavery won't be just about growing cotton and tobacco anymore. We'll see it in the mining camps and in building the railroads. We'll see it in the new factories that inevitably will be built. And as more territories come into the Union as slave states, the balance of power in Washington will shift more and more in their favor. If matters continue as they're going today, America's destiny is more inclined toward slavery than toward abolition."

"But people around the world still want our cotton, don't they?" Adam asks. "Isn't slavery part and parcel of why America is the leading producer of cotton?"

"It is, Adam. But what does slavery say about us as a nation," Simon counters. "The rest of the civilized world has rid itself of slavery. Most of Europe outlawed it a century ago. And just in the last ten years there's been successful abolition in Denmark, Peru, and the remaining French colonies. It'd been stopped in Mexico since 1829 until we nearly reinstated it there with our war with them a few years ago. Today America is emerging as a bastion of bondage. The Slave Power is taking over our presidency and our Congress and our courts and our nation's very decency. It's as if something evil has infiltrated our country and put men in power whose motives are at odds with everything America has stood for since its birth."

"I can't say I disagree," Adam says.

"What you say surprises me, brother, I admit."

"Maybe I've been naive till these past few months," Adam says. "I've believed slavery would just die away when the slaveholders found it more trouble than it was worth. Now I'm not so sure."

The meal over, Hannah and Anne begin collecting dishes until Simon asks them to stop. "There's one other thing I'd like to say before we leave the table. It won't take long, but it's important." Then he asks the others if they're familiar with the Fugitive Slave Act.

"Simon, do you remember Hannah writing you in March about the men who'd captured a young runaway slave and stopped here for water?" Adam says to his brother. "A few days later, I got an explanation from our federal marshal—the one who brought that slave boy here—as to how the fugitive law works, usually to the benefit of lawmen and slave catchers and judges. So, in answer to your question, yes, we're familiar with it."

"Then you know the law's been on the books for four years now," Simon says. "It's used frequently in places like this where runaway slaves are being hunted down and returned to their masters or sold to someone else for substantial profit. But farther north, the Fugitive Slave Act rarely comes up because far fewer runaways get that far. That all changed just two weeks ago."

Simon tells the others how he'd arrived in Boston at the end of May to attend a meeting of abolitionists. "We knew Pierce was going to sign the Kansas-Nebraska Act any day, but most of Boston was already in an uproar over a runaway slave named Anthony Burns. He'd fled last year from Richmond up to Boston, where he'd found a job. Somebody found out about him and he was arrested under the Fugitive Slave Law. Of course people in New England hate that law, and the arrest threw the city into an uproar. A couple of days later a group of abolitionists stormed the courthouse where Burns was being held, and a lawman got stabbed to death. Next thing, the president ordered federal soldiers into Boston to put the slave on a ship back to Virginia. Pierce wanted to make an example of Burns."

"It sounds like the president also wanted to make an example of Boston by enforcing the fugitive law," Anne volunteers.

"Yes, enforcing it to its fullest extent," Simon went on. "It used to be that a state like Massachusetts didn't have to cooperate in returning a runaway slave, but the fugitive law has changed all that. And Pierce seems bound and determined to enforce that law at any cost. I tell you, Franklin Pierce is either the stupidest president this nation has ever seen or its most wicked."

"What about the slave?" Hannah asks.

"Try to imagine this." Simon again places his palms on the table in front of himself. "When people knew Burns was going to be put on a ship back to Virginia, they draped black crepe from the buildings and wrapped all the lampposts in black along State Street, from the courthouse to the harbor. There must have been twenty thousand people lining the street, shoulder to shoulder. Others looked out from the windows and crowded the rooftops. People were shouting 'shame! shame!' over and over. The more the soldiers tried to push back the crowd, the louder the people shouted."

"Where were you, Uncle Si?" the boy Robert wonders.

"Well, I was right there on State Street with my friends, and it was the most remarkable sight. A thousand or more soldiers marching row after row down the street, and in the center of them—surrounded by marshals and deputies and militiamen and federal troops with sabers drawn and bayonets at the ready—was this one tiny man."

"The slave?" John asks.

"Yes, Johnny, the slave. Not much older and not much taller than you. When he passed, a hush fell over the street. All we could hear was the tromp, tromp, tromp of a thousand boots. And we could see the fear in that young slave's eyes." Simon sits silently for a moment. "All this to escort one young black man back to a life of captivity. This is what our nation has become."

CHAPTER THIRTY-SIX

THOMAS

"IT AIN'T A GOOD SIGN, MISTER PIKE GETTING KILLED like that," Nettie says to William as they stumble along the darkest road they've ever traveled. The humid night closes in on them as hidden creatures scurry through the brush and bats flutter unseen above their heads. "Now we got no hope cuz of a skunk."

She shifts Lucy from one shoulder to the other. "All alone. No idea where we headed. These children and those two sacks is all we got in the whole world."

William has carried Dan on his back since the boy grew too weary to walk. Martha is of no help, so frightened that she too clings to William.

"I know where we headed," William tells Nettie. "This here's the road where Bobby Hill took me into Washington town to see that judge's room. It changes to farmland pretty soon and then there's the town after that. It ain't far."

"Makes no difference," Nettie says. "We got to stay away from people." With that, she turns abruptly and walks with Lucy into the woods. William follows with Dan still riding on his back and Martha tagging along. Alfred and Richard lug the two gunnysacks as they follow the others.

A few yards into the woods, Richard trips in the darkness and sprawls onto the ground. He feels around frantically among the rotted leaves to find the hunks of ham and cornbread that have spilled from the gunnysack. He can no longer hear the others walking ahead of him. Holding the gunnysack tight against his chest, he stands alone and listens to the thousand strange noises that fill the night. An owl hoots close by and he bolts in fright, heedless of the brush crackling underfoot and the branches whipping his face. He can barely make out the shapes of the others ahead in the dim starlight as he runs toward them.

"Makes no sense to go on in this dark woods," Nettie tells the others. "I say we stop here and try to get some rest."

Hours later, the sun peeks over the horizon, aglow in the fog hovering over the treetops. The dew has made the forest floor slippery as William and Nettie prod the boys and Martha to move faster. "Mister Leyden sure to have men out looking for us by now," William mutters as he ducks and dodges limbs and underbrush.

Soon the group reaches the crest of a ridge. Martha suddenly stops walking. "What you going to do with me when we get over the river to the free side?" she asks Nettie.

Nettie stops to catch her breath. "Don't know what's happening to any of us now or then."

Martha holds back a thin maple branch. "You don't want me with you. I just know it." She releases the branch and it whips close to Nettie's face. The girl turns and marches defiantly ahead of the group.

"Let her go," William says.

Alfred stumbles with a gunnysack and falls to his knees. Nettie helps him to his feet. "The boy's too small to be carrying this big sack."

"Martha's supposed to carry it," William says.

Alfred hoists the gunnysack higher above the ground. "She said I had to carry it."

William waves to Richard. "Go fetch her." The boy disappears among the thickets. William and Nettie rest on a fallen tree trunk with Dan and Lucy while Alfred digs through the sack.

"Where's the food?" Alfred demands.

"We ate it. You know that," William tells him.

"I'm hungry."

"We all hungry."

Several minutes pass before Richard returns. He says he found Martha up ahead with an injured foot. "She been trying to walk back here but her foot hurts too much," he says.

William shakes his head. "Show us where."

They find Martha seated against the trunk of a sycamore. She holds her right foot in both hands and whimpers as she tells how she stepped over a log and landed on the stub of a branch. It sliced through the thin leather of her shoe and tore a gash in the arch of her foot. Nettie kneels down and examines the girl's foot to make sure there are no splinters in the wound. She rips a strip of clean linen from a shirt in the gunnysack and bandages the foot as best she can.

"Try to walk," Nettie orders.

Martha gets up slowly and avoids putting weight on her foot. She takes one limping step and cries out in pain. "I can't walk. I just can't."

"You can and you will," William says. "I'll make a crutch." It took time but he was able to locate a branch of suitable size and shape for Martha's crutch. He scraped off the bark with his knife and handed the crooked stick to her. "You got to keep up."

But walking any distance is difficult in a forest overgrown with brambles and littered with fallen timber. Mosquitoes and horseflies attack faces and bare arms. They climb hill after hill in hopes of seeing the town in the distance, but with the passing of the morning, the forest remains dense and no town comes into sight. Finally they stop. They are exhausted and covered with scratches and insect bites. There is only enough water in the canteen for one swallow apiece and they eagerly drink it dry. William is worried, not knowing what direction they're headed or if they're wandering in circles.

The bugs are too aggravating for them to remain at rest so they push on. They struggle up another ridge, badly eroded with nothing to stabilize the soil. The dirt breaks away underfoot and they slide back down the slope again and again. Sweat streams down Nettie's face and drips onto Lucy as the child clings to her mother's neck. Nettie finally pulls herself to the top of the ridge by grabbing the trunks of saplings.

She motions for everyone to be silent. William crawls up beside her.

At the base of the ridge flows a shallow creek. On its opposite bank stands a white man—scrawny and shirtless with black straggly hair and beard—hoeing plants in a sparse garden. Farther back are his shack and a corncrib. A mule grazes near a small stable while a dilapidated wagon provides shade for two hogs lolling on the damp earth near the creek bank.

"We got to get clear of him," William whispers as he gazes along the ridgeline.

"We need food," Nettie says.

"From him?"

"Just anything."

"Let me go down," says Martha as she hobbles up to where they're watching the man. "He won't hurt me right off, even if he's so inclined. I won't let him get that close."

Martha's offer surprises Nettie and William and they agree to let her try. William edges his way down the hillside ahead of Martha. Halfway down, his foot launches a small avalanche of gravel. The man stops hoeing and listens. Then he hacks at the ground once again. William slides behind a slender cottonwood and motions for Martha to join him.

She inches her way down, propped by her crutch.

The man hears her before she reaches the bank. He squints toward the hillside and drops his hoe. He hurries to his shack and reappears a moment later with a musket in his hands. He walks slowly toward the creek and keeps his eyes on Martha.

"What you be doing there, girl? You alone?" he shouts.

"I need help, sir. I'm hurt."

"Hurt your leg, did you?"

"My foot, sir. Hurt it bad." She keeps moving down the slope and closer to the water. "You got any food, sir?"

"You want food, do you?"

"I'm awful hungry, sir, awful hungry."

She hobbles within a few feet of where William is hiding.

"Even if I got vittles," the man shouts back, "I'm over here and you're over there. You got to come over here."

Martha reaches the bank of the creek. She dips the end of her crutch into the water.

"Can't swim, sir."

"Water ain't even to your belly. Just step in a ways and I'll meet you halfway."

"But I'm hurt. I'll bleed again."

"Naw, it'll just clean you up." He lays the musket on the ground and pulls off his boots. "Come on, girl, meet you halfway."

William's eyes meet Martha's and he sees the fear in them.

She sticks her bandaged foot into the water and winces. "It hurts," she moans. She shifts her weight onto the crutch and it sinks into the mud. She pulls it free and takes another step. The water soaks the hem of her dress.

The man wades in from his side. "Don't get wenches like you coming up into these hills."

"You sure you got food?" Martha says. The water rises to her waist.

"Plenty."

The man wades close to Martha and suddenly grabs her arm and yanks her toward him.

"You're hurting me," she shouts.

He stays in the middle of the creek and holds Martha as she struggles.

William dashes into the water, lifting his legs high. The man takes several steps backward to the creek bank and pulls Martha along with him. She tries to hit him with her crutch but he wrenches it away from her and throws it back into the creek.

William grabs it.

The man scrambles onto the bank with Martha in his grasp. William jams the crutch between the man's ankles and he tumbles to the ground. Martha breaks free as the man crawls like a spider toward his musket. William grabs the man's lank hair and pulls him backward into the water.

"You stay," William orders the man as he grabs the musket and points it at him.

"That was a damn darkie trick if ever I seen one." The man sits at the water's edge with his hands in the mud. "What you going to do? Kill me?"

"Not planning on even hurting you. We just need food."

"You were going to hurt me," Martha yells as she furiously limps toward him holding her crutch like a club.

"No," William says, grabbing the crutch before Martha can swing it. "We want food, that's all."

The man's shack is little better than a slave cabin. There are few pieces of furniture and his bed is a stained mattress on a broken trundle frame. An open fireplace provides heat for warmth and cooking. The pantry shelves are nearly bare.

"You said you had food," William says, keeping the musket trained on the man. "Don't see much here."

"I got enough." The man rummages through a cupboard and comes up with some potatoes and a slab of pork ribs wrapped in burlap. "You two trying to get away from some mean master, are you?"

"No, we ain't," William tells him. "This is my sister and we free. Traveling to Maysville to visit kin."

"Then what you doing in this here hollow?"

"Lost. We can't find the right road."

The man unveils the remains of a bread loaf, furry with mold.

"You can put that gun down any time, boy. I'm giving you my food, ain't I?"

William considers the situation. Nettie and Lucy and the boys are still at the top of the ridge. He can't get back to them without the threat of the man overpowering Martha, and she is too hurt to make it back across the creek and up the hillside herself.

"Going to have to tie you up for a bit," William tells the man.

"Like hell."

"Just until I can get up that hillside and back."

The man has some twine in a drawer and William ties him to a chair.

"What you got up that hillside? More darkies?"

William ignores him. He cocks the musket's hammer and leans the gun against the table. He tells Martha to stand near the gun but not touch it unless the man threatens to break loose. She hobbles over to the musket and touches its muzzle.

William glares at her.

"I ain't touching it. I just don't want to be too far away from it is all."

William wades back across the creek and claws his way up the side of the ridge to Nettie and the children.

"He's got food and water. Best we all go down."

He helps Nettie and Lucy down the slope. The boys run and jump and jostle the gunnysacks till they reach the bank. William picks up Dan and wades into the water.

A shot rings out and everyone splashes across the creek and runs to the shack. The man is still tied to the chai but it has tipped over backward. The room is thick with smoke and the smell of gunpowder.

"Damn you to hell," the man screams. "I'm shot!"

Martha stands wide-eyed with her hands over her mouth and the musket at her feet, smoke curling from its barrel.

William leans over the man.

"My leg, damn it!" the man growls.

William sees a rip in the man's trousers along his right calf. A small splotch of blood seeps through the cloth. He smells piss and sees a wet stain on the man's pants.

"You one lucky fellow. Shot skinned your leg. Cut you just a bit."

"It hurts like hell! You untie me, hear?"

William looks at Martha.

"It just went off," the girl sobs. "It fell over and went off."

"Lying bitch!" The man squirms against the twine that binds him. "She was holding the gun. Pointing it right at me. She pulled the goddamn trigger."

William spots the man's ammunition pouch. "I'm going to load that gun again. Then I'll untie you."

Eventually William releases the man. Nettie rips another strip of linen from the shirt in the gunnysack and binds the man's leg wound. Richard builds a fire to fry the pork and a while later they all share food from the man's rickety table. They learn his name is Thomas and he's lived in these hills since he and his bride arrived twenty years ago. Cholera took his wife and their two daughters in 1846.

"No women been in this place these eight years since my Emmy and the girls passed," Thomas says as he chews a piece of pork. "Never had no slaves myself. And don't you go telling me you ain't slaves. I got eyes and a brain both."

"Never mind what we is or ain't," William says as he gnaws a rib.

"Slaves is for them that's got money. I was born poor and I'll die poor. Hell, you probably had more when you was at your master's place than I got now."

William looks around the man's shack. "About the same, I'd say."

"Difference is, a slave is property and I ain't."

"We ain't property no more," Martha pipes up from where she's sitting on the floor.

"Are too," Thomas argues. "You'll always be that man's property till he sets you free. You get caught and you get took back to him and he can do what he wants with you. Hell, if I took you back myself I might get a reward. That's because you're property and I ain't."

William walks to the door of the shack. "You going to be my property for a little while more," he tells Thomas. "This gun says so."

"What you meaning to do?"

William says they're going to hitch the mule to the wagon, bypass Washington, and ride—all of them—to Maysville. "And you," he points to Thomas, "you be coming with us. You know this country and can get us there. Then you get your mule and wagon back."

"What about my firearm?"

"We'll see."

It's late afternoon when William slaps the reins against the mule's rump to get the wagon moving. He fears Thomas will try to alert people along the way and has again bound the man's wrists and seated him in the wagon bed with the others. The wagon creaks and groans as it lurches down the hilly road.

"You got to go right through Washington, like it or not," Thomas warns.

"Can't." William shakes his head. "Can't go through that town with a white man tied in a wagon."

"You got no choice 'less you plan on making yourself a new road."

William wonders if the wagon will even hold together. A bent front axle causes it to jerk and sway precariously. Several sideboards are loose and there's barely enough harness intact to keep the mule hitched. Soon the road intersects with a busier one and—just as Thomas had said—William sees no intersecting roads as they enter the town. Alfred and Dan shove each other for more room and push Martha closer to Thomas. The man lifts his bound hands and rubs them across the girl's arm.

"You sure a pretty one."

She swats his hands away.

Nettie glares at him. She holds Lucy with one hand and grasps the musket barrel with the other. "Don't you touch her. Don't be touching any of us."

"Why you doing this, anyway?" Thomas asks Nettie. "Your home so bad you have to put your little darkies at risk like this?"

"Just stop talking."

"Seems God made you a slave. Didn't have to, but he did. Now you're running away against God's will."

"God made me a slave? No, sir. Mister Leyden made me a slave. He bought me and didn't see fit to free me. Wasn't God."

William turns back to look at Thomas. "Don't go talking to this man. He just wants trouble."

"God doesn't make slaves," Richard says.

"God made your skin dark and put black blood in your veins, ain't that right, boy?"

"Don't pay him no heed, Richard," Nettie says.

"Ain't that right, boy?"

"He made me colored, but that don't—"

"Don't what? Don't make you a slave? Look around you, boy. Look in this wagon." Thomas nods his head at each person. "Slave. Slave. Slave. Slave. Now when we get into town you look at the darkies on the streets. Slave. Slave. Slave. Don't that tell you something?"

"Some coloreds are free," Richard argues.

"That's because white people set them free. God gave white people the power to keep slaves or set them free. That's because you're property."

"Quit talking to my boy," Nettie says angrily. "God didn't make us slaves and God didn't make us property. It's people like you who done it and you'll burn in hell for it." She yanks the gun out from beneath her skirt. "Now shut your mouth."

They roll into Washington and share the dusty road with a number of carriages and other wagons. They pass the old courthouse where Bobby Hill had taken William to show him the judge's chambers. Farmers and a few slaves loiter by the storefronts as brawny men load bags and crates into wagons. A couple of carriages stir up dust as they speed past the old wagon.

"We going straight through this town and we'll see what's God's will," William says as he flicks the tattered reins.

"You there," a man yells at William as a buggy pulls alongside. "You, boy!"

William sees a white-bearded man in a tall black hat in the driver's seat. "You know your wagon's got a bad axle?"

"Yessir. I can feel it."

"Have the smith down the street fix it," he shouts. "It's going to break and spill your family onto the road."

"I'll do that, sir."

Suddenly Thomas squirms upward and shouts. "Help me! They tied me up. Help!"

The man in the buggy jerks on his reins and strains to see into the wagon. "What's going on there, boy? Who's that man?" he shouts.

"My master, sir," William shouts back. "Gets liquor in him and he don't act right. Got to get him home."

"Good thing," the bearded man yells back. "Liquor puts the spell of Satan on some men. Sorry you've got to live with that." The man's carriage pulls ahead of the wagon and continues down the road.

"Looks like God ain't too mad at us after all," Nettie chides Thomas.

They travel another two miles north before William turns the creaking wagon onto another road and stops at a secluded grove to let the mule rest. Everyone climbs down from the cramped wagon bed. Thomas jerks his arm away when William tries to help him.

"This where you're going to kill me? Plug me with my own gun?"

"This is where I let you go."

"He'll come after us," Nettie warns. "He'll get some other men and they'll chase us down."

William puts his face close to Thomas. "You listen. I'm freeing you right here. We going to drive that wagon a couple more miles north and then I'll leave it with the mule alongside the road. You don't tell nobody nothing and you can have it back."

"And you'll be gone off again on foot?"

"Just don't you come after us."

"You got my gun."

"I'll leave it in the wagon."

Thomas scrunches his eyebrows. "So all I got to do is walk down the road and get my wagon?"

"William?" Nettie's expression is doubtful.

"It's only right," he tells her. "He got shot in the leg. We ate his food. We should just let this man be."

With that, William piles his family and Martha and the two gunnysacks back into the wagon and drives off as Thomas rubs his wrists and watches from the grove.

"How long you think he'll stay put?" Nettie asks.

"Not long."

Nettie looks behind the wagon. "You really going to leave this wagon for that man?"

"I ain't a fool," William says and drives on toward Maysville.

CHAPTER THIRTY-SEVEN

HIDEOUT

WILLIAM RESTS ON HIS HANDS AND KNEES AT THE EDGE of the cornfield where they've spent the night. He fingers a tiny green stalk rising crookedly from the cracked dirt. "Needs rain or this crop's going to blow away."

"We don't need to be worrying about crops," Nettie scolds. "You say you want to get to Mister Pike's home. So how we going to find it?"

"I got no answer just yet."

Martha hands a fidgety Lucy to Nettie and says, "We got to find somebody to help us. Somebody in that town."

"The girl's right," William agrees.

They board the old wagon as the sun climbs higher. They're hungry and thirsty and even the old mule has found little to graze on. They ride in silence for three miles as the road twists and slopes steadily downhill—a good sign they're nearing the river basin. At midmorning William steers the wagon around a sharp turn and for the first time they see the town of Maysville spread out below them. From high on the hill they can see clusters of roofs and the streets lined with stores. Smoke rises from factories and packing plants and an occasional church steeple pokes above the carpet of trees.

On the far edge of town the Ohio River sparkles in the morning sun.

"Praise God," Nettie shouts. "Look to the other side of that river, children. That's the free land."

Maysville is bustling with people and traffic. William tries to negotiate the wobbling wagon among the briskly moving carriages and wagons but becomes the brunt of shouts and jeers. He spots four black men in coarse slave clothing standing beside the road. He halts the wagon beside them.

"Can you help us?" he asks the nearest man.

"Help how?"

"You hear of James Pike? Man makes harnesses? We got to find his house."

"Nope."

"What you want with him?" another man asks.

William was uncertain of what to say. "He helps black folks."

"Helps how?" the first man asks.

"You be careful," a third man warns. "Lots of people say they help. Next thing you wake up on a boat going downriver with chains on your feet."

"Mister Pike's a good man," William says. "We got to find his house."

The first man points to a building across the street. "Go to the mail place over there with a yarn about how you need to find this man. They got to know where he lives."

William moves the wagon closer to the building where the man had pointed. He tells Richard to hold the reins. Nettie puts her hand on his sleeve. "You take care, William. If they don't want to tell you nothing, you just come back."

He finds himself in a small shop with colorful boxes of stationery tied with delicate ribbons such as he has never seen before. Pens and bottles and blotters sit on glass shelves and polished tables. A woman with white hair pulled into a tight bun stands behind a counter and fans herself while two other women in elaborate bonnets examine small bottles of colored inks.

The shopkeeper puts down her fan when she sees William. Her eyes narrow and she asks, "What do you want?"

"Need help, ma'am."

One of the other women steps aside as he approaches the counter. She pinches her nose with her fingertips. "Good heavens, don't you people ever bathe?"

He removes his hat and clutches it with both hands. "Sorry, ma'am. I been traveling a long while."

"Why are you here?" the shopkeeper demands.

"You do the mail here?"

"No, we do not 'do' the mail here. Do you see any mail here? This shop caters to those who compose the mail."

Confused, William looks around. "I'm trying to find a man," he blurts.

"Do you see any men here?" the shopkeeper says. She clearly enjoys her own repartee. "We do not 'do' men here either."

The two other women giggle.

"James Pike. I'm trying to find Mister James Pike."

The customer who had pinched her nose looks at William. "Now what would you want with Jimmy Pike?"

"You know him, ma'am?"

"I'll ask the questions, thank you. Now once again, what do you want with Mister Pike?"

He tightens his grip on his hat. "Carpenter work. I'm a carpenter and Mister Pike hired me to do some work in his house. Said he liked my work. He wrote down how to get there." He looks at the floor. "But I can't read, ma'am, and I don't know how to find his house in this big town."

The woman steps closer to William. She again turns her head away in an exaggerated movement of avoiding his scent. "Let me see the paper he wrote for you." She holds out her gloved hand and wiggles her fingers.

"It's lost. Lost like I am, ma'am. I got my family and we been traveling a long ways to get to Mister Pike."

She steps away from William. "And what, pray tell, does Mister Pike look like?"

William remembers James Pike lying dead at the edge of the road with his skull smashed in by the horse's hoof. "Tall man, up to here." He lifts his hand several inches above his own head. "Got a beard on his chin. Good clothes, ma'am, good clothes. And a bad leg from the war."

"That's Jimmy all right," she concedes.

"You know his house, ma'am?"

She tells him Pike lives a short distance northwest of town along the riverfront road. She describes his brick house in some detail.

"So," the woman's friend asks her, "who exactly is this James Pike you seem to know so much about?"

"I met him at church some years ago. I can't really remember."

"He doesn't sound like a man you'd easily forget," her friend adds.

"I didn't say I forgot him," the woman counters. "I just said I can't remember when I met him." She smiles coyly at her friend.

"Thank you, ma'am," William says as he backs out of the store.

"Tell him Edith helped you."

"I will, ma'am. Miss Edith."

"And tell Jimmy to give you a bath."

William steers the wagon into the stable behind the brick house and squeezes it between Pike's carriage and an empty stall. He wants to keep the mule hitched until he's certain his family will be safe. He closes the large doors, engulfing the stable in muggy darkness and rank odors.

"What you expect to find at this dead man's house?" Martha asks as she adjusts the bloodstained bandage on her foot.

"A place to hide till we find how to cross that river."

Once again they find themselves biding their time in a sweltering and cramped space in fear of being discovered. This time the three younger children are so exhausted that Nettie gets them to nap in the wagon.

"Got to get inside that house," William whispers to Nettie as she rocks Lucy in her arms.

"What you looking for?"

"Food. Maybe some clothes. I ain't sure."

He leaves the hot stable and dashes to a small white porch at the rear of the house. He stands in the shadows with his back pressed against the brick wall until there are no passersby on the road. He finds the door unlocked and enters the house. Lace curtains filter the afternoon sun to reveal a plushness that reminds him of the Leyden house. He finds the dead man's desk—a heavy piece made of golden maple—and runs his hands over the polished wood. He examines stacks of correspondence and newspapers on the desktop but they mean nothing to him. He walks into the bedroom and notices the bed's tall and intricately carved headboard. He sits in a chair in the corner of the bedroom and removes his hat to wipe his forehead.

A horse whinnies in front of the house.

William crouches and moves toward the parlor where he can see the road through the windows. Directly in front of the house is a one-horse buggy with a second horse tethered behind it. He watches a man wearing a high-crowned straw hat step from the buggy and help a woman climb down. It's Edith from the stationery store.

The two walk toward the front porch. William creeps behind a chair to avoid being seen through the door's etched-glass window. The man raps on the door and waits.

William hears Edith speaking. "I felt there was something strange about Jimmy hiring that colored man to do carpentry around here."

He strains to hear more.

"You did the right thing, Edith," the man says. "The darkie could've seen Jimmy anywhere and found out his name and that he was from Maysville. He could steal Jimmy blind."

The man knocks again.

"And, of course, silly me, I told him right where Jimmy lives."

The man knocks once more.

"See? I don't think Jimmy's home," Edith adds.

William ducks lower as the woman cups her gloved hands around her face and presses them against the window glass to see inside.

"I'll have a look around," the man says. "I want you back in the carriage, Edith." He leads her back to the buggy and helps her climb into it. He reaches behind the seat and pulls out a rifle.

William scurries on his hands and knees to another window.

The man walks along the side of the house and uses the barrel of the carbine to poke at bushes along the foundation. Whenever he comes to a window he peers inside. At the last window the man suddenly stops.

Martha's voice rings out, "You get away from there!"

The man spins around.

William slides across the wooden kitchen floor to see what's happening.

"Put that gun down," Martha orders. She's holding Thomas's musket at the level of her hip.

"Whoa, there, missy," the man says. "You don't want to be pointing that big gun at anybody. It's liable to go off and somebody could get hurt."

Martha takes another step forward. "I already killed one man. Did it yesterday. I blew a big hole in him. He died like a stuck pig."

"That's quite a story, missy," the man responds with less confidence. "How do I know it's true?"

"Don't do as I say and you'll see."

Then William hears Edith's voice.

"Good heavens," she exclaims as she approaches. "You don't imagine that gun is loaded, do you?"

Edith and the man talk but their voices are too low for William to hear. He storms out the back door near the couple, startling the man, who turns and points his carbine at William.

"Stop," Martha yells at him.

William quickly grabs the carbine's muzzle and yanks the gun from the man.

"See? See?" Edith cries. "That's him. I knew he'd come here to steal from Jimmy."

William releases the hammer on the carbine. "I didn't come here to steal."

"Then who's that?" Edith says as she points at Martha.

"My sister, and she's just protecting me."

"Protecting you from whom?" the man says.

"I'd say from you, sir. Mister Pike hired me to do work here and I was looking to where I'm supposed to build his bookcase. Mister Pike knows I'm here." William steps closer to the man. " How long you think I'd be alive, sir, if somebody like you carrying this here gun found a colored man in this house? How long before you'd pull that trigger?"

"Are you implying I would shoot you without first asking questions?"

William tosses the carbine back to the man, who catches it in midair. Then William walks over to Martha and takes the rifle from her and slings it under his arm. "I need to get back to my work."

They all hear a braying sound and look to the road to see a rider in a black coat and wide-brimmed hat astride a dusty mule.

And Martha shouts, "Reverend Shem!"

CHAPTER THIRTY-EIGHT

CROSSING

REVEREND SHEM DISMOUNTS AND BRUSHES THE DUST from his clothing. He walks with his mule toward the man with the carbine and the woman.

"Is there trouble here?"

William takes the mule's reins from the preacher. "I was in town this morning and told this woman Mister Pike hired me to do some carpenter work. I come here to look at the house and they showed up. Martha stopped him before he used that gun on me."

The preacher wipes his forehead with his bandanna and replaces his black hat. He steps closer to the man. "Are you satisfied that everything here is good?"

"Who's asking?" the man says.

"My name is Shem Marshall and I'm a preacher. Baptist mostly. I've known James Pike for years. I put him in touch with this man here," and nods toward William. "He's a fine carpenter."

"Do you know where Jimmy is?" Edith asks the preacher.

"Down by Mays Lick. He didn't tell me the nature of his business but said he'd be home tomorrow evening."

"You must understand that we were just looking after Jimmy's property," Edith says. "I don't know this man at all. I was worried after I gave him directions to Jimmy's house."

"Completely understandable, ma'am." The preacher bows his head to her. "I'm sure the Lord appreciates you being your brother's keeper."

Edith and the man depart, she full of apologies and the man clutching his carbine and shaking his head. The preacher looks at William. "Where are Nettie and the children?"

William and Martha lead him to the stable.

"Thank the Lord you're all unharmed," he says when he sees the family huddled in the shadows. "We don't have much time."

Reverend Shem tells them he was preaching at one of the farms when he heard that a man's body had been found near a wrecked wagon on the road to Washington. "It took a whole day before the lawmen would let me look at the body. I've been searching for two days but you covered your tracks well. I figured maybe you'd come here if you knew where James lived. It seems the Lord's been guiding us all."

"We didn't know where else to go," Nettie tells him. "We don't know nobody and don't know how to cross the river."

The preacher reassures them, explaining he'd accompanied Pike twice before to help slaves make crossings. "I'm pretty certain I can remember where he hides the boat. We'll wait until night. Slave catchers are all over this river like vermin."

They settle back into the stable, knowing it'll be two hours before they can head out. Reverend Shem admits he's worried. "It's just a matter of time before someone identifies James's body, bless that good man's soul. Then somebody's sure to show up here."

Then the preacher pulls a folded paper from his coat pocket. "I found these posted in Washington and Maysville," he says as he unfolds the paper. "Mister Leyden's put up a reward on you all. People say he's mad because no slave has ever run from his place before. They say he wants you back and he wants everybody to see what happens when one of his slaves tries something like this."

Time crawls as they sit in the dark stable with flies feasting on their sweat. Just before sunset Reverend Shem and Nettie venture into the dead man's house to look for food. When stars appear in the evening sky, William opens the stable doors and pulls the wagon into the muggy night air. Soon Reverend Shem is back astride his mule and leading the creaking wagon and its passengers westerly along the riverfront road. "Keep watch for a large oak standing by itself right next to the road," the preacher tells William.

A mile down the road a lone rider approaches and slows his horse's gait as he comes nearer. William can only make out that he's young and white.

"You lost?" the rider asks. "Where you all headed?"

"Prayer meeting near Charleston," Reverend Shem tells him. "How much farther?"

The young rider studies the black man and then stands in his stirrups to examine the wagon. "Not far. Two miles maybe."

"God bless you, sir," Reverend Shem says and nudges his mule onward.

The boy spurs his horse and rides off.

Only a hundred yards farther Reverend Shem dismounts next to a towering oak. He walks past the tree and disappears down a slope toward the sound of the river. A matter of minutes later, they all are standing on a thin strip of sandy riverbank with black water lapping at their feet. They stare in the moonlight at the boat moored to a broken-down dock. "It'll be tight with seven of you," Reverend Shem says. They pile into the boat, with the smaller children balanced on the older ones' laps.

The preacher steadies the rocking boat with one hand and points across the dark river with the other. "Now listen to me, all of you. Row across the river as straight as you can."

"I never rowed a boat before," William says.

"You'll catch on. Your life depends on it. When you reach land, go that way—west. There's a town called Ripley four or five miles downriver and folks there willing to help you. But keep in mind—you listening to me? —slave catchers are all over that shore."

Still holding the boat's rope, the preacher says, "Pray with me." He kneels on the splintered dock and bows his head. "Dear Lord, thank you for bringing these people this far in safety. Deliver them, Lord, into the hands of those who will help them. Guide and protect these your children, my sweet Lord."

William slips the long oars into the oarlocks as the preacher shoves the boat away from the dock. He struggles to turn the bow toward the Ohio shore. He pulls hard on the oars and lifts them from the water as he leans forward and then sinks the oars into the water and again pulls hard. He soon finds a rhythm and remembers the preacher's prayer.

"My Lord," he says as he pulls on the oars.

"Guide us," he says as he leans forward and lifts, swings, and dips the oars.

"My Lord"—pulling back.

"Protect us"—leaning forward.

"Amen," Nettie chants in William's pauses. Soon Richard, Martha, and Alfred join with her.

The boat moves smoothly through the water as if propelled by the prayers of its passengers. William lifts his voice to the night sky, as do the others. He sees in the moonlight Nettie's smiling face and knows their prayer will carry them across the water in a farewell to the painful land they are leaving and a joyous greeting at the shore welcoming them.

"My Lord, guide us."

"Amen."

"My Lord, protect us."

"Amen."

The Ohio shore comes upon them suddenly, its steep embankment looming in the darkness. William lets the boat drift until he spots a small stretch of beach and then guides the boat toward the bank. He hears the boat's bottom scrape the shore and jumps into the shallow water to pull the bow onto the land.

He falls to his knees.

"Thank you, dear God."

A match is struck nearby and its sputtering light reveals the face of a man standing a few feet from the shoreline. The man touches the match to a torch that bursts into flame.

"Stop right there," says another man, stepping in front of William and pointing a rifle at his head.

"Jesus, where'd all these coloreds come from?" says another man.

William quickly counts three men—one holding the rifle, one with the torch, one other standing in the darkness.

"Round 'em up," orders the man with the gun.

Two of the men splash into the water beside the boat, one of them still holding the torch aloft. The other grabs Alfred and then Dan and flings the screaming boys onto the riverbank like bags of grain. Nettie stands up and holds Lucy as she tries to keep her balance in the rocking boat. The man with the torch lunges for Martha. Richard grabs an oar and jabs at him.

William watches in horror as the men seize his children. A man lunges for Nettie and she suddenly loses her grip on Lucy. The child splashes into the water and Nettie screams, "My baby!"

William pushes the man's rifle aside and dashes into the river. He reaches into the muck and weeds to find his daughter. He wades farther into the river but still cannot find her. With water up to his chest he plunges beneath the surface and sweeps his arms back and forth and finally touches a flimsy lump. He clutches the fabric of Lucy's clothing and pulls her small body toward him.

Holding the child above his head he breaks the surface several yards from where the boat was landed. "Oh, baby, come on," he cries as he shakes her. "Breathe!"

He still hears the commotion around the boat, his family crying and men shouting over and over, "Where'd that buck go?"

William realizes the men can no longer see him. His search for Lucy has taken him beyond the light of the torch. He wades to shore and falls onto the mud with the child in his arms. "Please, God, help my little girl."

Lucy coughs and then spits water and gasps and then bursts into tears. William clamps his hand over her mouth to silence her as she struggles for more air.

The man with the torch moves closer and then stops. "He ain't down here. Musta drowned. Both of 'em."

"Come on back," orders the man with the rifle. "We got these ones. Let's go."

Nettie screams William's name.

Richard cries out in pain.

Then they are gone.

CHAPTER THIRTY-NINE

CARE

WILLIAM SCALES THE EMBANKMENT WITH LUCY'S SHIV-ering body tight against his chest. Finally reaching the road at the top of the slope, he tries to remain unseen in the darkness but move quickly enough to reach the slave catchers and the rest of his family. But he sees nothing in the darkness and hears only the sounds of bullfrogs and crickets and the chattering of his daughter's teeth.

The night has swallowed his family.

He walks westward for miles alongside the river until its ripples reflect the soft pink of dawn. His clothing is damp, first from the water of the river and now with sweat. Lucy no longer trembles but remains limp in his arms.

"Come on, my baby, talk to me," he whispers over and over.

He reaches the town of Ripley as sunlight breaks over the hills behind him. He walks past houses and fences with trellised roses sweetening the scent of the early morning. He steps to the side of the road as wagons roll past but he sees no trace of the one that carried away his family.

At one house a white-haired woman stands in the yard with an egg basket slung over her arm, and he calls out, "Ma'am?"

She turns. "Yes?" She studies him. "What is it?"

"My little girl, ma'am. She's sick."

"Bless her heart," the woman says and steps closer. "Does she need a doctor?"

"Don't know, ma'am. She fell in the river."

"Oh my goodness. She's breathing, isn't she?"

"Yes, ma'am. She just don't seem right."

The woman examines William more closely. "Are you a slave? Did you just come across the river?"

He lowers his eyes and doesn't answer.

"Never mind," she says and goes on to describe a house that fronts the river in the center of town. "Find that house and knock on the door and rouse whoever you can. Tell them you need help. They're good people. But get going. You're not safe on these streets."

William dodges wagons and carriages and horses as he makes his way past a boatyard and several stores to reach the house where the woman had said the people would take him in. The house is stately and he approaches it cautiously. The man who answers the door—stout with gray hair and beard, dressed in wool trousers and broadcloth waistcoat—quickly leads William and Lucy up a flight of stairs.

"You must stay up here and be perfectly quiet. You understand? We must be certain you haven't been followed."

William climbs the stairs behind the man and smells the aroma of bacon and coffee coming from the rear of the house. In the hallway at the top of the stairs he again tells the man, "My girl Lucy needs help."

"Yes," the man replies. "As I said, I'll tell my wife. She knows about these things." The man pushes aside a chest-of-drawers to reveal a doorway no more than three feet tall. "Through there. The attic gets hot this time of year but at least you're out of harm's way."

Soon the man's wife comes to the attic with a plate of bacon and bread. She wears a crisp white blouse and gray pleated skirt that matches the thick bun of her hair. She examines Lucy and says, "The child should be fine when she gets some food in her. I'm going to get some bedding for her." She stoops to leave the attic. "It'll get warm up here, but that should be good for her. I'll bring some tea."

A few moments later the man returns to the attic carrying two blankets and a pillow and a chamber pot. Then his wife returns with a bundle of cotton diapers, a kettle of tea, and two cups. "She certainly is a quiet child," the woman says as she tips a teacup to Lucy's lips.

William strokes Lucy's head. "This ain't like her."

The woman puts a blanket on the wooden floor for Lucy to lie on and then fluffs the pillow under the child's head. With practiced hands, she replaces Lucy's diaper and fastens the clean one with straight pins. "You watch her. If she starts to sweat, moisten her face with this towel. We want her to sleep."

William nods.

"If there's any trouble—if you think she's getting worse—come downstairs and find me. But only if you have no other choice. I'll be back in a while."

Then the woman leaves. For the moment—in this hot attic with its dusty plank floor and steeply pitched rafters and a single beam of morning sunlight streaming through the small gable window—he feels safe.

CHAPTER FORTY

REFUGE

BY AFTERNOON THE ATTIC IS SWELTERING AND WILLIAM
can barely breathe. Lucy wakes from a sweaty nap with a full-
throated cry. He looks into the child's tearful eyes and sees her spirit
has returned.

An hour later the woman returns to the attic. "Lucy's much
improved, but not out of the woods," she observes. "We can go downstairs now." They leave the attic and slowly descend the stairs—the air
becoming wonderfully cooler with each step—until they reach the
main hallway and then hurry to the kitchen at the back of the house.

The man is there with his waistcoat unbuttoned and shirtsleeves
rolled up on his pale arms. "I'm assuming you want to keep heading
north," he says. "I've made arrangements."

"Can't, sir. The rest of my family—"

" The rest?"

"They got caught when we crossed the river—my Nettie and
my boys and a girl." He gestures toward Lucy. "We the only ones
got away."

"This isn't good," the man says. "Do you know where they were taken?"

"I thought they headed this way. I tried to catch them, but they was too fast. Or they didn't come this way at all. It was dark, sir."

The man lowers his head. "I know you don't want to hear this, William, but your family could be anywhere by now. It's been too many hours. The men who caught them could be taking them back to your old home, or they could've put them on a steamer headed downriver. They could be taking them to auction in Louisville or someplace beyond. I'm afraid the possibilities are many and none of them good."

The man tells William he and Lucy must get to a safer place and then decide what to do. To stay in Ripley is to remain in jeopardy. "As soon as it's dark, I'll take you to another home where you'll be a little safer. Then they'll take you somewhere where you'll be safer yet. It'll be that way as you continue to travel farther away from the river. This town is overrun with slave hunters and sympathizers, as you've unfortunately witnessed."

The man leaves and says he'll return in a while. William sits in the kitchen for an hour while he and the woman care for Lucy. The woman gives William three more diapers to take with him. By the time the man comes back—wearing a long linen duster and a hat with the brim pulled low—William realizes evening shadows fill the kitchen.

"I know this is sudden," the man says, "but we need to go right now. Get your daughter and stay close to me."

The man leads William through an alley and past a row of houses and into another alley. Dogs bark and hogs snort as they pass. They hide in doorways and behind trees until they finally reach a steep hillside on the north edge of town. "It's a long climb up this hill— maybe a thousand feet—and you need to stay off the road," the man says. "Keep going and at the top you'll find a farm. There may be a lantern in a window facing the river. Go up to the house and ask for Reverend Rankin. Say the name."

"Reverend Rankin."

"The Rankins are expecting you and your daughter. But be quick and don't stop for another living soul." The man pats William's shoulder. "God be with you. Now go!"

The hill is steep and seems endless, just as the man had said. Trees and saplings are so close together that William can see only a few feet ahead in the rapidly dimming daylight. He bends low with Lucy against his belly and moves forward with one hand outstretched to protect them both. Finally he breaks through to a small clearing. Far below he sees lamps glittering in the windows of the tiny houses. He's high enough above the town to still see the sunset's orange sheen on the Ohio River as it winds westward through the dark Appalachian hills.

On the far side of the clearing William spots a brick house and a barn overlooking the river valley. He hoists Lucy higher on his shoulder and runs toward the house. He steps onto a small porch and through one of the windows sees a woman and two men carrying dishes from a table. He knocks softly on the door. One of the men opens it with a lamp in his hand.

William struggles to remember the name. "Reverend Ran … Reverend Rang …"

"Rankin," the man says and quickly looks beyond William into the twilight. "This is the Rankin home. Come inside."

William brushes Lucy's hair away from her face and follows the man into the dining room as Jean Rankin closes the heavy curtains over the windows. "I've been told you've been through a terrible experience," the minister's wife says. "You'll need sleep so you can think clearly. Let me look at the little one." She strokes Lucy's forehead to soothe her as she tells William that her husband is expected home the next day and that two of her grown sons are staying with her until his return.

She leads William and Lucy to a small upstairs room with a bed and a trundle bed stored beneath. "My son will bring you some food."

She starts to leave the room and then turns back.

"We've had hundreds of slaves stay with us over the years, so please listen to me," Jean says. "Before you sleep, take time to thank

the Lord for your own safety and your daughter's. Ask Him to protect the rest of your family. I tell you, William, it will help."

CHAPTER FORTY-ONE

DROUGHT

HANNAH JAMS HER FISTS INTO THE MOUND OF DOUGH on the tabletop and kneads it this way and that. She hears Adam cross the kitchen behind her and leave the house without a word. She brushes the flour from her hands and follows him out the door. She watches him stride past the barn and swat his hat against his leg and then disappear behind the hedgerow bordering the cornfield.

She wipes her hands once more on her apron and looks up. Again the sky is cloudless. It is still early and already the damp heat presses into every pore of her skin. She understands Adam's forlorn hope about the cornfield.

Everything there is dying.

She now fears the weather. Everyone she talks to fears it. The past winter had been bitterly and unrelentingly cold and often at night she had wondered if warmth ever would return to the land. Then the arrival of warmer weather brought strong thunderstorms that pelted people and plants with hard rain and hail. But the last storm she can recall was on the night so many weeks ago when Anne brought the runaways Nancy Blue and David to the farm. She remembers how the rain had pounded her back and bonnet as she drew water from the well for the two fugitives.

It seems that when the rain finally stopped that night, it stopped forever. There have been a few overcast days when thunder rumbled overhead and nights when lightning flickered on the horizon, but these were only false promises.

A week ago Adam had taken her to the cornfield to show her how the soil had turned to rows of lifeless clumps. He picked up a clump and crushed it in his fist, letting the dirt sift between his fingers and float away in the breeze. Now even the clumps are breaking down and turning to dust that gusts of wind lift to the treetops in dirty clouds.

These days people often part from one another with the words, "Pray for rain." Even the religious doubters are praying along with everyone else as people across Ohio and the neighboring states call the drought of fifty-four the worst in memory. Everyone knows the cloudless sky foretells trouble for their families. With no harvest they will not have enough food, for people or livestock, to last the winter.

Hannah runs her hands over her rounded belly. This child will be born in the middle of the winter. She knows the baby adds to her husband's concern about the family and she remembers how he'd promised her one evening that they'll have enough food and warmth. She realizes he was trying to put her at ease.

Hannah looks again toward the cornfield and imagines her husband as she has seen him so many times in recent weeks—pacing the cracked ground in search of some sign that the stunted cornstalks will magically renew themselves.

Then she returns to her kitchen.

CHAPTER FORTY-TWO

HOSTAGE

THE SLAVE CATCHERS' WAGON ROLLS THROUGH THE
night, heading east along the river. Nettie cries out once for her
daughter, and the man sitting at the rear of the wagon strikes her
head with a leather strap.

"Quiet, I told you!"

There is no silencing Dan. He bawls and keeps pulling at the iron
collar locked around his throat.

"I said shut him up," the man yells at Nettie and threatens her
again with the strap.

She reaches over Alfred and Richard to touch Dan. All three boys
are in misery. At the riverbank the men had quickly herded Nettie
and the boys and Martha into the wagon with its bed littered with
iron collars and shackles and lengths of chain. The men had clamped
the collars onto the two younger boys and Martha and then locked
heavier ankle shackles on Nettie and Richard. They had strung a
rusty length of chain through all of the collars and shackles—linking
them together, throat to ankle, to hamper any movement—and then
anchored the chain to the sides of the wagon with heavy padlocks.

The man bossing the others is named Walker. He calls the rifle-man sitting next to him George and the man who had struck her is Amos.

"Ever seen anything stupider than runaways singing out as they row across the river?" George says to Walker with a chuckle.

Walker flicks the reins again. "How about these here slaves pray-ing so loud you could hear them a mile—"

"For deliverance right into our hands," George says with a laugh. He clasps his hands together in mock prayer. "Thank you, oh Lord."

Walker tells George he wants to get the fugitives to Maysville and determine if there's a reward on them.

"Put them in jail there?" George wonders.

"Not on your life. I don't want the law getting near them. They could be worth a pretty penny. Just wish that buck hadn't got away."

"Bet he drowned along with that baby."

The man's words stab Nettie like a knife to her heart. The pos-sibility that both Lucy and William are dead jolts her so badly she chokes and coughs fiercely.

Amos slaps her with the strap. "Stop that!"

The wagon rolls through the main street of Aberdeen past dark houses and storefronts. Walker steers it down a dark hill and into a narrow lane. He reins it to a stop in front of a riverbank shanty where the air is thick with the croaking of bullfrogs.

"Get 'em out of this wagon and into the shack," Walker orders Amos. "We'll cross over when it gets light."

Amos unlocks the chain from the wagon and then locks the chain's ends together with its links still strung through the collars and shackles. "You do this right and nobody gets strangled," he tells the prisoners.

Nettie sees the problem as soon as they began to move. The chain still runs up and down through the several ankle shackles and iron collars, hampering all movement. Martha clutches Dan and is the first to climb out of the wagon. Richard is forced to hold his shackled leg high in the air as he crawls over the side to avoid choking Martha. Nettie too has to keep her leg high so she won't choke her younger sons. Halfway over the side of the wagon she loses her grip and tumbles to the ground and drags Alfred onto the gravel with her.

"Got to do better than that," Amos chides. He looks over at the man with the rifle. "Hey, George, you got to see this."

George comes closer. "Now that's a hell of a thing, ain't it? Just like a bunch of black crawdads wiggling about on the shore. Guess we don't have to worry about nobody making a run for it." Both men laugh.

The slaves huddle together on the gravel and begin crawling toward the shanty. The sharp stones cut their palms and knees. No one can move faster than the slowest person—and that's Dan, squatting on the gravel, whimpering, and tugging at his iron collar. Martha still can put no weight on her injured foot and she groans as the sharp stones dig into her flesh.

"Faster!" Amos shouts. He kicks Richard's ribs and then turns his boot on Alfred and knocks the child flat on the gravel.

"Mercy, sir," Nettie pleads. "They just children and can't keep up."

George lifts his rifle. "Can't you keep your yap shut, woman?" and then presses his boot onto her hand to grind it into the gravel. She cries out until he finally steps back. She rubs her bloodied hand against her leg to remove the stones and grit from the wounds.

They soon reach the shanty and quietly agonize over their cuts and scratches. An oil lamp throws light on the shanty's crude table and two chairs. Walker sits and reaches for the worn deck of playing cards on the table and cuts the deck twice. "Still three hours before light and I say we get some sleep," he says. "Somebody's got to keep watch. Low man."

George loses the draw with a three of diamonds. He slides a chair to face the fugitives bunched together and sits with his rifle propped upright on his knee. He pulls a plug of tobacco from his vest pocket and bites off a chunk. Amos blows out the lamp and fills the shanty with darkness.

CHAPTER FORTY-THREE

REWARD

BY DAWN NETTIE AND THE BOYS AND MARTHA ARE ALL splattered with George's stinking tobacco spit and Dan's pants are soaked with piss. The wounds on their hands and knees from the sharp gravel still sting. The men herd them onto the skiff as soon as sunlight hits the Ohio. They huddle in the bottom of the boat as Walker guards and George and Amos row to the Kentucky side of the river. Bystanders on the Maysville wharf gather to examine the catch.

"Better clean them up afore the auction," a man tells Walker.

"Mind your own business." Walker glares back at the man. "All you people, move on."

A squat woman pushes her way toward Walker and hands him a wrinkled handbill. "Looks like maybe these here are your runaways." Nettie recognizes the paper to be like the one Reverend Shem had shown them when he told them about Philip Leyden's reward. Walker and Amos examine the handbill then look at their captives.

"That's them, by golly. Fifty dollars for you and you," Amos says as he points first at Alfred and then at Dan. "That little drowned girl woulda been another fifty."

"And two hundred for each of these three," Walker says as he looks from the handbill to Nettie and then to Richard and to Martha. "Two, four, six hundred and two at fifty—that's seven hundred dollars if we get them back to this Leyden fellow."

"Question is," George muses, "could we get more by just selling them?" He turns to the bystanders. "Anybody give me seven-fifty for the lot? Do I hear seven-fifty? Seven-fifty?"

He and Amos laugh heartily along with a few of the men standing nearby.

"Give you a hundred right now for that girl there," says a sallow-faced man with dirty overalls tucked into broken boots. He points at Martha.

"You joking? She's worth a hell of a lot more than a hundred and you know it," Walker tells the man. "Her owner's offering two hundred just as a reward."

"Just trying to save you the trouble of taking her back," the man says with a grin.

"Hell you are."

Amos and George step closer. "What you think, Walker?" Amos asks. "Think we ought to just sell the bunch of them here in Maysville and be done with it?"

Nettie overhears the suggestion and panics. "Please don't, sir. Keep us together. Please, sir!"

Amos dangles the strap in front of her bruised face to quiet her.

George spits brown juice on the ground. "What you think we'd get?"

"A heap of trouble," Walker says. "We got to honor that they belong to this Leyden fellow, otherwise we're no better than thieves. Know what I'm saying?"

"So where's the Leyden place?"

Walker again scans the handbill. "South end of the county, near Mays Lick. Sure to take a better part of the day at least. But let me tell you this. When we get down there, we won't just take them right to this man's doorstep. First I'll tell him what we got and tell him we want a thousand for them. Not seven hundred."

"Think he'll go for it?" George wonders.

"Never know till we try."

The three men load the fugitives into a wagon rented from the livery and head south out of Maysville in the clear morning air. Walker divvies out portions of cornbread and jerky to Nettie and the boys and Martha. Nettie is too heartsick to eat. She sees the despair on the faces of Richard and Martha and the younger boys.

Richard slides closer to his mother. "What'll Mister Leyden do?"

"She don't know nothing, boy," Amos barks.

"What they saying?" Walker asks.

"The boy here wants to know what their master's going to do with them."

"Let me tell you this, boy." Walker pulls the reins to stop the team in the road. "Now just think about your master—this Leyden fellow. He's going to pay a thousand dollars to get all you back and he's going to be damn mad about it. So he needs to get his thousand dollars out of your hides one way or the other. Hell, boy, he might get a thousand dollars for your momma on the block. He might want to get an extra thousand's worth of work just out of you—but it'd be faster and a lot less trouble just to sell your black ass."

George holds out his rifle with one hand and points the barrel at Martha. "You look at her, boy. Your master could get his thousand back just by selling that one as a fancy girl. She's still young and her equipment's coming along real nice."

Martha pulls the tatters of her skirt over her legs.

By the time they reach the town of Washington the sun has made the chains and shackles hot to the touch. Amos opens a canteen and moves from person to person. He tips the bent metal spout into their mouths and spills water as he goes. Alfred reaches out to grab the canteen and Amos slaps his hand.

"Please, sir, let the children have more water," Nettie begs. "They're like to die of thirst."

"Nobody's dying of thirst." He pours water into his cupped hand and flings it in Alfred's face. "That better?"

CHAPTER FORTY-FOUR

POSSE

ADAM LIFTS THE BAG OF NAILS FROM THE COUNTER AND John Pope hands him a few pennies in change. "I have no answer to thy question," the storekeeper says. "No one but the good Lord knows how any of us will fare in the months ahead. Many face the same predicament as thee. Some of thy neighbors are asking me to extend them credit without limit."

"I understand, John."

"Thee can well appreciate that extending credit to my customers—and I know I should do so if I'm to call myself a Christian—gives me nothing to buy goods for keeping the store stocked. And with no goods to sell, the store will wither and die as surely as the corn is dying in thy fields."

Abruptly the door at the front of the store swings open. The floorboards creak as Klemmer marches into the store. Again he wears his heavy coat and slouch hat despite the heat of the day. He motions to Adam.

"Come."

Then Klemmer looks at John Pope and mutters, "You I do not want."

At that moment Summerfield walks into the store. "Klemmer, what are you—"

"We must have as many men as we can."

"Hold on, Klemmer," the marshal orders. "You trying to gather some kind of posse?"

"To get three coloreds and maybe more," he tells the lawman. "They are running across the Billings farm."

"Who says?"

"Billings's own boy. He saw them, three bucks, fugitives. He rode here to tell me just now."

Summerfield asks, "You got your hounds, Klemmer?"

The big man shakes his head. "No time."

Summerfield stands back as Klemmer walks past him and out the door. The lawman turns to Adam. "You'd better come, too. You got your horse, right?"

"You must be kidding," Adam says, startled. "I'm not going with Klemmer. You know my sentiments." He follows Summerfield through the door.

The marshal puts his hand on Adam's shoulder. "Listen to me, Porter. Just come with us. Don't raise a fuss and don't rile Klemmer. Just ride along and be part of the group. There probably aren't any runaways anyway. And if there are, I doubt we even get near them."

"But Klemmer knows I don't—"

"Just do as I say. Who knows? This might get Klemmer off your back."

Klemmer returns to the storefront where Adam and the marshal are standing. "We must go."

Adam turns toward Klemmer. "I'll not appease—"

Summerfield's eyes flash and he tightens his grip on Adam's shoulder. "You're coming with us. Whether it's by your own free will is your choice."

"The fugitive law?"

"That's right. You refuse to come and you're looking at one hefty fine. Be reasonable so we don't have to go down that path."

Adam steps into the sunlight where his black gelding is hitched amid swirling dust. Five mounted men mill about in the road as Klemmer waves his hat in the air. Adam recognizes Abe Williams. Ira Ogden gnaws on a turkey leg as he sits astride a scrawny chestnut nag. Then he recognizes Joshua Billings and recalls the night he lied to Billings to uphold Anne's alibi. Riding next to Billings is a young man not yet twenty. Adam and the marshal mount their horses and fall in with the group.

Joshua Billings reins his horse alongside Adam. "What you doing here?" He turns in his saddle and shouts to Klemmer, "He don't belong here!"

Summerfield calls over to Billings. "Let him be, Joshua. We may need every man we got."

Quickly assembled, the group gallops west with Klemmer in the lead and sends an even larger cloud of dust high into the air. As they near the Billings farm the young man with the group—Adam suspects he is one of Anne's brothers—draws close to Klemmer and points to the meadow.

Klemmer slows his horse to a walk and waits for the others.

"The boy says he saw them at about there"—Klemmer points to an open area south of the road—"and they were running"—he sweeps his arm across the road until he points northward—"over to there. Now we find their tracks."

"All right, men," Summerfield orders. "Spread out. Keep your eyes open and your mouths shut till we see something."

The horsemen move from the road into the meadow as the young man rides up to Adam. "My sister, how is she?"

"You're one of Anne's brothers?"

"Ben, the younger one. How is she?"

Adam sees the resemblance between Anne and her brother—the blond hair and well-sculpted face. The boy is small and Adam recalls Anne's stories about having to wear Ben's clothing when she worked in the fields.

"She's well. She helps my wife considerably. She—"

"Still with Jacob Pope?"

"Very much."

"They still, you know, helping the runaways?"

Adam shakes his head. "Nope."

"My pa, he'll be glad."

The boy nudges his horse past Adam and joins his father.

With the skill of practiced hunters, the horsemen line up along the edge of the meadow at intervals of several yards and move slowly forward to search for telltale signs of the fugitives—matted grass, broken stalks, footprints—anything that will put them on the trail. The men guide their horses, one plodding step after another, toward a far row of trees. Ogden spots something and gives a birdlike whistle as Klemmer rides over to meet him. Klemmer dismounts and kneels close to the ground. With cicadas droning in the distance, Klemmer rises and shakes his head indicating no luck.

The horses and riders continue moving, silently and methodically, through the parched grass. Grasshoppers spring up around the horses at every step. One lands on Adam's leg and he catches it in his hand. He feels it flutter against his palm and then he opens his fingers and watches it fly away. He rides on, slowly, feeling the heat rising from the meadow up to his hands and face. He shakes his head at the absurdity of being a member of Klemmer's posse, wondering if Simon or Anne or Hannah could even understand. He realizes none of it matters at all on this sultry afternoon. He is so drowsy he begins to sway in the saddle with the rhythm of his horse's steps.

"Sssst! Watch for the coloreds," Klemmer hisses at him from a few feet away. "That's why you are here."

Just then Ogden whistles again and Klemmer trots off to investigate. Ogden points to the ground and Klemmer again dismounts and sweeps his hat from his head. He crouches in the grass and puts his face close to the ground, sniffing it. He rises quickly and says, "This is something."

"And look't over there," Ogden says and points at something few yards ahead.

Klemmer waves his arm as a signal for everyone to join him. "You see," he calls out as the other horsemen gather, "this is where the coloreds had their rest. Where the grass is flat. They rested and we rode up and they could see our dust." He walks to where Ogden had pointed. "This mark in the dirt—this is where they took to running." He smiles. "Now they know Klemmer is after them."

Klemmer jams his hat onto his head and pulls himself onto his horse. He draws his rifle from its saddle holster, points it at the line of trees, and says, "They are there." Summerfield and Billings spur their horses behind him. Adam follows by several yards and then the stillness of the afternoon is split by the crack of a rifle shot.

Adam rides between the trees and into the meadow where the other men are gathering. Klemmer and Billings and the marshal are dismounted and standing over a body in the tall grass. Billings calls out for his son. Ogden and his ancient horse join the group as Ben Billings dismounts and runs to his father.

"Is this what you saw?" Billings says.

Adam nudges Othello closer and sees a doe lying dead on the ground, her skull shattered by Klemmer's shot.

"No, Pa," the boy answers. "I saw three of them running across here."

"Three bucks?" Summerfield asks. "Are we talking bucks as in coloreds or bucks as in this here?"

"Three coloreds," Ben yells angrily. "Not deer."

"Here's the problem," the marshal goes on. "We came through those trees and saw this grass moving and Klemmer decided to—"

"To scare them," Klemmer says as he reloads.

"Klemmer took a shot at the movement in the grass and then two bucks took off toward those woods. And I'm talking about deer bucks."

"Well, damn it all to hell," Ogden fumes.

"But you said you saw a footprint back there in that field," the boy says to Klemmer. "You said the coloreds were resting and started running when they saw us. You said that yourself."

"I saw what I saw," the big man answers defiantly.

"I'd say what we got here is just some hungry deer," Summerfield says.

"But I saw them," Ben insists.

"You saw something," his father says.

Adam looks at the doe and at the blood-soaked dirt and then looks at Klemmer. "If that would have been a woman or a child hiding in that grass—"

Klemmer stares at the doe's carcass and suddenly stomps the skull with his heavy boot. He stomps it again and again until he's mashed the bones to a pulp against the hard earth and covered his boot with the animal's brains. He storms over to his horse and slams the rifle back into its holster. "Now I go back with my hands empty!" Bloody tissue dangles from his boot as he sticks it into the stirrup and pulls himself onto the saddle. He wheels his horse around and gallops toward the road.

Adam glances at Summerfield.

"Let it be," the marshal says as he swings onto his saddle.

"Well, I ain't going to let this be a goddamn waste," Ogden tells the Billings boy. "Help me sling this deer over my horse. I got a hankering for venison."

CHAPTER FORTY-FIVE

RETURN

TWO MILES SOUTH OF THE TOWN OF WASHINGTON THE wagon begins to jerk violently with each turn of the left front wheel. "Goddamn it to hell," Walker grumbles as he and George climb down to examine it. "Look at these goddamn spokes."

"Can we keep going?" George asks.

"Can't risk it. It could give at any time. One of us needs to go back to Washington and get another wheel," Walker says. "We'll flip for it."

"What about me?" Amos shouts from the wagon bed.

"You stay here with your new friends," Walker tells him. He takes a coin from his pocket and sets it on his thumb. "Loser goes back. Call it."

"Heads," says George between spits of tobacco juice.

Walker flips the coin into the air. "Heads, damn it."

Within minutes, Walker is gone. George steers the wagon off the road and orders everyone out. He and Amos march Nettie and the boys and Martha to a grassy grove and chain them to a sycamore tree. Then George props himself against a fallen limb with his rifle slung under his arm. "Well, here we are," he says as he tucks a new wad of tobacco into his mouth.

Amos pulls a knife from a sheath on his hip. He picks up a small branch, leans against the wagon's tailgate, and whittles one end of the stick to a point. Then he skins the bark until the branch is only a shaft of yellow wood. Then he whittles the other end to a point. Shavings litter the ground at his feet. He whittles the shaft to make it thinner and then reshapes the first point.

"Jesus, Amos, why don't you carve something worthwhile?" George gripes as he takes off his hat and wipes his forehead with his arm. "Make a rabbit or something."

"What's it to you?"

Nettie prays her boys or Martha do not start trouble. One hour stretches to two as the afternoon grows muggier. Leaves droop on the branches as cicadas buzz in the treetops. Flies and mosquitoes torment slave and slave catcher alike.

"When's Walker coming back?" Amos frets.

"Another hour, maybe two. How the hell do I know?" George stands and keeps hold of his rifle. "I can't take this. I got to do something." He spits in the grass and turns to Amos with his hand outstretched. "Give me the key."

"What for?"

"Just give me the damn key."

Amos hands him the key and George gives Amos the rifle. Then George walks to the sycamore and unlocks the padlock chaining the fugitives to the tree. The boy Dan slides forward and starts to stand. "I got to pee, sir," he says.

"You sit back down, now!" George yells at him. A wet stain spreads across the front of the boy's pants as he sits down, whimpering.

George then slips the chain out of the iron collar around Martha's neck as the girl slides farther back against the tree.

"What you think you're doing?" Amos demands.

"You just keep an eye on these others," George says as he locks the chain and then grabs Martha's arm and pulls her to her feet.

"No!" Nettie cries.

"Let her go," Richard shouts. He grabs George's ankle but the man shakes his foot free and kicks Richard's forehead.

"I never been with no man, sir," Martha pleads.

George slaps her face with his open palm. A smear of blood appears on her lip. He shoves her toward the woods. "Nobody needs to see. We want to be decent about this."

Nettie watches them disappear behind the trees and brambles. She feels the world slipping farther and farther from all that is good. How much more pain can any of them bear? She thinks back to Reverend Shem and his prayers for their protection and how they had all prayed so joyously as they rowed across the river. But something has gone terribly wrong and she does not know why. All she knows this moment is that the world here in this clearing is terribly still and unbearably hot. Her sweat runs into her eyes and the iron chain and shackle burn her skin. She cannot escape thoughts of Hell and its endless pain and torture, the way Reverend Shem had described it to her.

Abruptly two men approach from the road and startle Amos. Walker has returned with a burly stranger lugging a wagon wheel.

"Where's George?" Walker asks. He looks at the sycamore tree. "And where's that slave girl?"

Amos points toward the woods where George had pushed Martha a few minutes earlier.

"We've got a wagon to fix, dammit," Walker fumes as he marches to where Amos points. Within moments the three emerge, with Walker ordering George to help mount the repaired wheel and Amos to chain up Martha again. Nothing more is said.

Nettie studies Martha. The girl sits on the ground and toys with the links of the chain. Nettie sees no injuries on the girl other than the cut lip from when George slapped her. She leans close and whispers, "Did he hurt you?"

"I'm alive, ain't I?" Martha says as she stares straight ahead. "There ain't nothing to talk about."

An hour later the fugitives are again chained together in the wagon bed. They ride through a wooded stretch with ravines on either side of the road. Though it was dark at the time, Nettie knows this is where James Pike died. A while later she recognizes the hills and meadows—bathed in the same serene, golden light—she had seen a lifetime ago when her family rode with James Pike toward the free land.

A few miles farther and Walker looks back at Nettie. "Up there," he says, pointing. "See that? Must be the Leyden place."

The distant, familiar silhouette of the house stands framed by the sunset. "Yessir, that's it."

Walker tells George, "I'm going to walk up there and talk to this man. I'll tell him we got his slaves and we want a thousand dollars. Listen to me"—he grabs George's arm—"any trouble and you get these darkies out of here as fast as you can. Worse comes to worse, I'll meet you in the morning back where we fixed the wheel."

Walker climbs down and heads toward the Leyden house.

George spits tobacco juice onto the lane. He glances back at Martha. "Hell, if Leyden don't want you, maybe I'll keep you myself. Seems like we was just getting to know each other."

Walker returns at twilight and announces, "He went for it." He climbs onto the driver's bench and slaps George's back. "A thousand dollars."

"He pay you?"

"He said to drive up there and we'd finish the deal when he laid eyes on them."

No one says a word as the wagon rolls up the darkening lane toward the house.

CHAPTER FORTY-SIX

HAVEN

WILLIAM TIPTOES OUT OF THE BEDROOM WHILE LUCY sleeps with her eyelids fluttering. He creeps down the stairs to find the two Rankin sons dressed in work clothes and eating flapjacks in the sunlit kitchen. Their mother, Jean, pours more batter onto the hot griddle. They exchange greetings, then William looks at the woman and says, "Ma'am, I don't know what to do."

"First thing is to get you and your child to a safer place," Jean Rankin tells him. She explains that Reverend Rankin has been in Cincinnati and is expected home perhaps later today. "But we mustn't delay."

"We're pretty familiar with what needs to happen," one of the brothers, Samuel, tells William. "We'll get you and your daughter to your next stop, a place some miles north of Red Oak."

The other brother, Calvin, says, "You'll go along what some call the Underground Railroad, something our father helped set up several years ago, such as it is."

William shudders as he recalls talking with James Pike about the Underground Railroad, when Pike reassured him that the escape route actually was aboveground, and a few minutes later, Pike was lying dead on the road. "I know about the Underground Railroad," William says with a pained expression.

To reassure William, the Rankins explain how runaway slaves have been crossing the Ohio River into Ripley for fifty years and how those who help the slaves have grown more cautious with adoption of the Fugitive Slave Law four years ago. "We can never be too careful because the slave catchers are crawling all over these parts," Jean says. "But, poor man, we don't need to tell you about that."

"You've helped other slaves get away?" William asks.

"Hundreds," Samuel says.

They tell William how their father, a Presbyterian minister, moved from Kentucky to Ripley thirty years earlier and immediately began helping fugitives. "He's the best-known abolitionist in these parts," Samuel says. "For years Kentucky slaveholders have put a price on his head, dead or alive. He tends to ignore it but it makes our mother sick with worry whenever he leaves home. That's why Calvin and I try to stay with her whenever he travels."

"Those hunters ever come up here to this house?" William asks anxiously.

"They've been known to," Samuel answers. "Mostly a bunch will show up on horseback and yell and charge around the house and then ride away."

Calvin takes up the story. "We had an especially bad night a few years back when our cousin John was staying here. I'd seen a number of Kentucky roughnecks hanging around Ripley earlier in the day, so John and I slept in our clothes that night. Sure enough, about two in the morning I heard somebody whistle in the yard. John and I got our guns and crept out the back door. I rounded the corner of the house and a man standing right there fired his revolver at me. It felt like he'd hit me with a log. I looked down to see my shirt on fire—he was that close when he fired at me—but the shot itself just grazed my shoulder. The burn was worse than the bullet."

The brothers then tell how their cousin John ran around the other side of the house and confronted another man who also fired at him point-blank. Both of the Kentucky men ran back to the fence. "They tried to climb over it and John fired at them," Calvin says. "One of them fell backward onto the ground and began screaming his head off. A half-dozen others came out of the woods to carry him away."

"Our poor mother," Samuel adds with a nod in her direction. "She thought surely Calvin and John had been killed. She locked all three doors and wouldn't let me or our older brother Lowry go out. I remember her standing right over there with tears streaming down her face and saying, 'We can do the dead no good—we can only preserve our own lives.'"

Samuel says he and Lowry climbed out a back window to see if their brother and cousin were still alive—which they were, though Calvin was wounded. Then they spotted a fire in the barn. "Lowry got a pail of water from the cistern and threw it on the fire. Thank the Lord it'd rained earlier in the day and that kept it from spreading."

Calvin nods in agreement. "We could have lost everything— the barn, the house, and the whole year's crop. To say nothing of our lives."

Their mother, silent until her sons' account ends, turns to William and says, "I learned there's no pain greater than knowing a loved one has been killed, and no joy greater than finding the loved one still alive."

CHAPTER FORTY-SEVEN

CONFINED

WILLIAM STANDS NEXT TO THE LARGE HUCKSTER wagon heaped high with hay in the Rankin barnyard. He jiggles Lucy in his arms and watches Calvin Rankin tighten the harnesses on the two mares hitched to the vehicle.

"Now look at this," Samuel says and motions for William to join him behind the wagon. He slides two slats from the wagon's rear gate and steps back. William sees the wagon has a false floor with just enough room beneath the mound of hay for a person to lie flat and be hidden from view.

"You and your daughter will ride there till we're far enough from town to be out of danger," Samuel says.

William stares at the cramped hiding place.

"You say we got to be in there?"

"It's safer this way. Especially when we go through town."

William crawls into the concealed space. It's so tight he has to lie on his belly and cannot roll to his side or back. Suddenly he feels the fear of confinement. Samuel slides Lucy into the space next to him. Calvin hands him a canteen and some diapers and then slides the two slats back into place. He and Lucy are enclosed in stifling darkness with no room to move.

The wagon jerks forward and Lucy sobs. "Hush, baby," William whispers as he tries to comfort her.

He feels the wagon enter the long and twisted lane from the Rankin farm heading steeply to the town below. Several minutes pass and he knows by the tilt of the wagon that Samuel has yet to reach the streets of Ripley. Each lurch and pitch causes hay dust to sift through the boards above him and Lucy. They can't avoid inhaling it. They cough and sneeze and he hears Lucy choke as dust lodges in her throat. He struggles to open the canteen and pour water into her mouth. Even then, the child gags and spits until she can breathe again. William covers her head with his arm to protect her as best he can.

The heavy mound of hay above them radiates the heat of the day and the temperature in the hidden compartment soars. William fights his own terror. His lungs tighten and each breath is shorter than the one before. He senses the weight of the hay pressing down on the boards above his head and he's scared the boards will give way and a ton of hay will crush Lucy and him. The darkness is unrelenting and the dust is suffocating. William knows the only way out is to scream for help, scream as loud as he can.

The wagon rolls ever so slowly and the surrounding sounds of horses, wagons and carriages, and people's chatter mean they now are in the center of town. William knows that for Samuel to unload a slave concealed in a trick wagon would mean certain capture.

"Oh, my baby, I don't know what's going to happen to us," he gasps to Lucy as tears run down his face. He tries to recall some hymns from Reverend Shem's services and hum them in Lucy's ear as dust coats his nostrils and throat.

At some point—William long ago lost track of time—he realizes the wagon is no longer moving and someone is tugging at the slats on the wagon gate.

"You all right in there?"

He recognizes Samuel's voice just as a wave of pure, cool air engulfs him and Lucy.

Night has fallen while William and Lucy have been confined in the wagon's secret compartment. When they resume their journey, William sits atop the wagon's big pile of hay with Lucy on his lap. Overhead is the dome of the star-filled sky and all around is the cool night air. From the driver's bench Samuel says only a few miles remain until they reach their destination. Calvin, astride his bay, follows several yards behind the wagon.

Another hour passes and Samuel turns the wagon onto a different road and then onto yet another one. Each turn brings the wagon onto narrower lanes until they reach a small house set far back from the road and hidden by vines.

"Wait here." Samuel climbs down from the wagon. He wades through the grass and knocks solidly on the door to the house. He soon motions for Calvin to bring William and Lucy. They enter the house and walk through one room and then into another where— amid the shadows cast by a single oil lamp—William sees a small man with long black hair. He is dressed in a white nightshirt and props himself upright with two canes. Nearby stands a black boy with a wide smile.

"Welcome to Chateau Childress," says the peculiar man as he gracefully bows.

CHAPTER FORTY-EIGHT

TROUBLE

ANNE REINS OTHELLO TO A HALT IN FRONT OF POPE'S Store and dismounts with an eye toward the four other horses already tied to the hitching rail, two with rifles protruding from saddle holsters. She brushes her hair from her face and pats the dust from her blouse and then wraps Othello's reins around the rail.

She steps toward the storefront where a stout woman peers into the store through a window in the closed door. "You should stay back," the woman tells her. Anne ignores her and opens the door into the store and confronts the backs of two large men blocking her view.

"What's going on?" she demands.

"You should leave, Miss," a man warns.

"What's the trouble, Abe?" another man asks, and she recognizes her father's voice. She pushes beyond Abe Williams to see her father standing alongside two other men in front of shelves of fabrics. It's the first time she's seen him in three weeks.

One of the men approaches. "Ma'am, I'm the marshal here and I think you should wait outside."

"She's my daughter," Joshua Billings tells the lawman. "She better hear this, too."

Moving still closer, Anne sees Jacob Pope, disheveled and leaning against the shelves. One of the strangers holds Jacob steady with a hand on his shoulder. "Jacob?" she says.

The man releases Jacob and turns to face Anne. He is large, burly, and wears his hat pulled low over his eyes. He looks her up and down. "You know something maybe?"

She looks past the man and calls to Jacob, "Have they hurt—"

"Let her by, Klemmer," her father says to the man. "My daughter was with the Pope boy when he went to the Childress house. They went there together."

"Stupid," Klemmer says as he steps aside.

Summerfield speaks up. "The point is, Miss Billings, the law of the land—whether you agree with it or not—says you've committed a criminal act by transporting fugitives. You've admitted as much to your family. But your father and I believe you were influenced by the Popes here—abolitionists who would do their damndest to hide runaways."

"That's not true," she protests.

The lawman removes his hat and rubs his brow with a bandanna. "Let me tell you what can happen even in a little place like Buford." He replaces his hat. "Let's say somebody decides they're going to give shelter to these fugitives. Word gets back across the river and pretty soon more start coming this way till we've got a steady stream of slaves coming at us. You get these slaves breaking into people's homes and stealing their food and valuables. Sometimes doing harm to good people. Then you get the slave owners chasing after them and you get more slave catchers and bounty hunters in these parts. Pretty soon you got neighbors shooting at each other and people getting killed. If you doubt me, Miss Billings, just spend some time around Ripley or Cincinnati or Marietta. Go to any of the river towns. You'll see a war going on in those places—the kind of war we don't want here."

Anne's eyes meet her father's and he addresses her in a tone almost tender. "The marshal says nothing will happen to you if you just stay away from the Quakers and anybody else breaking the law. Just forget this slave business, Anne, and come back home."

"You should do as your father tells you," Klemmer says gruffly.

John Pope clears his throat and straightens his glasses. He says to the marshal, "I don't believe thee has any proof of anything illegal here. All thee's determined is that we sell free-labor goods here. No law is being violated. Now please let my son be."

Suddenly the words "I will show you the truth" reverberate through the store. Klemmer grabs Jacob's shirt and violently yanks him forward. Then he slams Jacob hard against the wall with enough force to topple tinware from the shelves. Jacob groans and clutches at the back of his head.

"Jacob!" his father shouts. The storekeeper reaches toward his son but Klemmer pushes him away.

"Make him stop," Anne cries to the marshal. She turns to her father. "Stop him!"

"Tell me where you get the runaways!" Klemmer threatens. "Is it from Childress?" Again he shoves Jacob against the shelves. "Tell me where you take them. To Blanchard? To Porter?" He grips Jacob's jaw and twists it until Jacob groans. "Tell me before I break down this wall with your stupid coward body!"

Summerfield lifts his hand. "Klemmer, that's enough!" Turning to John Pope, the lawman adds, "You see how people get hurt? Your son's involved in something he shouldn't be, and the law says I've got to put a stop to it."

"Not God's law," Jacob says.

Anne speaks to Summerfield. "This is my fault. I shouldn't have said anything to my father about any of this. I didn't know who his friends were," and she glances at Klemmer.

"Come on, Klemmer," the marshal says. He motions for Anne's father and Abe Williams to follow.

Joshua Billings pauses as he passes his daughter. "Forget these people, Anne, and come home." She says nothing as he walks out of the store.

John Pope tends to his son and asks, "Is there some reason those men know about the aid thee has given to fugitives? Is there some reason thee has not even told me?"

"We didn't want you to worry," Anne interjects.

"Are thee certain that's why?" John says. "Or was it because thee knows I would warn thee against it?"

CHAPTER FORTY-NINE

TRUST

NETTIE NERVOUSLY FOLLOWS BOBBY HILL THROUGH the Leyden house to her mistress's sitting room. He pushes her through the doorway and closes the door behind her. Grace Leyden stands at a window in her blue silk robe staring at the morning sunlight on the fields.

"Ma'am?" Nettie whispers.

The woman spins around with her face drawn and eyes narrowed.

"How could you? That's what I want to know, Nettie. How could you have done this to us? After all we've done for you. After all I've done for you all these years." She pulls her robe tight and marches around the small room with her voice raised. "You've humiliated us. You know we pride ourselves in treating our servants as well as we possibly can, and in all these years since my husband started this farm with his bare hands, not one of our people has run away. Not one!"

"Ma'am—"

"Don't even think of arguing with me."

"I thought—"

"No! You didn't think. You and that stupid husband of yours."

Nettie's anger flares momentarily but she confines it to her eyes.

"You've hurt us, Nettie," Grace goes on, her voice becoming more subdued. "Can you understand that? Our friends have told us we were treating our property too well, livestock to servants. But we said this was the way we believed. Now you go and betray us."

Nettie watches every step as Grace paces.

"William was not stupid, I know. I'm sure you feel a loss. And I feel a loss as well. I took you in—not Sallah, not Glory, not Ellen—just you. I gave you pretty clothes and good work here in this house. I kept you away from the fields. I brought you into my bedchamber, no less, and into my very confidence. I trusted you to care for my daughter, for gracious sakes." She returns to the window and turns her back to Nettie. "Do you understand betrayal? Do you know how deeply it cuts? Do you have any idea what it's like to put your trust in someone and have that person break your trust?"

Nettie's eyes drop.

"And what have you done to your family by this foolish running away? Philip tells me William and Lucy are dead—that they drowned in the Ohio River. Just think of that dear child. Did your little Lucy ask for this?"

Nettie's lips quiver.

"That little girl was loved here," Grace says, her voice becoming more intimate. "She was well cared for. Did she go without food? No, she did not. Did she go without clothing? No, she did not. Did she live with her mother and her father and her brothers under one roof? Yes, she did. And now you've killed her."

A fierce cry wracks Nettie. "Stop talking about my baby!"

"Nettie, you as much as held that child's little face under those cold waters when you took her from here!"

Nettie covers her own face and feels the pain of the still-raw cuts on her palms.

"You have much to atone for, Nettie. Much to repent."

From behind her hands Nettie asks, "Ma'am, can I go?"

Grace straightens her robe and cinches its belt still tighter. She strides to the door and puts her hand on the knob. "Where do we go from here, Nettie? I suppose that's the question we must ask."

"I can get clean and—"

"You cannot come back into this house."

"Ma'am?"

"You may be back at this farm, but we all know it's against your will. I cannot trust you around my belongings and I cannot have you near my daughter. You have destroyed the trust—the beautiful trust—that existed between us for all of these years."

Nettie sobs, "I'm sorry, ma'am."

"You should be. Now go."

CHAPTER FIFTY

QUESTIONS

BOBBY HILL TAKES NETTIE BACK TO THE BARN AFTER her encounter with Grace Leyden. The boys and Martha are still chained to the posts where they spent the night after the slave catchers returned them to Philip Leyden.

"Seven days gone by since you and William drove away from here in that wagon you stole," Bobby Hill tells Nettie. "Seven days and now look who's back. Each one of you will see your life has changed more in those seven days than you can even imagine."

Nettie kneels beside Dan and Alfred. She gives them water from a ladle and tries to soothe them.

"I wouldn't get too close," the overseer chuckles. "Those boys stink to high heaven from sitting all night in their own filth."

"Let me clean them, please, Mister Hill," she begs. "It ain't their fault. We took them away. William and me. This is worse than you treat the animals." She sees Richard trembling. "Those men hurt Richard, sir. Kicked him in the head real hard. Let me help him."

Bobby Hill ignores her.

Nettie moves closer to Martha. "And this poor girl's been hurt worse than anybody. You got to let me take care of her."

"I don't 'got to' do a thing except what Mister Leyden tells me."

"That's exactly right, Bobby." Philip Leyden struts into the barn wearing his trousers tucked into riding boots and carrying a leather riding crop. He stands over Nettie as she crouches in front of the children. "You're all going to hear what I have to say." He swats the crop against his thigh. He tells them Nettie and her two youngest— Alfred and Dan—will return to their cabin, now to be shared with Willis and the ailing Ellen and their sons. Nettie will work in the fields and no longer in the Leyden house. Richard will live with Rufe and Sallah because he cannot share quarters with Willis's sons—the troublemakers Reuben and Ben—and will still help Rufe with the hogs. Martha will live with Glory and take care of the small children.

"And as you'll soon see, the first order of business is to save our tobacco crop from this drought." Leyden looks down at Nettie. "I'm certain you'll come to realize the great losses you've incurred by your foolish actions. You've lost your work in the house. You've lost your own cabin. You've lost the privilege of keeping your family together." He pauses. "And you've lost your husband and your child—all for no good reason."

Martha stirs at the post where she's chained. "Mister Leyden, sir?"

"I'm not finished." He steps back to stand beside his overseer. "Running away was unforgivable. Such behavior can destroy a farm like this one—a farm I've spent my entire life building. First one servant runs off. Then another and another." He points the crop at Nettie. "You're the only one here who can comprehend the magnitude when I say I paid one thousand dollars to get all of you back."

"I know, sir."

"I'm sure you do. And I'm sure those scoundrels boasted all the way here about how much money they'd milk me for. Well, it worked. I was willing to pay because there's one good way to stop more coloreds from running away. And that's to show what happens when you get caught."

"Examples," Bobby Hill grins.

Richard squirms against his chains. "Like getting beat near to death."

Leyden stares at Richard. "I won't beat you—even though you deserve it. No, you'll work in the fields like you've never worked before. My crops are dying and the only way to save them is with water. So, Nettie, you'll carry water to those plants. You'll keep them alive."

Martha speaks up again. "Mister Leyden?"

He looks at her.

"Mister Leyden, you need help in the house now Nettie can't work there no more?"

"You heard—" Bobby Hill begins.

"Wait," Leyden says. "Let's hold that thought in abeyance for the time being."

Nettie gapes at Martha in disbelief, but the girl keeps her eyes on the two men.

"Now listen to me very carefully," Leyden says and slowly shifts his gaze from Nettie to Richard to Martha. "I have questions and what happens to each of you depends on how you answer me."

He again smacks the crop against his thigh. "I want to know who helped you run away from here. You made it all the way to the Ohio and you couldn't have done it by yourselves. You couldn't have figured it out. I know you had help and I want to know who it was. I want to know if the man they found dead on the road to Washington had anything to do with you. I want to know if that preacher Shem Marshall helped you."

"Sir?" Martha asks again.

"What is it?"

"Sir, what you mean by what we say and what's going to happen to us?"

"You asked me a moment ago about whether we need help in the house. Maybe we do—if I get the answers to my questions. I'm going to take each of you outside this barn so you can answer the questions. Just you and me. Lying will make things far worse for you than what I've already said. So think carefully about what you tell me. And I'll start with you."

He points the crop at Martha.

CHAPTER FIFTY-ONE

AMBUSH

FROM THE DRIVER'S BENCH OF THE SINGLE-HORSE-BUCK-board, Anne peers back at the lone horseman she first spotted following them a mile earlier. "He's still way back there," she tells Jacob, beside her. The afternoon is hot and hazy and she watches the horseman through ripples of heat rising from the road.

"Are thee certain he's following us?" Jacob asks. "Couldn't he just be traveling in our direction?"

"But he never gets closer. He just keeps pace and stays far enough back so I can't see who he is." She glances back again. "I wouldn't be so nervous if we weren't headed to the Childress house."

Jacob flicks the reins to quicken Pony's gait. "Marcus said we should be there in time to leave with our passengers right at dusk."

Anne again looks back at the road behind them. "I'm still afraid it could be Klemmer. The rider's big enough."

"If thee's right, then he's following us for certain."

They round yet another curve—the bend in the road takes the horseman out of sight for a few moments—and Jacob quickly steers Pony and the wagon off the road and into a thicket of trees and brush.

They jump down from the wagon into the underbrush. Jacob grasps Pony's bridle in one hand and strokes her muzzle with the other. They remain silent with only the humming of insects in the air.

Soon they hear the steady clopping of the approaching horse. Anne squints between the branches and recognizes Klemmer in the saddle. He looks around as his horse plods past the thicket. Anne and Jacob wait without speaking, without moving. By the time they return to the dusty road, Klemmer is nowhere to be seen.

"He could be hiding anywhere along the roadside just as we hid from him," Anne says.

"We could turn back if thee wants."

"But didn't Marcus say they must be moved tonight?"

"That's what he said. But I worry about any harm coming to thee, Anne." He reaches out for her hand.

"I know."

Dusk has settled over the land by the time they reach the Childress house. Marcus takes them to the room where Wendell Childress sits at his desk amid a disarray of papers.

"Greetings." He rises slowly with the familiar oak canes supporting him. He points one of them at Jacob. "Your shoulder has mended, I presume?"

"For some time now," Jacob says and blushes. "It'll not happen again."

"I myself am reluctant to make such claims," Childress responds. "Just consider yourself fortunate that you suffered a mere dislocation."

Childress hobbles toward them with his stringy black hair swinging from side to side. Again his clothing is rumpled—the yellow linen waistcoat open, white shirt sleeves rolled up unevenly on his arms, tan trousers deeply wrinkled. "I've been cataloguing the tribulations of my current guests," he says with a gesture toward the desktop.

"A most unfortunate account, I must say. May all these damn slave hunters burn in hell, God willing."

"One may have been following us," Anne blurts.

"We hid along the road and he passed by," Jacob adds.

"Excuse me." Childress clamps shut his eyes. "I presume this man doesn't know you're here?"

"We can't say," Anne answers. "We didn't see him after a while."

Childress makes his way to a plush chair and drops into it. He clenches his forehead for a minute with his right hand. "You don't know where this man—" he stops with his eyes closed for several seconds—"where he is, but you evidently know who he is, at least to the extent you can label him a slave catcher."

Jacob nods. "Julius Klemmer and he—"

"I know of Klemmer. And, yes, he certainly has earned the sobriquet of damn slave catcher!"

Jacob tells about Klemmer coming to the store and pummeling him for details of transporting fugitives.

"And how, pray tell, did Klemmer suspect you having anything to do with fugitives?"

"My father," Anne answers. "He heard it from my father."

Childress continues to rub his temples. "I would like to understand why you told anyone anything at all about this activity. I do recall telling you that these are matters of utmost secrecy, literally of life and death. I'm not dreaming, am I?"

"Please," Jacob jumps to Anne's defense. "Many things happened that led to her telling—"

"Telling too much, obviously."

"Yes," Anne agrees. "Too much."

Childress rests his chin on the curved handles of his canes. "As the bard says, 'What's done is done.' Still, we cannot ascertain damages until they are inflicted. And that may never happen."

A puzzled expression comes over Jacob's face. "Does thee think we should go ahead with transporting the fugitives tonight?"

"Why do you ask?"

"Klemmer."

"Good point," Childress responds. "And what about tomorrow night?"

"Tomorrow?"

"Could our furtive slave catcher be out there tomorrow night—waiting for you in the shadows?"

Jacob weighs the question. "I suppose he could."

"And the night after that?"

"Yes, I see."

"If Klemmer suspects I'm sheltering runaways—and I'm sure he has suspected as much for some time—he could maintain a ceaseless watch on this place. He's a deranged and dangerous man. His motivation is a mystery, but we know he's intent on annihilating the Negro as well as those of us who want to help our black brethren. He wants us stopped at the very least and preferably removed from the face of the earth."

"Kill us?" Anne asks.

Childress shrugs. "When you first visited me I told you how the underground's routes were changing. One reason is because Klemmer and his band of degenerates have been frightening people out of their wits. Burning people's barns is a favored tactic. After all, the screams of roasting livestock have a way of intimidating. And I cannot say how much further Klemmer will go."

Marcus returns to the room. A black man holding a small child to his chest follows the boy.

Childress continues talking. "I'm certain there are effective ways to stop Klemmer and his ilk, all of them illegal." With one of his canes, he points first at Anne and then at Jacob. "Never forget that, in these insane times in which we live, Klemmer has the full force of the law on his side. While we may wish to help people like these"—he swings the tip of his cane toward the two fugitives—"it is we who are the criminals. Not Klemmer."

Anne reaches out to touch the child's hair but the child buries her face in her father's chest.

"She's scared, ma'am, that's all," the man says.

"Such a little sweetheart," Anne murmurs as she strokes the child's back.

"She's Lucy," the man offers. "I'm William."

"How long have thee been here?" Jacob asks.

"Three, maybe four days. Can't really say."

Childress grapples with his canes until he again stands upright. "William, these two are going to take you and your daughter on the next leg of your journey. To the man I told you about."

"Thank you," William says to Anne and Jacob as he backs out of the room, still tightly holding Lucy.

"That man has suffered a tragedy of enormous proportions," Childress says softly when William has left the room. "He has a woman he considers his wife and their sons as well as that little girl—an unusually stable family in the slave world. Their owner threatened to sell one of their boys, so the whole family took flight. They didn't know where to go or how to get there or what to expect once they got there. But they kept heading north. They stole wagons and walked heaven knows how far. They even witnessed the death of an abolitionist friend. Somehow they reached the Ohio River, rowed across the river to Canaan's welcome shore, and who's there to greet them? A damn slave patrol." Childress settles into the chair at his desk. "That little girl fell into the water and William dove in after her. He managed to rescue her from those dark waters and somehow eluded the slave hunters in the process."

"His family?" asks Anne.

"Captured. Even the boy they were trying to save from being sold. We've no idea where they are. They could have been taken anywhere for the highest dollar."

"I can't imagine the grief he must feel," Jacob says.

"He talks about trying to find his wife and boys."

"Are you going to let him?" Anne asks.

"Let him? I have no say—or even any advice—in the matter. That's why I want to get him to Henry Blanchard tonight. Blanchard has a certain perspective on these things and can level with the fellow in a way I never could. Henry can make him see the awful reality of the situation."

They gather beside the wagon as fireflies sparkle close to the ground and the moon shines through the treetops. Marcus loads straw into the wagon and lays out a canvas tarp for concealing William and Lucy.

Childress says something to Marcus and the boy goes to the house and returns with a hunting musket. He hands it to Jacob.

"I thank thee, but I cannot use this."

"Just have it with you in case someone surprises you," Childress tells him. "Consider it a precaution."

"But I could not use it."

"A true Quaker," Childress mutters.

"But I can," William says as he takes the gun from Jacob.

William moves to the wagon bench next to Jacob with the musket resting across his lap. Anne climbs into the wagon bed and nestles in the prickly straw as Marcus hands Lucy to her.

Suddenly shouts and neighing break the evening's calm as two horsemen with torches gallop from the darkness. One horse rears and nearly throws Klemmer from its saddle as the other horse veers away from the wagon and causes its rider to drop his flaming torch.

"You will stop!" Klemmer yells as he wheels his horse in a circle and brandishes his torch.

"Go, go!" Childress shouts.

The men's horses circle the wagon and kick up thick dust. Jacob slaps the reins and Pony yanks the wagon forward. For one terrifying moment Anne sees Klemmer looking directly at her as he struggles in the torchlight to control his rearing horse.

"I tell you to stop, damn you!" Klemmer calls after them.

Childress raises one of his canes and swats the rump of Klemmer's horse. The animal bolts and pitches Klemmer backward in the saddle.

The other mounted man kicks Childress and sends him sprawling in the dirt.

"Get down!" William shouts to Anne. He turns backward on the seat and points the musket over her head as Jacob steers the wagon along the dust-filled lane.

She waits for the roar of the gun but William does not fire. Then she sees the boy Marcus running to help Childress as Klemmer circles them both on horseback, holding his torch high.

CHAPTER FIFTY-TWO

ABDUCTION

"DON'T YOU GO BACK TO THAT PLACE," HENRY Blanchard warns Anne and Jacob. "I'm telling you, don't go." Only moments earlier they had delivered William and Lucy to the Blanchard home and Jacob had told Henry about the slave hunters and the surprise attack on the Childress home. "I'll see to Childress and the boy. Now you two get home," Henry orders.

They ignore Henry. They turn the wagon southward and ride through the warm night for an hour back to Childress's house. Once there, they hide Pony and the wagon a short distance from the house and pick their way on foot through the darkness.

"Does thee smell smoke?" Jacob whispers when they are still a hundred yards away. The smell of burning wood grows stronger as they creep closer. They find the remains of the stable standing like a blackened skeleton against the starry sky. Embers glow and charred wood whistles and pops as they run past it toward the house.

The small house is intact with its door wide open.

"Wendell?" Anne feels her way in the darkness around over-turned chairs and books strewn everywhere. "Marcus?"

A muted voice comes from the bedroom. "They've got him," Childress says weakly. "They took Marcus."

Jacob lights an oil lamp and carries it to the bedroom.

"Did they hurt you?" Anne asks as the lamplight falls across Childress, slumped against a wall.

"That dear boy will perish. He's as good as dead as we speak."

Childress's lips are crusted with blood. His clothing is dirty and his linen shirt is ripped. Anne lifts him to his feet and feels his bird-like bones through his shirt and waistcoat. She and Jacob guide him to the living room, where he collapses into his overstuffed chair.

"The others. Did you get them to Blanchard?"

"We did," Anne answers.

"You told Henry about Klemmer?"

"We did. Henry says he'll be here soon."

Childress puts his fingers to his temples. "They grabbed the boy. I told them Marcus was free and Klemmer told me to prove it. We came in here and like a fool I showed him the boy's papers. The moment he saw them, Klemmer grabbed the papers away from me." Childress covers his face with both hands for several seconds. "That other man torched the stable while Klemmer tied the boy hand and foot. I went at them—I tried to intercede but Klemmer flicked me away like a miserable bug. I lay there in the dirt with my stable on fire and my horse galloped out with his mane on fire and nearly trampled me. I heard Marcus calling for help and I could do nothing."

"They just rode away?" Anne asks.

"There was so much smoke and yelling. I heard the boy screaming." Childress shuts his eyes and his skinny shoulders heave as he starts to weep. "They rode off with Marcus slung across Klemmer's saddle like the carcass of a deer."

Jacob wanders into the kitchen and peers out a window. "Does thee have any idea where they've taken him?"

Childress looks up and his black hair falls across his face. "The answer is no. Klemmer left here, what, nearly three hours ago. Marcus could already be in the hands of a trader and—"

"We understand," Anne says.

From his chair Childress looks out a window toward the stable's smoldering rubble. "Have you ever actually seen an iron shackle?" he asks no one in particular. "They take many forms, you know. Some have chains that bind the wrists together and others are for the ankles. Some bear cruel spikes and some have chains bolted to an iron ball heavy enough to impede one's mobility, not unlike—"Childress wipes away his tears with his shirtsleeve—"not unlike my own wretched condition."

"Anne," Jacob calls from the kitchen. "Come here."

She finds him standing next to the table and staring at it. Even in the lamplight she can see his face is ashen. The papers designating freedom for Marcus are crumpled and bloodied on the tabletop. Jacob reaches down and turns over the papers to reveal the boy's severed ear.

CHAPTER FIFTY-THREE

ORDEAL

ALL ACROSS NORTHERN KENTUCKY, ACROSS PHILIP Leyden's farm, weeks of no rain turn the fields into webs of cracked soil and wither the tobacco crop. Morning dew alone cannot slake the thirst of the young plants under daytime's fierce sunlight.

From dawn till darkness, saving the plants is the only thing that matters in Leyden's fields. The slaves have rigged an ox-drawn wagon with eight oak casks to haul water. They fill the casks—bucketful by heavy bucketful—from the well near the cabins and then drive the creaking wagon to the fields. There they pour the water from the casks into large buckets attached to wooden yokes. Slaves strain under the weight of the yokes to carry the water down the rows where other slaves use smaller buckets—or ladles or tin cups or even their cupped hands—to wet the soil around the plants. So it goes, plant after plant, row after row, acre after acre, day after day, as they try to stave off the sun's destruction of the parched plants.

Nettie struggles under one of the yokes. She understands this is her punishment and she knows her body is being broken by it. When the four large buckets tied to her yoke are filled with water, she cannot stand upright. She bends beneath the terrible weight and shuffles one foot in front of the other as she struggles down the dusty rows. Her load lightens as she travels down the rows, but her strength ebbs even faster. By the time her four buckets are empty, she can barely stand. And then she returns to the wagon to get more water and the agony starts all over again. She is the only woman Philip Leyden has forced to carry a yoke. Men carry the other yokes and even Willis—strongest of all the Leyden slaves—groans under the weight when his yoke's buckets are full.

For Nettie, the only pain worse is watching her boys suffering alongside her. Richard has been taken away from the hogs to help transport water. He lifts water from the well and pours it into the casks on the wagon. Then he rides to the fields where he helps empty the water into the yoke buckets—filling and emptying countless buckets of water from dawn to dusk. Alfred and Dan both work in the rows. Alfred fills his own bucket from the yokes and pours water onto the plants throughout the day. Little Dan works on his hands and knees to pull tenacious weeds so they can't suck water away from the tobacco plants.

"Your hands any better?" Nettie whispers to Richard as he dumps water from a cask into one of the buckets hanging from her yoke.

"Sallah put these on them." He shows her the wet rags covering the bloody blisters on each hand.

"My poor boy," she says.

"Stop lollygagging!" Bobby Hill prods her with the four-foot willow switch he now carries. "Move along, Nettie. Can't you hear those little plants just crying for water?" He cups his hand to his ear and bends toward the tobacco plants. "Hear them? Hear their thirsty little throats just calling for you?"

"When you going to whip me, Mister Hill?" She leans forward and puts her hands on her knees to lessen the yoke's weight on her shoulders. "Just beat me and get it over with."

"Why would we do that, Nettie? I know some owners beat their runaways," the overseer tells her. "They beat them or lock them in stocks to teach them a lesson. But we figure whipping's no answer to our problem. We're better off putting you to work watering the tobacco and maybe saving the crop. It does nobody here any good having you lie around mending from a beating."

"You going to work me to death out here."

"Work you to death?" he says with a grin. "No, no, Nettie. We'll only work you like this till the rains come." He takes off his straw hat and looks up at the sky. "And it's another beautiful day. Yessir, not a cloud in the sky."

CHAPTER FIFTY-FOUR

DEPARTED

"SHE AIN'T GOING TO MAKE IT," WILLIS WHISPERS AS HE places his hand on Ellen's forehead. His wife is lying on the bed—the same bed and same cabin that belonged to Nettie and William just a few weeks ago.

"She still burning up?" Nettie asks and then calls to the boy sitting at the table. "Reuben, get a wet cloth for your momma's head."

Nettie lies crumpled against the wall like a rag doll. She can't move without pain flooding her limbs. Blisters still ooze across her shoulders from the weight of the yoke. Years working in the Leyden house left her feet tender and now fieldstones have bruised and bloodied them. While she hears her boys washing at the well, she has not bathed in days and the grit of the fields has worked its way deep into her flesh.

Her friend Ellen is dying. Something has gnawed at the woman's insides and shrunken her like dried fruit. Ellen no longer speaks but fills the cabin day and night with moaning and the rasp of strained breathing. Willis tries to comfort what's left of his wife while Reuben and Ben watch in horror as their mother suffers.

Willis places the damp cloth on Ellen's forehead. Suddenly her frail body arches sharply and she makes a muffled sound, as close to a cry as her windless lungs can emit. Nettie struggles to her feet and limps to Ellen's bedside, next to Willis. She watches as Ellen's eyes wildly scan the cabin's ceiling. She puts her hands on Ellen's body and feels the brittle ribcage. Then—as suddenly as she had arched and stiffened—Ellen collapses and releases her final breath.

Willis steps back from the bed as Reuben and Ben rush toward it. Willis grabs his boys and pulls them close. All he can say is, "She's gone."

Later that night, Bobby Hill orders Ellen's body taken to the barn. Nettie helps Willis wrap his wife in a blanket and the big man carries the body there and places it on one of the benches used for Sabbath worship. Bobby Hill lights a lantern and then stands a few feet away, arms crossed.

"Oh, there was a time when we had a carpenter here who could've built Ellen a real fine coffin," the overseer remarks with a grin. "But now he's gone too, long gone. May he rest in peace." He lights a second lantern for more light. "That being the case, Willis, I want you and Rufe to build a box for Ellen first thing in the morning. With the heat these days, we better get her in the ground right away."

Philip Leyden enters the barn with his vest unbuttoned and no hat. "So Ellen has passed on," he says and glances at the wrapped body on the bench. He puts his hand on Willis's shoulder. "You have our sympathies, Willis, my wife's and mine."

Willis keeps his eyes on Ellen's body and says nothing.

"Shall we bury her tomorrow, say about midday?" Leyden asks.

"If that's your wish, sir," Bobby Hill answers. "We can stop work for a while."

"Ellen was with us a long time," Leyden says and then glances at Nettie. "Always loyal she was, right to the end." He marches out of the barn past Nettie without acknowledging her. Then he turns back. "With Ellen's passing, it appears you have a new family, Nettie."

She looks up at him, puzzled.

"With Willis. You'll remain in that same cabin. Now it's yours again, this time with him."

She begins to understand what he's telling her. She looks toward the bench to see Willis standing by Ellen's body, the glittering streaks of tears on his face.

Leyden calls out to his overseer, "Let's see to it that Reverend Shem performs this burial. Have somebody fetch him in the morning."

"I'll do it," Bobby Hill answers.

"Excellent," Leyden says. "I believe we have some unfinished business with the good reverend."

CHAPTER FIFTY-FIVE

DELIVERANCE

REVEREND SHEM ARRIVES ON HIS MULE AS THE LEYDEN slaves gather on a rugged scrap of ground marked by hand-hewn crosses and faded slabs of carved wood. He walks under the midday sun to the crude pine coffin, sets his black hat next to the open grave, and opens his Bible. "Gather round," he calls out and looks across the graveyard to where Philip and Grace Leyden stand with their heads bowed. Bobby Hill stands next to his sister and stares back.

"Lord, send thy mighty spirit down upon us," Reverend Shem shouts with his face turned toward the hot sky. Then he lowers his voice as he scans the faces before him. "Our sister Ellen is in a better place. Yes, my brothers and sisters, a better place. As the Gospel tells us, she has arrived in—"

His eyes fall on Nettie and he stops praying. It's only for a moment but Nettie sees the stunned recognition in his eyes. Then he goes on.

"Yes, Ellen has arrived in the good land."

Nettie watches as the preacher's eyes—confused, filled with disbelief—return to her.

"Pray, my people, pray for the these loved ones Ellen has left behind," he intones. "Offer your prayers for Willis and for their loving sons, Reuben and Ben. Pray, my people, pray to Jesus Christ to watch over them in their pain and in their sorrow."

He closes the Bible and steps to the edge of the grave.

"Our sister Ellen is done with this life. No more dues. No more pain. Rejoice for our sister!" Sweat trickles down the preacher's face. He kneels beside the coffin and stretches his arms across it. Softly, he begins to sing.

"We're a-marching to the grave,

We're a-marching to the grave, my Lord,

We're a-marching to the grave,

To lay this body down."

Several of the slaves weep openly as Ellen's coffin is lowered into the grave. The preacher guides Willis as he scatters a handful of dirt onto the coffin's lid. His two sons do the same. Reuben is solemn. Ben cries loudly and drops his dirt beside the grave instead of onto the coffin. The others file past the grave and toss more soil onto the pine box as Ben sobs.

Nettie and Richard follow in line with heads down as they near the preacher. He reaches out for Nettie's arm.

"What happened?" Reverend Shem whispers urgently. "Why are you—"

"They got us at the river. My William and my little girl—" She sucks in a deep breath. "They didn't make it, Reverend Shem."

"Dear God," the preacher says as he releases her arm. "What have they done to you?"

She and Richard drop their handfuls of grave dirt and walk away without answering.

Now Reverend Shem preaches more boldly than before. "My brothers and sisters, remember that Jesus went to Bethany and there He talked with Martha. The Gospel tells us Jesus said these words to her. He said, 'I am the resurrection and the life. He that believes in me, though he be dead, he shall live. And whoever lives and believes in me shall never die.'"

The Leydens and their overseer watch silently.

Soon the preacher says his final "Amen."

Bobby Hill orders the slaves back to their work. "You can do your mourning later," he tells them. "Right now, you've got a crop to save."

Nettie watches Philip Leyden take Grace's arm and lead her on the path back toward their home with Reverend Shem following several paces behind. She turns to see Bobby Hill coming toward her and Richard.

"Come with me, both of you. Mister Leyden wants a word." They follow the overseer up the path to the small barn closest to the house. He gestures for them to go inside. Their eyes adjust to the deep shadows and they see three men—two with pistols on their hips, the third holding a coiled rope—waiting for them. Richard balks and the overseer shoves him inside.

"Wait here," he commands and then calls to someone outside the barn, "Get in here!" Martha nervously enters the barn and squints into the gloom. She wears the powder-blue cap and apron of a house servant. She recoils when she spots Nettie. "Don't be mad at me," she pleads.

"You Missus Leyden's servant now?" Nettie whispers through clenched teeth. "Are you?"

"I work in the kitchen with Sallah. I don't help with the lady or her child, not—"

"Shut up, you two," Bobby Hill barks.

Nettie moves closer to Martha. "I hope you proud of what you done."

"Shut up, I said."

They hear Philip Leyden approach as he talks to the preacher at his side. "Yes, Shem, you remind me of Paul when he says that the man who's called to the Lord is the Lord's freeman. Something like that."

Entering the barn, Reverend Shem sees the men with their guns and stops abruptly.

"Our guest of honor," Leyden announces as he closes the barn door.

CHAPTER FIFTY-SIX

ANSWERS

DAYLIGHT ENTERS THE BARN ONLY THROUGH A SINGLE window several feet away from where Philip Leyden stands facing the black preacher. The air in the barn is dirty with dust and the stink of the horse stalls.

"We're going to settle this right now," Leyden says. "Reverend, these sheriff's men and I have questions about your involvement in the escapes from this farm."

The preacher studies the three men. "I know him," Shem says and nods toward a beefy man with a red face and thick beard. "He was there when I went to see the man who was found dead."

"Sure enough," the man replies. He crosses his thick arms across his chest and rocks back on his heels.

"It's my belief somebody helped my slaves run away," Leyden says. "They're no smarter than my hogs and certainly don't know north from west or east from south. They don't know the Ohio River from the Licking River. But somehow they made it all the way to the Ohio and then across it. Also, Reverend, we have the matter of the dead man's body you were so eager to view. It turns out he was from Maysville and was a man of decidedly abolitionist persuasion."

Reverend Shem stands silently in his wide-brimmed hat, further obscuring his face in the shadows. He clutches his Bible.

Leyden keeps talking. "These three runaways surely know if you helped them. So I'm going to ask you—as I've already asked them individually—about what happened. I'm relying on your being a man of God to tell me the truth."

No one speaks.

"Reverend?"

"What is the question?" the preacher asks.

"Did you help these slaves run from my farm?"

"I did."

"No," Nettie gasps.

Two of the sheriff's men move forward.

"Wait," Leyden says. "I want details."

Reverend Shem takes a step closer to Leyden. "You called me a man of God, sir, and that's what I am. My mortal mission is to bring the Lord's message to my people. Scripture talks of freedom through and through. So, I ask you, how can any man or woman who's chattel, who's another man's property, listen to the stories of the Hebrews' quest and not have a God-given thirst for freedom? So, I do confess to encouraging them through my preaching, just as your good friend Reverend Barry encourages his own flock when he preaches from the same Bible. The word of God can set my people free."

Leyden stares at the preacher. "Be that as it may, did you help them escape?" He holds up a hand. "And be careful how you answer. I've already heard details from these three slaves."

"Did I help them run from this farm? Did I take them northward? No, I did not, other than what I just said about planting the dream of freedom as I find it in the Bible."

The man with the bushy beard quickly speaks up. "Wasn't you trying to see if that dead fellow was your Maysville friend?"

"The man was not who I thought he might be," Reverend Shem answers calmly. "The reason I insisted on viewing the body was because you wouldn't permit me to see it. If you'll recall, sir, I had to come back to the sheriff's office three times before you let me into that room where you'd put the deceased. If you'd done so the first time, there would have been no need for my persistence."

"Who'd you think it was, got killed along that road?" the man wants to know.

"I thought it could have been Philip Leyden. The description I'd heard certainly fits this man standing right here."

"You thought it was I?" Leyden says.

"That was my concern," the preacher answers. "And I couldn't understand why I wasn't permitted to see the body. I suspect these men thought I was going to put some sort of hoodoo curse on it. Me being a colored preacher and all."

Bobby Hill moves closer to Leyden. "Don't believe it, sir. They're all lying—these three and the preacher alike. I don't care what they say. I'm sure he helped them somehow."

Nettie looks at Martha and the girl returns the look, her eyes steady.

"What, then, is your solution to all of this, Mister Hill?" Leyden asks the overseer. "More whippings and beatings?"

The bearded man speaks up. "Well, Mister Leyden, whipping's been known to produce a goodly share of confessions."

"The lash," Reverend Shem interrupts. "It's been known to produce many confessions consistent with what the master wants to hear. Not necessarily the truth, but confessions to anything just to make the whipping stop. The flesh is weak."

"There will be no whipping and no more talk of it," Leyden says as he abruptly turns and storms past his overseer. "We're done here."

CHAPTER FIFTY-SEVEN

RETALIATION

DUSK HAS FALLEN BY THE TIME THE SLAVES CAN GATHER to mourn Ellen. Philip Leyden's insistence on watering the tobacco plants has delayed until now the customary funeral procession to the graveside and communal meal and wake. The exhausted slaves gather at the well to rinse off the day's dirt and then grab pieces of ham and bread Sallah and Martha have brought down from the Leyden house. Most collapse on the ground with their food amid the blinking of fireflies.

Willis stands by the bonfire. He begins to sing a hymn but falters tearfully after one verse and disappears behind the cabins. The slaves are sullen. Some talk in small groups and others sit in silence. The days of watering the tobacco crop have proved excruciating, draining everyone's strength and spirit. They know many of the plants are dead and more will die tomorrow.

Nettie sits on the hard ground with her three boys huddled by her side as they eat their ham and bread. She lies back, closes her eyes, and succumbs to the warm night air.

Richard speaks up. "Rufe's back, ma."

Rufe had been ordered earlier in the day to carry water with one of the yokes. He'd stumbled under its weight and Bobby Hill had beat him with his willow switch—one stinging blow after another as Rufe cried out and the spilled water seeped into the soil.

Nettie opens her eyes to look at Rufe but instead sees Martha standing close by as she hands Alfred and Dan more ham. Nettie props herself on her elbows. "So you didn't tell them nothing about Reverend Shem after all."

"They couldn't beat it out of me if they tried."

"We thought you told them," Richard says. "We thought that's why they let you work in the house."

"Mister Hill put me there and I know why."

Richard wipes his mouth. "So it looked like you told."

"They's all bad," Martha seethes. "Those men who brought us back and these men working us to death—just look at your momma here—white devils, all of them." Martha's eyes grow dark as she speaks. She crouches close to Richard. "They killed your pa and your little sister, you know. This ain't no life, never knowing what bad thing's going to happen next."

"Shush, girl!" Nettie sits upright. She sees Bobby Hill sitting on a stump several yards away. Richard gets to his feet and wanders off. Nettie watches him as he walks beyond the slaves and beyond the light of the fire until she can no longer see him in the dark.

"Why'd you shush me?" Martha demands.

"Don't want you getting riled. You supposed to be thinking about Ellen, bless her soul."

"They killed her, too. And you know it."

"She was sick. Been sick a long time."

"They didn't give her no care. They used her up, just like they using you up."

Nettie stares at the bonfire. "It's because there's no rain."

"You listen to me." Martha leans close to Nettie. "Did they bring me and those two boys to this farm and then sell them boys because it wasn't raining? Was they going to sell your boy because the ground was too dry? Rain's got nothing to do with it. They'd still be finding some way to work you to death if it was raining forty days and forty nights. That's what Sallah says."

Willis returns to the firelight. He holds a tin cup in one hand and tosses another log onto the bonfire with the other. He hums softly and watches the sparks fly upward into the night. He walks over to Nettie and Martha and kneels down.

"Brought this for you." He hands Nettie the cup. "It'll help."

She sips and is startled by the searing liquid. "Liquor!" She flutters her hand in front of her mouth.

"Do you good."

"Where'd you get it?"

"Ned, over at the mill. Brought it with the lumber."

"Don't you let Bobby Hill see this." She looks around for Richard. "Who's all been at this drink?"

"Why you ask?"

"Our boys?"

Both Nettie and Willis scan the area for their sons.

"I'll go." Willis rises to his feet.

"Over there," Martha says. "It's Richard."

Richard approaches until he stands between Nettie and the bonfire so all she can see is the silhouette of her son. "Sit here and be quiet," she tells him while patting the ground by her side.

He remains standing. "We didn't get a funeral."

"What you mean?"

"We got people who died and we didn't get a funeral. Pa and Lucy."

"Sit here, now."

"I ain't."

She struggles to her feet and groans at the aches in her back and thighs. She reaches for the boy's wrist and whispers, "You been drinking that liquor?"

"Leave me be." He wrenches free from her grip. "We don't need bodies for a funeral. We could still have one."

"Leave it be, Richard. We got troubles enough."

"She knows," Richard points at Martha. "She knows they as good as killed Pa and Lucy."

"You listen to me," Nettie says in a firm whisper. "I know you hurting from lifting all those buckets of water and I know you can't understand about your pa and Lucy. Lord knows I can't either. But we got to go on. We got to find the strength."

Richard's chin quivers.

She puts her arm around her boy's shoulders and guides him toward the cabin she shares with Willis and his sons. "Just come with me, my poor boy."

"Whoa, there!" Bobby Hill calls as he marches toward them. "That boy's not going in there."

"Just let me talk to my boy," she begs.

"That boy doesn't belong with you. You'd better—" Shadows fall across the overseer and he turns toward the bonfire. Standing against the firelight are Willis and Rufe and Sallah. Reuben and Ben stand farther back.

"Let them be together, sir," Willis says. "Just for a while. He's still her boy."

"You just don't understand, do you?" Bobby Hill snaps. "This is a penalty. You run away, you get punished. Sallah, you get Richard out of here. Take him back to your cabin."

Sallah steps toward Richard, but Nettie raises her hand. "Let me be with my boy, Sallah."

Bobby Hill grabs at Richard, who ducks and runs to Reuben and Ben. "We're not going to have trouble here, are we?" the overseer says. "Get these boys in their beds, now!"

Richard, Reuben, and Ben scatter into the darkness. Willis chases after them but can only grab Ben. Bobby Hill tries to head off Richard and Reuben near the fire. They skirt his outstretched arms and Reuben dashes into the darkness between the cabins. Just then, Richard pulls a stick from the bonfire and heaves it in a fiery arc toward the new building. It strikes a pile of stacked lumber with a spray of bright sparks falling onto the tinder-dry grass.

"What the hell!" Bobby Hill yells.

Richard races after Reuben between the cabins.

Bobby Hill shouts to the others. "Find those sons of bitches, all of you!" The slaves rise and walk around with no sense of urgency as the overseer frantically searches around the cabins.

Moments later Philip Leyden runs down the path from his house. "Bobby, damn it, look over there," he shouts. "Fire!" Flames are spreading through the dry grass and licking at the stacked lumber. "Get water!" Leyden shouts. "Get every bucket you can find!"

"No buckets here, sir," Rufe calls back. "All we got is still out in the field."

Bobby Hill stands speechless as the fire takes hold of the lumber pile.

"Get the damn buckets, Bobby!" Leyden again yells. "The rest of you get blankets!"

Some get shovels and throw dirt on the fire. Some others grapple with the lumber pile and pull it apart to save what timber they can. Nettie drags a blanket across the smoldering grass as she keeps watch for Richard. "What have you done, my boy," she quietly cries. "What have you done?"

Bobby Hill returns with four empty buckets. Leyden approaches him and the overseer lets the buckets fall to the ground as the slaves stomp out the last of the blaze.

"Where's the boy now?"

"Ran away, last I knew. With Willis's boy."

"Find them. Bring them to me when you do," Leyden says, hammering his fist against his open palm. "And I mean it, Bobby. You will find them."

CHAPTER FIFTY-EIGHT

INFERNO

FIVE BLACK BUGGIES ARE HITCHED TO THE RAIL between John Pope's home and store. A summer haze hangs lazily in the windless morning air as Quaker men in their dark hats and coats quietly guide their bonneted wives and their children into the house for Sunday worship. Across the road Anne ties Othello to the rail in front of the white Methodist church. She holds Hannah's hand as her friend steps carefully from the buggy with one arm resting protectively over her belly.

She leaves Hannah at the church—Adam has remained at the farm with their sons—and walks over to the Quaker meeting. Jacob comes out of the house and meets her in the road.

"It's so good to see thee, Anne. I've missed thee terribly."

"It's been almost two days," she says with a smile.

"It's difficult to be apart from thee at all."

"My goodness, Jacob, you're romantic today."

"It's because I love thee."

She is surprised by the boldness of his declaration, but Jacob simply takes her arm and walks with her into the house.

The small dining room is crowded with people on benches and chairs, sitting silently as they begin their worship. A woman Anne knows as Emily stands to speak with head bowed and hands clasped in front of her. "Dear friends, I ask thee to join with me again in asking the Lord's help in the months ahead as we face the toll of our failed crops. Ours is destined to be a difficult winter. It will call for our love and friendship and compassion. Let us ask the Lord to give us the strength to share whatever bounty we have with those who are less fortunate and to remember how blessed is the act of giving." She resumes her seat on the bench, next to her husband.

A moment later, a man rises to his feet behind Anne. She recognizes Abner Blair's voice as soon as he speaks. "In the words of the prophet Isaiah," he begins as usual. "'And the Lord shall satisfy thy soul in drought, and make fat thy bones. And thou shalt be like a watered garden and like a spring whose waters fail not.' Fifty-eight, eleven."

The Quakers absorb these thoughts in silence. Several dab at the sweat on their faces. Anne hears a slight rustling from two women near an open window. She peeks to see one of them lean toward her husband and whisper. He shakes his head with eyes still closed. She whispers to him again. This time he stands and walks quietly from the room.

Three more people turn toward the window and finally a man speaks up. "Forgive me, John, but I believe I smell smoke."

The man who had left the room suddenly returns. "John, thy stable is on fire! Everyone, come!"

They dash from the house to find the stable spewing smoke. Flames lick one wall and climb toward the roof as sparks spiral upward into the breezeless sky.

"We need water!" a man shouts.

The men strip off their coats and hats. Horses harnessed to the buggies stomp and whinny as the women guide them up the road and away from the billowing smoke.

Jacob and his father rush from the store with several buckets. People grab them and run to the rain barrel at a corner of the stable but find it dry, so they dip the buckets into the horse trough and fling the scant water onto the flaming wall.

Abner Blair pumps furiously at the nearby well as men and women frantically pass buckets between the well and the stable. Abner suddenly pauses to turn his eyes to the sky and shout, "For it is fire that consumeth to destruction and would root out all of mine increase. So saith the prophet Isaiah—"

"Pump!" a man yells at him.

A woman runs across the road to the Methodist church. Within moments another dozen people are joining the Quakers, grabbing blankets from their own buggies to beat back the flames. Smoke curls around the eaves as more fire breaks out along the roof.

Anne is aghast at what she's seeing and recollects the fire that had consumed the stable at Wendell Childress's home. She immediately thinks of Klemmer and his torch and of Wendell Childress telling her and Jacob how the slave hunters had taken to burning down stables and barns. She grabs a bucket from a Quaker woman and throws water onto the flaming stable wall and then quickly seizes two more empty buckets and runs them back to the well where Abner is still pumping and quoting Isaiah. She sees Jacob run from the store with more buckets and blankets and then drop them on the ground. He frantically looks around.

"I'm here," Anne shouts to him.

"Pony," he yells back. "Where's Pony?"

Anne cannot see the horse and watches Jacob disappear into the smoke pouring from the stable.

"Jacob!" his father shouts after him.

Anne runs toward the stable but a man grabs her as she reaches its open door and orders, "Stay back!"

"What's he doing?" another man shouts over the roar of the fire.

"His horse!" Anne answers.

"There's no horse in there," the man yells back.

But within moments Pony runs from the stable, snorting and sneezing, eyes wild and coat singed and smoking. Someone grabs the mare by her mane and someone else throws a blanket over her scorched back. Everyone watches the stable door.

Jacob does not emerge.

A moment later, a man from the Methodist group throws a bucket of water onto a blanket and pulls the wet cloth over his head and shoulders. He charges into the fiery stable just as a section of roof crashes down. The man is knocked backward by the cascade of flames and sparks and then regains his bearings and jumps over the fiery timbers to disappear deeper into the smoke.

Anne steps back with eyes stinging and lungs burning. Someone grabs her shoulder.

"Where's Jacob?" Hannah says, her arm raised to shield her face from the heat.

"In there," Anne cries. "He went in after his horse."

The man with the wet blanket stumbles out of the smoke with Jacob slung over his shoulders. He staggers and drops to his knees and lets Jacob slip to the ground.

"Dear God," Hannah moans.

A group of people—faces and arms smudged with soot, clothing soaked with sweat and water—block Anne's way as they rush toward the man and Jacob. A woman puts her hands over her eyes. Jacob's face is badly blistered with patches of blackened skin peeling to expose pink tissue beneath. His blond hair is burned away and his clothing is charred. He does not move.

Anne turns away. She cannot comprehend the scene. Through the blur of her tears she watches two men holding John Pope as his legs give way.

She slumps to the ground herself and Hannah kneels over her. "Hannah?" she asks calmly. "Jacob will be all right, won't he?" She turns her head and looks at Jacob. A man bends over him with his ear close to the burned face. Then he draws a blanket over Jacob's head.

As the world dims around her, Anne hears a man's voice coming closer.

"Our holy and our beautiful house, where our fathers praised thee, is burned up with fire." Anne looks up to see Abner Blair standing above her with tears on his face. "And all our pleasant things are laid to waste." The last thing she hears is, "Isaiah, sixty-four …."

CHAPTER FIFTY-NINE

CALAMITY

THE MORNING IS ALREADY MUGGY AS REVEREND SHEM rings the bell for Sabbath worship at the Leyden farm. Several of the slaves trudging toward the big barn are covered with field dust from the day before.

Nettie gathers strength to climb the path toward the preacher. Willis catches up with her. "I ain't seen Bobby Hill and the others leave here, not this morning so far. Maybe they going to give up trying to catch Reuben and Richard."

Nettie stops to catch her breath. "Been two days. You think our boys got away?"

"Don't know," he answers. "Don't know what I want. They get caught and they sure to be punished bad—but they'd be back with us. They get away and they might make it across the river like you tried and then they'd be free. But we'd never set eyes on those boys again."

"I know," is all Nettie can say.

They start up the path again and then see Reverend Shem running toward them with Bobby Hill several steps behind.

"Your boys," Reverend Shem gasps. "Where are they?"

"You mean Richard and Reuben?" Nettie says.

"Where are they?" the preacher demands. "Did they bring them back?"

"What you saying?" asks Willis.

The preacher sees Bobby Hill approaching and speaks quickly. "They found your boys yesterday near my place. I heard horses and some yelling and I went out and saw them. They must've been trying to reach me and those men were there waiting."

Bobby Hill steps in front of the preacher. "It's none of your concern, Reverend."

Nettie suddenly feels the sun suffocating her. Her breath grows short and she begins to swoon. She clutches Reverend Shem's arm to steady herself.

"Where's my boy, Mister Hill?"

"I've got nothing to say to you," he tells her and then looks at Willis. "Nor to you. You got questions, you take them to Mister Leyden."

"I got to know where my boy is." she shakes her fist weakly in the overseer's face. "You tell me."

"I told you I got nothing to say."

She pushes past the overseer and hobbles toward the Leyden house with Reverend Shem and Willis closely following. She lurches through the back door and limps through the pantry and into the empty dining room. She grabs the edge of the mahogany table to keep from falling.

"What you done?" she cries out to the empty room. "What you done with my boy?"

Willis and Reverend Shem try to pull her back.

Right then, Philip Leyden storms into the dining room. His black cravat is untied and his waistcoat unbuttoned. He clutches a small silver pistol in his right hand. "What's going on? What's the meaning of this?"

"Our boys," Willis tells Leyden. "They say you found our boys."

Leyden looks at the three of them and then composes himself. He slips the pistol into his trouser pocket and straightens his waistcoat. "I take it you heard this unfortunate news from your preacher here." He crosses his arms across his chest and glares at Reverend Shem. "I must admit I never was convinced of your innocence in the attempts of my slaves to run away, so I had my men stake out your barn. Isn't it coincidental that those two rascals ran straight to you?"

Nettie slumps to her knees. "Give Richard back to me. Please, sir."

The door to the hall opens and Grace stands in the doorway, looking at Nettie kneeling on the floor with Willis and the preacher standing over her. "Philip, are you all right?"

"Leave us, Grace." He closes the door and shuts out his wife.

Reverend Shem pulls Nettie to her feet and steadies her. "Trust in the Lord," he whispers in her ear.

"I've sold your boys," Leyden says.

"No!" Nettie gasps. Willis and Reverend Shem stand in stunned silence.

"They are troublemakers, through and through," Leyden goes on. "They assaulted my overseer and tried to burn down my new building. I warned them and I warned both of you. But things have gone too far and I have no desire for them to come back here—ever."

Leyden keeps his eyes on Willis and slips his hand back into the pocket containing the pistol. The big slave seems unable to comprehend his owner's words. Nettie buries her face in Reverend Shem's shoulder and the preacher asks, "Can we know where they—"

"You know all you need to know. Now leave my house. There's nothing more to say."

They walk back into the sunlight with Reverend Shem guiding Nettie as Willis follows. The other slaves are clustered around the barn door. Just as the three reach the barn, Bobby Hill grabs the preacher's shoulder.

"You go in there and preach a fine service, Reverend. We don't want anybody getting all riled up. You tell them it's God's will or whatever it is you say to keep them in line. You hear?"

Reverend Shem wrenches free and enters the barn.

CHAPTER SIXTY

INTENTION

HENRY BLANCHARD HEAPS A HEFTY PORTION OF GREENS and fried pork onto his plate as Sarah waits to hand him the tin of cornbread. He passes the pot of greens and pork to William, seated across from him at the table with Lucy on his lap.

"William, you ain't hungry?" Henry asks.

"I am, but I got something to say." William straightens the child on his lap. "I'm going back to get Nettie and my boys. If they at that farm, I'll get them away from there. If they been sold, I'll find them or die trying." He stares at Henry and Sarah across the table, waiting for their response.

"Dish up your food," Henry says. "You be needing it."

"I mean it," William persists. "I been thinking about it for two days now."

"What about that child?" Sarah asks. "What if you go back down there and don't come back?"

"I know all that. But when I look at this child, all I see is her ma."

"Sounds like the man's made up his mind," Henry says as he spears more greens from the pot. "Sounds like he's dead set on going back south—not north."

William turns to Sarah. "Can you keep my girl while I go? Find her a good home if I don't come back?"

Lucy squirms on his lap. "It's all right, baby," he says and pats her hair.

Sarah watches Henry devour the rest of the pork on his plate.

He glances at her. "What you looking at?"

She continues to gaze at him silently.

Finally Henry clears his throat and asks, "You want me to go with you?"

William shakes his head. "Down to Mays Lick? You be a fool—a big fool. You could end up a slave again or at the end of a rope. You got no reason." William takes a hunk of cornbread from the tin. "But I'm grateful for you asking."

"I do things you don't know." Henry pushes himself back from the table.

"What things?"

"Steal slaves. Bring them back here so they can go north. Done it for years now."

William stares back at Henry with a furrowed brow. "What you telling me?"

"It's like this. I go across the river into Kentucky and find folks who want to run away and I help them. I bring them up here and then get them going toward Canada. I'm telling you, I got people who help me and I know my way around. Never been caught at it even once."

"How many?"

"How many what?"

"How many slaves you stole?"

"Enough to know what I'm doing."

William says nothing as he tries to feed a piece of pork to Lucy. She pushes his hand away.

"William," Sarah says, "it's going to be hard to get your family back and Lord knows I don't want Henry in danger. But two's better than one. Think what you be up against back at that awful place all alone."

William keeps trying to feed Lucy. "Don't know why you want to risk your life for my family like that." He looks up at Henry. "You really got help?"

"Some," Henry answers. "Somebody to get us horses. Somebody to hide us. Somebody with a boat."

"I can't pay you."

Henry leans forward, puts his elbows on the table and thrusts his finger at William. "Don't you go demeaning me with talk about money. I never asked no slave for so much as a penny."

"What about my girl?" William asks again.

"She'll be here with me," Sarah tells him. "You'll only be gone a few days, Lord willing." She reaches for Lucy. "Let me take her. She needs to be fed proper." She puts Lucy on her lap and wiggles a fork with a morsel of pork in front of the child's mouth. Lucy eats it and then grabs for more with her tiny fingers.

William watches the scene and says, "I'll take your help, Henry."

CHAPTER SIXTY-ONE

REQUEST

HORSEFLIES SWARM AROUND ADAM'S HEAD AS HE brushes Othello's black coat in a stall in the barn. It's midday and the insects are drawn to the scent of horse and man. Adam swats at a noisy fly to keep it from the gelding's eye. Then he hears the sound of hooves near the house. He sets down the curry brush and walks to the barn doorway, where he watches a hefty man near the watering trough dismounting from a bay mare.

"Henry Blanchard," Adam calls out. "Surprised to see you here."

Henry strides toward the barn and touches the brim of his frayed straw hat.

"Got something to ask."

Adam moves into the glare of the sun to meet Henry, who removes his hat to brush dust from it.

"I'll get right to it," Henry says. "I got to cross the river and try to bring some people back, slaves." He replaces his hat and pulls the brim low over his eyes. "I'm asking you to come with me."

Adam is speechless.

Henry continues. "Got to go down into Mason County. Me and another man, a runaway. If things work out, we'll be coming back with more—maybe four or five, all told. But we got to be looking like slaves if we going to make it."

"I don't follow."

"Me and that man got to be able to move around if we going to get those people away. The only way to do it is to look like slaves and we need more than papers. We need an owner."

Adam sits down on the bench by the barn wall. Henry stands in front of him with his hands on his hips and his shadow falling across Adam.

"Just so I understand what you're asking," Adam says, squinting up at Henry's silhouette, "you want me to go into Kentucky with you and pose as your owner so you can bring back a group of slaves."

"That's about it."

"Why me?"

"Got nobody else—no other white folk anyhow. We got to leave tomorrow."

"Henry, I don't think so. I can't put myself in such danger. I got to think about my wife and my sons."

"Funny thing, that's what this man says too. So we going down there to get his kin, his wife and boys," Henry explains. "This man and his woman and children ran from the farm down in Mason County because their master wanted to sell one of their boys. They got over to this side of the river and the hunters were waiting for them. The man and his little girl got away but the hunters got his woman and boys. Now he's got to try to get them back. Says he can't go on living with himself if he don't try."

"And you're willing to risk your own neck for him?"

"He's a good man. But not the kind can do this sort of thing all alone."

"You've done this sort of thing before, Henry, you told me so. Why's it different this time?"

"Told you. There could be a bunch of us and we got to cover considerable ground. Folks going to be asking questions. That's part of it anyway."

"And the rest?"

"And I've gone too many times into that land by myself and now they keeping watch for a colored man looks like me. I hear there's a price on my head. So if I go there with my master, I'd look like any other poor slave and nobody'd pay me any heed." Henry lowers himself onto the bench beside Adam and reaches into the pocket of his baggy trousers. He pulls out a worn sheet of folded paper. "We can use this."

Adam unfolds the paper. "Bill of Ownership" is printed in black script at the top of the document, which certifies that the bearer— one Lucas McClure of Nicholas County, Virginia—is owner of this Negro man, Henry Blanchard.

"Had that for a good many years now," Henry says with a smile.

Adam stares at the words on the page. "Strange, isn't it?" he muses. "Given a mere twenty miles, this document could be entirely legal. If I were this McClure fellow, you'd be my property and I could work you and beat you however I wanted. I could destroy you and your family and still be abiding by the law."

"Would you?"

"Would I what?"

"Do those things. If you lived those twenty miles south."

Adam refolds the paper. "There was a time—not too long ago, I'm ashamed to admit—when maybe I could have put myself in the position of a Lucas McClure and could argue the question this way or that. I can't do that anymore. In my mind, there are no longer two sides of the issue. So the answer is no. I could not own you or anybody else. But that doesn't mean I'm going with you." He holds out the folded paper. "Here, take this back."

"You keep it till you make up your mind."

"I can't, Henry."

Henry is silent. He looks out across the meadow toward the wooded hills.

"Take your paper," Adam repeats.

"You got a fight going on in you. Seems part of you wants to help. Part doesn't."

Adam stares at the ground as Henry takes back the certificate of ownership.

"It's getting worse, you know," Adam says. "There was a fire last Sunday in Buford. The young Quaker man whose father owns the store there was burned to death."

"The one helping Childress?" Henry asks as he folds his certificate. "Him and that girl Anne brought the runaway man I'm telling you about, brought him and his little girl to my place. You telling me he's dead?"

"The stable caught fire and he tried to save his horse."

"I know about these fires." Henry stands up and again casts his shadow across Adam. "I know this makes what I'm asking you to be all the harder. We'll be leaving my place at midday tomorrow. You decide you want to help us, you show up by then."

CHAPTER SIXTY-TWO

JUSTIFICATION

HANNAH HAS CLEANED UP AFTER THE EVENING MEAL and bathed both of her sons and tucked them into bed with Anne's help. Back downstairs she gathers her sewing basket and sets an oil lamp near the sofa so she can do her mending. Adam comes in from tending the animals, lowers himself into a chair by the oil lamp, and tells her he's leaving in the morning to travel to Kentucky with Henry Blanchard.

"Why would you do that," is all Hannah can say.

"We're bringing back some slaves."

For a moment she doubts she's heard him correctly. "I don't understand."

"I can tell you what I plan to do, but I don't know if I can tell you why I'm doing it," he says as he slips off his vest and brushes some dust from the front of his shirt.

"Well, please try." She picks up a pillow beside her on the sofa and holds it close to her chest.

"You know the Blanchards help runaways. And you know sometimes Henry goes into Kentucky and finds slaves who want to escape.

I told you what he said about bringing them back across the river and getting them started on their way north."

She shakes her head and says, "And you'll recall I said a colored man going into that country to rescue slaves is courting his own death." She rises from the sofa and the pillow tumbles to the floor. She walks to the window and stares at the dusk settling across the countryside. "What has this to do with you?"

"Henry says it's not safe for him across the river. They're on the lookout for him and there could be a price on his head. So he's asked me to pose as his owner."

"And you said?" She turns to face him.

"I want to do this, Hannah."

At that moment, Anne comes down the stairs from the boys' bedroom. She picks up the pillow Hannah dropped and then begins unfolding blankets to place on the sofa for her bedding. Hannah breaks the silence, addressing Adam partly in anger, partly in confusion.

"I've heard your words and pledges about keeping our sons and me safe," she says. "I know you mean these things. But you also know this trip you're talking about would be dangerous. For heaven's sake, Adam"—and she looks over at Anne, who stands with her face lowered—"we've all just witnessed what can happen to people who oppose these slave hunters. That fire at John Pope's place was no accident. There is evil around us."

Adam watches Hannah brush away tears on her cheek. He lifts himself from the chair and joins her at the window. "Remember when we came to this farm and I didn't want to be involved with the outside world? I appreciated how remote we are here and I just wanted us to have good lives. Quiet lives. And you remember the day when the men showed up with that boy in the wagon?"

"Of course."

"Do you remember what you told me that evening? You said it made no difference how much I didn't want trouble coming around here. Things would happen whether I wanted them to or not. And you told me we hadn't done well by that poor boy."

"I remember."

"You were right, Hannah. I know now that I can't turn my back on the world and expect the world to leave my family alone. I don't have the power to make it so no one will be hurt or no one will die."

He turns toward Anne. "Remember when you brought those two slaves here? That old woman had joy in life like nobody I'd ever seen—despite everything she'd been through. She was filled with love. She just sang her songs with total happiness and gratitude. And I picture her grandson carrying her in his arms all those miles so she could finally feel free soil under her feet."

"She was a wonderful person," Anne says.

"They both were," adds Hannah.

"And the Blanchards," Adam continues. "They're doing what they can and putting their lives at stake every step of the way. I've thought about you, Anne, and about Jacob, how you both put yourselves in terrible danger to help these people. And, yes, I've thought about my brother and his abolitionist beliefs and all the pain and bruises he's suffered for voicing those beliefs. I know he can be a burr under the saddle but his heart is filled with good."

"Very much so," Hannah says.

"Words fail me, but I know deep down that something isn't right," he goes on. "The world surrounding us has gone awry somehow. We have laws that pay rewards to brutes like Julius Klemmer for hunting down a sweet grandmother like Nancy Blue and returning her to a living hell. We have a president ordering a thousand soldiers to escort a single man to a ship carrying him back to another man who claims the fugitive as his property to do with as he pleases. I can no longer believe this is the way things are supposed to be."

Adam returns to the chair and leans forward with his hands clasped. "Till now I've only stood witness to the courage of you Anne, and Jacob, and my brother, and Henry Blanchard, and that man Childress—all of you. I may have felt the terrible fear of being hunted by those men who chased me through the woods that night down by the Blanchard farm, but these runaways are frightened day in and day out. And even though I've felt the fear, I've done almost nothing to make things better."

Adam's jaw begins to quiver. "I tell both of you, I can't stop thinking about that boy in the wagon. I see him lying there, bloodied and chained up. I keep seeing his eyes and all the fear in them. Hannah, you tried to help him, but I—" He takes a deep breath to steady himself.

Hannah takes his hand. "Adam, it's over."

"No, Hannah, it's not over. I keep seeing the look on that boy's face, like a calf being led to slaughter. You told me about Jacob's terrible death. All of this is why."

"Why?" Hannah asks.

"Why I need to go with Henry. If we bring back ten slaves, twenty, a hundred, it still won't help that boy in the wagon. It won't help Jacob. But at least I'll be doing something."

CHAPTER SIXTY-THREE

JOURNEY

THE THREE MEN ON HORSEBACK RIDE FROM THE Blanchard farm steadily south toward the Ohio River. They travel the narrow roads and trails and cross dense forests of oak and poplar and hickory. Always they follow the downward slope of the terrain through hollows and alongside creeks, always lower toward the river basin. In three hours they reach the road into Ripley, with wagons and carriages and other horsemen joining them as they pass cabins and frame houses and finally the storefronts in the center of town. With the day's sun now well past its height, they look beyond the packinghouses and boatyards to see the flowing river and the dense haze shimmering against the Kentucky hills beyond.

"Beautiful," Adam says. "For something dividing two very different ways of life, it really is a beautiful river."

They ride to the riverfront through streets bustling with vehicles shuttling merchandise to and from the wharf.

Henry turns to William. "Any of this look familiar?"

William scans their surroundings. "Some people living down that way let me and my girl spend time in an attic," he says, pointing west. Then he points toward a distant hilltop to the north. "And then we went way up there, where some folks kept us a day and then got us on our way again."

Soon the three ride out of Ripley and head east toward Aberdeen in the late afternoon heavy with heat and humidity. A few miles out of Ripley, they turn from the main road onto a wooded lane leading away from the river. They come to a cabin and two barns. A black man with a gray-flecked beard and wearing worn overalls is chopping wood and stacking it beneath a massive oak.

"This here's Tuck," Henry tells the others. "We leave our horses with him."

Few words are exchanged.

"Wagon at the spot?" Henry asks.

"Yep," Tuck answers.

"Boat in its place?"

"Yep."

"Be back in three days, I figure. Could be longer."

"I see you when I see you," Tuck says and nods to the men.

They sling their carpetbags and saddlebags and canteens over their shoulders as Tuck leads their horses toward one of the barns. The men walk back down the lane as Henry explains that Tuck keeps a wagon hidden a half-mile away in a grove near where Eagle Creek enters the Ohio. A skiff is moored at the same place. They'll row the boat across the river—about two hundred yards wide at that point— and dock near the mouth of Lawrence Creek on the Kentucky side. They'll walk to the home of a man named Gibson who'll loan them horses. When they return, they'll leave the horses with Gibson and row the same boat back across the river then retrieve their own horses and the wagon from Tuck and ride back to Henry's farm.

"That's how you done it before?" William asks.

"That's it. Even if something bad happens to me, Tuck and Gibson stay safe because nobody knows about them. They don't even know about each other. Everything got to be kept quiet."

"But now we know," William says. "What your friends going to think of that?"

"It's all right. They know if I do something stupid I'm a dead man."

The men soon reach the riverfront and find the wagon in a clump of poplars with brush piled over it and two long oars lying in its bed. The rowboat is tied nearby in a stand of cattails. Adam wades into the river up to his knees and boards the boat. The other two follow with Henry using one of the oars to push the boat away from the shore. The skiff drifts free as Henry slips the oars into the rusty oarlocks and rows to the Kentucky shore.

They land in a small cove shielded by trees near the confluence of the river and Lawrence Creek. They tie the boat to a stake and stash the oars in a thicket. Adam and William follow Henry up a twisting path through an unkempt apple orchard until they reach a ramshackle house with wild roses scaling the porch and walls. A single section of picket fence remains upright while the rest lies flattened in the dry grass.

"Gibson's place?" Adam asks.

Henry steps over the remnants of the front gate and then walks to the front door. He thumps a couple of times and the door creaks open. A skinny white man in his late twenties with cropped brown hair and a haphazard beard stands in the doorway. His blue pants are cinched around his waist with a rope, and his unbuttoned homespun shirt reveals his sunken chest.

"Meet you out back," Gibson says with no greeting and then shuts the door.

Henry leads Adam and William around the side of the house. Somewhere deep in the barn they hear Gibson talking to someone. Adam looks at Henry, who says, "Don't worry." They find the scrawny man conversing in the barn shadows with three horses. Adam watches as Gibson strokes their muzzles, buries his head in their manes, and nuzzles them with words of affection.

Gibson soon hands the men the reins for three healthy stallions. "This one's Jess," Gibson says of Adam's horse. "This here's Sam," of Henry's, and, "This fellow I call Ben," he says to William.

Adam extends his hand to Gibson. "Adam Porter."

"I don't know you and you don't know me," Gibson replies in a drawl. "Just be careful with my boys."

They mount the horses and when they reach the road Henry turns west.

"Not that way," William shouts. "We got to go this way."

Henry sits still on his horse as William wheels around and rides up beside him. "Why you want to go this way?" William asks. "It's not the way to Mays Lick."

"We going a roundabout way," Henry tells William and explains he wants to take a longer route to the Leyden farm because it's the same route he wants to use for the return trip and they should become familiar with it. "We get your family and we can't be going straight up to Washington and Maysville where every slave catcher in the county be looking for us. We got to come back up through Germantown and Minerva where I got somebody who can help us."

"It'll put a whole day or more on everything," William protests.

"Could be," Henry says. "But if it's safer, it's worth it."

CHAPTER SIXTY-FOUR

SEARCHERS

ADAM IS NERVOUS AND SWEATING FAR MORE THAN THE day's heat warrants. Still on a Kentucky winding road hugging the Ohio River, he rides up to William and reminds him, "Better start calling me Mister McClure from here on."

Adam, William, and Henry proceed as the road veers away from the river and the countryside becomes hillier. They ride past large farmhouses surrounded by shade trees and see tiny figures of workers toiling in distant fields. Near the crossroads village of Minerva they spot four horsemen ahead in the road. They watch as the men linger, move on a ways, and then linger again. Two of them carry rifles reflecting the sunlight.

"They're looking for something," Adam says.

William halts his horse. But Henry motions him forward again and tells Adam, "You talk to them."

"How do, sir," one says to Adam with a noticeable slur. "Been on this road long?"

"Five miles maybe."

"As for us, we're looking for coloreds run away from a farm five miles from here. Back same direction you came from."

"When did they escape?" Adam asks.

"Escape?" The man looks hard at Adam. "They wasn't in jail. I said they was at a farm and run off."

"So you did." Adam responds. "I assure you that neither I nor my own coloreds here have seen anything. When did you say they ran away?"

"Afore light."

"And how many again?"

"Three bucks and two wenches."

"I surely doubt they made it this far on foot."

"Hey, Mister, can I ask where you're from?"

Adam is suddenly unsteady, weak with fear. "Nicholas County, Virginia. West part of the state. My name is Lucas McClure."

"Didn't think you was from here."

"Well, men, good luck finding those fugitives," Adam says as firmly as he can. "I'm here to buy a few more coloreds myself. So maybe I'll find those runaways before you do and I'll come out way ahead on this deal." He smiles and tips his hat to the men.

The men laugh and one chimes in, "Go ahead and take the Africans if you find them but don't go taking our reward or we'll track you down for sure."

"Wouldn't dream of it." Adam nudges his horse forward and looks back at Henry and William. "Come along, boys."

They reach the village of Minerva with the sun just above the western horizon. A half-dozen men and boys on lathered horses are charging up and down the main road and brandishing firearms above their heads. Henry rides alongside Adam to guide him and William to a smithy next to a livery. They dismount as the black-smith emerges from the dark interior. He's a large black man with huge arms and a scorched leather apron covering the front of his body. He carries an armful of iron rods.

"Zebulon," Henry says as he hitches his horse, "why all these men got guns? Is it the runaways?"

"Ain't seen you in a while, Henry," the smith answers with a grin. The men all move inside where the fire in the forge joins with the heat of the evening to make the small shop unbearable. Piles of unfinished horseshoes clutter the ground and a nearby workbench is piled high with hammers and tongs. The blacksmith drops the iron rods at the base of the forge. "Some slaves run off from the Anderson farm near here," he says as he wipes sweat from his round face. "That's about all the hands Mister Anderson had. So all these fellows been deputy-ed to find them."

"Did you know they was going to run?" Henry asks.

"Nope. I believe it just sort of happened."

Henry moves closer to Zebulon and pulls William with him. "This man here been down on a farm by Mays Lick and ran with his family. Hunters got his family at the river and now we going down there to get them back."

"And him?" Zebulon gestures toward Adam.

"He's saying he's our owner so we don't have to be hiding all the time."

"You'd best be hiding anyway," Zebulon says with narrowed eyes. "This ain't no time for black folk to be on the road—white master or no. These men been drinking and yelling and galloping around here all day on excuse of those runaways. They just keep waving those guns. Word is Mister Anderson put up a couple hundred dollars to get his slaves back and these men's liable to stop anybody for anything. Heed what I'm telling you, Henry."

Henry shields his eyes from the low sun. "We headed toward Germantown. Maybe we should get off the road and put up around here."

"You don't want to be out on the road this night, that's for sure." The blacksmith points south. "Go that way two miles and there's an old inn. Man name of Raleigh will let you sleep."

Henry puts his hand on the big man's shoulder.

"What about you, Zebulon? We got the boat all ready. You could be in Ohio by Monday. I'm sure they need smiths up in Canada."

"Not this time. I told you before."

"And I'll keep asking."

They leave the blacksmith and turn their horses in the direction of the inn. Along the way, Adam asks Henry, "Why wouldn't your friend just cross the river himself if he wants to move north?"

"You think Zebulon's free? He ain't. An old man owns him—owned Zebulon's pa before him—and that old man takes the money from the smithing and gives Zebulon a bit back for his family. Zebulon got a woman and some little ones and his pa is still around. He'd just as soon stay as that old man's property as leave his family behind. And them's too many to take with him anyway. That's what he tells me."

They come upon a rambling structure with shutters askew and a crooked "Inn" sign. "Me and William be out here," Henry tells Adam. "You say you got two slaves need somewhere to sleep. If they say we can't stay, you just keep in mind that you a Virginia man. Do what they say and don't be making trouble."

Adam finds the inn's owner to be a stooped man with a silver mustache drooping crookedly at the sides of his mouth. "Pleased to have you," Raleigh says as he watches Adam sign the McClure name in the register. "You're upstairs on the left and your hands can stay in the shed off the back of the house. My boy will show them."

"I pay for two rooms?" Adam asks.

"Course not." Raleigh eyes Adam with amusement. "This ain't Virginia. You just pay for your room. I just was telling you where your darkies can sleep."

"I understand that," Adam says with an attempt to chuckle. "It's just that we've come across some innkeepers not as fair as you, sir." He tips his hat and swats a mosquito as he heads up the warped stairs in search of his room.

CHAPTER SIXTY-FIVE

SUSPICION

DAWN'S PALE LIGHT STRIKES THE WINDOW OF HIS ROOM in the old inn as Adam quickly dresses and goes outside to find Henry and William. He raps on a door hanging crookedly on a lean-to tacked onto the back of the inn. Henry opens the door—shirtless, eyes red with fatigue—while behind him William is curled up on a torn mattress with blackened straw poking out. Adam waves away the stench of urine and rot that floats from the hovel.

"Good Lord, Henry, couldn't you find someplace better?"

"No place else so we bedded down in this shithole," Henry tells him. "Tried to sleep with the door open, but critters kept coming in so we had to shut it."

They leave the inn as soon as Henry and William have washed at the well and saddled the horses. There's no traffic on the road to Germantown at this early hour of the Sabbath. Heading south, the land becomes flatter and the fields larger, though drought has marred acre after acre with cracked soil and shriveled crops. As they ride, they devour hunks of bread from the loaf Sarah packed.

They travel seven miles to Germantown, where they see carriages hitched in front of a brick church and a throng of people wearing Sunday clothes. A few slaves standing near the hitching rails stare at Henry and William on horseback. The three men continue, Adam leading, to the far edge of town, where a man steps abruptly from the wooden sidewalk into the road in front of them.

Adam tries to steer his horse around the man, who holds up his hand and says, "A word, please." He wears a black frock coat and a tall-crowned beaver hat that adds to his already substantial height.

Adam's stallion dances nervously in front of the man.

"Step over here," the man orders and points to the nearest hitching post.

"May I ask why?" Adam says from his saddle.

The man pulls back the lapel of his coat to reveal a badge pinned to his vest.

"I'm VanArman. Deputy sheriff here. I need a word."

Adam is wary of the lawman, but he swings down from the saddle. The deputy towers over him and Adam sees his threadbare clothing and a Colt holstered on his hip. VanArman squints at Adam and then turns to the two black men.

"And who might you all be?"

"Lucas McClure from Nicholas County in Virginia."

"I know Nicholas County. My wife's got kin near there, around Charleston. Nice country."

"Yes, it is," Adam says.

"Traveling through?"

Adam removes his hat and wipes its sweatband with his handkerchief. "I came to Maysville with my main driver—that's Henry there—to purchase that other colored. We're going back home now."

"Maysville's that way," VanArman says and jerks his thumb toward the east. "Not the way you're headed."

"We've got some idle time so I thought we'd—"

"Why'd you come all this way to buy one buck, if you don't mind me asking? Seems there'd be a thousand of them for sale between here and Nicholas County." The lawman purses his lips and studies Adam more closely.

"It's a long story," Adam replies.

"I got time."

"Well, I don't, I'm sorry to say." Adam puts his hat back on his head. "I'd hoped to cover quite a bit of ground today. May I ask why you stopped me in the first place? We've done nothing wrong, bothered no one."

"Thing is, we've had a fair number of hands running off lately. Especially with this damn drought. I got a farm myself with a few bucks. Some of us think there's abolitionists down here giving our coloreds a helping hand."

"So why stop me?" Adam repeats. "I've got slaves of my own and don't cotton to abolitionists. And sure as God's in his heaven I wouldn't be stealing your coloreds. I've no need to."

"Look at it from my view," VanArman says. "Here you are coming through town—a stranger with two healthy bucks. Given a certain political persuasion, you might be inclined to no good."

"Well, Deputy, I hope I've convinced you of my intentions," Adam says as he puts his foot in the stirrup and grabs the pommel to pull himself up.

"Hold on," VanArman says. "You said you just bought that buck."

"Yes, that's what I said."

"Then showing me his papers shouldn't be a problem."

"Actually, it is a problem," Adam says. He removes his hat again while he collects his thoughts. "So here's my paper for Henry." He hands VanArman the creased certificate of sale from his vest pocket.

VanArman studies the certificate and holds it up to the sky. He refolds it and hands it back to Adam.

"But that's not the one I'm asking about." He points to William. "Where's his papers?"

"That's the long story." Adam senses the lawman is losing patience while his own throat is parched with nervousness. "I won him. His name's William and I won him in a bet. Truth is, I don't have any papers for him. Not yet."

"Well, when?"

"When I get back to Nicholas County." He replaces his hat. "William's part of a gambling debt from a fellow back home. I won him there, but he was here in Kentucky. In Maysville. He'd been loaned out."

"For what?"

"Well …."

"Carpenter work," William calls from his saddle with voice shaking. "My old master—he had me build a new office for a judge. Made his bookshelves and cabinets and all. I got a good name back home for building things."

"That's right," Adam adds. "So I came to Maysville to pick him up and take him back with me. His papers are waiting for me in Nicholas County. So everything's square, as the carpenter would say." He leans closer to VanArman. "You'll have to trust me when I say I got a damn good deal on this buck."

VanArman lifts his tall hat and he too wipes his forehead with his coat sleeve. "Must be you did to make you come all this way."

Adam again puts his foot in the stirrup and pulls himself onto the saddle. He turns the horse toward the road and looks down at VanArman. The deputy frowns and then waves the three men away with a flutter of his hand.

They ride another hundred yards with Adam in the lead before any of them says a word.

"Good thinking back there, Mister McClure," Henry says as he comes alongside Adam.

"Let's just get the hell away from here," Adam mutters and kicks his horse to a gallop.

CHAPTER SIXTY-SIX

CLOSER

THE NARROW ROAD OUT OF GERMANTOWN CLIMBS
steeply then dips precariously and then climbs again in an unending
series of twists and turns. A dozen miles later William looks around
from his stallion's saddle and shouts, "I know this land!" He kicks his
horse fiercely and the animal lunges ahead and nearly tosses him off.

A couple hundred yards farther Adam and Henry catch up with
him and yell, "Whoa, stop!" They all dismount with dust stuck to
their faces. Henry angrily grabs William's arm. "You want to find your
family?" he growls. "Then you stop stampeding around this country
like some fool. Somebody sure to spot us. That what you want?"

William hangs his head and takes the canteen Adam hands him.

Finally Henry calms down enough to ask, "So you know where
we are?"

"That preacher that helped us. His place is close."

They rest a while longer in the stillness of the afternoon, watching a flock of sheep drink from a shrunken stream. Henry decides
they should ride overland for the next few miles. They mount up and
begin picking their way slowly across several pastures. They veer in

wide arcs away from farmhouses and barns. A while later they reach a swath of forest and walk the horses through the woods until they reach another road where William suddenly becomes excited again and yells to Henry, "This is the preacher's road!"

"Which way?" Henry asks.

William points and they ride south for another half-mile and then spot the big barn with the painted cross on its side. They dismount and hide in a thicket across the road. Henry tells Adam to ride up to the barn and circle it and then ride farther down the road. "Anyone watching the barn will want to find out what you doing," he says. "We'll know if anyone's keeping an eye on this place."

Adam steps away from the thicket and swings himself up onto the saddle and nudges his horse across the road toward the barn.

Still concealed in the bushes, Henry puts his hand on William's shoulder and says, "William, you got to keep hold of yourself. I know this ain't easy. But we this close"—he holds his thumb and index finger an inch apart—"we this close to finding out about your people. You hear me, William?"

William nods and crouches lower.

Adam steers his horse toward the rear of the barn and then circles it. Coming around to the front of the barn, he stops his horse and removes his hat to wipe his forehead with his shirtsleeve. He drinks from his canteen. He turns his horse and rides slowly around the barn again. Then he rides back to the road and away from where Henry and William are hiding. He nudges his horse to a trot and disappears down the road.

"Either nobody's watching that place or they don't care about that man," Henry says.

William and Henry watch the road for Adam's return. They swat at the insects and drink the remaining water in their canteens. Shadows of the trees stretch across the road as the sun drops lower.

"Where's he gone?" William asks without averting his eyes from the road. "You suppose he got caught down the road someplace?"

The shadows of the trees have reached the far side of the road when Henry and William finally see two riders coming toward them at an unhurried pace. "Looks like he got the preacher with him," William says as he cranes to see through the brush. "Don't that look like a man on a mule?"

The two riders part by the barn. Reverend Shem rides toward his stable. Adam rides to where William and Henry are hiding and then dismounts.

"What'd he tell you? What'd he say?" William asks as he bounds onto the road.

"He said he's got to look around, wants to make sure nobody's watching his place. He'll come out to the road when it's safe." Adam points to the thicket. "We've got to keep hiding."

"You come back in here," Henry tells William.

"What about Nettie? The boys?" William demands. "What'd he say?"

Adam pulls his horse away from the road. "I didn't ask him, William. I didn't even tell him you were here. I just said I had two men who need his help on the underground."

William stares at Adam. "Why?" he asks. "Why didn't you tell him I'm here?"

Henry yanks William back from the road. "That close, remember?" He holds up his thumb and finger again. "You got to keep hold."

They wait several more minutes in the fading light. Then they watch as the preacher walks to the center of the road and stands there.

"That's the signal," Adam says. "Now we can go."

Adam and Henry take the reins of their horses and step onto the road. The preacher motions for them to follow as he turns his back and walks back toward the barn.

William runs up behind the preacher.

"Reverend Shem," he calls out. "Reverend Shem, it's me—William."

The preacher stops and turns back slowly.

"William?"

William runs to the preacher and the two men embrace as Reverend Shem shouts, "Thank you, dear, sweet Lord!"

Then Henry and Adam watch the two men crying in each other's arms.

CHAPTER SIXTY-SEVEN

REPORT

THE PREACHER QUICKLY LEADS THE THREE MEN INTO his coop, where William collapses onto a wooden chair and wipes his eyes. "Nettie and my boys?" he gasps. "They at the farm?"

"They are, William, they are."

"They all right, his family?" Henry asks.

Reverend Shem holds up his hand and remains silent. He ignites the wick of an oil lamp, throwing a golden light over the men's faces. He sits down close to William and puts his hand on his arm.

"William, you must listen to all I have to tell you," the preacher says calmly. "I figure you intend to get Nettie and the boys and go back across that river. For you to be able to do that, you must understand what's happened at the farm. You must understand everything."

William stares at the preacher. "What is it, Reverend Shem?"

"Richard's gone. He's been sold."

William does not move and does not change expression. He continues staring at the preacher as if time has stopped.

"Richard and Reuben," Reverend Shem goes on. "They started some trouble at the farm and they ran away."

"Sold?"

"Leyden's men must have figured they'd come here. So they kept watch on this place and the boys did show up. I saw those men grab both of them and carry them off."

"Nettie know?"

"She knows."

"Dear God," William says and lowers his head.

"Leyden must have sold them right away because the boys never made it back to the farm. Nobody knows where they are."

"Richard was why—"

"I know, William."

William takes a deep breath and then asks, "Nettie?"

"She's at the farm with the other two boys and has been since the slave catchers brought them back. They must've come straight back because they were at the farm just a couple of days after I last saw you." Reverend Shem wipes his forehead with the back of his hand. "It hasn't been good for her, William. She's suffered greatly."

"They beat her?" William asks, clenching his fists in his lap.

"Not as far as I know. But it's been terrible work. Leyden's been trying to save his crop by having his hands water all those acres. He's made Nettie carry water under a heavy yoke up and down the rows all day long. It's broken her."

William moans. "She hurt bad?"

"I saw her this morning when I preached there. She comes to worship and that's a good sign. But I can tell she's been worked near to death."

William stares at the lamp's sooty chimney.

"My boys?" he asks.

"They're with her. Everybody's been worked hard and those two boys have done their share. But they're all right."

"And not sold—yet."

Reverend Shem tells the three men that all of the Leyden slaves are concerned about being sold, same as all slaves through-out Kentucky. Drought has ruined the crops, and farmers fear the coming cash shortage. More slaves are being sold every day. Traders from Lexington and Louisville roam the countryside making deals.

Reverend Shem puts his hand on William's shoulder. "You need to know Nettie's been living with Willis."

"Willis and Ellen? What you saying?"

"Leyden put Willis and his family in your cabin and put Nettie and your boys in there, too. Ellen has passed on and Leyden ordered Nettie to stay there."

William shakes his head and thumps the table with his fist.

"William," the preacher tells him, "you've got to understand—to Nettie you're dead. And Lucy's dead. She thinks you're both at the bottom of the Ohio with your souls in the hereafter. And that thought has been more hurt to her than all the pain she's suffered in those fields."

CHAPTER SIXTY-EIGHT

ACTS

ON HER WAY TO THE HENHOUSE ANNE HEARS A BOY IN the barn shouting, "Get away! Get out, damn it!" She drops her egg basket and rushes into the barn, past the stalls, to find John standing with arms outstretched between a frightened cow and the pig named Hamlet. Tipped over at John's feet are the milking stool and the bucket with its warm milk seeping into the dirty straw.

"Damn pig!" John shouts.

"Your mother wouldn't like your language, Johnny."

"Ma won't like this spilled milk!"

Something moves behind Anne and she hears a man's voice, "Then we won't tell her."

She spins to see Simon walking toward her.

"Uncle Si!" The boy runs to Simon and nearly knocks him over.

"You're getting too big for this, Johnny," Simon says as he staggers backward. He regains his balance and smiles at Anne. "Good morning."

At that moment the big pig bumps against Anne and her legs collapse. She tries to catch herself but slips in the puddle of milk.

She topples and then rolls beneath the cow as the commotion sends Hamlet scurrying.

Simon rushes to Anne and crawls beneath the cow. He protectively wraps his arms around her. "Are you hurt?" he asks and bumps his head against the cow's swollen udder.

Anne looks up at the teats dangling on Simon's head and begins to giggle. She feels his arms around her and she laughs until tears run down her face. Then her laughter turns to sobs that wrack her body. She buries her face against his chest to muffle her cries. The misery she has endured silently for a week pours out in wrenching gasps as her grief crests like a fever breaking.

"Just cry, Anne, just cry," he tells her. He slides out from beneath the cow and pulls her with him. For several minutes they sit together in the straw, his arm around her until her crying subsides.

Anne raises her hands to her face to hide her swollen eyes. "I'm so sorry."

"No need," he says and gently brushes straw from her hair.

She stands and straightens her dress and apron. "Oh, dear. I hadn't really cried since Jacob—"

He nods. "I heard."

She lifts her apron and wipes her face. "I'll be all right."

Soon they join Hannah in the kitchen as she stirs a kettle of oatmeal. Simon tells her he hopes to spend a few days at the farm, and Hannah replies, "That'd be wonderful."

"Adam gone into Buford?"

"He's in Kentucky, Simon. He went there to rescue some slaves."

Simon's brow furrows. "What are you saying?"

Hannah tells him about Henry Blanchard and the fugitive man and his child who traveled to the Blanchard farm and how Henry had asked for Adam's help in trying to find the man's family.

Simon still is baffled. "He went along just because this fellow Blanchard asked him to? That doesn't sound like Adam."

"I didn't want him to go, Simon. It's much too dangerous. But he insisted it was something he had to do. There was no talking him out of it." Her voice drops to a whisper. "He's been gone two days and I'm so worried."

Anne pauses as she helps clear the dishes after the morning meal. "Isn't today the sewing circle?" she asks Hannah.

"It is," Hannah answers. "But I didn't think you'd feel ready to go yet."

"But the clothing," Anne says. "We have those baskets at the church and we need to get them to Sarah Blanchard. I was thinking perhaps Simon would come with me."

"Certainly," he says with a shrug.

"What on earth is Simon going to say to the likes of Mary Franklin or Eleanor Crowley?" Hannah wonders aloud. "They've made their feelings about abolitionists clear."

Anne sighs. "I suppose you're right. It's probably a bad idea."

"Quite the contrary. It'd be a pleasure," Simon says, grinning. "It's been awhile since I was part of a sewing circle."

Within an hour they've hitched Simon's horse to the buggy for the trip to Buford. Leaving the Porter farm, Anne keeps her eyes on the road but says to Simon, "You helped me this morning and I want to thank you for it."

"I feel badly about what you're going through. I'm glad I could help in some way."

"I haven't told this to anyone, but I believe Jacob was killed because we tried to help those runaway slaves," Anne says. "There's an awful man around here who hunts fugitive slaves. His name is Klemmer and I believe he's responsible for the fire that killed Jacob. That's how these slave catchers frighten people against helping the fugitives, by setting fire to barns and stables and maybe even people's homes. Klemmer did it to Wendell Childress and it was just a few days later when the Popes' stable caught fire."

"Why haven't you said anything to the sheriff or somebody?"

"Because I can't prove it. And I'm sure I'm not the only one who's suspicious of Klemmer anyway. But nobody will do a thing to stop him. Why would they? We all know the law's on the side of the slave hunters, and the people helping the runaways are the criminals."

"My dear, you have our sympathy," Elizabeth Rumsford says as Anne enters the little room at the rear of the Methodist church. "I know you were so fond of the Pope boy."

Anne nods and then introduces Simon to the five women of the sewing circle, telling them she and Simon want to pick up the clothing collected for fugitive slaves. She walks to the closet where the baskets have been stored. "It's good of all of you to do this."

Mary Franklin steps close to her and asks, "You won't be telling anybody where these clothes came from, will you? My husband wouldn't tolerate it."

"No, Mary, nobody will know where the clothes came from."

Eleanor Crowley—her ruddy face now even redder with sunburn—glares at Simon. "You the one Anne and Hannah talk about? The one from Boston who runs with Garrison and his abolitionists?"

"I'm actually from Ohio," he says, smiling. "But, yes, I've been in Boston a couple of years now with the Anti-Slavery Society."

"This ain't Boston," the woman snaps and goes back to her sewing.

"I realize that," Simon responds. "I know some people around here don't agree with our beliefs."

"Well, my name's Eleanor Crowley and—"

"My pleasure."

"—and there's a whole lot of people around here who feel you abolitionists are tearing the country apart."

"I'm aware."

"Fanatics," she persists. "We even heard your friend Garrison used Independence Day to burn a copy of the Constitution in public.

That makes him a traitor in my book along with that crowd of his traitor friends who cheered when he did it."

Anne spoke up. "Eleanor, this isn't the time or place—"

"No, it's all right," Simon interrupts. He sits in an empty chair next to Elizabeth Rumsford and reaches out to hold a bolt of blue-checked gingham while Abby Dillon cuts the cloth with her scissors. "Let me tell you what happened that day and then you make up your minds. With your permission, of course."

"We'd like to hear, yes," says the widow Rumsford.

Simon spends the next several minutes recounting for the women how the scene unfolded at the 1854 annual Independence Day meeting of the American Anti-Slavery Society at a park twenty miles from Boston. He describes the long list of speakers and the mid-afternoon temperature above a hundred degrees. He tells them how the large crowd fanned themselves in anticipation of hearing Garrison, the controversial abolitionist leader.

"I can describe what happened with some accuracy because I was there," he tells the women. "So, yes, Garrison finally stepped up to the podium—I beg you to trust me on this—and he praised the virtues of America. He spoke of America's great influence for eighty years now and how this country is an example to people everywhere who love liberty."

"How comforting," Eleanor Crowley blurts with evident sarcasm.

"Please go on," the widow tells Simon.

"So Garrison held up a sheet of paper and told the crowd it was the Fugitive Slave Law. Before we realized what he was doing, he'd set fire to it. And as it turned to ash, he called out, 'And let all the people say Amen.' And everyone within earshot shouted 'Amen' like it was a revival. Then he held up another document and said it was a copy of the judge's ruling ordering the fugitive Anthony Burns to be taken from Boston back to Virginia. He set fire to that one too. The people were still cheering when he held up a copy of the Constitution. When he announced what it was, everyone grew quiet. He said our Constitution had become—and I quote—'a covenant with Death and an agreement with Hell.' Then he set it on fire and shouted, 'So perish all compromises with tyranny.'"

Eleanor Crowley nods. "So it's true."

"Yes, it's true. Garrison burned the Constitution."

"What about the crowd?" Abby Dillon asks. "Did they really cheer?"

"I admit many did. But there were others who hissed at him and shouted out against him."

"And you?" the widow asks, looking up from her sewing. "Did you cheer?"

"No, I did not," Simon answers. "But I'll tell you honestly that I agree with what Garrison said. I too fear what America is becoming in the eyes of the world. I believe most of us aren't even aware of the evil that's consuming our country and is costing us the respect of civilized countries everywhere."

Mary Franklin looks at Anne. "What about you? You've certainly suffered as a result of all of this slavery trouble. What do you think?"

"I don't know about all the speeches and burning pieces of paper." Anne lifts up one of the baskets of clothes. "But this is what matters. It's through kindness and charity such as what you've done here that will make it so we can live together in peace. I know that each of you—regardless of how you feel about slavery and the laws protecting it—each one of you brought some clothing to help these unfortunate people. Now I don't know my Bible as well as any of you do, but I know that this is what Jesus was talking about when he said to help the least of our brothers and sisters. That much I do know."

Then Anne and Simon carry the three baskets of clothing to the buggy.

"That was a beautiful thing you said in there, Anne. You helped them feel good about what they've done. I'm very proud of you."

Anne ties on her bonnet to hide the blush rising in her cheeks.

CHAPTER SIXTY-NINE

SLAVEHOLDERS

ADAM PULLS HIMSELF ONTO THE STALLION'S SADDLE and stares at the morning sky to calm himself. Henry and William stand on one side of him and Reverend Shem on the other, all of them behind the barn and hidden from the road.

"It's all in your hands now," Henry tells him.

"Make him believe you," William says.

Their statements—intended to be encouraging—only make Adam breathe more rapidly. The four of them have devised a plan where Adam will go to Philip Leyden's farm this morning and approach Leyden as a fellow slaveholder. Adam knows their whole purpose for being here in Kentucky and trying to make contact with Nettie now depends on convincing Leyden of that lie.

"Trust in the Lord," Reverend Shem shouts after Adam as he nudges his horse forward. "Trust!"

The tree leaves overhead already are limp from the morning heat as Adam rides along and rehearses his speech to entice Philip Leyden to let him get close to Nettie. An hour later, despite his planning and rehearsing, Adam reaches the Leyden farm with no more confidence than he felt when he left the preacher's barn.

He rides slowly up the lane and sees to his right a scattering of four small cabins and a couple of slaves hammering siding onto a larger, new building. Before him are three barns and a pigpen and fields stretching to the horizon. To his left sits the Leyden house on a bluff a hundred yards away, large and solid with its broad front porch and the sun reflecting blindingly off its white paint. A servant girl wearing a light blue apron and cap and carrying a large basket stands beside the summer kitchen. She watches Adam as he approaches, one hand above her eyes to block the sun's glare. He dismounts and hitches his horse and then notices the girl is gone.

Adam stands beside his horse to collect himself. He takes off his hat to brush away the dust and then brushes still more dust from his vest and trousers. He straightens his clothing and glances again at the sky and then walks onto the front porch and raps on the door. A moment later the door opens. It's the same servant girl he'd seen moments earlier in her blue apron and cap, now standing in front of him.

"Is this the home of Philip Leyden?"

She answers, "Yes," and draws out the word as her eyes narrow.

"I'd like to see him. I have a matter to discuss."

He hears a woman's voice in the hallway behind the girl. "Martha, who's there? Is someone at the door?" The woman appears behind the servant and assesses Adam's appearance. "I'm Grace Leyden. Can I help you?"

Adam introduces himself as Lucas McClure of Nicholas County, Virginia. He tells her he's been searching for owners interested in selling slaves and was given her husband's name in Maysville.

"I'm afraid I don't know," she answers and seems bewildered. "I suppose it's possible. Let me see if my husband will talk with you." She steps away from the door. "Martha, please show Mister McClure to the parlor."

Adam walks into the entryway and smiles at the girl. William had described Martha to him, telling of her encounter with the man named Thomas and then her wielding the rifle to protect him at the Pike house in Maysville. In this hallway, without saying a word, she does nothing to conceal her dislike for Adam.

With a flick of her wrist, she gestures toward a sofa in the parlor, where Adam is to sit and wait. She mutters something under her breath and then leaves him. Adam notes the heavy draperies on the two southerly windows blocking the sun and giving the parlor a somber mood. White linen doilies rest on well-oiled tabletops, and an intricate Persian rug covers much of the wood floor. Three oil paintings decorate the walls, two depicting Jesus and the third a mountain stream. He realizes this room could just as easily be in Cleveland or Boston as in the home of a Kentucky slaveholder.

Several minutes pass and Adam wonders if his presence has been forgotten. Then Grace Leyden returns. "I apologize for keeping you waiting, Mister McClure. My husband was indisposed but will receive you now."

Adam follows her down the hallway until they reach a doorway where Grace steps aside.

"Mister McClure, please come in," Leyden says as he rises from his chair behind a large desk stacked with papers. He holds out his hand and introduces himself. Adam notices that they are dressed nearly identically—white linen shirts, dark vests, tan trousers— though Leyden's clothes are immaculate and of higher quality.

"My wife tells me you're seeking to buy chattel and were given my name," Leyden says as he resumes his seat behind the desk. "May I ask by whom?"

"I can't say for sure." Adam's mind races for an explanation. "I was talking with a group of men in Maysville and I asked if they knew planters who might want to sell their hands and they started giving me names one after the other. I was writing them down and didn't see who gave me each one."

Leyden smiles. "Well, whoever it was has the gift of prophecy. The idea of selling more of my hands occurred to me only yesterday in earnest. Please, have a seat."

Adam figures this is the room William built for Leyden. He can see the mastery in the joinery, the well-proportioned cabinets and bookcases, how the wainscoting mates perfectly with the room's trim in every corner. He realizes he has underestimated William's carpentry skills.

"Tell me, Mister McClure, have you been a slaveholder long?"

Adam sits upright in the chair. "It seems like forever."

"I know the feeling. I certainly do," Leyden says. "So why are you looking for slaves here in Kentucky, seeing that you're from Virginia? I take it you're expanding your holdings?" Before Adam can respond, Leyden goes on. "I don't intend to intrude into your personal matters, Mister McClure, but I—"

"Please just call me Lucas."

"A good strong name." Leyden relaxes back into his chair. "No, I don't want to sound like an inquisitor. We can get to the business at hand in a moment. But I beg your indulgence."

"Concerning?"

"I've been doing considerable thinking about economic considerations. I'm trying to foresee what the future holds for people like you and me. I seek perspective and the best way I can get it is by exchanging thoughts with gentlemen such as yourself."

"I don't know if I'm up to an exchange of ideas."

"We shall see." Then Leyden tells Adam of his discussions with bankers and businessmen in New Jersey. "These men had energy like the wheels of a locomotive," he says and makes pumping motions with his arms like the coupling rods on the wheels of a steam engine. "Action, power, speed, commerce, profit. Industry is everything and growth is the fuel, always more growth."

"Yankees do seem obsessed with making money," Adam interjects with a smile.

"To be sure, Lucas, to be sure. And when I returned home, I honestly felt the absence of all of that drive. Instead of simply settling back on my land and enjoying the quiet life, I felt consumed by a foreboding—a sense of threat. Can you understand what I'm talking about?"

"Please go on." He sees Leyden becoming more comfortable with him.

"I fear we southern planters are at risk of being swallowed up by our northern neighbors. It may seem unimaginable, but one day our way of life could be devoured by their manufacturing power."

"Unlikely, I'd say. We have our cotton and our tobacco. We produce huge amounts of wealth with cotton alone. With wealth comes power. You and I both know, Philip, that we planters are the economic strength of this country. Everything is secondary to cotton."

"But for how long? Look at this matter of slavery." Leyden leans forward with his elbows on his desk. "That's what I want to discuss with you, Lucas. This is where I want to hear your thoughts."

"We've just met," Adam says. "For all you know, my thoughts could be worth absolutely nothing."

"Never," Leyden counters. "You're a fellow landowner and an agriculturalist facing the same challenges as I. It's not that I would change my beliefs based on what you alone tell me. On the contrary, I take my guidance from the preponderance of facts and opinions I hear. That and from the good Lord, of course."

Adam feels sweat trickle down his back. "You're telling me a trip up north and a talk with a couple Yankee bankers have made you doubt your livelihood and your very heritage? Many more conversations like that and they'll turn you into a flaming abolitionist." He speaks rapidly to head off Leyden's objection. "And if that should happen, I can clear your conscience this very moment by taking your coloreds off your hands for a damn good price."

"Ha!" Leyden laughs and slaps his hand on his desk. "I bet you would, too."

Leyden rises and moves to the front of his desk, leaning against it a couple feet from Adam.

"I'm certain you're aware, Lucas, as I am, that the real growth in our economy is along the Mississippi delta where the cotton growers are pushing westward. There's an increasing demand for labor and those planters are willing to pay more per head."

"So I've heard. But I'm not certain I can match their price, if that's where you're going with this."

"No, no," Leyden says with a wave of his hand. "But I admit to giving serious thought to supplying coloreds to those planters."

"You don't appear to be a typical slave trader," Adam says with a grin.

"That's very astute, Lucas. I'm certainly not a slave trader in either practice or temperament. So let me ask you this. Who would you rather deal with, some scurrilous character who might peddle you stock that could be inferior or diseased or ill tempered? Or would you rather buy from someone with a reputation for selling good, strong, obedient chattel who have had some exposure to Christian values?"

"What's the price difference?"

Leyden suddenly claps his hands together. "Lucas, my friend, you have cut to the chase. That is precisely what I need to know. Would you be willing to pay more for higher quality stock? Is it really worth it to you?"

"There are times," Adam responds as he carefully selects his words. "Yes, there are times when I would pay a higher price. It would depend on a number of things. There are other times when I'd go for the best price I could get and I'd go to auction and hope the rain kept everybody else away." He tries to chuckle.

Leyden seems to ponder Adam's words. "These things you mention. What are they? You said you'd pay more depending on certain things?"

Adam knows he is visibly sweating. He hates this conversation. It's taking too long and he knows the longer they talk the greater the chance the ruse will be revealed.

"Maybe if I wanted someone suitable to be a driver. Maybe if I needed someone good with horses or a good carpenter or a good cook. It boils down to this: Why would I buy one buck or wench and not another. I buy what I'm looking for and I pay accordingly."

"You would pay more to find what you need."

"If I had the assurance I was getting what I want, then he or she is worth the higher price to me. Of course."

"I'll tell you what this means to me," Leyden continues as if thinking aloud. "I've got to establish a reputation as a discerning seller you can trust. Planters who want just brutes can buy them anywhere. But when they need—"

"I see your scheme here."

"Excuse me?"

Adam leans back in his chair. "You're setting an elaborate stage for me to pay top dollar for whatever slaves you're willing to sell me." He wags his finger at Leyden. "I've got to say you're far cleverer than any trader I've ever met."

Leyden bursts into laughter. "No, no. I'm not that devious. Not yet, anyway." He takes a moment to collect himself. "I've no intention of becoming a run-of-the-mill trader or breeder. My wife wouldn't stand for it. But I know there's a way to provide chattel that's in keeping with the rules of successful property exchange. I must say, you've been most helpful, Lucas. Much more than you probably realize."

Adam draws his handkerchief from his pocket and pats his forehead. "You say you have hands to sell?"

"Ah, yes, to the matter at hand," Leyden says. "Let me tell you the situation and then you decide if you're interested."

Adam feels his tension mounting as Leyden long-windedly recites his philosophy of slave ownership: his preference that his slaves live as families, the Christian guidance in humility and obedience he provides. He explains that he rarely beats a slave. "Of course, to be consistent with all of this, I'd never sold a slave. Never until a few weeks ago."

"That's remarkable," Adam says. "Why the change?"

"To see how my plan might work. You could call it practice. I bought some slaves at auction. I sold them to a man representing a consortium of planters and made a decent profit in the process."

"Now you have others?"

"This is different." Leyden crosses his arms over his chest. "Just look around at this room."

"I have. It's a fine room."

"One of my slaves had a gift for woodworking. He built this room for me just a few weeks ago."

"I know something about carpentry myself and I can tell you he's done a good job. How much would you want for him?"

"Bear with me," Leyden goes on. "The woman this man lived with was my wife's maidservant. My point is, this couple had good positions here with good futures."

"Had?"

"They ran off. Took their children and one of my other girls and headed off to Ohio. I've never had that happen in the twenty-nine years I've owned this farm. They got it in their heads I was going to sell one of their boys."

"Were you?"

"If the truth be known, I'd considered it. The boy was running with a pack of rascals and giving us fits."

"So now they're gone?"

"By some stroke of luck a patrol nabbed them on the Ohio shore. Unfortunately for the fellow who built this room, he and his daughter drowned."

"He should have stayed put."

"Very true. We got the woman and her sons back, along with the other servant girl. As you can well understand, I needed to make an example of them. So I put the woman to work in the fields. It's extremely hard work for a former house servant."

"Are you going to bring her back to the house to work?"

"That's the point. My wife and I—especially my wife—feel deeply betrayed by this woman, considering all Grace had done for her. As things now stand, Grace doesn't even want to set eyes on her."

"So you're selling her?"

"If you're interested."

"You say she has sons?"

"She had three but I sold the one a few days ago. The other two are quite young."

Adam pauses to weigh the situation and then says, "Yes, I'd like to examine her. And the boys, too. Then we can talk price." He stands up and faces Leyden. "If we can agree, I'll take them tomorrow morning."

Leyden clasps Adam's shoulder. "I started out asking for your indulgence and you've been most gracious and informative. I thank you, Lucas, for sharing your thoughts with me."

"Well, time's flying, Philip. Can I see her now?"

"Of course," Leyden says as he walks toward the hallway. "Of course you can."

CHAPTER SEVENTY

REVELATION

NETTIE UPROOTS SOME PIGWEED NEAR A BEANPOLE with her hoe and looks up to see Bobby Hill barking commands as he approaches. "You—all three of you." He gestures at Alfred and Dan working nearby in the beet rows. "You come with me." He flaps his hat to swat flies away from his face.

"My boys, too?"

"That's what I said."

Alfred and Dan drop their handfuls of weeds.

"Where?" Alfred wants to know.

"Just come like Mister Hill says." Nettie brushes dirt from the boy's ragged pants.

Bobby Hill leads them past the hog pens to the toolshed near the house.

"Wait in there."

Nettie takes hold of the boys' hands and steps into the shed. It's stifling and dim, with cobwebs hanging thickly from the rafters like decayed drapes. She shudders at the sight of the heavy wooden tool chest William so often used. Alfred and Dan stray farther into the shed till there's a loud clatter and Nettie calls out, "What you boys doing?"

She looks deep into the shadows—dust floating upward through the thin shafts of sunlight—to where the boys have overturned a stack of tobacco baskets. She senses something and turns suddenly to see three men standing near the shed door. She recognizes Bobby Hill and Philip Leyden with a man she doesn't know.

"Boys, come back here." She keeps her eyes lowered.

"This is Nettie," Leyden tells the stranger. "Nettie and her boys."

The stranger bends down toward Alfred.

"These boys—how old are they?"

No one answers and the man looks at Nettie.

"How old?"

"He's my second oldest." She shoots a pained look at Leyden. "He's eight." She rests her hand on Dan's head. "And this one, he's near six."

"Good," the man says. Then he turns to Leyden and asks, "You're sure these are healthy stock?"

Nettie suddenly throws her arms around both boys and pulls them close to her. "No!" she shouts at the stranger. "They all I got!"

The stranger looks again at Leyden. "You said her name is Nettie?"

Leyden nods.

The stranger turns to Nettie and removes his hat. "Nettie, my name is Lucas McClure and I own a farm in Virginia. I'm here to buy servants and—"

"No!" she cries out. "Not my boys!"

She pushes past the stranger—still clutching both boys to her—and falls to her knees in front of Leyden. "Please, sir, don't sell my boys to this man. Please!"

"Stop it," Leyden orders. "Just stop your yelling and listen to him."

"Calm yourself, Nettie," the stranger says. "I have no intention of separating you from your boys. I'm interesting in buying—"

She looks at Leyden with tears welling up. "Why you going to sell us? You know I work real hard for you—me and my boys. We won't cause no more trouble."

"Having you here is no longer good for either of us." Leyden reaches down and puts his hand on her shoulder and she cowers at his touch. "Ever since you were brought back I've had to prove to the others that running away has its consequences. Do you understand me?"

"But I done the work, sir." She looks at the overseer. "Mister Hill, you tell him. I hauled that water till my back was broke."

Leyden gestures toward Adam. "Mister McClure here just told you he'll take both you and your boys. He'll keep you together. I'd say that's very fair."

Nettie struggles to think clearly. "You keep me and my boys together like Mister Leyden says?"

"That's what I'm trying to tell you," the stranger replies. "I'll keep you and your boys together and give you work in my home. Not in the fields."

"Sir, I pray to God you're a good man," she says and pulls her sons even closer.

The stranger steps back into the sunlight and motions for Leyden to join him. They talk in low tones, saying things Nettie cannot decipher.

Bobby Hill stands as a silhouette against the bright sunlight and bends close to Nettie. "Looks like you'll be moving on, assuming those two gentlemen can agree on a price." He grabs her arm and roughly pulls her to her feet. "This here's still more proof that your little idea to run off has turned out different than you thought. You lost your baby girl. You lost William."

"Don't say these things, Mister Hill. Please." Her tears again fill her eyes.

"And Virginia is mighty hard slave country," the overseer goes on. "They don't tolerate uppity behavior there. Not one bit. They whip you till you got no skin left. You misbehave and they'll cut off your hands. You try to run away and they'll—"

She clamps her hands over Dan's ears. "Stop."

"They'll burn off your legs. One leg at a time. They cut out your pink tongue for lying. Maybe poke out an eye just for looking wrong at your master." He leans close to Alfred. "You hear me, boy? That's going to be your new home."

The stranger comes up behind Bobby Hill. "What are you telling them? What were you saying to that boy?"

"About Virginia."

"Mister Hill," the stranger says with visible anger. "I am a Virginian and we are not monsters. Like Mister Leyden, I want my property to feel safe and secure."

"Begging your pardon, but you'll find that treating them—"

"Mister Hill, I am not going to debate plantation management with you even though I have considerably more experience. Now go out there with your boss while I talk to Nettie."

Bobby Hill traipses to the yard to join Leyden.

The stranger comes up to Nettie, who's still on her knees. He takes her chin in his hand and moves her head one way and then the other. She tries to pull away. But his fingers tighten on her jaw.

"Open your mouth, Nettie," he whispers to her. "Open like you're showing me your teeth."

Slowly she bares her teeth.

"I'm with William. He's alive," the stranger tells her. He grips her jaw so tightly she can't move her head or speak. "We've come to take you and your boys away from here." He brings his face closer to hers. "Do you understand me? William is alive and so is your daughter."

Nettie wants to scream with joy but the man puts his other hand firmly over her mouth. Her jaw trembles in the man's grip and tears run down her face.

"Don't be afraid, Nettie. I'll be back tomorrow morning to get you and the boys. Do you understand what I'm telling you?"

He slowly releases her jaw and she reaches out to clasp both of his hands. She nods as her tears fall to the ground.

"What's he saying, Ma?" Alfred asks.

"He's saying we going to be all right, my boy," she sobs softly. "We going to be all right."

CHAPTER SEVENTY-ONE

READY

WILLIAM HOLDS THE REVOLVER CLOSE TO HIS FACE AND makes sure each cylinder is loaded. The sharp stench of gunpowder hangs in the air. Henry calls to him, "Now hit the tree one more time." William steadies his stance and points the gun and fires. The recoil knocks the Colt upward in his hands as a hunk of bark flies off the trunk of the nearby maple.

The sound of the shot reverberates across the meadow behind Reverend Shem's barn.

"You sure you know how to use that thing?" Henry asks. "If you got to shoot somebody, you do it with no second thought. Can you do that?"

"If I got to."

William squints into the sun and listens as Reverend Shem and Adam hitch two horses to a wagon. The preacher is asking if Philip Leyden haggled over the price Adam offered for Nettie and the boys. Adam says Leyden accepted a thousand dollars for Nettie and six hundred for each of the boys and seemed to be relieved things were settled so quickly.

The men finish fastening the harnesses. Without a pause, Henry announces, "It's time."

William shoves the revolver into his belt and mounts his horse. Henry gets into his saddle and looks down at Adam standing next to the wagon.

"We'll be there. Right close by. You just won't see us."

With that, William and Henry steer their stallions onto the road under a gray sheet of low-hanging clouds that muffle the horses' hoofbeats. The two men speak little for the next hour. Sweat has soaked their shirts by the time they reach the lane leading to Leyden's farm. They tie their horses to saplings several yards from the road and William leads Henry on foot through the trees. They sneak past the slave quarters where wisps of smoke hang motionless above the cabins.

"Where you think this'll happen?" Henry whispers as he pushes aside the brush.

"Don't know. Maybe close to that bell pole there," William says.

They drop to their knees and then to their bellies in the stiff grass. Thorny berry vines curl overhead and buzzing horseflies seek their sweaty skin. William draws the Colt from his belt and sets it in the grass near his head, making grasshoppers spring away.

"He should be coming now with the wagon."

"We got to wait," Henry says. Once again, he holds up his thumb and index finger—this time with only a sliver of space between them—"Now we this close."

Some time later they hear the wagon rolling slowly up the lane. They watch as Adam drives past the slave quarters and then past the bell pole and on toward the house, a distance from where William figured he would stop.

"No, no," William whispers in alarm. "Now we got to get up there, closer."

Both men study the groomed land where Adam has stopped the wagon.

"No place to hide up there," Henry says.

They watch Adam climb down from the driver's bench and walk toward the house. William grabs Henry's arm and tells him their only chance is to run in a wide arc in the open and then cut close to the house so they can hide beside the porch.

"Then we got to go now," Henry says.

William picks up his Colt and the two men run, crouching low and covering the ground as rapidly as they can. They make it across the front field and then stop to catch their breath before the final dash across the lawn.

They see Adam now standing on the porch near the front door.

"Now!" Henry orders. Together they rush to the side of the house and duck below the windows and then throw themselves on the ground next to the porch's foundation. William puts his hand over his mouth to muffle his gasps and waits for his heart to stop pounding. Henry lies close to him, his chest also rapidly rising and falling.

Moments later, William raises his head and looks between the porch-rail balusters. Adam is standing four feet away. Their eyes meet briefly and William sees the startled look in Adam's eyes just as the front door opens and Grace Leyden speaks.

"Mister McClure? Good morning to you."

"And to you, ma'am."

"Before you see my husband, I'd like a word." She steps onto the porch and closes the door behind her. "My, how uncommonly still the world is this morning." Then she turns to face Adam. "I know you're here to buy Nettie and her boys. My husband believes you're a man of good heart and you'll be reasonable with them. You'll keep Nettie and her sons together? Is my husband correct in that?"

"He is. I intend to provide a decent home for all of my hands. Like you and your husband, I've prided myself in having few runaways and I'm sorry to hear of your recent misfortune. I don't know what gets into these coloreds sometimes."

"How right you are, Mister McClure. Philip probably told you Nettie was my maidservant for years. I trusted her."

"And you've been hurt."

"So true. I can't take her back into the house and I can't bear to see her in the fields. Too much has gone on between us. I simply cannot bear the pain I see in her eyes."

"This is for the better."

Grace's words pierce William like nails driven into his heart.

"Thank you, Mister McClure." She moves to the door. "Now please come inside."

Right then, Philip Leyden appears in the doorway. "Grace, I didn't realize Lucas was here already."

"I was just talking with him about Nettie."

"Well, good morning to you," Leyden says, smiling. "We can be done with this quickly. I see you brought your wagon. Are you alone?"

"I am. I have shackles."

"Then come inside and we'll conclude this matter."

"I'd prefer to see them again first."

Leyden stops and turns in the doorway. "Excuse me?"

"I don't mean to be difficult, but I want to see the woman and the boys just one more time before I buy them," Adam tells him. "They've had the night to think about all of this and I want to know their frame of mind this morning."

"Looking for what, if you don't mind me asking?"

"It has nothing to do with anything you or your wife said. I just want to see them again before we conclude the sale."

"I suppose that's reasonable," Leyden concedes. He walks toward the edge of the porch. "My overseer is out in the fields. I can take you to the cabin myself."

"Have Martha bring them up here," Grace suggests.

"Yes, good idea."

Leyden calls for Martha. Almost immediately she steps from the house onto the porch. Leyden tells her to go to Nettie's cabin and bring her and her sons to the house. "Make sure they bring whatever belongings they're taking with them."

Leyden waits until Martha is sauntering on the path toward the cabins before he speaks again. "That girl Martha ran away with Nettie and her family," he tells Adam. "I must say, she seems perfectly glad to be back here. I don't think she liked what she saw as a colored girl on the run."

"She's your new maidservant?" Adam asks Grace.

"She's house help. I don't think I could have a real maidservant ever again after Nettie. Not for a good long time anyway."

Another period of silence follows and then Grace says, "I'm going inside, Philip. I don't want to see any more."

William and Henry huddle closer against the porch as Grace steps within three feet of their hiding place as she goes back inside the house. Then William hears Leyden speak the words that set his hands trembling.

"Here they come—Nettie and her boys."

CHAPTER SEVENTY-TWO

RESCUE

WILLIAM AND HENRY CRAWL CLOSER TO THE PORCH stairs so they can see the area in front of the house. Henry pulls his pistol from his belt and nudges William to do the same.

"Nettie," they hear Adam say, "do you and your boys still want to come to Virginia with me?"

She nods. "We ready."

William peers over the top of the steps. He can see Nettie in front of Adam with a large bag at her feet and Alfred and Dan standing behind her. She's stooped and her dress and head cloth are ragged and stained. He's never seen her so tired and spent. He feels rage rising and he lifts his revolver higher just as Henry puts his arm out to restrain him.

"I want you and the boys to get in the wagon," Adam tells her.

William and Henry watch Adam lead Nettie and the boys to the wagon. Just then they hear hoofbeats and see dust rising as Bobby Hill appears on his chestnut mare.

"Can't say I'm going to miss the likes of you, Nettie," he calls to her as his horse dances in a circle.

"Shackles," Leyden says. "You said you were going to chain them. You'd better do that before we go into the house."

Bobby Hill steers his horse alongside the wagon bed and looks down. "No chains here. You forget something, mister?"

"One moment," Adam says. He walks to the wagon and reaches under the driver's bench. He turns around with a rifle in his hands and swings the muzzle toward the overseer. "Get off your horse and go stand next to your boss."

"Lucas, what are you doing?" blurts Leyden.

Bobby Hill slowly dismounts. "He's stealing them, that's what."

"Put that gun down," Leyden demands. "This makes no sense."

"Stand back," Adam says and glances nervously toward the house.

William and Henry jump up and run toward the wagon.

"Pa!" Alfred shouts.

Nettie puts both hands to her face and struggles to stand in the wagon bed.

"Well, well," Bobby Hill sneers. "Look who's back from the dead."

William runs to the side of the wagon. He jams the Colt back into his belt. Nettie climbs over the side of the wagon and falls into his arms.

"You alive," she cries. "Sweet Jesus, it's true. Alive!"

Alfred and Dan try to climb down from the wagon as they yell, "Pa! Pa!"

Henry keeps his revolver trained on Leyden and Bobby Hill. "Back in the wagon," he calls to the others. "We got to get away from this place."

"I see what's happening here," Leyden says. "Bobby was right, plain as day. You're stealing them."

Adam turns to William and Nettie. "Hurry. We need to—"

Henry's revolver explodes.

William drops to his knees and pulls Nettie down with him. He yanks the Colt from his belt and holds it at eye level. He looks at Bobby Hill. The overseer looks at his own right shoulder as a small pistol falls from his fingertips.

"Bobby?" Leyden says, reaching toward him.

Bobby Hill lifts his hand to his wound. Blood trickles between his fingers and he slumps to his knees.

"Damn fool!" Henry yells. "Couldn't let well enough alone."

The front door opens and Grace dashes onto the porch. "Philip? Was that a gunshot?" She hurries down the porch steps.

"Bobby!"

Leyden moves behind the wounded man to hold him upright. Adam runs to help and together they lay him onto the grass. Adam grabs a handkerchief from his pocket and tries to stick it under Bobby Hill's shirt.

"Get away from him!" Grace shouts as she kneels beside her brother. "Who did this?" She spots Henry and his smoking revolver.

"Murderer!" she screams and reaches for Bobby Hill's derringer in the grass. Adam shoves her and she topples backward against her brother. Something catches Grace's eye and she says in an oddly distracted voice, "William, is that you?"

"Better take care of him, ma'am," William answers.

The woman is in a daze, her arms and legs spread awkwardly on the grass, her brother's blood soaking her skirt.

"Grace!" Leyden barks. He tries to staunch the overseer's wound. "We need bandages and water. Get Sallah!" Grace gets to her feet just as Martha comes running from the side of the house and sees the overseer and the blood.

"Mister Hill hurt? Dying?" She puts her hands to her cheeks. Then she looks up and says, "William?" She looks at Grace Leyden and then at William and Nettie. She walks toward the wagon.

"No, Martha," William says. "Not this time. Get Sallah so she can tend to Mister Hill." The girl doesn't move. "Get her now!" Martha walks backward slowly in the direction of the house, her eyes riveted to the scene unfolding in front of her.

William helps Nettie back into the wagon and climbs in after her. Alfred and Dan both cry and clutch at their father. Adam and Henry—still keeping their guns trained on the Leydens—climb onto the driver's bench.

"Let us go peacefully so nobody else gets hurt," Adam tells Leyden.

William wraps his arms around Nettie and his sons and looks back to see Leyden still bent over Bobby Hill with his hands and forearms smeared red. Grace leans over them both with one hand on her brow.

The wagon creaks all the way to the foot of the lane. There's rustling in the thicket and Reverend Shem steps in front of the wagon's team.

"I heard a shot."

"Henry had to shoot Bobby Hill," William says.

"Dead?"

"Not yet," Henry says.

They all climb down from the wagon. The preacher leads Adam's horse into view and ties it next to the other two stallions. He puts his arm around Nettie and explains, "These horses will be much faster." She frantically digs into the large bag she brought and pulls out shoes for her boys and one of the dresses Grace had given her.

"You got to leave them," William tells her. "That whole bag."

"But these are—"

"Only things," he says.

William mounts his horse and pulls Nettie up behind him and realizes she feels as brittle as a bundle of sticks pressed against his back. Reverend Shem hoists Alfred up to Henry and then Dan up to Adam. Then the preacher leaves the wagon and its team in the road and climbs onto his mule. He looks at everyone and waves his wide-brimmed hat.

"God be with you!"

And they part.

CHAPTER SEVENTY-THREE

FLIGHT

HENRY FORCES ADAM AND WILLIAM TO RIDE HARD TO put distance between themselves and the farm, where they know Philip Leyden is gathering hunters determined to track them down. After a long and dusty ride the group reaches the road to Germantown and stops to let the three heavily lathered horses cool down.

"We got to hide someplace till dark and then get to Minerva and find Zebulon," Henry tells the others.

They search for a hideout. A mile down the road they cross a slow-moving stream and Henry says, "Let's see where this creek takes us." The drought has shrunk the stream to a languid ribbon with blacksnakes sunning themselves on its warm banks. The riders steer the three horses into the creekbed, where their hooves make sucking sounds in the mud. They follow the creek a quarter-mile as it meanders around a bluff topped by a stand of oaks.

"Tie the horses here," Henry orders as he tethers his own horse to a sapling. He climbs the bluff and posts himself at its highest point. Then they wait. Adam sits beside him and watches the countryside between the bluff and the distant road. They take turns as lookouts and watch the slow arc of the sun. Only a couple of wagons and a handful of riders on horseback travel the far-off road.

"Why haven't they come after us?" Adam wonders.

"Don't know. But it don't mean we got away," Henry says. "Not yet."

At dusk they leave the bluff. A flight of swallows veers and swoops in giant loops above their heads as they follow the creek back to the road. By the time they reach it, a bank of clouds has rolled in to block the rising moon and they struggle in the darkness to see the edges of the road.

A mile farther they hear dogs howling in the distance.

"Hounds?" William wonders.

"Let's hope they just some farmer's animals and that's all," Henry says.

They ride on. Adam feels Dan's head slump forward as the child drifts into sleep. A few more miles and the road starts to climb and drop and twist through the darkened terrain.

"Hold up," Henry says and reins in his horse. Adam and William halt their horses alongside him. They all hear the steady clop-clop-clop of a rider approaching a hundred yards behind them. Henry whispers for everyone to take cover away from the road. He lifts Alfred down to the ground.

"What about you?" Adam asks.

"You just keep this family together," Henry says as he turns his horse toward the sound of the oncoming rider.

Adam makes sure everyone is concealed, then orders, "Stay here." He again mounts his horse and trots off to find Henry. He soon finds him with the unknown rider, both on horseback in the middle of the road. He calls out, "Everything all right here?"

"Seems this road's pretty busy considering the hour," the other man muses as he leans forward in his saddle to see Adam. The man's slouch hat hides his upper face and a thick beard covers the lower part. Adams spots the man's mud-spattered his boots and wonders if he'd followed the creekbed in hopes of tracking the group.

"I'm just curious what this one's doing out here this time of night," the man says as he eyes Henry.

"And I told you I'm a free man and can go where I want."

Adam straightens himself in the saddle. "This is not a good time or place for a colored with that attitude. Free or not."

"Not when we got runaways who near to killed their boss," the man continues as he rests his hand on the stock of a rifle slung next to his saddle.

"What are you talking about?" Adam asks.

"Leyden farm. Back near Mays Lick."

"Good lord, I know Philip Leyden," Adam says. "Is he hurt badly?"

"Not him. 'Twas his kin, the overseer. Darkie pulled a gun and shot him when they was running away. Poor fellow near bled to death."

"I been nowhere near Mays Lick," Henry says. " I'm only headed that way now."

The man keeps talking. "Lots of people out looking for those runaways this night. Spread out all across the countryside, we are. I want to know if either of you seen a darkie family along this road. They're supposed to be with a white—"

The man looks at Henry and then at Adam and then slowly slips the carbine from its sling and levels it at Adam. "I'll bet you do know Leyden. Bet you stole his slaves right from under his nose."

Adam raises his hand. "Sorry, friend, you got the wrong man. Now put the gun down. I can't vouch for this buck here, but I got my own coloreds and don't need to steal another man's, especially a friend's." He struggles to keep his voice steady as he waits for the burst of flame and the bullet to tear into his body.

The man keeps the rifle leveled at Adam as he steers his horse in a circle around him and Henry. "Maybe we should just go back to see Leyden hisself. Find out what he's got to say about you two."

Adam turns in his saddle to face the man. "I told you I had nothing to do with it. And I will not have you or anybody else push me around the countryside at gunpoint."

"I'd say you got little choice."

Henry speaks up. "I got papers. I can show you who I am. Look here." He waves his right hand high in the air and spurs his horse close to the man.

"Stay back," the man orders and swings his carbine around. Then Henry brings his arm down solidly across the man's shoulder and knocks him from the saddle. The man tumbles to the road with a yelp and his rifle clattering beside him. Adam and Henry jump to the ground and pin down the man. A piece of metal protrudes from the man's collar and Henry rips open the man's shirt to find a Bowie knife strapped to his chest.

Henry pulls the long-bladed knife from its sheath and holds it against the man's throat. "You got to learn to treat people better when you meet them on the road," he growls with his face close to the man's.

"I will," the man whispers as he struggles for breath.

"What should we do with him?" Adam asks.

"Don't cut me," the man pleads with eyes wide. "Just go on your way and I'll say nothing."

"We intend to," Henry says. He slices the leather thong that had held the knife's sheath in place and then uses it to tie the man's hands behind his back. He cuts a strip from the man's grimy shirt as a gag and another one to tie his ankles together. Then he and Adam carry the man several feet from the road and leave him hog-tied in a gully.

"Now it's between him and the critters," Henry says.

The incident has unnerved Adam. He can't stop his hands from shaking. "I got to say, Henry, I never had a gun pointed at me till I met you," he says, as if trying to make light of the situation. "The first time ever was that night I first met you, when those two men in the road took out after me. Then the drunken slave catchers whooping it up in Minerva. And it could've been me Leyden's overseer wanted to shoot back there. Now there's this scoundrel."

"Worst part," Henry responds, "is there's bound to be more on their way soon as word gets around about what happened at Leyden's place."

"Henry, I don't know if I can go on."

"Well, you can't just sit here in the road."

"That's not what I mean. I'm not sure you need me anymore. You've got friends who can help you get back across the river."

"Plan is for us to stick by one another all the way. But I can't stop you if you want to leave. That's for you to say."

The two men ride back to where the others are hiding and Henry calls out to them. William and Nettie and the boys step from the darkness and William lifts Alfred onto the saddle with Henry. Then he leads Dan to Adam's horse and hoists the boy onto Adam's saddle.

"I know you got boys of your own," William says as he hands his son to Adam. "So you got to know how I feel about a man who's willing to carry my boy to a safe place or maybe die trying." William reaches up, clasps Adam's arm, and squeezes it tightly. "I'm just trying to say thank you."

Adam positions Dan on the saddle near his lap and wraps an arm tightly around the boy. Then he calls out to Henry, "We're ready."

CHAPTER SEVENTY-FOUR

CAUTION

A STIFF BREEZE FROM THE SOUTH SHREDS THE CLOUDS and lets the first light of day fall across the countryside. The dawn carries the scent of wood smoke as the exhausted riders enter Germantown.

"People beginning to stir," Henry says to Adam.

"But we're miles from where we should be, Henry. We need to get through here without encountering the likes of VanArman again."

They look back to see William riding wide-eyed while Nettie's head lolls against his back. Adam and Henry slow their horses until William catches up.

"Just keep hold, William," Henry says in a low tone. "We got to get past this place with no ruckus."

They keep their pace painfully slow to soften the sounds of hooves. The sky brightens overhead, making the group visible to anyone who'd happen to glance toward the road. They all continue past the houses and storefronts and liveries as roosters crow one after another with the morning sun.

Finally they pass the last house along the road and see a man walking toward them. He's black and wears the baggy homespun clothing of a slave and carries a pitchfork on his shoulder. He steps to the side of the road as they approach and then lifts his straw hat and smiles.

"We got to hide again," Henry tells the others as sunlight spreads across pastures and woodlands. They are all exhausted.

Adam points toward a wooded hilltop to the east. "I say up there."

They follow a gulch away from the road until they reach the base of the hill. They dismount and guide the horses up the steep incline. Stumbling and sliding—Adam and Henry still carrying Dan and Alfred in their arms—they reach the crest, where they all sprawl onto dew-drenched grass.

Henry looks over at Adam. "Soon, you go see Zebulon."

"I'm so tired I—"

"Folks won't bother with you like they would me. You got to find out where Zebulon thinks we should go—with this daylight and all. Men going to be looking for us."

"And food," William calls out.

"And get some food," Henry says. "I know you got to sleep. But you got to do this first."

An hour later Adam stands with his horse in front of the blacksmith shop in Minerva. His body aches and his eyes burn and his mouth tastes of dust. He waits for Zebulon and grows nervous as the sun climbs higher. A wagon drawn by an ancient mule—a drowsing old man limply holding the reins—creaks past the blacksmith shop and scatters the chickens pecking in the road.

Adam realizes it is now Wednesday. He has been away from home five days.

"That you, Henry's friend?"

Adam turns to see Zebulon holding a ring of keys and a small cloth bag. The sleeves of his coarse brown shirt are torn off raggedly at the elbows to reveal strong forearms with burn scars. He looks Adam up and down. "You all right?" Without waiting for a reply the big blacksmith sticks a key into the padlock. He pushes open the door and gestures for Adam to follow. "You get that man's family? The ones Henry was telling about?"

"They're all resting on a hill a few miles south of here."

Zebulon opens the big door wider and lets sunlight fill the front of his shop. "Just act like we doing business here."

Adam relates the details of the rescue and the group's flight through the night.

The blacksmith dons his heavy leather apron. "I heard nothing about any slave stealing down by Mays Lick. It'd be those wild-assed fools you saw here last time that'd know. They still all hot after those Anderson slaves. Same as when you was here before."

Zebulon pokes the coals in his forge and piles kindling and coal on them. He picks up his bellows and puffs life back into the fire.

"I know where they is, those other runaways. You got to take them with you."

"Now wait. I don't know. We've got—"

"You all going the same way. Got to cross the same river. Maybe more is better than what you got right now."

"You mean if we run up against these hunters around here."

"That's what I'm saying."

Adam tells the blacksmith Henry will know what to do.

"I got to know now," Zebulon replies. He pokes the fire and sparks fly into the funnel-shaped hood above the forge. He tells Adam the Anderson slaves still are hiding in the woods east of Minerva instead of risking crossing the Ohio with so many slave catchers watching its banks.

"How many are there?" Adam asks.

"Five in all. Two men and a boy and two women, one with child." He curves his hand out over his own belly.

"Can she travel?"

"That's what she's been doing. She don't want her child to be nobody's slave."

Adam steps closer to Zebulon. "This complicates everything and makes it more dangerous. Now there'll be two groups of fugitives who need to be taken across. I don't know what Henry will say."

Zebulon continues to stoke his fire. "How many horses you got? Three?"

"Three horses, six people."

The blacksmith again picks up his bellows and blows air into the embers. "Where you intend to cross?"

Adam tries to remember. "Is there a Lawrence Creek in these parts?"

"Over by Charleston. Runs into the Ohio there."

"That must be it. The boat's near there. By an orchard."

They decide to wait until late in the day and then Zebulon will bring a wagon to the hilltop where the others are resting. Then by wagon and horseback they'll travel to where the Anderson slaves are hiding and all of them will travel through the night to reach the river.

"It'll be more dangerous with that many people, Zebulon. Don't you agree?"

Zebulon sets the bellows on his tool bench. "It's always dangerous. Any way you look at it."

Nettie cradles William's head as he sleeps. They're huddled together at the base of a towering oak and she can feel the rise and fall of his chest against her arm. Nearby her sons chase grasshoppers. She strokes William's face and feels the roughness of his stubble against the calluses on her hand. She watches as he slowly wakes. "You a brave man, William, and a good man."

William looks up at her and smiles and begins humming. Nettie recalls how Willis loved to sing. She remembers lying on her mattress in the cabin with her back bloodied and nearly broken and listening to Willis sing as he cooked a meager meal for her and the boys.

"William, I got something to say."

He stops humming and sits up.

"I want you to know that Willis was good to me that whole time. He never made me do a thing that would hurt you. Even when we thought you was dead. I never want you to think unkindly of that man."

When he returns to the hilltop, Adam tells Henry about Zebulon's plan for them to join up with the other runaway slaves.

"No good. No good at all." Henry's voice rises. "That's too many. That's two trips or more to get everybody across." He kicks the ground with enough force to send a chunk of sod flying.

"We'll just tell him no," Adam says.

"That ain't right either. Those people need help just like we do. We just got to get some sleep. I can't think straight right now."

Adam holds out the small cloth bag Zebulon has given him.

"What's that?"

"Food from Zebulon. He'll bring more tonight."

CHAPTER SEVENTY-FIVE

DEFENSES

THE CONDITION OF THE BLANCHARD PLACE IS FAR worse than Hannah imagined. The ramshackle farmhouse reminds her of the drawing of a haunted house in one of her childhood books.

"Let's get close to the porch," Anne says as she navigates the buggy toward the house. She climbs down from the seat as several hogs lumber toward her and hens flutter against her skirt. She jumps onto the rickety porch and pounds on the door. She waits and then says, "I'm going out back."

"I'm coming with you," Hannah tells Anne. "But what about the clothes?"

Three large baskets sit on the buggy floor holding clothing the women of the sewing circle have contributed. Hannah herself added two of her own dresses and a pair of Adam's worn trousers. She had come across her blue shawl while she was sorting—the very one she had worn the day the men brought the slave boy in the wagon—and had run her fingers over the soft wool and then put it with the other clothing in hopes it would find its way to another slave in need.

"Leave the baskets here for the time being," Anne says.

Hannah, heavy with her pregnancy, holds out her hand and Anne helps her down. The two women follow the dusty path around a corner of the house with pigs and chickens trailing behind. They walk toward the barnyard with its clouds of flies. Near the back door of the house they see four hogs nudging their snouts against the carcass of a hound. The pigs poked at it and gnaw at a gaping wound in its side.

"How awful," Hannah says and puts her hand over her face.

Anne moves closer to the carcass as a boar with a blood-smeared snout eyes her. She looks beyond the dead dog to the barns across the yard.

"Sarah!" she calls out. "Sarah! Are you here?" Two sheds stand beyond the tumbledown barns. The door on one of them opens slowly. "It's me, Anne Billings." The shed door opens farther and a musket barrel emerges. Finally Sarah steps from the shed with the musket on one arm and Lucy held tightly against her chest with the other.

"Get inside!" Sarah shouts as she runs toward the house with the child jostling against her shoulder.

The three women enter the darkness of the keeping room and Sarah lays the musket on the table. Hannah's eyes adjust to the dim light as she scans the large room with its stone fireplace and heavy drapes covering the windows.

"What's wrong, Sarah?" Anne says as she lifts Lucy from Sarah's shoulder. "The gun. That dead dog."

Sarah draws her forearm across her brow. "There was this man. Maybe more than one. But I seen only him and his dogs. He came here early this morning when I was asleep with the child. I heard a howl and it scared the daylights out of me and set the child to crying. So I got the gun and tried to keep an eye on him out front. He come up close to the house and then comes round back." She walked to the back door to show what had happened. "He comes to right there and I says, 'What you doing?' And he says he knows we hiding slaves in here. I tell him we're free folk and we got no slaves in here and for him to go away. Then he turns and hollers like he's got somebody with him. He says he's coming in the house. So I point the gun and say no he ain't. He pulls out a pistol and starts toward the door. Then his two dogs started fighting like they was going to bust their leashes and one of them jumped up so I shot and killed it. Then I got behind the door so maybe he'd think I got another gun—one that's still loaded. I told him to get away or he's a dead man."

Sarah closes the door and latches it.

"Did he leave?" Hannah asks.

"Appears so. I waited a while and then got scared again. I took the child and the gun and went to that shed out there. The one with the hiding place. There's a room in there where folks can hide. We was in there all morning when I heard somebody call my name and it was you."

Hannah looks at Sarah and sees her hands still trembling. "Does the man know Henry's not here?"

"He likely figures it since it was only me tried to stop him."

Anne and Hannah suspect the man with the dogs was Julius Klemmer. They describe Klemmer and his hounds to Sarah. She nods and says, "Sounds like. And I got to think he's coming back. He was seeking something and it could be this child and William."

Anne and Hannah tell Sarah they could all return to the Porter farm or go into Buford. "But that man could come back here any time," Sarah tells them. Then they tell Sarah about Klemmer's penchant for burning down buildings and she says, "Then we got to make sure he can't burn this one."

Hannah holds Lucy for the time it takes Sarah and Anne to rush through the outbuildings to collect every water bucket and milk pail they can find that's not rusted through. At the well they pump water into the buckets and lug them into the house. Soon buckets of water stand on the floorboards by each window. The dining table is littered with carving knives and a sickle.

"You should load the gun again," Anne tells Sarah.

"Don't know how."

Hannah looks up. "Maybe I can." The other women look at her with surprise. "Adam taught me. If I can remember." She lifts the musket and turns it over. She squints down the barrel. "It's quite like ours and has the same parts."

Sarah gathers together a dented brass powder flask and a small cotton bag.

"First I do this," Hannah says as she pulls the hammer back a notch "Then this," as she removes the percussion cap. She opens the powder flask and taps it gently on the edge of the barrel until the grains of black powder start to flow. She stops and then changes her mind and taps a bit more powder into the barrel. "For luck."

Sarah hands her a gray conical slug from the cotton bag.

"I need a piece of cloth, a little piece." Sarah goes to the kitchen to snip a piece from a rag. Hannah pulls the musket's ramrod from under the barrel. "Now, I do this," she says as she wraps the bullet in the cloth and slips it into the barrel. She jams the rod up and down several times to push the bullet firmly against the powder. "And I need one of these," she says as she replaces the old percussion cap she had removed. "That as good as I can do."

"Should we try it and see?" Anne asks.

"No need," Hannah answers. "I don't want to waste a shot. It's all in God's hands anyway."

CHAPTER SEVENTY-SIX

HOSTAGES

HOURS LATER THE WOMEN HEAR HORSES ON THE LANE leading to the Blanchard house. Sarah rushes to a front window and peeks through the drapes and says, "Please God, let it be Henry."

She quickly turns away. Hannah and Anne see the look on her face.

"Klemmer?"

"And two others."

Hannah carries Lucy around the heavy cupboard they've pushed against the front door and between the buckets of water on the floor so she can join Sarah and Anne at the window. At the top of the lane she sees the three horsemen with the sun low behind them.

"The one with the straw hat is Ogden," Anne tells the others, "the horrid little man who owns the inn. The other one I don't know."

"I do," Hannah says. "He came to our farm the day they had the runaway boy in the wagon. Abe Williams I think they said."

"He was with Klemmer and my father the day they beat Jacob at the store," Anne adds.

Sarah picks up the musket. "What do I do?" There was nothing Hannah or Anne could tell her.

The men dismount a distance away from the house. Klemmer hands his reins to Ogden and strides toward the house with his rifle cradled in his arms. He kicks at the hogs and pokes a boar with his rifle and sends the animal scurrying.

Sarah lifts her musket higher.

"Wait," Anne says. "Let me talk to him. He's friends with my father so he might listen."

Klemmer steps onto the porch and stops at the door. "You remember the child's story?" he calls loudly to anyone who can hear. "I will huff and puff and blow this house down." He chuckles and then suddenly shouts, "Open this door!"

Anne unbolts the door and opens it only as far as the cupboard propped against it allows. Klemmer cranes to see her.

"So," he says, "Miss Billings. A good surprise. You will know what I'm after."

"There's no one here."

Klemmer suddenly throws his full weight against the door and breaks it open with a crash that sends the cupboard sliding across the floor. The force knocks Anne and Sarah backward and in the confusion Hannah ducks into the bedroom with Lucy.

Klemmer squints into the darkened room with his rifle at his hip. "It is a cave in here." He grabs the drapes nearest him and yanks them. The heavy fabric tears loose and falls to the floor. A blaze of late afternoon sun pours into the room.

Sarah aims her musket at Klemmer, her hands trembling.

"Put it down," he orders and ignores the muzzle pointed at him. "You will find Klemmer is harder to kill than his dog."

"Get out," Sarah says and motions with the muzzle toward the splintered door.

The women hear Ira Ogden yell, "Klemmer? You all right?"

"I am good," he shouts back.

"I told you to get out," Sarah says as she swings the musket back toward Klemmer's head. "Our men be back here any time now. Henry and the others."

"Maybe they bring more runaways for Klemmer, yes?"

The man pays no heed to Sarah and her musket as he strolls across the room and glances at the knives and sickle on the tabletop. He grins as he sits in a wooden chair and props his rifle on his knee. He again wears his heavy wool coat and wipes its sleeve across his sweaty face. He cocks his head and listens. "What is that I hear?" He listens more intently and then smiles. "I say bring the child out here. Now!"

In the bedroom Hannah puts her hand over Lucy's mouth.

"Bring the child!" Klemmer frowns at Sarah and Anne. "Someone is in there with the child?"

Hannah slowly carries Lucy into the room and stands beside Sarah and Anne.

"So it is you—more surprise," Klemmer says.

Sarah struggles with the weight of the musket and its barrel dips toward the floor.

The movement does not escape Klemmer's eye. "I tell you one last time to put the gun down. You put it down and I will put mine down."

Sarah cautiously lowers the muzzle.

Klemmer lays his own rifle on the floor beside the chair. He reaches into his coat pocket and pulls out a small pistol. He holds it up for the women to see and then sets it next to his rifle.

"My father will hear of this," Anne tells him. "He won't like you threatening us this way."

"Ah, you are wrong about your father. You anger him. Why do you piss on the law?"

"Because the law is wrong."

Klemmer removes his battered hat—revealing unevenly cropped, matted black hair—and lays it on the floor beside his rifle and pistol. He opens his wool coat wider and leans forward with his hands on his knees. "Two things I want. No, maybe three." He points at Lucy in Hannah's arms. "I want that child. But the child is not the big thing.

The child will be more trouble than the reward is worth. It's the man I want. I know this is where you brought them both."

Anne glares back at him. "You mean the night you stole that poor boy from Wendell Childress and cut off—"

"I stole nothing."

"You know very well that boy was legally free."

"No matter!" Klemmer grips his knees tightly. "I want the man and this child." He looks through the drapeless window. "And I want any other runaways your men bring here. Am I right? They are bringing more?"

"You're wrong," Hannah tells him. "They'll be back from town any time now. And they have friends with them. You'd better leave while you still have the chance."

Klemmer rises from the chair and remains unfazed as he walks to the doorway.

"Ogden!" he calls. A moment later Ira Ogden is at the doorway. "Put the horses in back. I want one of you there and the other one over there." Klemmer points to the two ends of the house. "If you see Blanchard or any others, you tell me."

"Got any idea when they might show up, Klemmer?"

"The women say their men are in town. So they could be home soon. But I think they're coming from the river and bringing more runaways to this place."

"What if there's a whole bunch of them?"

"Then we will still get what we want." He gestures toward the women. "Because now we have something they want."

CHAPTER SEVENTY-SEVEN

NORTH

THE RED SUN SLIPS BELOW THE HORIZON JUST AS Zebulon arrives at the base of the hill in a wagon drawn by two dusty mules. The group pops up from the gullies on both sides of the road. Henry and Adam lift Nettie and the boys into the wagon and then mount their horses to ride ahead. William ties his horse to the tailgate so he can sit with his family beneath the ragged sheet of canvas arching over the wagon bed. In a matter of minutes the wagon is rocking along the road in the dusk.

"Pork and some bread in that basket," Zebulon calls over his shoulder. "Just save some for the others."

For the next hour they skirt Minerva on a rutted lane and then rejoin the main road to head north toward the forests where Zebulon believes the Anderson slaves are hiding. "They been deep in these woods for days now and scared to death the whole while," he tells William. He slows the wagon and studies the area to the left of the road. "I dropped off some food yesterday but don't know if they got it."

Abruptly Zebulon stiffens and pulls back on the reins.

"Put those blankets over you," the blacksmith orders. "Someone up ahead."

"Coming this way?" William wonders.

"Got torches. It don't look good."

William covers Nettie and the boys with the blankets. He perches in a front corner of the wagon bed so he can see past Zebulon's broad back.

"Henry or Adam up there?"

"You lay low and stay quiet," Zebulon says. "And no, I don't see them."

Torches flicker in the road ahead and William hears the sounds of a man yelling and then the muffled scream of a woman amid whinnies and the scuffing of hooves. Dan sits up and Nettie pulls him to her. The blanket falls off both of them.

"Lord, it's them slaves," Zebulon mutters. "Hunters got them."

A man shouts close to the front of the wagon.

"Whoa there, boy!"

Zebulon pulls the reins and the mules halt.

William sees the glow of torches through the canvas, like a dull sun through clouds.

"That you, Zebulon?" a man asks. "It's you, ain't it?"

"Yessir. You catch them fugitives?"

"What you doing out here, Zebulon? You wasn't coming by to pick up these darkies by any chance?"

"Not on your life, sir!" The blacksmith's mules are skittish in the torchlight and he calls out to them, "Easy now." He turns his attention back to the men near the wagon. "No sir. Fellow hired me to fix his wagon. Says it broke down somewhere on this road. You seen a busted wagon along here?"

William slowly lifts an edge of canvas an inch and peeks toward the roadside. He sees six or seven men with guns and torches running in and out of the woods and struggling with a man and a boy while holding a woman at the edge of the road.

"Ain't seen no wagon—broken or otherwise," the man says. "Zebulon, you wait here."

William watches as two more men emerge from the woods. Each holds one arm of a young man in tattered clothing. The slave struggles until one of the hunters whacks him with a pistol and knocks him to his knees. Then another man pounds the slave's back with the butt of a rifle until he collapses on the road.

"Any more back there?" another man shouts into the woods.

"Last one here," says a voice from the darkness.

William turns to Nettie. He can see her dimly in the diffused light of the torches as she holds both boys tightly against her chest. Her eyes are shining with tears and wide with fear.

One of the hunters shouts to another, "Goddamn, what'd you do?"

William peeks again from beneath the edge of canvas. He sees a pregnant woman stumble from the woods with blood seeping through the front of her dress. She holds her protruding belly with both hands.

"Oh Lord," Zebulon groans.

One of the men shoves the woman and she topples forward onto the road and cries out as she hits the dirt. She rolls over onto her back and the bloody splotch grows. The slave who's been knocked to the ground crawls toward her with his hand outstretched. The hunter with the rifle again slams the butt onto the man's back and pins him to the road.

"Get 'em all chained up!" orders one of the hunters.

William turns away from the scene and puts both hands over his eyes. His horse nickers at the back of the wagon and a man says, "Settle down." The canvas parts and the man peers into the wagon bed. "Give it here," he orders and then grabs a torch from another hunter. He thrusts the torch into the wagon and its light falls on William and on Nettie and the boys.

"More in here!"

At that moment Zebulon slaps the reins and the mules lunge forward.

"Whoa, damn it!" someone shouts and suddenly men are jumping onto the sides of the wagon as it rolls down the road. One lifts the canvas and swings his leg into the wagon near Nettie. William grabs the man's shoulders with all his strength and flings him backwards. The man clutches a handful of canvas and rips a long strip of it as he tumbles backward onto the road. Alfred cries out and William spins around to see another man climbing in. He grips the man's arm and twists until he feels the socket snap. The man screams as he falls from the wagon.

"Get your gun!" Zebulon shouts to William as he lashes the mules again and again.

William remembers his revolver is in his saddlebag, beyond his reach. Hunters are hollering in the dust behind the wagon and he can see some of them mounting their horses and grabbing torches. Zebulon's mules pick up speed and the torn canvas flutters and snaps in the wind as the wagon hurtles down the road. William grabs Dan and holds him tight against his chest to make the boy stop screaming.

"Keep going!" someone yells from the road.

William looks out the rear of the wagon and sees Adam and Henry on horseback in the middle of the road. A group of hunters gallops toward them waving torches and rifles. All at once, William sees several spears of fire shoot from his friends' revolvers. In the distance two torches fall to the ground.

Moments later Henry gallops up to the wagon.

"Stop!" he shouts to Zebulon, and again, "Stop!"

The frenzied mules finally come to a halt as Henry leaps from his horse. He runs to the back of the wagon and helps William and Nettie and the boys climb out and onto the road. "We go on foot from here through the woods." Henry leads his horse toward the cover of the brush as Adam rides up with his gun in hand.

William and Nettie and the boys follow Henry into the thicket. Adam and Henry linger to watch for the hunters they know are not far behind. Then Zebulon joins them with branches cracking loudly under his huge bulk.

Once more William and his family are stumbling blindly through woodlands at night—snagged, tripped, and bruised by unseen branches, vines, and thorns.

"You boys," Zebulon calls out to Alfred and Dan, both huddling beside Nettie. "You come to me," the blacksmith says. "I ain't nothing for you to fear." Then he reaches down with his big arms and scoops them up and clutches them to his chest as he lurches through the woods.

CHAPTER SEVENTY-EIGHT

ASSAULT

DAYLIGHT FADES THROUGHOUT THE ROOM DESPITE THE ripped-down curtain. Klemmer stands at the table where the women laid out the cutlery and picks up a butcher's knife. He runs his thumb down its broad blade. He sets the knife on the table and then lifts the sickle and swings it downward with force enough to stab its point into the tabletop.

The women are dazed. This man has quickly and without effort taken control of them. All of their talk about the knives and musket—could they actually kill a man and what would it feel like?—had been only words. He's left his rifle and pistol on the floor and walked away from them, confident the women won't grab his weapons, just as he knew Sarah wouldn't dare shoot him.

Klemmer slips off his woolen coat. Sweat has glued his grimy linen shirt to his body. Leather straps crisscross his chest to hold a knife's sheath near his left armpit.

"We will sit and we will wait."

No one moves.

He grabs two chairs from beside the table and heaves them noisily across the floor. Sarah stands open-mouthed as he marches toward her and wrenches the musket from her hands. It happens so quickly she does not resist.

"Sit, I told you." He tosses the musket onto the table, sending the knives and sickle clattering to the floor. Lucy begins to sob and Hannah tries to calm her.

Klemmer returns to his chair and unties the leather straps so he can slip off the sheath and lay it on the floor next to his hat and rifle and pistol. He picks up his coat and pulls a small bundle of red cloth from a pocket. He carefully unwraps it and selects a thick cigar. With a sweeping motion of his arm he strikes a match against the floorboards, holds it to the cigar, and puffs until a dense cloud of smoke surrounds his head. He picks up his rifle and lays it across his knees and settles back into the chair.

"Now we wait."

Klemmer studies the women and lingers longest on Hannah, eyeing her again and again as he tilts his head back to exhale pungent smoke. She hugs Lucy tighter and turns to face the bare window where the waning light penetrates blue tiers of cigar smoke.

Anne breaks the long silence.

"Why do you hate so?"

"No talking."

She persists. "What makes a man like you—you're not a fool, after all—what makes you hunt down people who only want to be free? What makes you—"

"You cannot hear?"

"What makes you want to take children from their mothers and—"

He flings his cigar and it hits the wall behind Anne with a spray of sparks.

"It is the law," he growls and reaches for another cigar.

"That's it?" Hannah asks. "You do these things because it's a law? Despite how unjust it may be?"

He spits a fleck of tobacco leaf.

Anne leans forward. "Then you're an animal. A horrible animal. No, you're worse than an animal because you have no conscience."

Klemmer rises from his chair and stomps toward the women with his rifle in hand. They cringe in their chairs and Hannah puts her arm over Lucy's head but Klemmer yanks Lucy from Hannah. He dangles the screaming child above the floor.

"This is the animal," he says to Anne. "This one is no better than one of the stinking pigs!"

Then he drops Lucy and the child hits the floor with a sickening thud.

Sarah lunges to the floor to grab Lucy and lands near a paring knife Klemmer had knocked from the table. She pushes the bawling child aside and grabs the knife and jumps to her feet. She jams the blade deep into Klemmer's shoulder and pulls it out to stab him again.

Klemmer spins around as she sinks the blade into his chest. He swings an arm blindly and knocks Sarah sprawling over the chairs. "Damn you!" He staggers backward toward the window as blood seeps through his shirt. "Damn you," he snarls again as he jams his bandanna under his shirt and presses on the wound on his chest to stanch the bleeding.

Hannah rushes toward the table and grabs Sarah's musket.

Klemmer sees her hoist the gun. "Ogden!" he bellows. He stares at Hannah and the musket. "Ogden! Come!"

"Get out," Hannah says firmly.

The musket's hammer clicks loudly when she cocks it. She walks toward Klemmer until the end of the barrel is so close to his body that she couldn't miss. "Get out of here."

"You are all dead," Klemmer says between clenched teeth as he backs out the door. Again he yells, "Ogden!" and stumbles into the twilight.

CHAPTER SEVENTY-NINE

PARTING

THE GROUP PUSHES ON THROUGH THE DARK WOODS with Henry leading the way. For hours they weave north till exhaustion overwhelms them. Gathered together in the cool night air—the three horses grazing nearby in a moonlit pasture—they wonder why the slave catchers haven't come after them.

"I know we scared the bunch of them," Adam says. "They stopped in their tracks when we fired."

Zebulon whispers with the boys asleep in his arms. "Those men likely went back for their reward. Better to collect that money than get a bullet in the belly."

"Smell that?" Henry says as he tips his head back. "Wind blows just right and you can smell the river."

They descend another heavily wooded slope, moving quickly and heedless of the brush and limbs. They know they're near the river when they reach the road where Gibson lives. Henry climbs onto his horse and tells the others to stay back from the road.

"You know where we are, Zebulon? Which way to Lawrence Creek?"

"Try that way." Zebulon points east.

Henry and Adam gallop off toward Gibson's place with William's horse in tow. William takes Nettie's hand and pulls her through the brush. He knows she's close to collapsing. He can hear Zebulon panting behind them as he carries Alfred and Dan. A quarter-mile farther and they reach the orchard where they slump behind a grassy mound surrounded by apple trees.

"I'm so scared," Nettie whispers as she presses her face against William's shoulder.

"We can't think of that other time. Not now."

William hears men walking toward them through the orchard and then Henry's voice calls out softly, "William? You here?"

He stands up. "Here."

"The boat still there?" Henry asks.

"Don't know. We waited for you."

They all climb down the steep slope to the riverbank and wade through the lapping black water amid the croaks of countless frogs. A few feet farther they find the skiff tied to the stake in the riverbank. Henry retrieves the oars he'd stashed in the bushes as Adam helps William and Nettie climb into the boat. Zebulon hands Dan and Alfred to their father and the boys crouch on the bottom of the boat between William and Nettie.

"We'll make two trips," Henry says. "I want to get this family over first. Adam, wait here with Zebulon."

"I ain't going." At the blacksmith's words everyone falls silent. "I ain't going," he repeats.

Henry drops the oars onto the shore and steps close to his friend.

"Zebulon, those men will hunt you down. Sure as anything."

"Maybe they will. Maybe they won't."

"I'll stay here with you," Adam argues. "Henry can come right back for us. It's less risky than you walking back into Minerva."

"It ain't that. I ain't ready to go."

Henry and Zebulon face each other.

Finally Henry speaks. "I know it's your family, Zebulon."

The blacksmith says nothing.

Then Henry smiles and says as if by habit, "You could be in Ohio by sunrise. I'm sure they need—" his voice cracks. "They need smiths up in Canada."

"Not this time."

"I'll keep asking."

The two men clasp each other until Henry breaks away to pick up the oars and climb with Adam into the boat.

As they leave the Kentucky shore the boys wave to Zebulon.

The blacksmith stands alone in the moonlight at the water's edge and waves back.

CHAPTER EIGHTY

TORCHES

IT'S NEARLY MIDNIGHT WHEN ANNE SEES THE MEN light their torches. "They're going to burn us out," she tells Hannah and Sarah.

Two hours have passed since Klemmer stumbled from the house clutching his wounds. Anne and Sarah have been keeping watch, stationing themselves at the front windows and staring toward the grove where the men tied their horses. Back by the table, Hannah holds a damp cloth on Lucy's forehead, bruised when Klemmer dropped the child to the floor.

Anne again peers through the window. "They've got three torches, now four. One of them is coming around the side of the house—that way."

Sarah rushes to the back door and takes the same position as when she shot Klemmer's dog so many hours ago.

A flaming torch suddenly shatters the panes of a front window. Anne sees Ogden's grizzled face in the firelight as he wiggles the torch to ignite the drapes. She cocks the pistol's tiny hammer and points the gun at Ogden's face and pulls the trigger. The pistol makes a loud pop.

Ogden stares back at Anne and then clamps his hand against the side of his head. He backs away and lets his torch fall to the ground. He takes his hand from his head and looks at his fingers.

"Shot my damn ear!" He again slaps his hand against his head and runs back into the night.

The room reeks of burning oil from the torch.

"Is that it? This thing has only one shot?" Anne tosses the pistol onto the floor and grabs Klemmer's hunting knife. She picks up the sickle from the floor and holds it out to Hannah. "You should take—"

Another torch crashes through the front window and this time ignites the drapes. Anne quickly rips down the burning cloth and stomps on it. She grabs a dented bucket and douses the drapes with water while the torch sputters nearby on the floor.

Then the sudden flash and crack of a rifle comes from the window. The bullet whistles past Anne to strike the hearth and send stone chips flying. She drops to the floor.

"Anne!" Hannah screams.

"It missed." Anne crawls back to the smoldering drapes and smothers the flaming end of the torch with the heavy fabric.

"They got the barn on fire," Sarah yells from the back door and watches as squealing pigs run from the flames. She sees Abe Williams walking toward the house with fire rising from his torch.

"Come on, come on," Sarah urges quietly. She raises the musket and cocks it as he comes closer. Then the roar of her musket shakes the house. Anne runs to Sarah's side and both look through the doorway to see hogs trampling the man's fallen body.

"Don't know if I got him or the hogs did," Sarah says.

The women watch as flames rapidly consume the barn walls. Pieces of flaming roof crumble and send great spirals of orange sparks into the black sky. The air is filled with the screams of the pigs still trapped in their fiery sties.

Suddenly sickened, Anne turns away. "It's like when Jacob—"

The women realize the attack has stopped. They can hear only the sounds of timbers crackling in the burning barn and the lingering squeals of the hogs. Hannah again loads the musket—measuring the powder, ramming in the bullet, fixing the cap—as they wait for whatever will happen next.

"I didn't see Klemmer this time," Anne says. "Maybe he's bled to death out there."

"No, that's a strong man," Sarah tells her. "He'll be back."

CHAPTER EIGHTY-ONE

DEATH

MOMENTS LATER THE FRONT DOOR CRASHES IN AND Klemmer charges through the doorway with his rifle in his hands. As Anne reaches for the hunting knife, Klemmer kicks her solidly with his heavy boot and she slumps to the floor in pain. Hannah curls over Lucy to protect the child from the raging man.

At the same time, Sarah slams shut the back door and holds it just as Ogden throws himself against it. He pounds and shouts, "Abe's dead! Klemmer, he's out here and he's dead!"

Klemmer—his left arm in a makeshift sling, his shirt a patchwork of bloodstains—strides across the room and swings his rifle at Sarah. She tries to block the blow with her musket, but the clash of the two barrels sends her musket tumbling. She reaches for it and Klemmer strikes her head solidly with the heavy stock of his rifle. She collapses unconscious to the floor, where Klemmer nudges her with his boot.

"Klemmer?" Ogden pokes his head through the back door and looks around before stepping inside. He has a plaid cloth tied around his head as a bandage for his wounded ear. He's holding an unlit torch.

"Light it," Klemmer orders. "Light everything in this place."

Ogden pulls a match from his pocket and strikes it against the stone hearth. He touches the match to the oily rags. The torch smolders a moment and then bursts into a smoky ball of fire.

Hannah watches Klemmer from the corner where she huddles over Lucy. He shakes his head. "Only you are left. And your men will find only your ashes. Such a shame."

Klemmer turns to Ogden and waves his good arm around the room. "Burn it all."

Ogden walks to the only window still hung with drapes and touches the torch to the fabric. Flames curl toward the ceiling. In a moment the ashes of the drapes drift to the floor and die out. He then rubs the torch against the damp pile of drapes already on the floor, where again the fabric only smolders. He looks around the room and says, "Sure ain't much to catch fire."

Hannah rises to her feet with the child in her arms. "You may burn us to death, but you won't prevail," she tells Klemmer. "Evil never does."

Klemmer points his rifle at Hannah's forehead. "Stupid speech for your last word," he tells her with a grin. "There will be not so much pain this way," he says as he cocks the rifle. "Now put down the child."

Then Ogden screams.

He's bent over and his torch falls from his hands as Anne pulls the sickle from his gut. She raises the bloody blade high and swings it down with all of her strength into the man's back. Ogden slumps to his knees and then crumples to the floor as blood soaks his shirt.

Hannah grips Lucy tightly and dashes toward the back door. Klemmer grabs her shoulder with his free hand and then yells when she punches the wound in his chest. She breaks free and runs through the doorway and into the firelight of the barnyard.

Klemmer chases her, still holding his rifle.

Anne grabs Sarah's musket from the floor. Through the doorway she sees Hannah holding Lucy and running in the firelight toward one of the sheds. She sees Klemmer stop and raise his rifle and aim it at Hannah's back.

Anne fires the musket with an explosive roar. The power of the recoil knocks her backward. The doorway is shrouded in smoke as she tries to see across the barnyard but can make out only a few roaming hogs.

She sees nothing else.

Hannah and Lucy are gone and so is Klemmer.

CHAPTER EIGHTY-TWO

REUNION

ONE BY ONE, THEY SLIP SILENTLY ONTO THE OHIO SHORE.

William steps from the boat with Dan in his arms and helps Nettie find solid footing as she frantically searches the darkness for slave catchers. Adam carries Alfred from the skiff. Henry then herds the family toward a swampy patch of cattails as Adam stands by with his Colt drawn.

Everyone waits in silence.

Soon Henry says he's assured they're safe. Minutes later he leaves for Tuck's farm. The family crouches in the cattails still in fear of the rough voices of slave catchers. But this time only the sounds of frogs and crickets fill the night.

A while later they hear the hoofbeats of at least three horses approaching. Nettie mumbles, "Oh, Lord," as she holds Alfred close to her.

"William," they hear Henry call in a low voice from the road, "Adam, come help."

Both men scuttle up the embankment to find Henry and Tuck on horseback with two mares in tow. Tuck climbs down from Adam's black gelding and walks to where the wagon is hidden in the poplars. Adam is giddy to see Othello and he nuzzles the animal's neck.

The men work quickly in the darkness. Soon the mares are harnessed to the wagon and Henry leads the team onto the road. The family climbs into the wagon as Adam keeps watch. Henry pulls himself onto the driver's bench and looks down at his bearded friend in the road.

"You best skedaddle, Tuck."

They roll through the eastern outskirts of Ripley with nothing to conceal the wagon's fugitive cargo. The town slumbers and the few men they encounter only glance at them before returning to their own nocturnal concerns. Adam rides alongside the wagon under the star-filled sky as Henry turns the team onto the winding incline away from the river basin.

Some time later, the road levels off and Henry slaps the reins and the wagon clatters along quickly to the rhythm of the jingling harnesses. For more than an hour no one speaks. They don't dare to risk even a sound.

Adam has not slept for two nights yet remains alert as he envisions being back home with Hannah and his sons. He spurs his horse a hundred yards ahead of the wagon. He sees a faint orange glow behind the distant hills and suddenly realizes it's too early for dawn to be breaking. He trots back toward the wagon and waves for Henry to stop.

"Is your farm in that direction?" He points toward the north.

"Just a few miles more," Henry says.

"Look over there," Adam says, pointing. "Something's on fire."

Daybreak is heavy with smoke as Henry steers the wagon onto the narrow lane leading to his home. William and Nettie clutch their sons as the wagon bounces violently over hardened ruts. Adam is first to reach the top of the lane where he finds three horses grazing, their riders nowhere in sight.

The Blanchard house stands starkly outlined by pale smoke still rising from the barnyard. Adam dismounts from Othello and Henry jumps down from the wagon. Both men stumble over confused hogs as they make their way to the house.

They find the front door splintered and hanging from broken hinges. A man lies moaning on the floor, curled up and holding his gut with both hands, blood gleaming on the floorboards in the early daylight. Henry and Adam glance at the broken windows and the flame-blackened patches on the walls. They see knives and a bloody sickle scattered about.

"Sarah!" Henry calls as he cocks his pistol.

Adam recognizes the blue wool coat and sweat-stained hat discarded on the floor. "Klemmer's been here."

"This him?" Henry crouches beside the wounded man and rolls him onto his back. Adam studies the man's contorted face.

"No. That's his friend Ogden."

"What's happened here?" Henry demands of Ogden, who only continues to moan.

"Sarah!" Henry shouts again.

At that moment William and Nettie and their boys reach the front doorway and peer into the house. "My god," William says and holds out his arm to block Nettie.

Nettie sees the man and the blood on the floor and suddenly screams, "Where's my baby?"

"Take her and the boys back to the woods," Henry tells William. "Get away from here, now!" William and Nettie grab their boys and run toward the grove of trees near the house.

Meanwhile, Adam crosses the room to the back door. He cocks his Colt and opens the door wider. He sees the smoldering remnants of the barn—beams and studs standing like blackened sticks amid charred boards—while hogs with singed hides roam the sooty rubble.

"Look over there," Adam says to Henry and points toward some hogs poking at two dark shapes on the ground.

"Lord, don't let it be Sarah," Henry groans as he runs past Adam.

They reach the first trampled body and Adam says, "Some sort of dog, maybe one of Klemmer's." The second body is a man's. Henry kicks at two bristly boars standing over their grisly prize. He and Adam examine the scraps of shredded flesh and fabric still clinging to muscle and bone. "It's not Klemmer," Adam says. "Too small."

"My lord, what's happened here?" Henry says as he looks around his farm in the smoky light. "Sarah!" he calls once again. Somewhere near the barn's smoking wreckage a rooster crows. Henry lowers his face into his hands and Adam turns away to allow Henry his grief.

Then Adam spots a buggy hitched near the Blanchard's garden. He walks closer and recognizes its damaged right side and knows the buggy is his own. He straddles the short fence and dashes through rows of beans and cucumbers to reach it. He examines the buggy frantically as he realizes with horror that Hannah and his sons must have been here among the flames and the death. He cries out, "Henry!"

Henry wipes his eyes as he walks toward Adam and the buggy. He stops near the well and suddenly falls to his knees. Adam rushes from the buggy to find Henry crouching next to Sarah, who is propped against the well's granite-block wall. Henry presses his bandanna against her head where her hair is matted with blood.

"You got home," she mumbles.

"Sarah," he says softly. He probes gingerly with his fingers to find the wound on her scalp. "Who did this?"

Before Sarah can answer, a ruckus erupts near the house as Nettie runs toward the barnyard kicking at the hogs. Behind her, William tries to catch up and shouts, "We'll find her, we will!" They reach the others at the well and Nettie kneels beside Sarah.

Adam is already leaning close to Sarah's face and asking, "Was Hannah here? My boys?"

"Hannah," Sarah whispers back. "She's here. And Anne."

Nettie puts her hands on both sides of Sarah's face and stares fiercely at the injured woman. "Who's got my baby? My Lucy! Where's Lucy?"

Sarah lifts her arm and points in the direction of a shed.

Adam jumps to his feet and runs toward the shed but stumbles over a hog and sprawls on the ground. He raises himself from the filth with Nettie close behind crying, "My baby, my baby!"

Adam reaches the shed where he spots a man motionless on the ground, his back against the wooden wall, one arm in a sling and the other draped over a rifle in the dirt. Two boars are thrusting their snouts toward the man's face and gnawing at his hands.

Adam recognizes Klemmer and nudges the body with his boot. Klemmer's body slumps over to reveal the gaping gunshot wound in his back. The boars warily resume nibbling the body. "Have a feast," Adam utters.

Nettie is several feet away, hands clasped before her. "Is she there?"

"Lucy? No."

Then Adam hears a woman's voice calling from behind the shed. He steps over Klemmer's body and sees a sliding wooden door in the rear wall and instantly remembers Henry telling him weeks ago about the shed's secret room. Just then a woman's hand and arm emerge from the opening as she calls out, "Adam, is that you?"

"Anne?"

"Oh, thank god!" Anne crawls out of the tight opening and frantically looks around. She jumps up and throws her arms around Adam.

"Anne!" He shakes her shoulders. "Anne, where's Hannah?"

She motions for him to follow. They step again over Klemmer's body and Anne dashes to the front of the shed. She reaches inside the ramshackle little building and tugs on a rope. A small door opens slowly in the scant daylight to reveal the hidden room. Adam and Nettie peer inside to see Hannah huddled in a corner—holding little Lucy.

CHAPTER EIGHTY-THREE

MERCY

ADAM LEAVES THE BLANCHARD HOUSE AND WALKS across the barnyard to the well. He leans against it and removes his hat. The sun is high and he gazes up at a sky the color of pearl. He closes his eyes and recalls the tears already shed this day. He and Hannah had cried when they embraced—as had Henry and Sarah—with the joy of being alive and together after terrible ordeals. Anne had wept as she recalled the terror of the slave catchers' assault on the women. But the tears shed most freely that morning were Nettie's as she held Lucy on her lap and cried over and over, "I'm here, my little one, mama's with you again."

A sudden hand on his shoulder breaks Adam's reverie.

"Porter, we need to talk."

Joseph Summerfield stands close. The marshal pulls a flask from beneath his vest and twists open the cap. He holds it out but Adam shakes his head. Summerfield sips from the flask and clenches his jaw as the whiskey bites.

"What are you going to do now?" Adam asks the lawman.

Summerfield squints into the sun and takes another pull from his flask. "Don't know," he says. "It was one of those strange things, running into your brother last night just when Ogden's missus was getting worried about Ira not being home."

"What was my brother doing in Buford?"

"He got worried when your wife and the Billings girl didn't come home so he headed into town to leave your boys with John Pope. He figured he might need a gun if he came out here." Summerfield chuckles. "And he was right in knowing old Quaker Pope wouldn't have one around. So he came over to the inn."

Adam puts on his hat and pulls down the brim to shield his eyes from the sunlight. "What'd Ogden's wife tell you?"

"Just that Ogden had gone off with Klemmer and should've been back hours earlier, the crazy coot. Then your brother comes in and asks if anybody can lend him a gun. Of course I wanted to know why and that's when he tells me the women had come out here to the Blanchard place and hadn't come back. Just like Klemmer and Ogden. So I decided to grab a couple men and come see what's what." Summerfield takes another sip and puts the flask back in his vest pocket. "Looks like it's been a long night."

"Very long for some of us."

"And apparently it was their last night for some others," Summerfield says. "Looks like Klemmer attacked the wrong people. And in this case, it happened to be women. We've loaded his body into the wagon alongside Abe Williams—what's left of him anyway."

"And Ogden?"

"I'm afraid Ira's probably done for, too," the lawman answers with a shake of his head. "I'm surprised he was still alive when I got here."

"You can thank Henry Blanchard for that. We found Ogden lying there in his own blood and you can imagine the thoughts that went through our minds. But Henry said we should just patch him up best we could."

"Blanchard was right. Not much chance of Ogden making it back to the inn. I'm likely to have three dead bodies in the wagon by the time I reach Buford."

Adam pulls a bandanna from his pocket and wipes the sweat from his face. "So, when you going to know?"

"Know?"

"Know what you're going to do about all of this. You got two—probably three—dead men and three women here who were forced to defend themselves. And you're the law. You decide what happens to people."

Summerfield looks beyond Adam, staring at the horizon. "Going to be another hot one." He reaches again for his flask but changes his mind.

"You know what Klemmer and the others were up to," Adam goes on. "They would've burned that house to the ground and—"

"Listen," Summerfield interrupts. "I'm not a stupid man. I know what Klemmer was, and I've got plenty of suspicions about things he'd done. He may have had the fugitive law on his side, and he used it with a vengeance. But I helped bury John Pope's boy after that fire in Buford. So you're not telling me a damn thing I don't already know."

Adam studies the marshal's red face. "Then can I take my wife home now?"

Summerfield turns to look across the barnyard at the wisps of smoke still curling upward from the rubble.

"Go ahead."

"And that slave family?" Adam says. "What about them? You have no idea what they've been through."

"Sorry, Porter, I didn't see any slaves."

With that, Summerfield walks off.

EPILOGUE

THE SEARING SUMMER OF 1854 FINALLY SURRENDERED
to autumn. Each September dawn in Buford brought an iridescent
fog the sun's rays soon burned off to reveal a landscape turned to
tinder. The few storms bringing rain to the Ohio Valley had come
too late. The crops had failed and there was not enough hay or oats
or corn to feed the livestock. Families were forced to slaughter their
animals to provide the salt pork and corned beef to survive the coming winter.

Across Ohio and Indiana, Pennsylvania and New York, farmers
sold parched acreage at painful losses. They moved their families
to Cincinnati and Indianapolis, Pittsburgh, Buffalo, and Detroit to
become clerks and mechanics, teamsters and mill workers—whatever could provide food and shelter and spare them the torment of
the dust and blazing sun. Others sold or abandoned their farms to
move farther west, where land was virgin and cheap and where they
could start new lives. A thousand families moved to the new Kansas
Territory in 1854.

The experience of recent months taught Adam Porter he was
not by temperament a farmer. For two years he had spent his wak-
ing hours cultivating fields that fought back with a vengeance. He

had battled rocks and stumps and ornery draft animals only to be defeated by a cloudless sky.

Then, in September, an unexpected opportunity arose from an unexpected source.

Ira Ogden somehow had survived his wounds but had lost much blood. He remained weak and seemed to exist in a haunted daze, scared of anyone who came near him. His wife wanted to leave Buford with her damaged husband and return to kin in Kentucky. Joseph Summerfield considered Ogden's incapacity sufficient punishment for his wrongdoings, and the lawman acted as intermediary when Adam negotiated with Ogden's wife to buy the Buford Inn.

Adam spent weeks preparing for his family's move from the farm to the inn. He repaired the inn's rooms where he and Hannah and their children would live. He constructed a sty for Hamlet—the family had agreed to spare the pet pig from the butcher despite their need for meat—and he rebuilt the main stable to house Othello and the horses of overnight guests.

Hannah was eager to move to the inn. She too had labored to make the farm a good home, but it had proven a hard and isolated life and she had no regrets about leaving it behind. They planned to put the farm up for sale within a month and be settled into their new home by winter—two months before the arrival of their baby.

Anne and Simon often helped Hannah and Adam stack the wagon with furniture and utensils, tools, and clothing destined for the inn. But on this day they stood beside another wagon—this one holding their own few belongings.

"I daresay this is the last time all of us will be together at this farm," Simon said to his brother and Hannah and Anne. Instinctively they tried to delay the farewells they knew were only minutes away. Adam and Simon drifted toward the barn and Anne followed Hannah into the house.

Simon in recent months had been working with the Ohio Emigration Society and talking to hundreds of people about opportunities in Kansas. He told them about fertile land for farming and pristine rivers bordered by cottonwoods. He described meadows and forests filled with game. New towns were rising on the prairie every week to provide opportunity for anyone willing to work. And there was that other matter—slaveholders still could turn Kansas into a land of pain and misery as it headed toward statehood unless enough anti-slavery settlers moved there to keep it free.

Simon became convinced that he too must move to Kansas. "I remember coming here last month and Hannah telling me you were down in Kentucky to rescue a family of slaves," Simon told Adam as they stood in front of the barn. "I admit it was hard to believe, but you'd told her it was something you must do. Well, this is something I must do."

"You take care in Kansas," Adam told his brother. "If things don't work out, you come back. We'll always have room for you."

Inside the house, Hannah wrapped a piece of cloth around a china serving dish and placed it carefully into a woven basket. She looked at her friend. "What do you think will happen, Anne?"

"I believe the slave owners will see all of us abolitionists coming into Kansas and know they could lose the vote to make it a slave state, so they won't risk moving their slaves into the territory—"she chattered nervously—"because if they get them there and Kansas becomes free, they'll have to move the slaves out again and maybe lose them in the process. So, us moving there could help discourage the slaveholders from—"

"Anne, I'm talking about you and Simon."

It was a question everyone had avoided.

"I'm more certain than ever that I need to leave Buford," Anne said.

A few days after the attack at the Blanchard farm, Anne's brother Ben had brought her a verbal invitation from her father to join them for an evening meal. She'd sat at the table and listened to her father try to justify his friendship with Julius Klemmer by saying he did not know the harm the man was capable of committing. Then he'd tried to express his remorse over his treatment of Jacob Pope. He'd stammered, with his eyes darting, but he would not tell her the two things she'd waited to hear—that he was sorry and that he loved her.

Anne suffered from Jacob's death. With him, she had never been happier. Without him, she had never been sadder. When Simon told her a week ago that he was leaving Ohio for a new life in Kansas, she'd said without hesitation, "Take me with you."

And without hesitation he'd answered, "I will."

"As for Simon," she now told Hannah, "we're close, but we've never so much as kissed. We'll be spending weeks together—maybe months—and I'm not sure what will happen. I'm not even sure what I want to happen."

Hannah handed Anne the basket with the dishes wrapped for protection. "These are for you."

"But you'll need all your dishes for the inn, Hannah."

"Please, take them. They're pretty and you'll want some pretty things out there in Kansas."

William and Nettie's first experience of living as free people was a gift from Joseph Summerfield. "Listen, Blanchard, I won't come after them, not right now," the lawman had told Henry the morning he left the Blanchard farm with a wounded man and two dead bodies in a wagon. "Just get them on their way as soon as you can. They're still runaways and I don't want you rubbing my nose in it."

Afterward Henry had warned William and his family that other slave catchers lurked nearby—Klemmer's death offered no guarantee of safety—so they must stick close to the house. For four weeks the family never stepped foot off the Blanchard farm.

Those weeks gave Nettie a chance to heal. She had arrived at the Blanchard farm more dead than alive. Her muscles and bones had been ravaged and her skin deeply scarred by the long days of carrying the heavy yoke. Her strength had come from the need to get her boys away from the Leyden farm and then the need to find her daughter. When she finally got her boys to Ohio and held Lucy in her arms, she'd collapsed.

Day after day, Nettie slept. William and Sarah fed her and rubbed ointments on her skin. Her children sat on her bed to keep her company. After two weeks she was able to walk outside. She gained strength as the sunlight took on autumn's golden hue.

But still there was pain. Her thoughts of Richard's fate seemed more than she could bear. She treasured each memory of her boy. Yet those same memories condemned her to misery. To make it from day to day, she knew she must concentrate on the life she and William would build for her other three children—the ones she could still embrace.

Meanwhile William built things. He'd left Nettie's bedside long enough to look over the charred barn and the broken pigpens and the ramshackle sheds. He'd found Henry's tools and soon stripped whatever usable lumber remained of the barn and stacked it several yards away. Henry saw what William was doing and told him to stop, to leave be.

William laid down the hammer and looked straight at the other man.

"I thank you and I thank God for the help you and Sarah been giving me and my family," he said. "I thank you for stealing my Nettie and my boys from Mister Leyden and for bringing us to this place. You're a good man, Henry Blanchard, but there's one thing you ain't."

"Meaning?"

"You ain't a carpenter. You let things slide. You can grow lots of fat hogs for sure. But they run wild. These hogs let you live on their farm, not the other way around."

So the work began. William figured Henry could get by without rebuilding the barn if the other buildings could be strengthened to fulfill their purposes. Working throughout each day the two men straightened and reinforced the crooked sheds. They replaced rotted siding and repaired sagging roofs. They hung doors and repaired windows. Then William turned his attention to the hogs. He used the salvaged timber to build three pigsties on the site of the burned barn. Now the pigs could have their place and the Blanchards could have theirs.

William then had turned his attention to the house. In a week he and Henry repaired the porch and the rotted windowsills. They patched holes in the outside walls to keep out the starlings and squirrels. It took three more days to repair the fire damage Klemmer and Ogden had inflicted in the keeping room. Then the two men and William's sons pulled a wagon through the yard and filled it with the junk strewn everywhere. They counted six trips to the nearby woods to dump the debris into one huge pile. Finally Henry swung a scythe and William a sickle to hack down the tall grass.

One evening William and Henry stood in the garden as the breeze scattered yellowing leaves at their feet. "We can't push our luck with that marshal," Henry said as he picked a ripe squash and laid it in a basket. "Somebody find out he's turning a blind eye to you folks and he could end up in jail. So I figure he's coming back here one day soon. And if he don't, others will."

At that moment, inside the house, Nettie was putting another log in the fireplace and telling Sarah she wanted to live nearby so they could always remain close.

Sarah walked across the room and took Nettie's hands in hers. "Maybe someday, when the law's different and we're all truly free, maybe then you can come back here," Sarah told her. "But you been through too much and you can't have it all happen again. You got to get those children to where they can be safe."

So, the four of them talked. Henry told William and Nettie of the two main routes for fugitives between Buford and Canada. One would take the family northwesterly into Indiana and on into